Praise for *Ryeport Redemption*

"I just couldn't put your book down…."

~ Pat Woods

"…readers will find a gripping, epic adventure within its pages."

~ Blueink Review

"Thanks to Cribb's vivid descriptions and smooth dialogue, the plot is engaging and the characters likable."

~ Kirkus Reviews

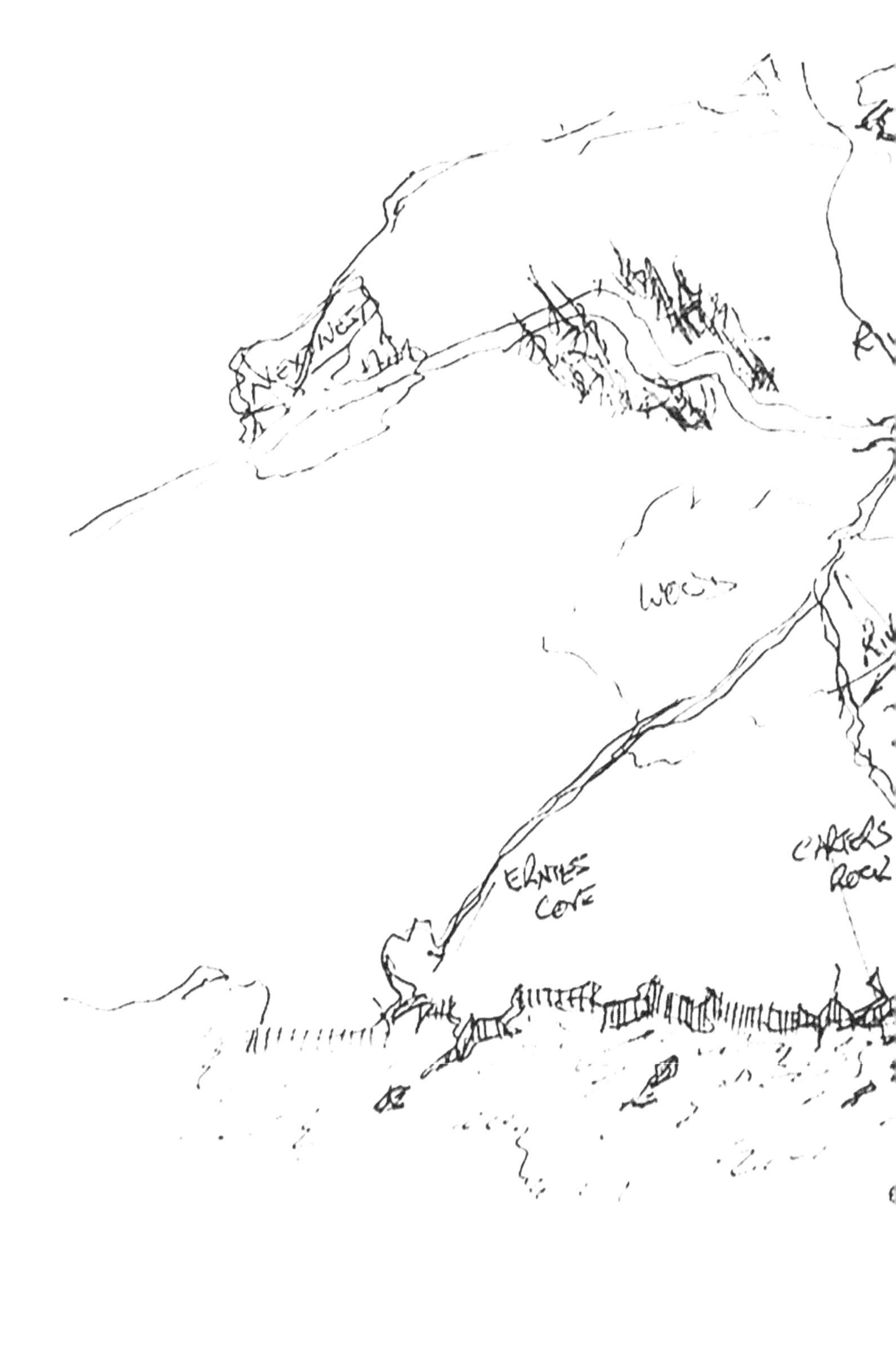

EXTINCT
WOODS
ERNIES COVE
CARTERS ROCK

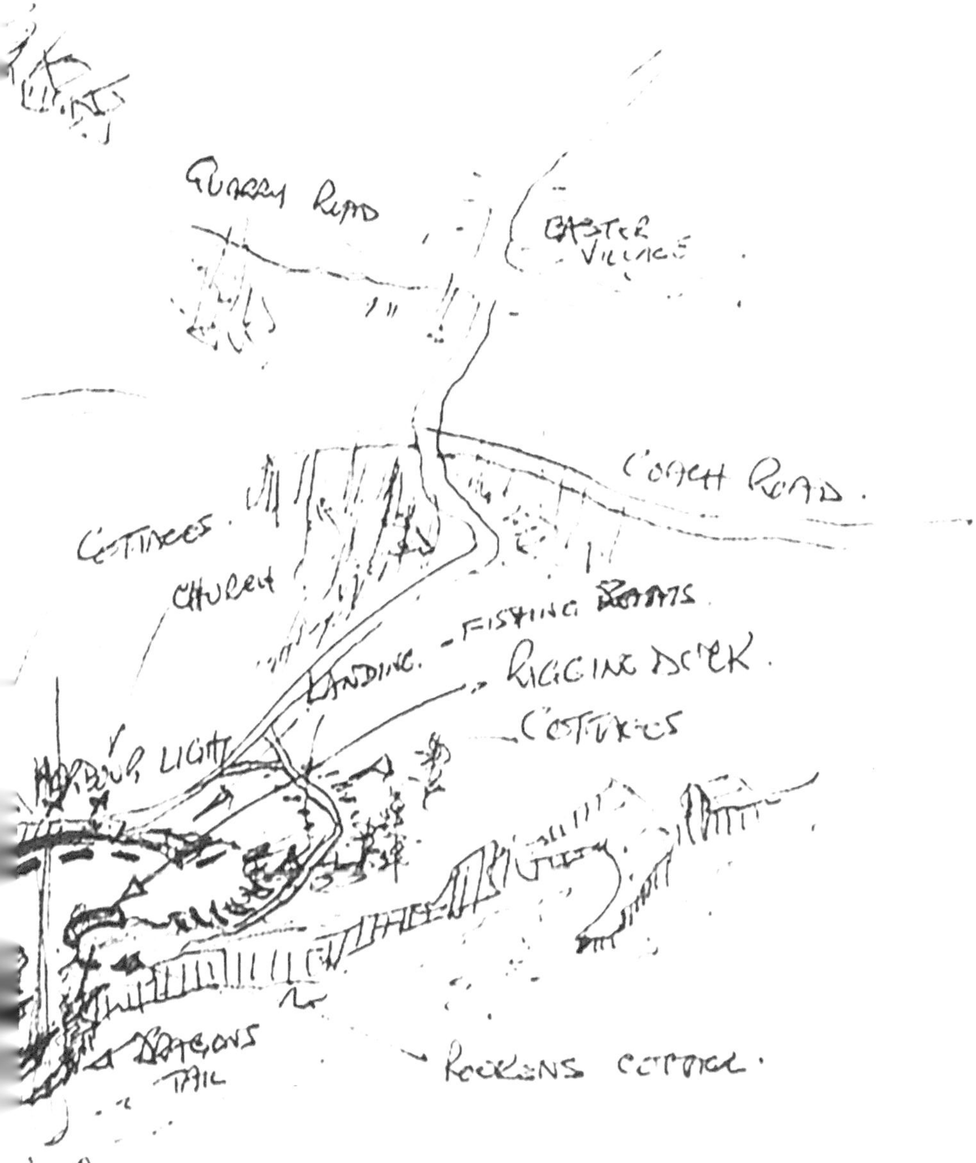

QUARRY ROAD

OYSTER VILLAGE

COACH ROAD

COTTAGES

CHURCH

LANDING — FISHING BOATS

RIGGING DOCK

COTTAGES

HARBOUR LIGHT

DRAGONS TAIL

ROCKENS COTTAGE

RYEPORT

Published by
Hasmark Publishing
www.hasmarkpublishing.com

Copyright © 2020 Les Cribb
First Edition

Disclaimer

This book is designed to provide information and motivation to our readers. It is sold with the understanding that the publisher is not engaged to render any type of psychological, legal, or any other kind of professional advice. The content of each article is the sole expression and opinion of its author, and not necessarily that of the publisher. No warranties or guarantees are expressed or implied by the publisher's choice to include any of the content in this volume. Neither the publisher nor the individual author(s) shall be liable for any physical, psychological, emotional, financial, or commercial damages, including, but not limited to, special, incidental, consequential or other damages. Our views and rights are the same: You are responsible for your own choices, actions, and results.

Permission should be addressed in writing to info@lescribb.com

Editor: Janet-Lynn Morrison
jjlmorrison@gmail.com

Cover & Book Design: Anne Karklins
anne@hasmarkpublishing.com

ISBN 13: 978-1-989756-62-1
ISBN 10: 198975662X

The Ryeport Redemption Trilogy

Book 2

Curse of the Seahorse

From the original novel
The Fo'c'sle Door by

Les Cribb

Hasmark
PUBLISHING
INTERNATIONAL

With much love and grateful hearts we dedicate this book to our parents, Les and Joyce Cribb.

This tale sprang from our Dad's ever active imagination. We watched over many years as finally with retirement, he had the time to use his gifts as a storyteller to create this wonderful, captivating adventure.

We are very proud of his achievement and delighted to see it in print despite the many challenges that were thrown into his path. But the greatest gift he left us was a legacy of love and laughter. All of his funny stories, funny hats, funny songs and funny faces that he entertained us with brought so much laughter. His love for, and fierce dedication to his family and every one of his "Papa Hugs" will be with us always. Our beautiful Mum, was right there through every celebration and every crisis. With her gentleness, eternal patience and quiet strength she was always our port in the storm and a "guiding light" to us all. We were well loved.

It is our hope in finishing this part of Dad's journey for him that the reader will have a chance to experience how wonderful it is to get lost in a good book.

Anne, Jackie, Lisa and David

TABLE OF CONTENTS

Roddy dove under the water as bullets splashed around him and wondered how things could have gone so terribly wrong. The 'Viking funeral' had not gone as planned. Despite all of Roddy and Sailmaker's efforts to warn off the villagers about the ambush, a small piece of wood had tumbled from the pile dislodging the long fuse. It was now wet and the only choice was for Roddy to remain behind to finish the job but he would no longer have the time afforded by the fuse to distance himself from the boat quickly enough.

Insisting upon Sailmaker leaving in the dinghy, he would light the fire by hand once he was out of sight and swim back alone. Thankfully, now Bannerman's old boat was blazing beautifully, but now that the soldiers had spotted him he desperately needed to escape their view.

Misjudging his bearings he had surfaced too far to the west and fighting the cold and fear dove again, this time resurfacing farther east but also closer to the beach and his pursuers.

He was numb and feeling the desperation as he realized he could not escape. As strong a swimmer as he was, he could now barely feel his arms and legs, his lungs were burning and musket balls were splashing dangerously all around him.

Then just as he felt he could move no more and was preparing to give up, he saw movement at the bottom of the cliff.

Ryeport Harbour

From the author's sketchbook

CHAPTER 1

Kill the informer

Goodman was desperate to learn the results of the Customs ambush and what damage might have been done to his organisation. However, his strict rules, following the event of a warned-off run, demanded that no members of his organisation were to deviate from their usual, legitimate routines. They were to be particularly careful not to contact other smuggling associates for news in case Customs officers were watching for such reactions. Goodman, aware that he was being watched, had to follow those rules himself and was, consequentially, out of touch regarding the success or failure of the warning-off of the boats and his shore parties, including Prudence. His only consolation at this time was that he had not been questioned by Customs officers. He hoped that 'no news' was 'good news'.

After assigning his staff their various duties, he took Mrs. Whatson's buggy into town for kitchen supplies and to check for mail at The Coach and Horses. He hoped that the gossip mill at the inn would provide some information on last night's events. He wasn't disappointed; the inn was abuzz with news and rumour. Some fishing boats had been boarded by Revenue cutters investigating a boat that had been set afire about a mile east of Nextwest. Those fishermen claimed to have been roughly handled, searched and treated as though they were smugglers. Once it was obvious that the burning boat had effectively 'warned-off' any attempt at a run ashore, members of the cutters' crew had told the fishermen the story of the failed ambush. One comment that particularly bothered Goodman was that a swimmer had been seen in the water near the burning boat and had been shot at by the soldiers on the beach.

The Customs officer that was 'tailing' Goodman duly recorded in his note-book that the butler seemed as astounded as any other patron on hearing these stories, and, after leaving the inn with some mail, had excitedly shared the news with vendors at the market. Goodman, of course, was well aware of his 'shadow' and acting for his benefit. He was very concerned about Prudence though, despite the fact that no mention had been made of any hay wagon or arrests involving a 'warning-off' party on the cliff-top. However, he needed to know if she had been arrested. He was concerned that she might crack under intense interrogation.

On returning to the house, he gave the news to a shocked Mrs. Whatson and her staff. His employer graciously allowed Goodman private use of her buggy for a personal visit to a sick friend, and Goodman left for The White Hart to see Prudence. He needed to see for himself that she was free. He was still being followed and would have to be careful not to throw suspicion on her. He pulled into the yard of The White Hart, entered the inn and, peering through a window, watched his 'shadow' ride past until he stopped behind some trees, about 50 yards farther on. "Well, he won't learn much from there. Or see whom I'm talking to," Goodman muttered. He was relieved when Pru answered the door herself. She gave him the details of the hay carts pursuit by the vicar, their efforts to make the interception appear innocent and their unloading of the tackle under the hay but she had no news of how the vicar intended to 'warn off' the boats at sea.

Goodman appeared relieved. He told Prudence that soldiers on the cliffs had claimed a boat was set afire about a half a mile out to sea. That was about 11 o'clock. The Customs men had no boat, so they were unable to put out the fire, and a swimmer certainly wouldn't be able to. Whoever set the fire had also put some explosives and grapeshot in the boat. Every so often, one of those little bombs would go off, scattering shot in all directions. It made sure the soldiers and the sloop's crew kept their distance. The sloop reached the boat shortly before it sank. Not much left of it, apparently. No name on the boat either; it had been shaved off.

"So all our people are safe?" asked Prudence.

"It would seem so. Godfrey's runners got the word out in plenty of time. The tough part of the job will be Ryeport. Whitestone is bound to be suspicious of the hay wagon. Especially since the vicar stopped you only yards from where you would have turned into the field. If the vicar had been a few minutes later, they would've had you dead to rights. Especially with that tackle aboard. By the way: why were you so early?" Prudence pulled a face. "Because of the tackle! Elliot, the man who was to have driven the cart before he broke his leg, said it was taken off the site by mistake. When it was dismantled for storage, the parts were set on the wagon, just to keep the parts together and make sure nothing was left in the field. Elliot assumed he had to take it with him. When Godfrey found out, he told Elliot to get it to the site early. He wanted the shore party to check that there was nothing missing. So we left as soon as possible." Goodman's expression was grim. "That's bad organisation. I'll have a word with Godfrey about that."

Prudence continued: "The ambush party was well hidden and didn't reveal themselves. But none of us were acting as though we suspected anything. We did nothing to attract suspicion. Jed was giving the vicar a hard time though until Mrs. Drew said: 'If you don't listen to the new delivery instructions – the cat will be amongst the ducks.' I wondered whom she learned that from."

Goodman was pacing back and forth. "She got it from me," he said. "We owe that lady a pile of gratitude. If I ever get my hands on that bloody informer, he'll wish he'd never been born. We would have all been in jail by now had it not been for the vicar and that Drew woman. The Revenuers could have captured about thirty people from hereabouts, plus the men in our boats. Prudence, I've been thinking; Sailmaker is the only man that was party to the details, who wasn't to be involved in the run. We let him know the time and place, so he would have the tackle ready on time. He has to be the informer. Most likely, he'll be getting a big reward too." Goodman pounded his right fist into his other palm, as he said this. His expression was malicious and Prudence, who was familiar with his explosive temper, knew that his anger would prevent rational judgement. Revenge was what he wanted now. Questions, if any, would come later. She felt sure that if he were to run into Sailmaker accidentally, he'd likely kill him on the spot. Very volatile was Mr. Goodman.

"I could go to Ryeport tomorrow and find out what happened," Pru said. Goodman seemed pleased with that idea, and his expression brightened. "Why don't I go with you?" he responded. "I might be able to eliminate our informer at the same time." Prudence shook her head. "What possible reason could you have to suddenly drop in on Ryeport? One that White-stone might consider innocent, that is? You've never had any business there and it's certainly not the place you'd choose for a day's outing. Our unexpected appearance there now would be more than suspicious. The Customs men may have failed with this ambush, but that'll only make them more determined to find our leaders and their contacts. Mrs. Drew already proved that you're a prime suspect. You say you were followed here today. If you go to Ryeport, it will add credibility to their suspicions."

"Aha! I've got another couple of boxes of clothes for your darling vicar," exclaimed Goodman. "That'll do. That's a reason to go to Ryeport." Prudence was thoughtful for a while. "It could be a reason for me to go but not you. Whitestone would never believe that you would only be delivering used clothing to Ryeport. I could go on my own. You'd draw too much attention. I can even include a couple of dresses of my own. I might even be able to get Reverend Tubbs to take me. That will help throw them off. I can say that I felt bad that I hadn't contributed any clothing and wanted to participate. That's a more likely story and a legitimate reason to visit both the vicar and Mrs. Drew." Goodman was silent for a few seconds. "You can't do what might have to be done."

"Neither could you if you're being watched. You were followed here remember. Besides, if you are right, and Sailmaker is the informer, he will most likely run when you confront him and that will certainly draw the attention of the men watching you. On the other hand, if you're wrong, and kill the wrong man, then we will be working under a false assumption of safety. Also, if Sailmaker was the informer, and is killed unexpectedly, Whitestone will step up his investigation even more." Goodman looked disappointed. "Sailmaker wouldn't know me," he said. "He only dealt with our crew as far as the tackle was concerned." He sounded disappointed but raised his hand in a gesture of submission. "Alright, you go. I'll have the clothes delivered to the church. You aren't allowed in the house. Find out where we stand as far as the villagers are concerned. Do you know who was in on the run?"

"I only know of one. His name is Bannerman." Goodman pondered for a few moments. "That's the one who recommended Sailmaker. It'll be hard to talk to him without raising suspicion, so don't even try. Just find out if he's in custody or being questioned. He doesn't know you. Let's keep it that way."

"I'll be careful," Pru said. Goodman looked out the window and saw his 'shadow' leading his horse into the yard. "I've got to go," he said. "I mustn't let the spy know I've been here with you. I'll have an ale and something to eat downstairs," he said and hurried from the room. Goodman chose a vacated table that still had an empty jug on it. To the spy, of course, it would appear that this was his second ale. Goodman felt pleased with himself at this small subterfuge. Drinking from someone else's jug was of no concern to him. A few minutes later, he paid for two ales and returned to the Whatson's. His shadow wasn't far behind, and Goodman caught a glimpse of him from time to time.

· · ·

Prudence's assumption that she could persuade Tubby to drive her to Ryeport was correct. Reverend Tubbs gladly drove his wagon to the Whatsons, loaded the boxes of donated clothing aboard the wagon and they soon departed for their surprise visit to Ryeport. They arrived at the vicar's cottage soon after 11 o'clock in the morning. Bessie's face lit up in a big smile when Prudence announced that she had brought more clothing. "Oh, 'ow kind. It's made such a difference to our church attendance," she said. "Those that are still waitin' to be fitted are 'chompin' at the bit' – as the saying goes. The women at least. The men are never as anxious to get 'togged-up', especially if it's to go to church." She gave her guests a knowing smile. "Thank you so much, Miss Prudence. You too, Reverend Tubbs. It's so kind of you to drive all this way for our benefit."

"No thanks necessary, Mrs. Drew, I assure you. It's been my pleasure and I've had the added reward of most charming company for the journey." Tubby was a little flushed but beaming with pleasure. Mrs. Drew turned to Prudence, looking a little puzzled. "Don't I know you, my dear?" she said, frowning as she studied Pru's face. "I've a good memory for faces as a rule and though I'm sure I know you, I can't remember when we met. Could it have been in Nextwest, perhaps when I was delivering pies, or perhaps at the Whatson's house when we picked up the first batch of clothin'?" Prudence smiled. "No, not on either of those occasions," she replied. "It's possible you may have seen me in Nextwest sometime. Perhaps in the market, but we've never actually been introduced. I would have remembered." She had to hastily change the subject. It might be acceptable for Mrs. Drew to know that she had been the young boy on the hay cart, but Tubby certainly should not hear about that. "Mrs. Drew, we'd heard that there had been some excitement here the other day. With Customs and Revenue men, I believe. Is that true?"

"Oh, yes." Bessie's expression became more serious. "A Captain Whitestone was 'ere with some soldiers. It seems that the soldiers were all set to trap some smugglers that night and to make sure that no one warned them off, they'd laid an ambush to arrest the smugglers' shore party and prevent them from lightin' a warning bonfire. Some'ow those smugglers got wind of the ambush and someone set a boat on fire, at sea instead of on the cliff. Almost 'alf a mile offshore from the landin' beach, I 'ear. Anyway, it was far 'nough out to sea that the Customs men couldn't put it out. This Captain Whitestone brought his armed men 'ere. 'e thought that our villagers might 'ave 'ad somethin' to do with it. I ask you, who could ever believe such a thing?"

"That must have been unnerving, Mrs. Drew. Did they arrest anyone?"

"Oh no, dear! They certainly tried to find a reason to, but there was no evidence of any wrong doin' 'ere. It was obvious though that this Whitestone chap thought some of our lads 'ad been in on the smuggling some'ow. 'e was questioning our men all through the night. The Sullivans and Bannerman came in for the worst of it. They'd been on a bit of a binge, they 'ad, and in the mornin', they were in no condition to fish, so they slept all day then sailed straight 'ome. To a big tongue-lashin' from Jenny Sullivan, I can tell you." Mrs. Drew gave a little chuckle. "Jenny can give you a talkin' to that'll singe your ears. You'd not likely forget it in an 'urry. Bannerman says she's where the expression 'fishwife's-tongue' came from. Anyway, Whitestone couldn't get the answers 'e wanted from those boys, so he spent a lot of time questionin' the innkeeper and the vicar. Me too, actually."

"Really! Why would they question you and the vicar?"

"Don't really know for sure, but it seems they were lookin' for someone who might've swum out to the boat and set it afire 'cos they didn't see anyone light it. Or even see the boat towed out there. It wasn't rigged for sail, and they saw no one aboard. Most of our men were away, sellin' fish along the coast, so they questioned anyone they thought might've been a good enough swimmer to get out to that boat. They'd 'ave seen another sailboat, you see. There was enough moonlight for a sail to show up real easy. There was a King's sloop out there watchin' and a couple of Revenue cutters too. They all say the boat wasn't there before dark, and no boats passed 'em after dark. So 'ow did it get there? A swimmer couldn't 'ave dragged it out there. Who could afford to burn a boat after all? And there's no boats missin' 'round 'ere. There weren't many men left in the village at the time. I suppose the soldiers thought the vicar was one of about three people left 'ere that might've been capable of swimmin' out to the boat."

"So, did they arrest him?"

"Oh no, they found 'im sleepin' in a chair, beside our doctor's bed. Doc 'udson 'appened to be sick and needin' some attention, so the vicar went and sat with 'im. Whitestone was mad. You could see that 'e thought someone 'ad put one over on 'im. They even questioned me. Now can you imagine me swimmin' out to a boat and setting fire to it?" She laughed. "And then I would've 'ad to swim all the way back again. I swim like a rock, I do. The whole village was laughing at this Whitestone chap by the time it was all over. He couldn't find grounds to arrest anybody.

"Whitestone was really upset though. One of our villagers over'eard some militia officers talkin'. They said it had cost a lot of time and money to set up this trap and that it was supposed to catch a whole lot of smugglers. But they didn't catch one. Whitestone's 'for it' apparently. 'is boss, some bloke called Corby, from London, will be mad as 'ell, this officer said. 'e blames Whitestone, or one of 'is men, for letting information leak out about the trap. Anyway, all's well that ends well. Now we can get back to our usual peaceful, boring life again. That's another reason why I'm so pleased with these extra clothes, m'dear. Create some new interest and excitement, it will. We still 'ave quite a few people who 'aven't been fitted. They really will appreciate it."

"You're most welcome, Mrs. Drew," said Prudence, but she still needed more information about the investigation and wasn't prepared to change the subject. Wasn't there some problem with a hay wagon too?"

"Well, yes, there was. But 'ow could you know about that?" Mrs. Drew asked, puzzled.

"Oh, I know someone who deals with the farmer who supplied the hay. They were talking about it. I believe the farmer's name is Pringle."

"That's right," said Mrs. Drew. "It was Jed Pringle brought the 'ay. Don't really know what all the fuss was about really. It seems that Pringle thought the 'ay was supposed to go to Archer's stable, not the inns. Storm in a teacup really. But Whitestone isn't satisfied. 'e wants to question the young lad that cadged a ride on the cart that day. No one knows who 'e was. Not even Pringle. Just gave 'im a ride, 'e said. In exchange for 'elpin' to unload the 'ay. Oh, look! 'ere comes the vicar now."

The vicar groaned when he saw Tubby's wagon outside his cottage. "I wonder what this is about. I hope it's not the bishop paying a surprise visit," he remarked to Sailmaker. "Maybe he's checking up on the stories of smuggling and the vicar being amongst those suspected." Sailmaker smiled as he clapped a comforting hand on the vicar's shoulder. He could see his friend was really troubled. "It won't be the bishop, Father. If he came at all, he'd be in his coach, not on a wagon. He'd send for you more likely. But I'd better leave you to it, Father," and, with a smile and a wave, Sailmaker left him. Tubby was quickly on his feet as Roddy came through the door, greeting him with a broad smile and outstretched hand. "Hello, old chap! You've had some excitement here, we understand. Nothing like the dull life I have in Nextwest." Roddy shook his hand before turning to welcome Prudence. "Good Morning, Miss Prudence. It's lovely to see you again. As for you, Tubby, please be assured that you are most welcome to my share of the excitement that we've had lately. However, that's behind us now. Good morning to you both, Prudence, Tubby. What a pleasant surprise. What brings you to our little village?" Despite his smile, he was still expecting bad news. Prudence returned his smile. "We had some more clothing, Father, and I thought I should take the opportunity that afforded to visit Ryeport. So, I pressured the good Reverend Tubbs to bring me here. How are you keeping?"

"Very well, thank you, Prudence. You appear radiant as always." Mrs. Drew was smiling during these greetings, anxiously waiting for an opportunity to break into the conversation. Finally, she said: "Look at all these clothes, Father. This little lot will likely finish out most of the ladies' needs. "Father, Miss Prudence asked if it might be possible to give 'er a tour of the village. After you've 'ad some refreshment, of course."

"Certainly, Bessie; it will be our pleasure. Why don't we go to the inn for a meal first? We can start our little tour after that. Ernie will be pleased to have extra patrons for lunch and it will give you a break from your chores, Bessie."

During the meal, Prudence managed to pluck at the vicar's sleeve without drawing anyone else's attention and whisper: "I have to speak with you in private. It's urgent. Maybe during our tour of the village?" Their opportunity came as they were leaving the church; Mrs. Drew and Tubby were a couple of paces ahead. Prudence and the vicar allowed that lead to grow until they were out of earshot. Then Pru said: "Goodman needs that tackle you put in the stable. He wants to run the goods ashore quickly, on the same beach. Most of the soldiers are already on their way back to their barracks and he's sure the Revenuers have given up on this run. This timing would catch them unawares. They won't be expecting it so soon after all the recent fuss, especially at the same beach. Too cheeky! But we must have the tackle. He wants you and Sailmaker to deliver it to the beach as soon as possible."

"That's all very well, Pru, but I'm not a smuggler, as you well know. Nor do I intend to be. You know my situation. I must stay well away from the smuggling business. You're talking to the wrong man."

"Well, you may not be a smuggler, but they consider you a friend, even though that will never be mentioned outside of four or five trusted people. You're off Goodman's blacklist, for sure. He would love to know who lit that fireboat and I imagine Whitestone would give his right arm to know how that all came about. That was a great idea by the way; who thought of it? Can you fill me in on those details, Roddy? I'm dying to know how the boat got placed and who lit it. And about how Whitestone questioned you too." And so the vicar gave Prudence all the details about the fireboat, including the failed attempt to light it with a fuse. Prudence stopped dead in her tracks, one hand clapped over her mouth. "How ever did you get back to Ryeport without getting caught?"

"Sailmaker waited for me under the cliff. He risked his neck for me. I'm lucky that he did. I'd never have made it otherwise. I'd stripped off for the swim and left my dry clothes in his dinghy, but they got soaked when he pulled me out of the water. So, I had to row back here naked. The soldiers were all over the place, on the cliff-top and on the beach. Others were spread out along the Coach Road, I'm told. It's a good thing there was only a short piece of beach just there or the soldiers on the shoreline would have caught us. The piece of cliff that we were hiding under was cast off that beach. I don't think they ever saw the dinghy. Sailmaker was great at finding shadows, and I had to stop rowing whenever he thought we were at risk of being heard. He dropped me off in Sorry Cove – the soldiers never got that far – and took his dinghy back through The Chute. By the time I got to Doc Hudson's, I was so cold, I was disoriented. I was warmer in the water than out. I'd left my clerical clothes at Doc Hudson's. Doc was great though, despite being sick and not having been told about our plans. He'd seen me change and hide my clothes behind his chest of drawers, so he knew something was amiss, and he kept an eye out for me." The vicar smiled. "He helped me out when I needed help really badly, despite not knowing what I was up to. He dragged me through his back door and helped me dress whilst he warned me that soldiers were going door to door. Then he crawled back into bed. I'd barely managed to flop into the chair beside his bed before the soldiers barged through the door. I made out I was sleeping. I don't know how I would have managed without Doc." Prudence raised her eyebrows. "So it was you who actually set fire to the boat?"

"Yes. Thank God, Sailmaker waited for me. I would have been caught for sure. I was freezing cold. I'd had to wait in that cold water until Sailmaker got his dinghy back to the cliff before I could even light up the boat. Then I had to swim to shore. They must have seen me because they started shooting. They came pretty close too. The coldest part though was in the dinghy coming back. I had no dry clothes and that breeze was really cold. If the soldiers that found me at Doc's had touched my skin, they'd have known I was the swimmer. I had a terrible struggle just controlling the shivers. We had a lot of help from unexpected sources, Pru, and we would have been done for without it."

Prudence smiled. "Well, thank goodness you're not involved with the smuggling, Roddy. But I think you'd be hard pressed to convince Bessie, Ernie, Sailmaker or Goodman, the Pringles and now Doc Hudson of that. It's a good thing it's a well-kept secret," she said with a smile. "All we need now is for Whitestone to find the lad who rode with Pringle that day and then you could be in deep trouble. By the way, Mrs. Drew thinks she knows me. Do you think she saw through my disguise the other day? Goodman said he told her: 'a young lady of the vicar's acquaintance, disguised as a farm boy' would be on the cart."

"I don't think she recognised you. But she will likely put it all together and very quickly. She's smart about people. Pru, I must let Bessie know, as quickly as possible, that you were that boy. If she puts it together on her own, she may blurt it out in front of Tubby. Let me talk to her now. I'll find some pretext to get her away from Tubby."

Prudence took his arm gently. "That's fine, but we also need you to talk to Sailmaker," she said. "See if he can arrange to get the tackle to the beach where you lit the fire-boat. We'll need him to rig it for us. He's the only one who knows how it should be set up now that Elliot has a broken leg. The capstan is the tricky part. He'll be well paid."

"When do you need it?"

"As soon as possible. We'll hide it until Sailmaker can set it up. He must let us know when that can be."

"Surely, it's too dangerous so soon after Whitestone's visit. He really suspects the village."

"Yes, he obviously suspects the village, but Goodman has arranged for a distraction that will draw their cutters and remaining officers west of here. He'll give them plenty else to look at whilst our goods are run ashore. And we'll make sure the villagers are seen to be in the clear." Her smile returned. "You really are a protector of this little flock, aren't you? Despite your protests about hating the village." Her smile lit up her face and her eyes twinkled with amusement, as though she had caught the vicar in some guilty secret. "I'll see what Sailmaker says, Pru," he responded rather sternly. "But how will I let you know what he decides?"

"We've arranged for Pringle to deliver another load of hay," she said. "Good quality stuff this time. The last lot was only meant to be burned in the warning-off fire. Don't worry about the money. Pringle will bring it with him and he'll repay the money paid for the last lot. Sailmaker just has to tell Pringle yes or no and name the time for delivery and setup. But since you refuse to be involved in the smuggling, I'd better not let you in on any more of our secrets." She laughed and her amusement was so genuine it shattered the recently tense atmosphere of the conversation. "Just listen to those two back there," Mrs. Drew said to Tubby. "It seems that they really enjoy each other's company."

"Yes indeed they do, Mrs. Drew," said Tubby turning to look at them. "They do indeed."

• • •

Narrow shafts of sunlight were slicing between gaps in the rough boards of Pringle's barn, lighting its gloomy interior with their bright, irregular beams. Dust particles sparkled and danced their way through these natural spotlights as they dithered over a place to settle. The three men sitting on sacks of seed, surrounding a wooden crate, were not spared the sun's decorative talent either. They too became part of its canvas, as it brushed ragged golden lines across their bodies. Jed and Bob Pringle were listening anxiously to Goodman as he ranted and raved about the informer that had nearly put them all in the hands of the Customs officers. The crate, set between the three men, served as a table for their earthenware mugs, a gallon jug of rough cider, homemade biscuits and cheese. The Pringles had recognised Goodman's angry mood as soon as he alighted from his buggy and Bob had led the Spotsman directly to the barn whilst Jed went to the house for food and drink, in what was proving to be a fruitless effort to pacify the ragged temper of their belligerent visitor.

The Pringles made a point of never discussing 'trade' matters within hearing of their wives. The ladies knew they were involved, of course, but the two men kept their families ignorant of any details. That was largely for their own protection but also to avoid accidental leakage of information. Goodman was aware of this and appreciated the fact that he was never introduced or identified to the ladies of the farm. The fact that he had appeared at the farm at a time of such unrest was a clear indication of his concern. The Pringle brothers were trusted members of Goodman's inner circle. They organised the receiving and efficient redistribution of the smuggled goods. Their responsibility commenced at the landing and continued to the selected dispersal points throughout the countryside. There was nobody that Goodman relied on more than these two tough farmers. No one in his group was more exposed to betrayal than they since they were known to a large number of smugglers and receivers in the operation. By contrast, he was known as the Spotsman only by his inner circle.

His small group of confidants also included Godfrey, his security overseer and, over the past year, Prudence, who had social access to wealthy prospects. Godfrey was responsible for controlling the discipline and security of the whole operation and was not above dirty deeds when required. Plenty of the smugglers were tougher than Godfrey, but few had the detached attitude needed for his occasional 'correction'. Godfrey was a man without conscience or compassion. To him, people were merely 'tools' to be used and discarded as the situation required. These four people were the only ones who knew the identity of the Spotsman and he confided in them in all details pertaining to a smuggling run. Now, because of a need to diversify landing sites, they'd arranged a run ashore at a previously unused and difficult beach. Special tackle was needed for this location and they had sought outside help. It had been Bannerman who had recommended Sailmaker's skills to the Pringles when they asked his advice for the new landing site. Now, for the first time in their organisation's history, they had given incriminating information to someone outside Goodman's trusted circle. Goodman had been on edge ever since the failed ambush. He prided himself on his thorough planning and to date that had always kept them safe. The fact that there was an informer in their group was driving him insane. An unknown informer was a hidden peril that he couldn't factor into his planning. Despite the danger of being constantly watched, he'd felt compelled to flush out the traitor before he struck again. His prime suspect was Sailmaker, and he was now pushing that point of view, forcefully, with the Pringles.

"Sailmaker was the only one who knew the time and place of the run who wasn't actually involved in it. He didn't want to be part of the operation. Remember that! Just wanted to do a job and get paid for it. Well paid too, I might add. He was safe. No chance of being shot at or arrested during the run. Everyone else was risking something by being involved. He's not one of us. I'm sure he went for a reward. There's always a reward. Even if none are posted, one would always be offered if you hinted to the Revenuers that you knew something." Bob Pringle wasn't convinced, and he shook his head. "Remember it was Sailmaker that came up with the idea of fixing up Bannerman's boat and setting it afire. Then 'e patched up that lumberin' wreck and towed it into place and lit the fuse. No mean feat that! If 'e 'adn't done that, we'd all be be'ind bars now. So much for not bein' involved. 'e didn't get paid for that risky bit of extra work, did 'e? I can't see where you get your suspicions from. Bannerman recommended 'im, and I'd trust 'is opinion any day. 'e's a 'ard man but straight up."

"Not true," said Goodman, wagging a finger at Bob. "It was the vicar's idea for a fire at sea. A Viking funeral, he called it. And the fuse that Sailmaker lit didn't work. It was the vicar that risked everything when he lit the boat, directly from an oil lamp. And that was after making sure Sailmaker was safely out of sight under the cliff. The vicar took all the risks and got shot at for his trouble. I think Sailmaker intended that fuse to fail. No risk to him if the boat was never lit. But it would make him look good in our eyes if we thought he'd done all that. Take you two, for example. You think he's a bloody hero." Jed Pringle nodded. "Well, 'im and the vicar too. Goodman, let's face it. Our goose was cooked until those two got their 'eads together. An' that Mrs. Drew, of course. That was a gutsy play on 'er part too. You'd be wearing 'eavy bracelets right now but for 'er. Let's cool down and look at things rational like. No sense in goin' off 'alf-cocked just because we're under a bit o' pressure." Brother Bob chimed in: "That makes good sense,

Goodman. Be really sure who the informer is before you do anything drastic. If you nail the wrong man, we'll still be targets for the real informer that you leave undiscovered. An' we'll 'ave created enemies amongst our local supporters in the bargain." Goodman stood and began pacing as he continued his tirade. "Oh, you two are easily taken in. I know it's the Sailmaker. If you won't help me solve this problem, I'll handle it myself."

Jed Pringle stepped in to change the subject, convinced that offering Goodman a second viewpoint at this time would be as productive as flogging a dead horse. "When do you plan to set up Sailmaker's tackle and get the hidden goods ashore then? That's what we're in business for. If the goods stay submerged or hidden long enough, the Revenuers'll eventually creep 'em up and we'll all be out a lot of money."

Goodman's shoulders slumped a little as he realised that the brothers were not about to accept his opinion on the informer. "Alright! Arrange for Sailmaker to set up the tackle then. Six nights from now; that'll be next Wednesday. We'll bring the goods ashore." Suddenly, his expression brightened, and he grew thoughtful for a few moments. "Let him set it up and lift a few rocks from the beach as proof that it still works. He can show Godfrey how to take the gear apart and setup for next time. Tell him the run ashore has to be the very night the tackle's set up. But, in fact, we'll set if for a later date. We'll wait and see if the Revenuers show up on the night Sailmaker believes we'll make the run. He'll be the only one with the false information. Don't mention that date to anyone else. That way, when the Revenuers show, we'll know for sure where their information came from. That's what we'll do. But you make sure and convince him that the run has to be on the night the tackle is set up. That'll give him almost a week to get word to his contact. Then, when the Revenuers show up, even you will have to admit I'm right. And, except for our concealed watchers, we'll all be safe in bed while they're scrambling all over the cliff. All it will cost us will be the tackle."

Bob Pringle gave Goodman a questioning look. "Talkin' about watchers: 'ow come you got away from yours then? We all know they're following you around like a newborn calf follows its mother."

"Godfrey's watching my back. He'll leave a signal for me if there's a problem. We checked for followers on the way here several times. There weren't any, and if there had been, Godfrey would have looked after it."

"You talk about things being 'looked after' and 'doing it yourself', Goodman. But I didn`t sign up for involvement in any murders. " As he made that statement, Bob Pringle leaned towards the Spotsman and raised a warning finger in his face. Goodman sneered, "No, I figured you for a talker rather than a doer, Bob. Don`t you worry about it. I won't ask you to dirty your hands." Goodman's temper was simmering just below the boil. "Slow to do the dirty work but quick to pick up your share of the profits."

"You won't shame me with that kind of talk, Goodman. We more than pull our weight, an' we've never shied away from a bit of rough stuff when necessary. But money ain't everythin' to us. It's just an 'elpin 'and in 'ard times. I'd be no 'elp to my family if I was rotting in some bloody jail, would I? Better off without the money. The only reason we came aboard was because your outfit was well organised and had a reputation for no violence or other troubles. Change that and you change the rules of the game. And I tell you right now – straight up – we won't be players." Bob's temper was flaring now. Jed agreed with his brother. "Bob's right. Find out for sure who the informer is and then we can all decide what to do about 'im. You just can't go around killin' people because you get a bee in your bonnet, or knock someone off, on the off chance that it might be them. That's not likely to solve the problem and it'll bring the constable into the act too. That'll mean more problems for us. That's not smart thinking."

Goodman's lips were set in a grim line. Realising that he would not make any headway with the two brothers, he drained his jug of cider, sat down and fell silent. Bob broke the silence. "As you know, I spoke with Sailmaker when we delivered that fresh load of 'ay yesterday. 'e refuses to get the tackle to us by towin it be'ind his boat. 'e says it's too dangerous with his small dinghy. And, should 'e be stopped by a Revenue cutter, 'e wouldn't have a leg to stand on. Imagine, tryin' to explain what 'e's doin', out at sea alone in a light dinghy, towing spars and tackle to a known smuggler's beach – especially when 'e's already a suspect in the fire-boat incident. Also, 'e says even if 'e was stupid enough to do it, it would be too dangerous and difficult to man'andle them long poles up that cliff. The tackle was meant to do the 'eavy lifting, not 'im. And I for one agree with 'im. So, I've changed the plan. I've arranged to buy a cartload of dry logs from Archer; that's the bloke who cuts firewood for the village and their beacons. Sailmaker acts as a general 'andyman for the village too, so 'e'll 'elp load the logs an' bury the poles for the tackle in amongst 'em. Then, if we're stopped, it will be over a cartload of firewood. There'll be no rope or pulley blocks on the cart. That stuff will be crated and delivered separately to our barn. Right 'ere, in sealed boxes. You can arrange for someone else to pick up the crates and get them to the beach on time. I'll drop the poles off in the field above the landin' area. Unless we're being watched that is. In that case, we'll make other arrangements. Alright? You can get Godfrey to have someone scout ahead of us, checking for spies." Goodman nodded. "Alright, you let me know how everything goes with that. I'll have Godfrey send someone as a scout. We'll get the gear to the field in time for Sailmaker. Splitting it up like that is a good idea. No one would find the separated items suspicious."

"Sailmaker's idea," said Bob Pringle. "That means nothing!" Goodman replied tersely. "We're all set then," said Jed. After the tackle's set up, we'll meet back 'ere, pay Sailmaker for 'is work and make it look like we're going ahead with the run that night."

"Fine. That could give me a chance to have a few words with him." Goodman rose from his seat, looking more content than he had all afternoon. The brothers exchanged anxious glances. Bob shrugged. "Keep in mind that we want no part of any violence, Goodman," Jed said. "Especially, we don't want any murders here on our property. Remember, you were wrong about the vicar. I'm sure you're wrong about Sailmaker as well."

• • •

It was Tuesday evening – the night before Sailmaker was to reinstall the tackle on the cliff-top. Dusk was falling and he was alone, sitting on a keg he used to hold the door of his rigging shop open. A light, pleasant, breeze from offshore carried the familiar sounds and smell of the sea to him as it rustled the leaves of the lone chestnut tree behind his shop. All things considered, a comfortable and tranquil evening, but Sailmaker wasn't in any mood to appreciate it. Almost two weeks had passed since the burning of Bannerman's boat and, despite the fact that they had all escaped unscathed from that adventure, his thoughts were very troubled.

"Well! You look as though you've inherited all the troubles of the world. What's up?" Sailmaker was startled. He'd been so engrossed in his thoughts that he'd not seen the vicar approach. His voice coming unexpectedly out of the fading light startled him. He jumped up; his right arm rose as though to protect himself. "Whoa, boy! It's only me!" The nervous reaction of his friend made the vicar jump too, and he also raised a protective arm as he took a step back. "Oh. Sorry, Father. I was miles away. You scared me."

"I could see that, Sailmaker. But it looked as though, wherever you were, you'd be better off here. Anything I can help with?"

"No, Sir. I was just thinking about a job I have to do."

"I've just had supper at the inn, Sailmaker. I'd hoped to see you there. Meg was asking for you too. Have you eaten?"

"No. Not hungry."

"You and Meg haven't quarrelled, have you?"

"No, Father, I'm alright, really. Just got things on my mind, that's all."

"Alright. Obviously, this is a bad time for a visit. I'll leave you to your thoughts." The vicar turned to go.

"Father, I'm sorry. Just got things on my mind."

"That's alright. Everyone needs time for private thoughts. If you ever need help with a problem though, I'd be pleased to help. The offer's always open." The vicar took a couple of steps, then paused and looked back. "You know, Sailmaker, whatever we discuss is always confidential. You've always made yourself available for me when I needed help. And I'd like you to know that I'd welcome the opportunity to return the favour. In fact, Sailmaker – and forgive me if this sounds a bit presumptuous or sloppy – I regard you as my closest friend. No one has ever put themselves out for me the way you have. I'll always be grateful for that."

"Thanks, Father. I enjoy working with you too." The vicar started to leave but had only gone a few yards when Sailmaker called him back. "Father! Perhaps it might help if we had a little talk. You're the only one who might understand. There's no one else I can confide in. But there is no one who can help me with this problem. Seems a bit silly really, but I feel nervous about something I have to do tomorrow." The vicar was soon by his side. "Got another one of those kegs? My feet still get sore walking over this rough ground."

"Sure. Grab this one. I'll sit on the crate inside the door." Sailmaker stepped inside the crowded shop, lit an oil lamp and placed it on the bench before seating himself just inside the doorway. The vicar cast his eyes over the confusion of pulley blocks, sailcloth, different sized ropes and other items of rigging revealed by the yellowish glow of the lamp. "It seems I'm making a habit of stealing your seat," he said as he settled on the keg. "Well, my friend: how might I help?"

"Remember the Viking Funeral?" The vicar grinned. "How could I forget?"

"Well, I'm not finished with that particular piece of business!" In the glow of the oil lamp, Sailmaker and the vicar's frowns deepened. "Really? Please go on."

"Father, those spars we unloaded right under Whitestone's nose were part of my gear. "

The vicar was looking increasingly concerned. "But the Revenue men won't have traced that back to you, surely?"

"No. That's not the problem. As you know, the smugglers now want to set the tackle up again. What you don't know is that they arranged to run goods ashore tomorrow night. Those goods are the same ones they intended to run ashore on the night of the fire-boat."

"But you're not part of the smuggling."

"I'm not. I refused to be part of that. But I did agree to set up the gear and they still owe me the money they promised me for that job. Now they say they'll pay me, once I reset the tackle and demonstrate that it still works. Because of the delay caused by the ambush, and the shifting back and forth of some of the tackle, they aren't sure they can rely on it anymore. I have to fit it up and prove it all over again. But they did promise me a bonus when the job's complete. Because I'm not part of the ring, I wasn't supposed to wait for my payment. They had agreed to pay me for the work I did once the run was over. I should've been paid long before this. But this problem with the informer put a stop on things."

"Sailmaker, I'm really surprised they'd trust you that far. You're not risking your neck during the run. Not likely to be required for future operations either. It's possible they may decide not to pay you. And, if you complain, they may even decide to shut you up for good. You're not a member of their crew, yet you know enough about them to get them hung. I think you should be very careful about trusting their promises."

"That was my feeling too. Now you know why I'm not good company tonight. If it weren't for the fact that Bannerman got me the job and that I trust him, and the Pringles, I'd cut my losses and try to forget it. I only took the job because it would have helped me 'n Meg to get a bit of a start in our life together. I'd feel better asking Ernie for permission to marry Meg if I could show some ability to support her.

"I really earned those two guineas. They should've paid me after the first setup. Now the Spotsman insists on another trial lift, to prove everything's in working order. He's arranged for some smugglers to help me and wants me to show them how to set it up and take it apart again.

"I'm really concerned about the run being on the same night I install the gear. It gives me no time to fix any unexpected problems. Ropes and blocks could've been lost or damaged. I've already set up all the tackle once, and everything worked fine then. But that time, I had more than a week before the run was due to take place and time to fix any problems. Then I had to dismantle it so they could disguise and hide it. They weren't supposed to remove it from the field. It was supposed to be left on the old, heavy cart looking like discarded junk. Anything could have happened to the winch or other tackle now. I shudder to think of what might have happened to me if the gear had failed. I've never met the Spotsman bloke. Bannerman arranged for someone to show me the site and tell me what was required. Some other men helped while I actually set it up. Apparently, there are only one or two people who actually know who the Spotsman is. But he'll be watching me tomorrow, Jed said – from a boat, through a spyglass. If he doesn't like what he sees – I don't get paid. I've never met the man, don't even know his name, but he controls whether or not I get paid." Sailmaker looked downcast. "What do you think, Father? Should I go and do the job or just not show up? On top of all this, Ernie would probably skin me alive if he found out I'm still involved. He stuck his neck out to help me the day we burned Bannerman's boat. And that was because he thought that night would end my connection with the smugglers."

The two men sat silently for a while as they pondered the situation. Finally, the vicar broke the silence. "We must keep this between us, Sailmaker. The less anyone else knows about it, the less chance for a loose tongue to cause trouble. The inn would be particularly dangerous. Strong drink and high spirits are a bad combination. Any information leak could lead to disaster. I'll come with you tomorrow. That way we can reduce the risk of some smuggler trying to curry favour with the Spotsman by silencing you for good. If you don't show up, now they've already set up the run, they might consider that a betrayal.

"Sailmaker, I believe I've met this Spotsman. At least, putting two and two together, I believe this man to be the Spotsman. That's a term I'd never heard before I came to Ryeport." Sailmaker abruptly stood up, looking at the vicar in disbelief. The vicar continued: "That meeting was quite accidental, my friend. In fact, the man intended to kill me. Fortunately, another smuggler persuaded him that might cause a big investigation. Not a good prospect for people who like to operate in secret. Anyway, that man was the one I had Bessie warn when we went to Nextwest. It seems I have this unhappy knack of being in the wrong place at the wrong time. Don't look so stunned, my friend. Remember, I told all of you about that meeting, at my cottage the night we burned the boat. Sailmaker, as you know, Bannerman and Ernie were first on the list of people threatening to kill me when I arrived. But they were closely followed by this smuggler. I had three death threats in one week. The people I met down here in those early days really made me feel welcome.

"Anyway, I'm fairly sure that the man I met is the Spotsman. Fortunately, the 'Viking funeral' put me in their good books, and I know that holds true for you and Bessie as well. The dangerous side of that is that very few smugglers know who was responsible for their salvation. And, of course, we're safer for that. The only people who know of our involvement are the trusted lieutenants of the Spotsman. So, if we were to appear in the wrong place, at the wrong time, the usual crew of smugglers might think we are Customs' spies and deal with us accordingly. That's why I think I should come with you. You need a neutral witness. The fact that I would be dressed as a vicar might also buy us some credibility. Where will you be meeting the person who is going to pay you?"

"I don't know for sure. It seems likely to be Pringle's barn. But you can't come, Father!" Sailmaker's tone was adamant. These men wouldn't know you were a friend any more than they'd know me. I bet there'll be more than enough of them to take care of us two if they'd a mind to. And clerical clothing ain't likely to save you. Besides, you don't want to become known as a 'smuggler's friend' by your bishop either. Loose tongues would get you sacked pretty quickly. The only time some of these men feel important is when they're showing off 'inside' information in a tavern. Your life might not be worth more than a free jug of ale from a Revenuer."

The two men were silent again for a few minutes. When Sailmaker spoke next, it was with quiet conviction. "I hadn't realised you knew the Spotsman personally. But he knows that it's because of you, Bessie and me that he's safe and that we risked our necks to keep it that way. I'm sure that whoever is in charge of the party tomorrow will be a trusted member of his team and will know we are to be kept safe. I feel better now, knowing that you know each other. Tomorrow would be a bad day for you to go for an early morning sail with me. I can't let anyone know where I'm going, and for you to be missing too would raise too many questions. Besides, Bessie was saying that you've got a busy day tomorrow. I just got the jitters over this business, Father. I'll be fine now. Tomorrow night, we'll celebrate my two guineas with supper and a drink at the inn. Then we'll always have this little secret between us." The vicar gave a worried little smile. "Are you sure, Sailmaker? Sure you can handle this business alone tomorrow?"

"Yeah! Thanks, Father. I'm really glad you came by." The two men stood, shook hands and left the shop; both were far more troubled than either was prepared to show. Sailmaker, however, decided to take comfort from the smooth delivery of the spars and tackle to the cliff top. Everything was again ready for him to reinstall. "Just a case of the jitters," he repeated as he made his way home.

• • •

The following morning, even before the Cobbe brothers were up and about, Sailmaker's dinghy slipped through The Chute, carrying her nervous owner and his backpack of hand tools. He knew that he could never carry enough spare equipment to cover all possible problems. He would have to trust that everything was on site and intact. That was, after all, the main reason for his nervousness.

The Pringle brothers, still nervous about Goodman's paranoid behaviour and uncertain of how things would unfold, had decided to absent themselves completely from the area of their farm. They planned to be conspicuously present at Nextwest Market and it was there that Prudence, unexpectedly, bumped into them as she made her way along the row of stalls in the town square. "Well, hello, Bob! Jed! Fancy seeing you here, especially today," she raised her eyebrows. "I thought you would have been busy elsewhere." Her unexpected appearance and exuberance caught the Pringle brothers off-guard. Bob took a furtive glance around, and his voice was little more than a whisper as, with a weak smile, he took her arm and steered her away from the people gathering at his wife's stall. "Well, normally we would be, Miss Prudence, but we don't want to be anywhere near our friend Goodman or Sailmaker today. And it's our guess they'll be at our barn this afternoon. Y'see: Goodman made it pretty clear at a meetin' in our barn that Sailmaker is to pay the price for being the informer." Pru's shocked expression caused him to hold up a warning hand to silence any comment. "Now me 'n' Jed know there's no proof 'e's the informer. We think the lad's on the up-n-up and Goodman 'as just lost it." He tapped the side of his forehead. "In 'is present mood though, there's no reasonin' with 'im." Bob's expression was grim. "Sailmaker's thinkin' 'e'll be paid for 'is work today – an' so 'e will be but not likely with coin. We think Goodman will likely do the lad in an' most likely, dump 'is body at sea. Me an' Jed, an' our families, are stayin' in town tonight, Miss, makin' sure that we're seen to be 'ere if and when that deed is done. We're worried that it might be done in our barn too. Against our protests, o' course, but Goodman's got the 'bit between 'is teeth' now. Sometimes ye think e's listenin' to reason. After a lot of arguein' like, 'e might seem to go along with ye', seem t' give in, sort of. But that's just 'is way of endin' the discussion. 'e'll ignore your concerns an' go 'is own way no matter what. 'is mind's made up, so it is."

Prudence's smile had long since been replaced by a look of deep anxiety. She remembered how hostile Goodman had been regarding Sailmaker, and she became very agitated. "I know he thought that Sailmaker was the informer, and Goodman can be violent and impulsive, but he promised me he would investigate and be sure before he did anything drastic. I was certain he'd find that Sailmaker has been true."

"Like I said, Miss Prudence, in 'is state of mind, there's no reasonin' with 'im. God knows we tried. Didn't we, Jed?" Jed gave a quick nod. Then, shaking his head, he added his concerns to those of his brother: "We want out of this business, Miss Prudence. Goodman'll get us all 'ung the way 'e's goin'. We didn't get into the trade to become killers or killers' accomplices. We told 'im that. But 'e just got madder with every word we said. So, we want out. Where there's no reason, safety goes out the winda', we say. We've got family to consider." Pru's anxiety was hard to miss. These tough, normally self-assured, brothers obviously believed they were out of their depth. "What arrangements has Goodman made to meet with Sailmaker then?" she asked.

"Well, don't know for sure. Goodman's at sea right now in a fishin' boat we understand, watchin' Sailmaker set the tackle an' do a trial run. Goodman's in a safe place, of course. The fishin' boat's crew will deny all knowledge of what's goin' on, on the cliff-top if a cutter hauls alongside an' asks questions. If Sailmaker's caught though, 'e won't 'ave a snowball's chance in 'ell of talkin' 'is way out of trouble. Broad daylight too. See 'ow crazy

Goodman is. If the lad gets caught, 'e could give us all up. Goodman says: if the gear works well, they'll meet to settle up sometime in the afternoon. The lad's no part of the trade really, as you well know. Just did a job for a fee, so 'e wasn't supposed to wait for 'is money like the rest of us. Our barn's my best guess for their meetin'. It's close to the landin' site. Depends 'ow long it takes for Goodman to get ashore as far as the timin's concerned. Of course, Sailmaker still believes the run will be tonight. So 'e'd want to leave as soon as possible.

"So, he's in no real danger from that then. The run won't be for a day or two yet. The date still hasn't been set," said Prudence. Bob looked a little puzzled. "Well, we know that Sailmaker was told it was for tonight, Miss, but that was so 'e was the only one that could give the Revenuers that false information. We've since found out that most of the goods are already ashore. Goodman set up several small runs over the last couple o' days, using boats that operate west of 'ere. A little trade goods each day, covered by tarps an' buried under the fish. Did the job real good apparently. Went to a lot of trouble, 'e did. Got some boats fishin' and others creepin' up sunken goods. Then all the boats shared the fish caught by them that was fishin'. Went real smooth, so they say. 'e didn't use anyone from east of 'ere neither. 'specially Ryeport, just to be sure Sailmaker didn't get to 'ear about it. We 'eard all this from Godfrey's cousin only this mornin' when we ran into 'im in The Coach'n' 'orses. 'is boat was in on this little game an' 'e thought we knew all about it. Went quite pale, 'e did, when 'e realised we'd been kept in the dark. They're all scared of Goodman an' is so-called master-at-arms. Honest, Miss, 'e was panickin' real bad, begged us not to tell anyone, but we thought that you'd know, for sure."

Prudence was absolutely stunned. Her expression was not lost on Bob, who realised that his news had caught another of Goodman's trusted lieutenants 'in the dark'. " 'e didn't tell you either, did 'e, Miss? Bob shot a quick glance at his brother, anxious to see if Jed had understood the broader significance of his question. Jed's wide-eyed look confirmed that he had. It was now obvious, to all of them, that Goodman was operating virtually alone, without the cautious input of his team leaders. That was even more evidence of his paranoid state of mind. Goodman and Godfrey, without any constraints, would be extremely aggressive. The farmers' furtive little group was totally engrossed now, conversing in whispers, and looking very conspiratorial. Bob had a sudden sense of being watched. A quick glance around confirmed they were attracting unwanted attention, including that of their wives. Their wives had already been shocked when they learned that their husbands were to stay with them for the whole market day. That was very suspicious since the men made no secret of despising the job of market vendors. Bob straightened up and gestured for his companions to do the same. Turning his back to the curious onlookers, he continued: "Goodman said 'e would prove to us that Sailmaker's the informer. " 'e gave 'im six days' notice of the run just to give 'im time to let the Revenuers know. That was why 'e was told the tackle had to be ready for a run tonight.

"Meantime, Goodman gets the goods ashore early. Those goods are safely 'idden now. All except for the stuff carried by the Ryeport boats. They weren't to be party to this little arrangement. If the Revenuers do show tonight – when there's no run – that'll be all the proof Goodman needs that Sailmaker's the informer. Mind you, in my opinion, even if the Revenuers don't show, Goodman would only say that Sailmaker 'adn't been able to make contact and kill 'im anyway. 'e's out of control – ain't 'e, Jed?" Bob's grim-faced brother answered with a quick nod. "We think either 'im or Godfrey'll knock-off Sailmaker this afternoon without waiting for White-stone's men to show up." Prudence was shifting from one foot to the other and looking very nervous. "Who else knows about this? Does the vicar know?" Her anxiety was now reflected in every word and gesture. "Calm yourself, lass," said Bob. "There's no use ye' getting upset about things ye can do nothing about."

"Does the vicar know?" She was insistent. "Can't see 'ow 'e would, lass. 'e wasn't at our meetin' when Goodman blew 'is top in our barn. Neither was Sailmaker. It's possible the lad may 'ave told the vicar about 'avin' to reinstall the tackle and the dummy run, but I don't imagine the vicar would be daft enough to show up for that. No point in 'im bein' caught in that sort of situation."

"Can one of you take me to Ryeport – right now?" Prudence looked anxiously from one brother to the other, but both men were slowly shaking their heads. "Sorry, Missy. We've got just the one 'orse and 'e's a cart 'orse. We sell our goods off the cart, as you can see, so we've no way of drivin' ye anywhere today. Besides, it's important that we both be seen 'ere all day. Don't know when or 'ow Goodman might do the deed. Or 'ow, or when, it'll be discovered. It could very well mean our lives, Miss." The Pringles looked a little shame-facedly at Prudence. She sensed that these tough men were embarrassed for stepping aside and allowing Goodman free rein in what would be the unjustified murder of Sailmaker. Obviously, they were scared of the hot-tempered Spotsman and his unscrupulous henchman, Godfrey. Godfrey's reputation was well known, and fair fight was never his style. A fatal, back-alley mugging when you least expected it was his preferred method of settling accounts.

"But this murder has to be prevented!" Prudence's face was flushed and her manner extremely nervous. "But what if Goodman's right?" Bob looked embarrassed even as he spoke the words. "I know he's not right!" Her voice rang with conviction. She turned away from them and, without another word, gathered her skirts and hurried, almost running, to the livery. Jed Pringle made to go after her, but his brother restrained him. "This is bad business, Jed. Best we stay out of it, for our families' sake."

CHAPTER 2

Blind vengeance

Sailmaker arrived at Wynos Beach, ahead of Godfrey and his helpers and, after hiding his dinghy, climbed the rough ledges to the cliff top. He was retesting the security of the steel anchors that he'd installed for the original setup when Godfrey's grating voice spoiled the tranquillity of the morning. "Well, well! Someone's up early this morning. Piss the bed, did ye?" Sailmaker turned to confront the rat-faced man as he hauled his wiry body over the cliff-top and ignoring Godfrey's remark, asked: "Where's the rest of the gear then? I thought it was to be here first thing."

" 'old yer 'orses! 'old yer 'orses! It's all 'ere – 'idden be'ind that row of scrub. In an 'urry, are ye? You must admit we did a good job of 'idin the stuff!" Two rough looking men soon followed Godfrey over the cliff-top and, with just a nod to Sailmaker, made directly for the bushes that Godfrey had indicated. Minutes later, they hauled a very heavy, low centred, flat-bed cart, loaded with spars and tackle and still covered with camouflaging brush, into the area where Sailmaker was standing.

Sailmaker examined the equipment and gave a sigh of relief. His fear of missing or damaged pieces proved unfounded; everything was there and looked to be in good shape. Godfrey's voice cut into his thoughts again: "Spotsman's watchin' from one of them boats over yonder." He nodded in the direction of two boats about a mile offshore. One of them appeared to be fishing already, whilst the other was tacking to an area, just east of the first. "We came in on the boat that's still tackin," said Godfrey. Sailmaker studied the two boats. On the stationary one, he could make out the figure of a large man, braced against the mast and holding a spyglass, but there was no way Sailmaker could distinguish his features at this distance. Godfrey's grating voice intruded on his thoughts once more. "Well, 'ow do we go about settin' this up then, matey? You're in charge. Tell us what to do, an' let's get goin'".

Sailmaker walked to a level spot near the edge of the cliff-top and, using both arms, indicated where the cart should come to rest. "Pull the cart into this spot between these anchors. Then I'll secure it while you unload the rest of the tackle."

"You 'eard the man. Let's get goin'". Godfrey waved to the men with the cart and, with a sweeping gesture, indicated the chosen spot. The men heaved on the shafts of the cart, grunting under the weight as they eased into position. "Be careful, lads. I wouldn't want to see ye' go over the cliff." Godfrey covered his eyes with both hands. Things were going well enough that he felt a moment of levity was in order.

Sailmaker was nervous. These men were, supposedly, his friends and colleagues in this venture, but he shared the vicar's concerns about their allegiance to him. Another concern was Whitestone and his Customs officers. Although Godfrey had assured him that he had kept the area under surveillance ever since the night of the failed ambush, and that no Customs men had been seen in the area in all that time, he knew that Customs riders often scouted coastal areas on a random basis. He and the tackle would also be very visible to a passing Revenue cutter. He did his best to put these negative thoughts behind him and focus instead on his return to Ryeport with his fee in his pocket. His skills had provided the smugglers with a means to run goods ashore at what had previously been an impossible landing site. The fact that the Customs officers would have shared that opinion was also its main attraction. Sailmaker's ingenuity had made this otherwise impossible beach possible and that should have earned him the respect of the smugglers. It was also true that these men would all be behind bars now had it not been for himself and the vicar. But they wouldn't know that. Half an hour later, the tackle was completely assembled and Godfrey's grating voice shook him out of his reverie. "Are we all set then?"

"Aye, all done," replied Sailmaker. "The lines are all rigged. The winch is set and the cart well anchored. We're ready for the trial lift. Are you sure that you know how to take this apart and put it back together again?" Godfrey smiled, revealing an unsightly batch of stained teeth. "Yeah, you're a good teacher and it really ain't that complicated, is it?"

"Alright then! Get your lads down to the beach and have them secure some rocks on the line the way I showed you, and then we'll haul 'em up." The lifting went smoothly, and they soon had several rocks from the beach on the cliff top. Sailmaker permitted himself a smile. "We're all done. I see one fishing boat is already heading back to harbour. Where do I have to go to get paid? You can look after things from here on."

"I'll show ye, lad. But first, we'll 'ave a drink an' a bite to eat. I've got a jug of scrumpi an' some fresh bread and cheese. It'll be a while before the boat arrives at the dock. Then the money man still 'as to drive from there to Pringle's barn. Let's walk over to the barn an' eat there. Just in case some nosy sod comes along an' wants to know what we're a-doin.'" Sailmaker smiled. "Got any pickles to go with that cheese?"

• • •

Prudence's sagging shoulders and downcast expression were clear evidence of her despair. All her efforts to find transportation had been in vain and much valuable time had been lost in the process. All carriages at the livery and the inns were already rented, and she could think of no private individual who might loan her a carriage. That is, no one other than those that wouldn't chivalrously insist on escorting her, Reverend Tubbs, being a prime example. But such an escort would expose her association with the smugglers and possibly result in violence on the body of her benefactor. Prudence was totally exhausted and well aware that her frantic search for a carriage of some sort had drawn some unwanted attention. She decided to return to The Coach and Horses in the faint hope that someone might have returned a buggy. She was but a few yards from the inn when a familiar voice startled her.

" 'old up Missy! 'old up! I managed to get a wagon for ye." She turned to see Jed Pringle jumping down from a small wagon drawn by a well-groomed chestnut mare. "Jed! That's wonderful. How ever did you manage that?"

"Tell ye all about it on the way, Missy. Let me 'elp you up. Time's gettin' short, I reckon". She accepted Jed's assistance as she mounted the small step and sank her weary body onto the bench seat with a sigh of relief. "Thank you, Jed." She reached for the reins. "I'll not forget this. When do I have to get it back to you?"

"No need to worry about that, Miss," he answered as he ran to the other side of the wagon and sprang aboard. He smiled as he took the reins from

her. "I'm comin' with ye, Miss. Giddap, Betsy!" The young mare responded smartly, and they were soon turned around and threading their way through the throng of shoppers in the marketplace. "But, Jed, you can't come with me. What about your need to be seen here and not being involved? And what about Bob; won't he be upset?"

"Yeah, he'll be upset right enough. But don't think badly of 'im, Miss. 'e's more worried about the consequences to our families really. Me too, to be 'onest with ye. But I just couldn't stand by any longer, Miss. My guts 'ave been in turmoil ever since our last meetin' with Goodman. Then you asked for our 'elp, an' we turned you down. That didn't sit well with me. After all, us two 'ave been comrades before, 'aven't we? So I went to the church and 'ad a word with their groom, Fletcher. I knew you couldn't do that 'cos that Reverend Tubbs would insist on drivin' ye. That wouldn't do either, would it, Miss? Anyway, Fletch' wasn't goin' to 'elp at first, but I reminded 'im of a few favours that 'e owed us, and 'ere we are, on our way to the farm. Too late now to go to Ryeport, Missy, wouldn't you say? I think we're on our own, young lady." By now, the wagon was clear of shoppers and Jed slapped the reins on Betsy's back. "Giddap, girl, get along now." Betsy responded admirably and soon they were moving at a pace that, considering the condition of the road, could only be described as risky. But neither rider wanted to slow the pace. "Won't the wagon be missed, Jed? At the church, I mean?"

"Well, Fletch' didn't think so, but that's always a possibility. So, 'e asked Reverend Tubbs if anyone would be needin' it. Said 'e'd like to do a personal errand. Tubbs said it was alright, and 'ere we are, travellin' in style. The bishop's away, ye see. In 'is fancy coach. The one with 'is coat of arms on the door." Jed gave a short, un-amused laugh. "Anyway, Missy, I think the wagon is the least of our worries t'day, don't you?" His raised eyebrows and the grim set of his mouth conveyed more meaning than his words. "Do you have any idea about 'ow to go about this affair, Missy? I imagine Goodman will 'ave some 'ands close by to 'elp with any 'clean up' that might be required. All the odds in our favour are dead against us, Miss." He gave her a quick, uncertain grin. "We'll 'ave to be careful. 'ave a good look around to see what we're up against before we do anythin'. Can't just go bargin' in like."

"Jed, I really don't know what to do. I thought at first that if the vicar and I were there, then Goodman would have to behave himself. Now it's too late for that. Judging by what Bob was saying, we may be too late to save Sailmaker even now."

"That's possible, Miss. We can't know for sure what's goin' on. Goodman's deliberately kept us in the dark. We must play it carefully though. Can't rush in blindly." He raised a cautioning finger to emphasise his words. "There could be quite a few of Godfrey's men at our farm. If it turns out that the lad's done for already, we'd best turn tail and sneak away. Better that they never know we were there. On the other 'and, if 'e's still alive, we're goin' to need a plan. Any ideas about 'ow we should go about this, Miss?"

"How can we plan when we don't even know where Sailmaker is or if he's still alive?"

"You're right, Miss. So we'll take a look first, careful like. I'll 'ide the wagon in the trees this side of our barn. Then I'll stick the nosebag on Betsy, just to keep 'er quiet, and slip around the barn and take a peek through a winda. You stay put. If you see anything bad goin' on, you slip away quietly in the wagon, back to Bob in Nextwest. And don't 'ang about 'cos they may come after ye."

"Nonsense, I'll not leave you to face these people alone. After all, I got you into this mess. I'll come with you to the barn. We'll both take a look, and then we'll make a decision."

"Now look 'ere, Miss Prudence, we're talkin' about some real 'ard cases 'ere. They won't care that you're a lady. They can be very 'ard – specially 'ard on wimmin' – if you get my meanin'".

"Jed, we're both going to the barn. No arguments now." Less than an hour later, the wagon was concealed in the small copse on the west side of Pringle's farm, and Betsy was quietly enjoying the extra oats that Jed had slipped into her nosebag when Fletch wasn't looking. Then, the would-be rescuers slipped quietly through the trees to the blind side of the barn. Jed motioned for Prudence to stay put as he took a quick look around the corner before slipping out of sight. Seconds later, he was back, motioning to Prudence to follow him around the barn. They stopped at a small window with a broken pane of glass, and Jed held a finger to his lips as he motioned her to look inside.

The barn was dimly lit by some small windows and an open door. As when Goodman had had his meeting with the Pringles, some sunlight had penetrated the gaps between the wallboards, and Prudence was able to make out the figures of Goodman and Godfrey behind some straw bales at the far end of the barn, but there was no sign of Sailmaker. Then she heard Godfrey's grating voice. "Why don't we just do 'im in now, dump 'im in the 'ole, an' go on 'ome? Why 'ang about when your mind's already made up?"

Goodman's response was angry and impatient. "Because, I want to know who he reports to and what he's told them, that's why! When he comes to, I'll question him, offer him his life if he cooperates and when I'm satisfied – not you – but me, I'll finish him and dump him in his smelly grave. I want you gone from here long before that though. Remember the plan, and make sure you follow it. No changes. And I particularly don't want your blokes seeing me. You make sure of that." Prudence nudged Jed, as he listened at a gap in the barn boards. "He's alive, but they are going to kill him," she whispered.

"Aye, lass, I 'eared," replied Jed and held a finger to his lips again.

Goodman was speaking again, this time emphasising his instructions to Godfrey by prodding him in the chest. "You make sure the men dig the grave under the edge of the manure pile outside the cow barn. Shovel the manure away from the edge and back onto the pile. Then dig the hole at the edge of the pile so that I can just dump him in it. Then back fill the hole, and fork the manure back over it. That way it won't be obvious. Leave the tools there for me - but make sure that the handles aren't left lying in the shit. The hole only needs to be about three feet deep, and the ground will be soft so it should be easy digging. No one will look under the manure for a grave and it'll be a year before the stuff's rotted well enough for the Pringles to use it. Even then, they'll just dump fresh stuff in its place."

Now it was Godfrey's turn to sound impatient. "We've already been over this. They're diggin' the 'ole already. What I don't un'erstand is why you don't plonk 'is body in 'is boat, tow 'im out to sea an' dump 'im over the side' with a couple of rocks for ballast. People will think 'e fell overboard an' drowned." Goodman's response was impatient: "Because I don't want to carry him all the bloody way to the cliff-top and then down the cliff-face. Quite apart from the chance of falling, I'd risk being seen. Besides, I don't know how long it will take to persuade him to tell me what I want to know. By the way, did you check on the Pringles?"

"Yeah, yeah. They're stayin' at The Coach an' 'orses tonight – both families. You got lots o' time." Godfrey shuffled uncomfortably under the big Spotsman's glare, finally settling in the path of one of the shafts of sunlight penetrating the barn boards. That drew a bright, angled line up his back, as though cutting him in two parts. Goodman continued: "When the grave is dug, take those two men to the cliff-top and set them up so they can watch the coastline. I want to know if any Revenue cutters show up, or if anyone else takes an interest in the beach or the tackle. Understand?"

"Yeah. We bin over this already. There's plenty of places for the blokes to 'ide an' watch the beach."

"Good. And your job after that is?" Goodman raised his eyebrows and one hand, in an assertive, enquiring manner.

"I goes down to the beach an' row Sailmaker's dinghy out to meet Penndyck's boat. 'e takes the dinghy in tow to a spot just west of Ryeport an' lets 'er slip, so's the tide'll carry it to a local beach where the villagers will find it', and they'll think 'e fell out an' drowned." Godfrey repeated Goodman's instructions in a bored, metered manner, nodding his head from right to left to punctuate the sentences, but he took a quick step backwards when he saw the angry colour rising in Goodman's face. "You make sure you get this right, Godfrey. If things go wrong and I get taken by the Revenuers, I'll make sure they know of your part in it. Your neck will stretch as well as mine."

"Alright, alright, I knows that. I'll be leavin' now. The 'ole should be finished an' I'll take the two blokes with me. Sure you can manage on your own?"

"Yes, I'm sure. And I don't need an audience for what I'm about to do." Goodman looked down at the floor. "He's stirring." He raised his arm and pointed to the door. "Get going. Right now!" Godfrey left the barn, calling over his shoulder as he went: "I'll be at The Coach 'n' 'orses later. Maybe we can 'ave a pint or two?"

Jed and Prudence quietly returned to the side of the barn shielded from the farmyard and perched on some logs stacked there. Prudence clasped both hands to her face as she turned anxiously to Jed. "Did you hear all that?"

"Aye, Missy, I did. 'e's alive, but it sounds like 'e's unconscious. They must've knocked 'im out before we arrived. The good news is the other bloke's will be leavin' soon, so we'll only 'ave Goodman to deal with. The bad news is we'll 'ave Goodman to deal with. If we could get Goodman to leave the barn though, maybe we could go in and 'elp Sailmaker escape." Prudence was biting her lower lip. "But we don't know if he's in any condition to escape. He could be badly hurt!"

"Aye, that's true." Jed peered around the corner of the barn just as the two men that had dug the grave stuck their tools upright in the soft ground at the edge of the manure pile. Then they wiped their hands on their clothes and walked out to the driveway. "Looks like Godfrey and 'is two 'elpers are leavin', Miss. Thank God, they're headin' straight across the road. They might've seen our wagon otherwise. Give 'em a couple of minutes an' they'll be over the rise, on the other side of the road and out of sight." Then Godfrey's voice rang out again, as he yelled after the two men. "I said don't leave the 'andles in the shit. I didn't say leave 'em stickin' up like bloody flagpoles, so's they'd attract attention. Why didn't ye stick a bloody flag on 'em, so's ev'ry passer-by would come to see what we're up to?" So saying he pulled the pitchfork out of the ground and threw it down, then kicked the spade over, causing a deep divot to fly up from the blade where it had been embedded in the manure moistened soil.

Jed pulled a face, and the two stared at each other, hoping for inspiration and painfully aware that time was their enemy. Suddenly, Jed sprang to his feet. "I've got it, Missy. I'll get the wagon, drive into the yard an' stop by Goodman's buggy – actin' all surprised like – then I'll go lookin' for 'im. If I call out: "Anyone there?" 'e's bound to come out of the barn 'cos 'e won't want anyone goin' inside. That'll give you a chance to slip in an' see if Sailmaker's still capable of walkin'".

"But Goodman will be mad. He thinks you're in Nextwest. He's bound to smell a rat!"

"That's right, Missy, but I've got me excuse. I'll tell 'im that I got talkin' to a bloke in the market who offered to buy me dad's old musket. So, I borrowed the wagon to come an' get it. Most likely, I'll be able to lead 'im away from the barn while I fetch it. I can ask 'im 'ow much I should sell it for."

"Have you got a musket?"

"Sure, I 'ave. Belonged to me dad, so it did."

"But you won't want to sell that."

"Don't 'ave to, Miss. There ain't no interested bloke at the market. Nobody would want it anyway. The trigger's broke. Later on, I can always say the bloke turned it down. I'm off, Missy. No time to waste now. When Good-man follows me to the 'ouse, you go down this side of the barn an' slip in that side door." He pointed. "See, it's always open. The top 'inge is busted. Bottom of the door's been stuck in the ground for years. Bob says it's taken root. You'd best wait 'til Goodman an' me are well away from the barn. 'e won't want me to see the grave by the manure pile, so I'm sure 'e'll lead me away from the barn towards the 'ouse. All set?"

Prudence was biting her lower lip and looking very worried. "You're a pretty lady, Miss. But if you keep bitin' on ye' lip like that, you'll soon 'ave it 'angin' in tatters. Then it won't look so good. I've gotta go." He hesitated a moment longer. " 'ere, Missy. Take me knife. They may 'ave 'im tied up." Minutes later, Prudence heard the sounds of hooves and steel rimmed wheels on the driveway. Then, Jed's voice rang out: "Whoa, girl. Whoa!" He brought his wagon to a halt, inside Goodman's buggy, and set the brake. " 'ello there. Anyone about?" He shouted. "Who's there?" He stood up and looked around, allowing time for Goodman to exit the barn before he climbed down. "What are you doing here, Pringle?" Goodman demanded. "I thought you were supposed to be in Nextwest."

"So I was. So I was. But I came 'ome for somethin'". Suddenly, his faint smile was replaced by a frown, and his manner became confrontational. "Is that alright with you, Goodman? Me comin' 'ome, I mean? Or should I ask your permission now, to come an' go on me own farm? And what are you 'ere for anyway? Waitin' for someone?" He cocked his head to one side, inquisitively.

"Of course. Sailmaker's coming. I've got to settle up with him. He should be here soon."

"Not goin' to do anythin' 'asty, are ye?" Jed cocked his head on one side again.

"No. The dummy run went well. We'll wait and see if any Revenuers show up. I've got watchers in place."

"So you'll be sendin' the lad away with a pocket full of money then?"

"Something like that. What did you come back for? I heard that you and Bob were staying in Nextwest tonight."

"That's right. We're goin' to 'ave supper with some friends, a few jugs an' a game o' cards. Lookin' forward to it."

"So why'd you come back?"

Jed grinned. "For me dad's old musket. Some bloke at the market was talkin' about old guns 'n' things, and when I chimed in about Dad's musket, 'e says 'e'd like to buy it." Jed raised his eyebrows and gave a smile. "Said 'e'd make me a good offer too. I don't need that old thing. Actually, the trigger's broke.

I didn't tell 'im that though. Let 'im knock a bit off the price, I thought to meself. I'll still be ahead of the game. So 'ere I am. 'ere why don't you come up to the 'ouse with me? You could tell me what you think it's worth."

"Can't. I've got to stay here and wait for Sailmaker."

"Alright, I'll bring it back to the barn an' show ye. Maybe Sailmaker knows a bit about these things too. Two opinions are better than one."

"Oh, alright – I'll come with you. But we'd best be quick."

And so the two men walked to the farmhouse, with Goodman walking half a step ahead of Jed, to block his view of the manure pile, whilst he kept him talking about the market, the musket or anything else that would keep the farmer's attention focused on him rather than the manure pile

● ● ●

Back in Ryeport, the vicar had been unable to focus on anything. Bessie kept looking up from her chores and watched him struggle with his next sermon. After scrapping two attempts, he abandoned that task in favour of his plans for The Guiding Light Church. But that too quickly fell by the wayside and he dumped his drawings back into his desk drawer. Suddenly, he announced that he was going to visit Doc Hudson. "Why?" Bessie asked.

"I'm concerned about him. He's looking rather frail; don't you agree? It's time we started paying him more attention. He's eighty years old after all and has been working very long hours since the night of the rescue."

"Whatever is your problem, Father? You've been fidgety all morning. You haven't been able to finish anything you started. Somethin's bothering you. What is it?"

"Nothing! Nothing's bothering me. Just need a change of pace perhaps. You're right. I can't concentrate."

"Why don't you just take a break? Don't visit anybody. Take the wagon and go for a ride. It's a nice day. Maybe go and visit Tubby if you've a mind to." Then her face brightened as she added: "If you do, then maybe I could come with you an' pay Marie a visit."

"No, no, Bessie. It's not that I wouldn't want your company, but I do need to clear my mind. Your idea of a quiet drive in the country might do just that. Thank you. I'll not be too long. Back for supper, I expect, maybe sooner – depends." And then he left, heading for the inn, Slondosh and the wagon.

"Well, look at that," Bessie muttered. "Never seen 'im like that before. Don't seem to know 'is arse from 'is elbow t'day. Wonder what's up."

The drive to Nextwest usually took about an hour and a half. Pringle's farm was a little over halfway along that section of Coach Road – almost an hour's drive away. The vicar expected to reach the entrance to the cliff-top field where Sailmaker was to reinstall the tackle minutes after that. He'd been unable to get Sailmaker off his mind all morning and had a sour, anxious, feeling in his stomach, as though something bad was going to happen to his friend. Premonition pains, his mother used to call such feelings, and he felt guilty that he hadn't gone with Sailmaker this morning. It was true that he had lots of things to do, but they certainly weren't as important as his friend.

Slondosh was hurrying over the now familiar Coach Road to Nextwest. The vicar needed to find Sailmaker but didn't know where to begin. The cliff-top perhaps? He knew the entrance was close to where he'd stopped the hay cart that day, but he had no idea what he might encounter there. He did remember Sailmaker saying that the field sloped up from the road, creating a ridge before falling towards the cliff and that hid the cliff-top from the road. He did remember where Pringle's farm was because Bessie, when pointing it out to him, had said: "Travellers appreciate landmarks on lonely roads."

But what should he do? He was sure Sailmaker would have finished setting up the tackle by now and that watchers could be waiting to deal with anyone showing an unwelcome interest in that cliff top. Sailmaker had also said that he expected to get paid in Pringle's barn. It made sense that Goodman would go to a convenient, friendly house rather than the exposed cliff-top for such a meeting; especially because the Spotsman made a point of remaining incognito and the watchers might deal with him as they would a spy. "So – Pringle's farm it has to be," he muttered. "But I must keep my eyes peeled for watchers." He coaxed Slondosh to a faster pace now that his mind was made up.

• • •

Prudence watched with bated breath as Jed and Goodman passed the manure pile. Jed was discussing the musket with Goodman and paid no attention to the 'grave'. It was time for her to act. Quickly, she slipped past the 'rooted' door with the broken hinge and made for the spot where

Goodman and Godfrey had been talking. Her first glimpse of Sailmaker sent a wave of panic through her whole body. He was lying on the floor, bound and gagged, his eyes were closed and the side of his face was covered with blood. Hurriedly, she knelt beside him. "Sailmaker, Sailmaker! Can you hear me?" His eyelids fluttered when she gently patted his face. Again she called his name, loosening his gag as she did so. This time he gave a low moan and his eyelids opened briefly. Remembering the rain barrel outside, she rushed out and quickly returned with a ladle of water. Sailmaker's head jerked as she splashed some of the cool liquid on his face and his tongue searched his lips for the moisture.

Reaching under her dress, Pru tore a piece of cloth from her petticoat, soaked it, squeezed some water into his mouth and then bathed some blood from his face. There was an ugly gash in his hair above his right ear, and the blood had started to congeal. She cut the ties at his wrists and ankles, grabbed the front of his shirt and pulled him into a sitting position, trying to twist him around, so he could rest his back against a crate, but he was too heavy for her. She knelt beside him, placed one knee behind his back and splashed water from the ladle onto his face. "Sailmaker, can you hear me?" His eyelids fluttered open again and it looked to her as though he was trying to focus. "Whe...where....where am I?"

"Pringle's barn. We have to get you out of here, Sailmaker, and quickly! Can you stand if I help you?"

"Try," was his feeble response. So Prudence got behind him and tried to lift him up. But, again, he was too heavy for her. "Too heavy," she said. "Can you roll over and get up from your knees?"

"Help me...roll." Prudence helped him roll over onto his knees, and he rested there awhile with his head hung low, appearing barely conscious. "We must hurry, Sailmaker. Let me help you."

Sailmaker raised his body to an upright position but remained on his knees. Prudence crouched in front of him and put her arms around his chest under his arms. "Put your arms around my neck, Sailmaker. I'll count to three and then we'll both stand up – alright?" Sailmaker nodded, but his eyes remained closed.

"One....two....three....heave!" Sailmaker managed to get one foot on the floor but was still kneeling on the other leg and Prudence was still bent over. "Once more, Sailmaker. You nearly made it. Once more...on three."

This time he managed to get both feet on the ground but stumbled and would have fallen had she not pulled his left arm over her shoulder and heaved upward. "We are going to walk out of the barn now, Sailmaker. We must get you into the wagon and to a doctor. I'll help you. Ready?" They began their slow, stumbling walk to the door, resting every two or three steps. Pru's heart was pounding in her chest, as she wondered how much longer Jed could keep Goodman occupied.

. . .

Jed purposely delayed finding his dad's old musket, looking in every unlikely nook and cranny as he tried to 'buy time' for Prudence. However, the Spotsman's attitude was making it clear that he'd worn that tactic too thin. The wily farmer was well aware that all the Spotsman wanted to see of him was his back as he drove out of the farmyard but, feigning innocence, he jovially offered to pour the Spotsman a drink whilst he continued searching. Goodman declined the offer and abruptly declared: "I'm going back to the barn! I have to meet Sailmaker." That seemed to jog Jed's memory, for he suddenly remembered where he'd put the old musket.

" 'ere it is. Surprise, surprise! After all that searchin', it's right where it should have been in the cubberd under the stairs. Me mem'ry ain't what it used to be." Despite Goodman's obvious lack of interest, the farmer managed to detain him a while longer as he showed Goodman the broken trigger. "Do ye think that'll take much off the price then? The broken trigger I mean. Should be easy enough to fix, don't ye think?" Goodman's patience was exhausted. "How would I know, Jed? Looks like an old piece of junk to me. Why don't you keep it? I'd say it's only value would be a sentimental one."

"Junk? Junk? Weren't you listenin'? This 'ere is a collector's piece. I've 'eard tell of 'ow these old pieces fetch a good price in London. Don't tell me it's junk." But Goodman refused to get further involved in the argument. "I'm going back to the barn, Jed. I don't want Sailmaker to walk on by this place. I can't afford to go looking for him if he gets lost. My time is valuable and frankly, I don't give a fiddler's fart about your bloody old musket," and with that, he turned to head back for the barn. Jed fell in behind him with a sick feeling in his stomach. He had no way of knowing how Prudence was faring in the barn. If Goodman walked in on them too soon, they wouldn't stand a chance. Jed knew he was no match for Goodman physically and his only weapon was the broken musket.

As the two men approached the barn, Goodman again tried to distract Jed's attention from the manure pile, pointing to a hole in the roof of the barn. "Better fix that hole in the roof of your barn, Jed. Squirrels'll get in there and make a real mess of your seed." Focusing attention on the barn was the last thing Jed wanted, so he ignored Goodman's remark, peered around the big man and pointed to the hole that had been dug beside the manure pile. His voice rose in pitch and volume as he cried out: "Well, just look at that. We've been robbed. Somebody's been stealing our cow shit," and then he laughed out loud as though that was the funniest joke he'd ever heard. That painfully artificial laugh was intended to warn Prudence of their approach and she did get the message.

Goodman gave Jed an angry look, realising that any hope of a secret burial in that particular spot had now vanished, but he wondered if Jed had realised the true purpose of the hole.

"Look at that", said Jed, pointing to the hole. "Up north they've got a sayin': 'Where there's muck, there's brass'. Maybe someone thought we 'ad valuables buried there, or maybe thought this was the end of a rainbow, an' just went diggin' for gold under the shit. But I don't see no rainbow!" He decided that justified another loud laugh as Goodman wondered how to handle Pringle, given this new situation.

Back at the barn, Prudence and Sailmaker heard the fresh burst of laughter just as they passed through the 'rooted' side door. "We must hurry," she said. "Jed is letting us know they're almost here." When they reached the corner of the barn, Prudence saw that Jed's wagon and Goodman's buggy were in plain sight from the manure pile, and Jed caught a glimpse of her when she sneaked that quick look. He thought they must be discovered and his stomach churned, but fortunately, Goodman chose that moment to check his watch. Now the farmer needed to turn Goodman's back to the escaping pair. It was time for a change of tactics. He stepped around Goodman and closer to the manure pile. " 'ere! This was your doin', wasn't it? Diggin' this 'ole, I mean. It's a grave, ain't it? Goodman, you said you weren't goin' to do anythin' 'asty. But you bloody well lied to us, didn't ye? You always intended to kill that poor sod and without waitin' for any proof. On our property too!" Jed was working himself into a mock rage. "You know we won't be party to your murderin' schemes, but it looks like you planned to bury 'im 'ere so's we'd get the blame for it. Maybe you'd even tell the constable where to find 'im, 'eh? Anonymous like. That's a clever way to get rid of people that don't agree with you. That's what you're up to, ain't it?" Even though it was an act, Jed's fit of temper was in keeping with his confrontational character, and Goodman certainly 'bought' his performance and turned his back on the barn to confront the farmer.

Prudence understood that Jed was trying to buy time for them but couldn't get Sailmaker to move any faster. "We have to get you into the wagon before the Spotsman turns around, Sailmaker. I can help, but you're too heavy for me to lift." Peering around the corner of the barn, Sailmaker mentally measured the distance to the wagon and nodded. "Chance it," he murmured, but he was still very wobbly.

Goodman took a quick look over his shoulder at the barn, so it was fortunate for the two escapees that Sailmaker paused to gather his strength before they stepped out from cover, or the game would have ended right there. Prudence also risked another look only seconds earlier as Jed continued playing for Goodman's attention. "Look at me, Goodman. What d'ye 'ave to say to your unwillin' partner in crime?" You're a traitor to your friends, that's what you are." A wave of panic had swept over him when Goodman had looked back at the barn but, fortunately, he had focused on the open double doors, in the middle of the barn, not the end where the wagon was.

But now, Goodman was getting angry. His face flushed and there was a grim set to his features as he faced his tormentor. "Shut up, Pringle; I'm tired of listening to your endless yapping. Yes, in case I might need it, that's a grave for Sailmaker. Or it could be for you if you don't shut your mouth. I'm sick of listening to you and your brother spout your petticoat values. I'm the one who's stuck with the job of keeping us all safe from the hangman's noose. Someone has to make the hard decisions and you and your cry-baby brother couldn't do it, that's for sure." Goodman's anger was mounting and, fists clenched, he took a couple of threatening steps towards Jed and towered over his smaller adversary in a very menacing manner.

Jed saw Prudence and Sailmaker stumble from the barn towards the wagon. "You promised us that you were going to wait. You were goin' to be sure you 'ad the right man before you did anythin' drastic. Looks to me like you 'ad no intention of doin' that."

"Well, with or without your approval, I plan to have a few words with this Sailmaker before I pay him, that's for sure. I may even keep him here until I'm sure that the Revenuers aren't going to show up tonight. Not that that would be positive proof of his innocence, mind you. But it could very well decide what currency I'll use to pay him off. And, if it turns out that I save his family the cost of a burial, that's more than an informer deserves." Jed lowered his eyes, as though he were scared to maintain eye contact with Goodman, but in those brief moments, he saw Prudence swing Sailmaker's legs into the wagon, climb in after him, and quietly close the tailgate. They were no longer visible from where he stood.

"Well, that's more like it. More reasonable anyway. All we wanted was reason, no 'asty decision. But you should've told us what you 'ad in mind. This is our bloody farm remember, not yours." Jed allowed the anger back into his voice and wagged a finger in Goodman's face as he spoke. He'd needed that little show of temper to restore his pride after having appeared to back down. "Well, I'll be gettin' back to the market then. See 'ow much I can get for me musket." He stepped around Goodman and headed for the wagon. Goodman turned to follow him, his face still angry and his fists clenched. Jed was nervous about turning his back on the bad-tempered Spotsman, especially after working him into such a rage, but he still ventured one more try at improving their chances. Turning to face the angry Spotsman again, he said: "Maybe you'd be better off waitin' at the road. It's a long way to the next farm and if Sailmaker ain't sure where to come, an' walks on by, it would be a long walk back."

"I'll wait in the barn. He knows this place well enough." Goodman's tone was dismissive, and he pushed Jed aside as he headed for the barn door. At the wagon, Jed took a quick glance over the side at the two figures lying on the floor between the seats. Sailmaker let out a low groan and Prudence looked up anxiously. Jed slipped the musket over the side, and Pru took it and laid it on the seat. Jed sprang into the driver's seat and slapped the reins on Betsy's back. "Giddap, girl. Let's go." But he'd made a bad mistake in pulling the wagon inside Goodman's buggy because that prevented him from making an immediate turn on the driveway. Now, just when he could have been making a mad dash for the Coach Road, he would have to lose time by driving away from it to make his turn around the large oak tree in front of the house. That lack of foresight would give Goodman more time to intercept them. Could he pass the barn before Goodman returned to confront them? They rounded the tree and Betsy was just hitting full stride when Goodman came running from the barn. Jed called over his shoulder, "We're found out, Missy. No time for talk now." "Ha! Ha!" he yelled and laid the whip across the horse's flank. Betsy leapt to obey the lash and Jed charged the horse straight at Goodman. The big man was too alert, however, and side-stepped the charging animal, grabbing her bridle as he did so. Jed whipped the horse again and she tried to break free, but Goodman was hanging his considerable weight on her bridle, and dragging her head low, he brought her to a stop.

"You interfering bastard!" Goodman fumed. "Who's helping you in this?" He stepped around the horse and pulled hard on the left rein, effectively controlling the animal as he moved towards Jed. The farmer stood up and lashed at Goodman with the whip, catching him across the face. Goodman fell back screaming as blood welled from a cut under his left eye. Betsy shied and tried to bolt. "You bastard, Pringle; I'll kill you for that. I'll kill you," screamed Goodman as he held the rein with one hand and covered his cut face with the other.

Jed lashed out again, but this time Goodman caught the lash and, in trying to jerk the whip from the farmer's grasp, pulled Jed off balance, causing him to fall from the wagon. He landed awkwardly wrenching an ankle. Goodman dropped the whip but retained his hold on the rein as he kicked Jed in the stomach. Jed groaned and rolled towards the manure pile in an effort to get away from his attacker. That suited Goodman just fine because he was able to pick up the fallen spade. "You bloody traitor," he yelled. "You shall share Sailmaker's grave." Goodman swung the spade, one-handed, at Jed's head, but the farmer ducked and the back of the spade struck him across the shoulders. The second blow also glanced off his back but struck his head on the follow through. The farmer was struggling to his feet when Goodman dropped the reins to leave both hands for the spade. He started to raise the spade, two handed now, but because his back was to the wagon, he didn't see Prudence stand up and swing the butt of the old musket at his head. Unfortunately, the rising spade deflected the blow. Goodman cried out in surprise, spun around and swiftly knocked the musket out of Pru's hands with one stroke of the spade. "So, you're a part of this too, Prudence? It seems I'm surrounded by traitors today. But I'll enjoy dealing with you, my girl. I'll be settling a few accounts this day."

Prudence tried to grab the reins, but Goodman got them first. He quickly looped their slack through the spokes of the wagon's front wheel, pulling Betsy's head down and hard left in the process. He then pulled the surplus into a quick knot, through the spokes. "Never seen a horse run with its head down like that," he said, smiling smugly. "You're not going anywhere, Miss. Meantime, you can watch the entertainment free of charge. I'll deal with you later." Seeing that Jed was still on all fours and only semi-conscious, Goodman looked over the side of the wagon and saw Sailmaker lying there, unconscious again. Goodman grabbed the front of Pru's dress and pulled her face down, so it was close to his. "I hate digging," he said. "And now I have to make this stinky hole big enough for all three of you. You will pay extra for that." He thrust her away and turned his attention back to Jed. "First, the bloody farmer," he said and rotated the shaft of the spade, aligning the edge of the blade so as to deliver an axe like blow with the edge, obviously relishing the task. He turned back to Prudence with a big smile on his face. "I think I should wear an executioner's mask for this, don't you, Pru? The end might've been easier for your friend though if the edge of his spade was sharper. It might take several hacking blows to sever his scrawny neck with this." Jed had managed to get one foot on the ground, but both hands and one knee were still on the ground as he struggled to stand. Goodman measured the distance and very deliberately checked the edge of his 'blade'. Prudence screamed: "You murdering bastard," and threw herself from the wagon at Goodman's head. However, her light weight did little to affect the big man's balance, and he easily shook her off. She had only delayed the inevitable. Goodman gave a chuckle. "You three are really making my day quite entertaining. I can't remember when I've had so much fun." Then he struck Prudence with a vicious, back-handed fist to the side of her face, knocking her to the ground where she fell stunned against the wagon wheel. "Back to the fun part," said Goodman as he again realigned his 'axe' in preparation for the execution of his defenceless farmer.

All this action and confusion had occupied the combatant's attention so completely that they had failed to notice a new arrival. Pringle's driveway was curved, with dense brush on the inside of the curve and this had hidden most of this action from the vicar's sight. But now, having rounded the dense brush, he had seen Goodman knock Prudence to the ground and set himself to execute Jed Pringle. Roddy leapt from his wagon, screaming: "NOO....NOO!"

Goodman whirled around, scowling at this fresh intrusion, but recognising that the rushing newcomer was his most capable adversary, he swung the spade at the vicar's head. Roddy ducked under that blow managing to grab the pitchfork, two handed, like a quarterstaff and blocked the blow.

However, the force of Goodman's blow drove him to his knees and the pitchfork from his grasp, leaving him struggling to retain his balance. A quick glance over his shoulder reassured Goodman that Pringle and Prudence were still no problem and he smiled disdainfully at the defenceless vicar as he said: "I was just telling Prudence how much I hate digging. Then you showed up. So now I'll have to make the grave big enough for four of you. I really regret that. But not as much as you will."

Roddy, still on one knee, managed a tentative, one-handed grip roughly halfway up the pitchfork's shaft, and then tried to swing that end towards him in an effort to regain his quarterstaff once more. Goodman swatted at the rising pitchfork with his left hand, intending to knock it to the ground and clear the way for his next blow, but one tine of the pitchfork snagged on a pocket of his waistcoat. Angrily, he tried again to knock it to the ground, but the snag held. However, he found that in moving forward, the vicar's weapon moved ahead of him, away from the vicar's grasp. Realising that this movement now controlled the pitchfork, he decided to taunt Roddy. He stepped backwards, allowing the shaft to draw within reach of the vicar's groping fingers, but just as he was about to close his hand on the shaft, Goodman stepped forward, pushing it out of reach again. Then he laughed and repeated the movements. After one more check over his shoulder, to verify that Jed and Prudence were still in no condition to bother him, Goodman realigned the spade for his fatal blow at the defenceless vicar. His eyes narrowed and his jaw clenched as he raised the spade above his shoulder and he took two, quick, short steps forward and with the butt end of the pitchfork's shaft skittering harmlessly ahead of him, he threw all his weight and strength into a swift, synchronised swing. Roddy stared into Goodman's crazed face and muttered: "This is where I die."

But that was the very moment when the butt end of the pitchfork shaft dropped into the deep divot left by Godfrey when he'd kicked the spade to the ground earlier. The pitchfork was now firmly embedded in the bottom of the divot and no longer harmless. Instead, it transferred all of Goodman's murderous energy to the business end of the pitchfork, impaling the Spotsman on the tines as they penetrated his waistcoat and rib cage, just as the vicar regained a tentative grip on the rock steady shaft. He watched in amazement as his assailant's crazed expression changed to pained surprise as his momentum lifted him off his feet before the angled shaft spun him, dying, onto the driveway.

Roddy remained kneeling, shocked and immobile for several seconds as he tried to understand how he had survived this grossly mismatched battle. To the recovering Prudence and Jed Pringle, however, it had appeared that the vicar, whilst still on one knee, had tossed Goodman aside like a forkful of hay. On regaining his composure, Roddy went to examine Goodman. The Spotsman's eyes were wide and staring, and the expression of shocked disbelief seemed frozen on his face. There was no pulse or sign of breathing. Roddy stood beside his dead assailant, motionless, apart from some trembling, until painful groans from the battered farmer and Prudence calling his name, re-awoke him to the plight of the other survivors of this battle.

Prudence was on her feet now, holding her bruised cheek and staring at the vicar with a look of absolute awe on her face. Jed too had regained his feet but was very unsteady and staggered to the wagon for support. "My God, Father! Where in 'eaven's name did you come from?" he said. "You were like an avenging angel. I'd best start going back to church." He stood half-crouched, with blood trickling down his face, holding onto the wagon with one hand and clutching his injured stomach with the other. The vicar ignored the farmer's question and hurried to Prudence. "Are you alright, Prudence?" He examined the colourful swelling building on her cheek where Goodman's heavy knuckles had struck. I'll be fine," she said. "I could use a drink of water but see to Sailmaker first." The vicar looked puzzled. "Where is he?"

"In the wagon. Goodman must've hit him really hard. His head is badly cut and he keeps passing in and out of consciousness." Sailmaker was trying to sit up but didn't look as though he knew where he was when they looked over the side of the wagon. Prudence unfastened the tailgate, climbed in and helped raise the young man to a sitting position. "You're safe now, Sailmaker. How do you feel?" Sailmaker was holding his head and kept squeezing his eyes closed and then blinking rapidly as though trying to clear his vision. "Think I'm gettin' better, Miss. But, God... my head hurts real bad. I've got a terrible headache. Where's the Spotsman?"

"Don't worry about him; he's no longer a threat." Prudence didn't want to say too much before she'd considered the possible consequences of the conflict.

Jed was also shaking his head as though trying to clear blurred vision. "Why don't we all go to the house?" he said. "We can get something to drink and clean up there." Then he almost fell as he let go of the wagon to untie the reins holding Betsy's head down. He gently stroked and patted the animal's neck as he spoke softly to her. "There, there, Betsy. I'm sorry I made you part of this, girl. It was none of your doin', was it?" He stumbled again and had to hold on to the horse for support until he could control his shaky balance. "Boy! I've 'ad better days than this, I can tell ye! Father, 'ow's Sailmaker?"

Then Sailmaker recognised the vicar. "There's the vicar. What are you doin' here, Father?"

"I thought I'd better check on you, Sailmaker. See what trouble you were getting into." The vicar was uncertain how to reply because Prudence, who was now supporting Sailmaker from behind, was shaking her head as she held one finger on her lips.

"Let's all get to the 'ouse then, right now!" Jed was taking charge again, assuming his usual assertive manner. "God, my 'ead's killin' me too, lad. What did that madman 'it me with?"

"It was only a spade," responded Prudence. "Why are you making such a fuss over a little smack with a spade?" But she smiled and reached out and gently touched the farmer's face. "Thank you, Jed, I'll never forget what you did here today." She gave a nervous little laugh and then winced at the pain brought on by the facial movement. Turning to the vicar, she said: "Well, my avenging angel: Thank you too! And Him who sent you! Aren't we a sorry looking bunch though? Why don't you put the nosebag on Slondosh, Roddy? Leave your wagon here." She laid her hand on his shoulder. "Jed was right; you certainly were our avenging angel. I was amazed at the way you tossed Goodman aside with that pitchfork. Someone up there," she raised her eyes skyward, "must have sent you. And just in the nick of time too. But now, of course, we'll have the earthly consequences to deal with."

She took Betsy's bridle, turned the wagon around and wearily led the mare back up the driveway to the house, talking softly to the animal as they went. Jed paused to check on Goodman. "You're dead right enough," he muttered as he gave the corpse a token kick. "But there'll be the devil to pay for this." He put his foot on the man's belly, heaved the embedded pitchfork from the Spotsman's chest and tossed it aside. Then he looked around for something to cover the corpse, but there was nothing handy. "Sod it! My 'ead hurts," he said, as he returned one hand on his head and the other on his stomach. "I can't be bothered with you right now," he said, and joined the survivors making their way to the farmhouse. Sailmaker was sitting up unassisted now, his legs dangling through the open tailgate, his elbows on his knees and cradling his bloodied head in both hands. Prudence, dishevelled and bruised, led the battered crew. The vicar paused long enough to drape the rain-cape from his wagon over the dead man's face, hung the nosebag on Slondosh and followed the others.

CHAPTER 3

The dangerously dead Spotsman

Godfrey had followed Goodman's instructions very closely and all had gone exactly as the Spotsman had planned. Carter and his sons had discovered Sailmaker's abandoned dinghy about one mile west of Sorry Cove. They searched the area for over an hour, checking in every cove and inlet and yelling Sailmaker's name until their throats were too sore to shout anymore. Finding no trace of him, they returned to Ryeport for more help, with his dinghy in tow. It was completely out of character for Sailmaker to take off without telling someone where he was going, but none of the villagers could shed any light on where he had gone. The fact that his small dinghy was found so far from the harbour added to their concern, leaving them fearful that Sailmaker had mysteriously drowned during some sort of secret errand.

Only Ernie, Bessie, Bannerman and Doc Hudson were aware of his earlier involvement with the smugglers and they weren't about to share that knowledge. O'Sullivan's was one of the first boats to return from fishing, and Ernie was waiting anxiously to speak with Bannerman privately. After they had been told the story of the abandoned dinghy, Ernie took Bannerman aside. "Bannerman, we've searched high and low but can find no trace of Sailmaker, and he's too good a sailor to fall overboard and drown in a sea as calm as today's. I wondered about that business with the smugglers. Is he still involved with them? It's the only other possibility I can think of." Bannerman was obviously shocked to learn that Ernie knew of Sailmaker's involvement with the smugglers, as the innkeeper quickly realised from his stunned expression. "Yes, Bannerman," said Ernie, in a disapproving tone,

"I know about the tackle and that it was you who connected him with the smugglers."

Bannerman took several thoughtful moments before replying. "Ernie, I know nothing about Sailmaker bein' involved with them anymore, honest. But, we tried a new fishing area today and, just by chance, met up with a boat from west of here that fish there regularly. They told us about boats from the west that had been runnin' trade goods ashore for a couple of days, in dribs and drabs, mixed in with their catch. That's a very risky move. Somethin' strange is goin' on, an' we ain't been told about it. We figured it had to be some of the stuff that was sunk on the night the boat was set afire. We didn't let on that we were 'traders', o' course, or they'd 'ave kept their mouths shut. At first, we thought that some fishing boat had just got lucky an' snagged someone's sunken kegs an' that the rest of the tale was a rumour that got exaggerated. Like I said, no one had mentioned anything to us about bringin' our goods ashore and ours is just as valuable as anyone else's. Anyway, they wouldn't 'ave needed Sailmaker's tackle for that job. Tell you what, Ernie, I'll ask Sully to take 'is boat to the cliff where Sailmaker rigged that tackle and see if anyone's about. Meantime, someone should take a run out to Pringle's place. They might know if anythin's goin' on."

Now it was Ernie's turn to look thoughtful. "You know – Bessie said the vicar was very restless today. Couldn't settle, she said. He and Sailmaker are getting pretty thick these days. Maybe he knows something he ain't telling. Bessie said she got tired of him pacin' about and suggested he go for a drive. He jumped at the idea. Maybe he went to Pringle's. Bannerman; I think you're right; someone should go to Pringle's." Then his shoulders slumped. "But the vicar took the wagon; we've got no way of getting there. Archer's old horse and wagon ain't no faster than walking. Apart from that, we don't want Archer, or anyone else, knowing that you or Sailmaker are involved in the trade."

Bannerman nodded. "Alright, Ernie, how about me takin' Sailmaker's dinghy right now, to the beach where Sailmaker rigged the tackle? I'll ask Sully to follow as soon as they've unloaded the catch. I can save more time by takin' the dinghy through The Chute. I'll climb the cliff an' if 'e's not there, I'll walk on up to Pringle's. But we've got to keep this side of the business real private, Ernie. I didn't realise you knew all this, but it mustn't go any further or a lot of good people could end up in the lock-up. Takes just a small slip of the tongue is all. Look, if it weren't for the slip-up that the coachman over'eard, a lot of us would be locked-up already. And even now, no one knows who the informer is. I'll be leavin' right away. Sully's boat won't take long to unload, but they'll be about an hour or so be'ind me at the beach I reckon.

• • •

Back at Pringle's farm, the injured 'comrades-in-arms' were gathered around the kitchen table, feeling very sore and very sorry for themselves. The vicar and Prudence were doing their best to treat Sailmaker's and Jed's wounds. Sailmaker's was very difficult because the gash above the ear was in thick hair. "This really needs to be stitched, but I don't know how to handle it," said Prudence. "We need to get him to a doctor."

The vicar was quietly concentrating on cleaning Jed's scalp wound when the farmer's assertive voice made him jump. "Speakin' of doctorin', Father, I think we could all use some medicine before we go any farther, an' it just so 'appens there's a bottle of real good medicine in the bottom cupboard of that old dresser by the side door. Glasses are in the cupboard above it. Like me, they don't look very classy, but they work real good." Jed turned his head to look up at the vicar and in response to Jed's raised eyebrows and smile, Roddy obediently retrieved the bottle of brandy and four glasses and brought them to the table. "I don't know if this is going to help, Jed," he said.

"Nor do I," replied the farmer. "But if the first one don't, maybe the next one will. I'm no quitter. I'll just keep on tryin.'" He pulled his shirt aside. "Just look at this bruise, Father. Spiteful sod, that Goodman, ain't 'e? Well, not anymore 'e's not, thanks to you." The vicar looked very worried as he examined Jed's head. "Jed, if you think that bruise is bad, you should see the split goose egg on your head and the bruise on the back of your shoulder. They're yellow and purple and changing colour almost as I watch."

"Well, I 'ave been told that I'm a colourful character," joked the farmer, examining each glass before pouring four stiff drinks. "Ladies first," he said, passing the best-looking glass to Prudence. "Then you, Father. You saved three lives today – four if we include yours, an' if you 'adn't saved yours, none of us'd be 'ere to tell the tale, would we? In fact, we'd be smellin' somethin' far less pleasant than brandy. So! 'ere's to your very good 'ealth." He downed the brandy in one swallow and immediately poured a refill. "Anyone else?" he queried, raising the bottle to his companions.

At this point, no one else had even taken a sip of the brandy, so there were no requests for seconds. Pru was gently soaking the congealed blood out of Sailmaker's hair trying to determine the full extent of his injury when Jed piped up again. "Use some brandy on that cut, Missy. I met a ship's surgeon once, who said how 'e always does that now. It seems 'e accidentally spilled whisky on a man's wound durin' a battle surgery and that was the only wound that didn't get infected that day. It cleaned the wound real good, 'e said. 'e always cleans wounds with whisky now. Burns a bit, mind ye." Jed was now pouring his third glass as the vicar patiently tried to clean his bobbing scalp. "Stop jumping around, Jed. How do you expect me to clean this wound with you bouncing all over the place? And you had better slow down on the brandy. You're getting through that stuff far too fast. Drinking all that alcohol so quickly and without food will hit you suddenly and hard."

"It's no problem, Father. I'm used to it and I've got a whole keg of this stuff in the pantry. More than enough to go around – and enough for you to spill some on my noggin too. I'd bet there was some cow shit on that spade. Oops! Sorry, Miss." But the vicar's thoughts were progressing beyond brandy and the dressing of wounds. "Jed, we will need your help to get Goodman's body out of sight pretty soon. If you are drunk, as well as sore, you may not be much help."

"You're right, Father. I'd forgotten about friend Goodman. I'm real sorry for neglectin' 'im, so I am. Thanks for remindin' me." He raised his glass to the vicar and promptly downed it before reaching for the bottle again. But Prudence beat him to it. "Jed, I'll be pleased to serve you all the brandy you want later, but right now, we do need clear heads. We have to get this Goodman business out of the way as soon as possible." Jed accepted Pru's rebuke as easily as he'd ignored the vicar's. He turned to Sailmaker. "You've got a real champion in this lady, young fella. Goodman's been sayin' for days now that you was the informer. Insisted on it, 'e did. None of us agreed, mind ye. There was no evidence, or reason, to believe that. We all said you was on the up-'n-up, 'specially after the fire-boat incident. But Miss Prudence 'ere, she said right out that you weren't the informer. She knew you weren't, she said, real positive like. Wouldn't let on 'ow she knew, mind ye. But I respect that. No blabbermouth is our Miss Prudence. You'd be dead but for 'er. Real champion, she is." Jed's speech was beginning to slur as he raised his empty glass to Prudence, but her feeble smile couldn't hide the concern she was feeling. She raised her hand to quieten the farmer, before looking intently into Sailmaker's face. "How do you feel, Sailmaker?

Do you think you could handle the ride home? I'd like to get you to a doctor to get that wound looked after."

"Not yet, Miss. I'm feelin' better, but I don't think I could climb down the cliff and sail my boat home. Not yet anyway. But I will have to make sure my dinghy is safe whatever happens. I tied her up below the cliff." He turned to the vicar. "You know the spot, Father; she's tied up where we hid that night. Besides, Miss, Goodman still owes me money. I think he's trying to beat me out of it, but I earned it, and I…want it!" His voice was fading with the last few words and his consciousness suddenly seemed vulnerable again. Prudence signalled the vicar and nodded discretely to the door. The shock of battle was beginning to wear off now and the desperate need to do something about Goodman's body was asserting itself in her mind. "Jed, keep an eye on Sailmaker for me, please. The vicar and I will check on the horses and take a look around. As soon as you're ready, Roddy, let's step outside. We'll not take long. In the meantime, Jed, please stay off the 'medicine' until we have everything settled regarding Goodman." She and the vicar left the house and, after ensuring that there was no unwanted interest from travellers on the Coach Road, they walked back to where Goodman lay.

"Why on earth would Goodman think Sailmaker was the informer? If it wasn't for him, the Revenuers would have all of you in jail by now. And, since he was so convinced it was Sailmaker, why were you so sure it wasn't him?" The vicar was holding his head on one side inquiringly. "I thought you and Goodman were a close team. What one knew, surely the other would also know?" Prudence was avoiding the vicar's eyes and remained silent for a few moments. Then, after giving him a rather worried look, she made a decision. "Roddy, there is no easy way around this, so I will have to trust you and tell you straight out. I knew it wasn't Sailmaker because…I'm the informer." She waited for the shock to register. "You're the informer!" The vicar's eyes now locked on hers. "So, it was you that let the information slip?" He looked perplexed and raised a hand in a questioning manner.

"Yes! I'm the informer…spy…traitor…whatever you want to call it. It's a long story, and we don't really have time for all the details right now. I was caught by the Customs officers several months ago when I delivered goods to a new client of Goodman's, who proved to be a planted Revenue spy. Once I gave him the goods, Whitestone stepped from behind a screen and arrested me. They knew that Goodman was part of the ring because he'd made the buying arrangements with their spy, but what they really wanted was the organisers and funders for the operation. At that time, I was just Goodman's courier. I didn't know the Pringles or any other smugglers, so I had nothing of substance to tell Whitestone. He didn't believe me when I told him my only involvement was in delivering goods as Goodman instructed and threatened to hang me. He described all sorts of unpleasant things they were going to do to me to make me talk, and he assured me that I would eventually tell him everything I knew. After they had their information, he promised to hang me anyway because I hadn't cooperated with them from the beginning. Then they left me alone for a couple of hours to reflect on the tortures they'd promised. But there was still nothing I could tell them, so they changed tactics and offered me a deal. Whitestone said that only because they wanted the Spotsman and his backers, they would give me a King's Pardon if I became their informer. They would set me free, give me the money to pay Goodman for the smuggled goods I'd delivered, after which I was to carry on as though nothing had happened. In exchange, I had to get them the time and location of the next run. They would set up an ambush for that run and catch enough smugglers so that they would find someone who would talk. Whitestone also suspected that I was Goodman's lady-love and said that, provided I used my womanly wiles appropriately, he would give me the information I wanted. That thought made me shudder. I agreed to get them the information but wanted the pardon first. At first, they refused saying I would get the pardon after they got the capture. I said I didn't trust them. After all, they had told me that they were going to torture me for information and then hang me anyway, once they had it. So, I wanted the pardon first. They left me for an hour or so but finally came back and agreed. I was to carry on as though all had gone well that day. But once I had the pardon, I would be working for them. I got the pardon about a month later, and gave it, in a sealed package, to a highly placed individual whom I knew I could trust. It was only to be opened in the event of my death or imprisonment, but then I had to go along with their plan. So, that's how I became their informer. No one else knows it, other than Whitestone of course." She fell silent, biting her lip and looking apprehensively at the vicar as she waited nervously for his reaction.

"Roddy, please understand, I didn't know you or Sailmaker then. Not even the Pringles. It was weeks after that that I met you at The White Hart. Whitestone knew he had to wait for the planning of the next 'run' and during that time, Goodman began to involve me more in the organisation, especially as far as upper-class deliveries were concerned. That was when I was introduced to the Pringles. Roddy, every man I'd ever been involved with had betrayed me, including my fiancé, the man who professed his undying love for me. He just lived off my money, sold my jewellery and, once I was penniless, tossed me aside. Even my own father abandoned me when I was in trouble. I had no reason to think any man, especially smugglers, would be any different. Apart from Grandfather, the only person I could ever rely on was myself. I didn't think it was reasonable that I should suffer torture and death to protect smugglers that I didn't even know. But now, Whitestone's impatience was growing. I had given him useless bits of information to this point, and now I had to give him valid details of a run soon or he would revoke my pardon, arrest Goodman and myself and force us to reveal details of our associates. Whitestone said that would be a hollow victory because the arrests would give the financiers the opportunity to cover their tracks and escape, and he promised that I would pay extra for that. It was after I had given him details of the run, I met you. You risked your life trying to save me, not knowing I was already working for the other side and would have been safe anyway. How could I possibly allow Goodman to kill Sailmaker after all your efforts to save us all? How could I?"

The vicar was standing before her, dumbstruck. "Pru…I…I just don't know what to say. Now we're in this awful mess with a dead body to explain away. What do we do now? Do you just give us all up to the Customs men?"

Now she got angry. "No! Haven't you been listening? I could have given you all up to Whitestone days ago if that was my intention. Instead, I got Jed to bring me here to try and save Sailmaker. But Roddy, please give me your word that you'll tell nobody about this. I'll be as good as dead if you do. Goodman's enforcer is Godfrey and his thugs will come for me, for sure.

"Of course not, Pru; I'll not say anything. But I don't know what to think now. I don't have any idea how to get out of this mess." He waved his hand despairingly at Goodman's dead body. "If they don't hang me for his murder, they will certainly tie me in with the smugglers. So, whatever happens now, any hope of reinstatement in my father's will is gone. But, if they hang me, I guess that won't matter."

"That's not going to happen!" Prudence was emphatic. "We will find a way around this and go on with our lives. Goodman was always violent and vengeful but, after the failed ambush, he became a raving lunatic, hell-bent on vengeance. Anyone would do. He just had to kill someone. He really was beyond all reason. But Roddy, this has to remain our secret. Please, promise me that." She gave the vicar an anxious look, as she waited for him to reassure her.

There was no response from the bewildered vicar, so finally, she said: "Let's load Goodman into a wagon and take him to my room at The White Hart. I'll contact Whitestone and tell him that Goodman found out that I was the informer and attacked me. I've got the bruises to prove it. I'll say I killed him in self-defence. I'll blame the Revenue service for leaking the information that I was the informer. I shall say it must have been them because I was the only other person, apart from them, who knew who the informer was. They will cover it up somehow if only to deflect attention away from their investigation. Eventually, they'll have to give up on me. With Goodman gone, the whole operation will collapse anyway." Roddy's frown was deepening with every word Prudence spoke. "But what about Sailmaker – the Pringles, all the villagers, and Bessie's sister? They too are at risk whilst Godfrey is around. What'll he do when he finds out Goodman's dead? You said he was here this afternoon. He's bound to find out that Sailmaker is still alive and Goodman is dead."

"Oh my God, that's true." Pru's anxiety deepened. "There are also the two smugglers that dug the grave; they're across the road, watching for intruders at the cliff-top and they know Sailmaker was here." The vicar hung his head as he tried to digest this new information. It seemed that he would never respond, but eventually he said: "Pru! I can't involve you in all these risks. I killed Goodman. Not intentionally of course, but you should not be at risk because of that. I'll find some way that doesn't involve you. In the meantime, your secret will stay between us alone. Too many people might be anxious to kill the informer. Sailmaker too almost paid the price because Goodman suspected him to be the informer. And Jed must never know. He is obviously a good friend and loyal individual, but I am nervous about his drinking habits. So, neither of them should ever learn about this."

"I agree. I think it would be dangerous for my new admirer to learn the truth, especially if he decided to defend me." She looked anxiously back to the farmhouse, then down the driveway. The vicar followed her gaze but, seeing nothing suspicious, continued: "So, you believe this fellow Godfrey was party to all of Goodman's intentions for Sailmaker and actually struck the blow that laid him out?"

"Yes. We heard him trying to persuade Goodman not to waste any more time but just kill Sailmaker out of hand and either dump his body at sea or bury him under the manure pile. But Goodman wanted Sailmaker's boat set adrift somewhere near Ryeport, so the villagers would think he'd drowned. Sailmaker doesn't know yet that his dinghy isn't where he left it." The vicar frowned. "That could be a major loss to Sailmaker if it isn't found. "What about the money that Goodman was supposed to pay him for the lifting tackle?"

"I don't know if he ever intended to pay it, much less carry it with him. I'm sure he wouldn't pay it if he could possibly avoid it."

"Let's see if he has it on him." Roddy dropped to his knees beside the dead Spotsman and began searching his pockets. Prudence stood at his side. "This feels like we're robbing the dead, Roddy." He gave her an anxious look. "Yes, it does, Pru, but Sailmaker earned that money and Goodman owes it. Now there's an idea. Why don't we take him out somewhere, rob him and leave the buggy close by and unfettered?" He will look like a robbery victim. We must arrange for Sailmaker to have an alibi though. And ourselves, of course."

"That won't work, Roddy. It still leaves Godfrey on the loose. He will realise that the tables were turned when he finds out that Sailmaker's alive. He and his thugs will go after Sailmaker at their convenience – may even turn King's evidence for a pardon or reward. We'll have to think this through very carefully." Roddy had found a guinea and some change in Goodman's purse. Apart from that, the only other valuables the man had on him were a handsome pocket watch, with fob and chain, and an expensive looking ring. "He has only one guinea here, Pru," he said, looking up. "Oh, my God! Here's Bannerman!"

The tough-looking fisherman was striding towards them wearing a very grim expression and carrying a club-like piece of wood in his right hand. He had obviously seen the vicar rifling through the dead Spotsman's pockets.

"Well, well, Mister Preacher man. I'm always finding you in unflattering situations. This man looks rather dead and here you are, going through his pockets."

• • •

Godfrey was at The Coach and Horses, and he was getting drunk. He considered he'd earned it and thought that Goodman should be paying for it. He thoughtfully reviewed the efforts of his day: He'd done a good job for the Spotsman and everything had gone as planned. The tackle was set up on the cliff top. He'd left watchers in place to spot spies or Revenue cutters and no one had seen Penndyck's boat take Sailmaker's dingy in tow or cast it adrift where the Ryeport boats were bound to find it. By now, Goodman should have dumped Sailmaker's body under the manure pile and be safely home. He smiled, thinking what a fitting ending it was for an informer – to be buried in a manure pile. "Just the sort of grave he deserves," he muttered under his breath. Godfrey was waiting for Goodman, just as he'd told him he would. " e'll most likely come to see me soon. Buy me a drink or two, just to show me a little appreciation. I deserve that at least," he muttered as he pushed his supper plate away. Ada, the barmaid, responding to his signal, topped up his tankard, holding her jug at arm's length, avoiding eye contact and focusing strictly on his tankard. She shuddered as she snatched up his plate, before hurrying away. In a barroom that had its fair share of unsavoury characters, this otherwise confident young woman found this particular man revolting. There were no saving graces or likeable traits about Godfrey. His grating voice, surly manners and mean features were well matched by his ill-kempt and grimy appearance. She shuddered again as she dropped his plate on the kitchen counter. "No wonder 'e always sits alone," she remarked to the cook as she turned back towards the bar. Cook screwed up her nose. "Godfrey?" she queried. "Who else?" replied the troubled barmaid.

Godfrey, though, was deep in thought. He wondered how Goodman had got on with questioning Sailmaker. "If 'e ever comes to, o'course," he muttered. "I'd 'ave finished 'im with that whack to 'is 'ead if that bloody bit o' wood 'adn't broke. Didn't notice it was already cracked. Just my luck." Godfrey had no friends, only a few cronies that would do his bidding for some free ale, so if he needed someone to share some conversations or confidence, he'd be out of luck. Possibly this was the reason that he would often talk to himself – usually very softly and guardedly – after checking for possible eavesdroppers. A few drinks, however, would lower his guard and, becoming less conscious of his surroundings, he would grow louder. Right now, as he waited impatiently for Goodman to arrive and 'show him some appreciation', he was getting quite chatty. "I don't agree with Goodman 'bout questionin' 'im," he said quietly. "Why waste time like that? Don't mess about. Just get rid of 'im, sez I. An' where does 'e get off gettin' mad at me just 'cos I 'it the bloke a bit 'ard? Well, what's done is done, sez I, as I ties 'im up. Goodman's got no bloody right bein' mad at me, 'specially after all I've done for 'im." He pulled a face – mimicking Goodman's expression – and his mumbling gradually grew louder. "You can't get answers from a dead man, you bloody fool, sez 'e." Godfrey's re-enactment of that last exchange with Goodman, in Pringle's barn, was taking on a life of its own and the patrons of the bar were being treated to a free show. "Then 'e starts proddin' me chest, like I was some bloody lackey, an' then 'e makes me repeat 'is instructions, treatin' me like some bloody kid. Needs to show me more respect, 'e does. Otherwise 'e'll be sorry. Well, I 'spect 'e'll cool off when 'e 'ears 'ow well ev'rythin' went t'day. 'e bloody well better or I'll show 'im what's what."

He suddenly became aware that the room had gone quiet and people were staring at him. He realised that he had been talking and wondered how much they'd heard or understood. Angrily, he addressed the closest table. "Well! What're you lookin' at then? Mind yer own bloody business, why don'cher?" His wild manner and crazy stare caused people to quickly avert their eyes and try to look disinterested. That seemed to satisfy him, and he took another glance at the door. "Still no sign of Goodman!" He started to fidget. "No bloody appreciation, that's what." He checked his pocket change, decided he had enough for another drink or two and waved his tankard in the air again. People at adjacent tables were giving him uneasy glances. Godfrey was an unpleasant looking fellow at best, but his reputation was even worse than his appearance. Impatiently, he waved his tankard at the barmaid again as she served a nearby table. She groaned but hurried to top him up. "Better you than me, lass," said one of the patrons, sympathetically. "Part o' me job," she replied. "But it's a part I'd gladly do without."

Godfrey spread his coins in a small puddle of spilled ale on the table. "I'll 'ave one more after this, with some bread and cheese next time. Take what I owe out of that." He nodded to the coins sitting in the puddle. Ada nodded curtly and swept some coins into a cloth that she carried for wiping the tables. "Nice manners you got," she said, as she headed for the kitchen, with the wet coins still in the cloth. Godfrey scowled. "Watch yer bloody lip," he called after her. The slur in his raspy voice, and his drooping eyelids, already betrayed the effect of too much alcohol.

The barmaid arrived with the bread and cheese and refilled his tankard, but Godfrey wasn't sure that he wanted the food anymore. However, he waved the girl away, nibbled on a piece of cheese and washed it down with more ale. A few minutes later, his head was on the table, resting in a fresh puddle from his spilled tankard, and he was quietly snoring. Minutes later, Ada brought John Shields, the burly innkeeper, to Godfrey's table. "We can't leave 'im 'ere like this, can we, Guv'ner? It's upsettin' the rest of the customers."

"You're right, Ada. Call Jack for me, lass. Looks like I'll need a hand to carry this classy gent outside." The barmaid hustled away as the innkeeper reached out and gently shook Godfrey's shoulder. "Wake up there, matey!" Godfrey awoke with a start and jumped to his feet screaming: "I'll kill you, Goodman, you ungrateful bastard" and reached for the knife at his belt. The room fell silent and the startled innkeeper jumped back. But John Shields had been part of many naval boarding parties before using his prize money to buy this inn and he recovered quickly. He had Godfrey's arm twisted behind his back before the drunken man could reach his knife. "Steady, man, steady. You were dreaming. Bad dream too, by the looks of things." John Shields had Godfrey well under control now.

"Let me go, you bastard. You're 'urtin' me arm." Obviously, the worse for drink, and with his ale-soaked hair plastered to the side of his face, Godfrey was an even more unpleasant sight than usual.

"I'll let you go, matey, when you're outside and on your way home," said the innkeeper. He was already propelling Godfrey towards the door when Jack, the stableman, arrived to give him a hand. "It's alright, Jack. He woke up. "I didn't think he'd have the legs to get outside, but 'e can walk. Can't you, matey?"

"Let me be, you big oaf. I 'aven't finished me ale. I'm a customer and I paid for my supper and the ale. Let me be."

"Aye matey, so you did. But I'd like you to take 'ome everything you bought 'ere. There's no need for you to be giving it back before you leave. It never looks as appetisin' second time around, does it now? Let's get you outside into the fresh air. Jack moved to Godfrey's other side, and the two men marched Goodman's Master-at-Arms into the street. "Too bad you're so upset with Mister Goodman, matey," said Shields, "but I suggest you try and sort out your differences peaceful like. I think Goodman would chew you up and spit you out in little bits." With these parting words of advice, the two men pointed Godfrey in the direction of his shop and gave him a gentle shove. He managed to stagger a few steps, before stumbling into the

From the author's sketchbook

side yard of the inn and landing flat on his face in a puddle. Jack moved to help him up, but Shields held Jack's arm. "Leave 'im be, Jack. Let 'im sleep it off. 'e's out of sight there and we don't want to risk 'im spewing up all over us. We'll clean up in the morning if need be. Hopefully, 'e'll be gone by then." The two men returned to the bar to a strong round of applause to which they responded with elaborate bows and gracious smiles. Ada, the barmaid, led the clapping most enthusiastically.

• • •

Jed Pringle was looking through his kitchen window, watching Prudence and the vicar rifle through Goodman's pockets, when he saw Bannerman arrive. "Good Lord! Pretty soon there'll be more people 'ere than in Nextwest Market. What's 'e doing 'ere I wonder?" Sailmaker was sleeping, but restlessly, so Jed placed two chairs against the couch where he was lying to make sure he wouldn't roll off and hurried out to join the trio gathered around Goodman's body. Bannerman looked up as Jed approached, keeping a wary eye on him whilst he continued to question the vicar: "What do you know about Sailmaker, Vicar? The Carter's found 'is dinghy, abandoned, just east of Carter's Rock. The whole village is out searching for 'im." Jed had hobbled into the circle in time to hear the question and responded for the vicar. "He's asleep in the 'ouse, Bannerman. Where'd you come from?" Bannerman looked at Jed's bruised and bandaged head, also noticing the way that he favoured his right side. "What the 'ell's goin' on 'ere? You all look as though you've been in a big fight. Is Sailmaker alright?"

"Well, 'e's been 'urt, but we think 'e'll be alright. He could do with a doctor though to stitch up a nasty 'ead wound. 'ow'd you get 'ere, in a buggy?"

"No, Sailmaker's dinghy. Quicker than a fishin' boat. The villagers thought 'e might 'ave drowned." Looking at the vicar, he added: "I came through The Chute. Ernie 'n' me thought maybe 'e might be workin' on the tackle again since 'e didn't tell anyone where 'e was goin'. Did you know, Vicar?"

"Yes. But he made me promise not to tell anyone – especially Ernie and Meg. He was nervous about going back to the cliff top, but said that was the only way he would get paid for the work he'd done. I tried to talk him out of it and then offered to go with him, but he refused. That was last night. I got worried about him and came out here, to make sure he was alright." Jed broke in. "Bloody good job 'e did too, or we'd all be dead now. You got anyone else followin' you, Bannerman?"

Bannerman looked confused. "Aye, Sully's boat's on the way by now. I don't know if any others'll tag along. They're all searchin' the water, coves and inlets, lookin' for Sailmaker." Jed looked concerned. "Then we'd better get this body out of sight and us back in the 'ouse so's we can get a story worked out. The goin's on 'ere t'day ain't somethin' we should be sharin'".

Bannerman looked around the injured group and said: "There's somethin' else: I ran into trouble at the cliff top. A couple of blokes set about me when I climbed up by the tackle. Is that part of what's goin' on 'ere?" Jed was holding his head again. "Come on up to the 'ouse, Bannerman. We can sit down and tell you all about it. Maybe we'd better cover up the body first though. Could you get some sacks from the barn, Father? I think I need another drink to ease the pain." Roddy nodded. "Whereabouts are the sacks, Jed?"

"Far end of the barn. Loose on the floor, they are. A couple of pieces of firewood would come in 'andy too, just to weight the corners down."

"I'll look after it. You three go to the house. I'll be up shortly." Bannerman put a restraining hand on the vicar's shoulder. "Coverin' 'im up like that won't do; it will still look like a covered body. Somebody's bound to take a look; they might even think it's Sailmaker. Let's get 'im into the barn, Jed. One of us on each corner should do it. We can 'ide 'im better in there. Jump to it; we could be gettin' company anytime." And so Goodman was hidden in the barn behind the crate that had so recently served to prop up Sailmaker.

Sailmaker was awake when Bannerman went in to see him. The young man was pleasantly surprised. Bannerman insisted on seeing his wound and undid the bandage. He was shocked by the size of the ragged cut. "That's gotta hurt," he said. "Somebody put good weight be'ind that – could've killed you. Who did it?"

"It had to be Godfrey," Sailmaker replied. "Goodman was talking to me when everything went black and there were just the three of us in the barn. Goodman thinks I was the informer. He said he'd got some questions to ask me, about who I'd been talkin' to about the tackle. He thought Cap'n Hawksworth was a Customs spy and that I was givin' him information back at the inn. I said it wasn't true and then everything went black. How did you know where I was? Did the vicar tell you?"

"No. The vicar kept his word to you. Boy – you stink of brandy. 'ow much 'ave you 'ad?"

"Only two drinks. But Jed insisted on spilling some in the wound – said it would clean it real good."

Bannerman smiled. "Sounds like a waste of good brandy to me." Then he began telling them how the afternoon had unfolded in Ryeport. After that Prudence explained their side of the story, and Jed told of the vicar's imitation of an avenging angel. Bannerman and Sailmaker both looked stunned. Bannerman shook his head as he said, "Seems I've been misjudgin' you, Vicar. Sorry! 'Give-a-dog-a-bad-name', as the sayin' goes. My first impression of you wasn't good – an' I still think you deserved that one. But I can see you've 'ad an up 'ill battle ever since. The village will be obliged to you for this."

"No, Bannerman!" There was panic in the vicar's voice. "The village mustn't know of my part in this. I would be sacked from the church for sure and I'll lose more than my livelihood if I'm in any way linked to the smuggling operation. Please, keep this matter just between us." Bannerman was silent for a while. "There is the small problem of Goodman, you know. Plus one, maybe two others."

"What others?" asked the vicar, frowning. Bannerman was thoughtful for a few moments. "Well, I guess we all know more about each other now than we would have shared normally, so I'll trust you with my little problem too. Remember I told you that I ran into some trouble on the cliff top today?" There was a quiet chorus of: Yeses and Ayes. "Well, I killed one of 'em." He briefly waggled his improvised club in the air.

"What!" The vicar wasn't prepared for any more shocks today.

Bannerman explained: "When I climbed to the cliff top, these two blokes were waitin' for me and did their best to knock me down onto the rocks. They weren't too good on their feet though. I think they'd been drinkin'. Smelled like it anyway. Luckily, I was able to dodge be'ind the tackle. This club belonged to one of 'em. From what you tell me, I think they must have been the blokes that helped Sailmaker set up the tackle. I imagine they were watchin' to see if any Revenue spies were around. Anyway, there was a fight, an' they lost. They're both at the bottom of the cliff now. One of 'em was still movin' when I looked down, but I didn't go down to check. After the reception I got, I was too anxious to see what'd 'appened to Sailmaker, an' it seemed like time was important. Sully will likely find 'em before anyone else anyway. The tackle made me think that Sailmaker 'ad been there. Then I wondered if the Revenuers 'ad posted men across the road like they did for that last ambush of theirs, so I didn't go straight up to the road but went along the cliff top instead, out of sight from the road, until I was opposite your farm, Jed. I remembered the big oak tree in front of the 'ouse, so I knew where to come out. Then the first person I saw was our vicar 'ere, robbin' a dead man." Roddy stood to object, but Bannerman smiled. "Sorry, Vicar, just teasin'". Roddy nodded and sat down as Bannerman asked: "But what are we going to tell Sully? They already know about the tackle 'cos we was goin' to run our goods ashore there. They also know the vicar 'ere burned my boat, ably assisted by Sailmaker, o' course. So, we can't keep 'em completely in the dark. By the way, Vicar, I never did thank you for that. I loved that old boat, an' I 'aven't worked out how to repay you yet. I 'ad plans to fix 'er up, so I did. You killed my dream." The last words were said in an accusing tone and the vicar looked troubled and about to apologise, but Bannerman smiled and raised a hand to stop him. "Bloody good job you did too. Otherwise, I might be danglin' in chains on some jetty by now. Thank you."

"Now the Sullivans are real good people but can get a bit loose-lipped when they've 'ad a few. Nothin' intentional, you understand. They're just not good at tellin' lies or keepin' secrets. We need a real good story, my friends, an' quick. One the Sullivan boys can believe. They shouldn't know what really 'appened up 'ere t'day, an' they're likely to be arrivin' soon. And they won't find anyone to delay them, when they climb the cliff, so they could be 'ere anytime."

The vicar spoke up. "Could you take Sailmaker back to his dinghy, Bannerman? If you leave now, you might beat the Sullivans to the cliff top. That could avoid a lot of problems. You could take him to Doc Hudson and get his wound looked after. That should be done as soon as possible. You could say that he fell, hurt his head on the rocks and was delirious when you found him. We'll look after Goodman."

"Good idea, Vicar. Are you up to it, Sailmaker?" The young man nodded.

"One more thing, Vicar," said Bannerman. "If I can get him to Sullivans' boat in time, I'm coming back 'ere to 'elp with Goodman." He nodded towards Sailmaker. "The Sullivans can get 'im back to Doc Hudson. There's too much to do 'ere for three beat-up old crocks like you. And Godfrey could be a real problem, no matter what story you come up with. We need to have a serious talk about Mr. Godfrey, vicious, cowardly, bastard that 'e is." Bannerman and Sailmaker swallowed the last of their brandy and left with Bannerman supporting Sailmaker as he walked wearily down the driveway. Their trip back to the beach was slow but uneventful. Fortunately, they arrived just as Sullivan's boat was heading in to the beach. They inspected the bodies of the two smugglers at the base of the cliff as they waited for Sully to beach his boat. Sailmaker confirmed that these men had been the ones that helped set up the tackle. Both were dead. The fall had finished whatever Bannerman had started as far as physical damage was concerned. The Sullivans were visibly shocked by the scene that confronted them. Big Dave Sullivan, 'Sully', stepped out of his boat into a foot of water, calling to the two waiting men as he pulled his boat onto the beach. "Bejesus; what's been goin' on 'ere, Bannerman? You alright, Sailmaker? Glad to see you're still breathin' anyway. Who are these other blokes then?"

Bannerman had a plan forming in his mind and needed to talk to the people at the farmhouse to see if it might work. He was impatient to get going. "Long story, Sully. Sailmaker 'ere was to set up this tackle for the run that got warned-off because of the informer. The Spotsman decided to set it up again – for tonight." He emphasised his next remark by using both hands to point to the Sullivan brothers. "But for some reason – he wasn't goin' to tell us. Now, lads, this looks like it ties in with the tale we 'eard from that boat we met today, remember? They said that smugglers 'ad been runnin' stuff ashore for a couple o' days." The Sullivan brothers nodded. "Well, the Spotsman got Sailmaker to set up the tackle again. But, instead of payin' 'im for 'is work, they set about 'im an' would've killed 'im, but luckily, the vicar just 'appened to pay the Pringles a visit an' that saved Sailmaker's life. Later, when I arrived on the cliff-top, these two blokes set about me. As you can see: they weren't up to the job. Now, lads, I've got to get back to the farm to see what I can find out about the goods that we sunk. I might even 'ave to go to Nextwest to do that 'cos we don't know for sure what's goin' on. But we do need to get Sailmaker to Doc 'udson, an' quick too! The lad's got a real nasty cut on 'is 'ead that needs patchin' up. Now, all that I've told you must stay just between us. The rest of the village mus'n't know the truth because they'll catch on that we're involved in the trade. That wouldn't do, would it?" He raised his eyebrows and spread his arms in a questioning manner. "One careless word could mean our necks! Un'erstand?" Sully looked perplexed.

" 'old on, Bannerman. You're movin' too fast. I thought we were just out lookin' for Sailmaker, and now, 'ere we are with two dead blokes an'

Sailmaker all beat up like. What 'appens about these bodies, an' what 'appens to us, if the Revenuers or the constable comes lookin' for them that knocked off these two blokes?"

Bannerman's shoulders slumped. "Look, lads, I know it's a lot to dump on you unexpectedly, but trust me. It's goin' to be alright. You won't be involved with these dead blokes; I'll look after that. But we must get Sailmaker to Doc pretty fast. On the way 'ome, you can cook up some story about 'im fallin' and crackin' 'is noggin' on some rocks. Say you saw 'im stumblin' about on the beach east of 'ere, delirious like. Remember – you never saw me – I'd gone to Pringles – but don't tell the villagers that either. They think I was just out searchin' for Sailmaker. Just remember: You didn't get this far west. So, you didn't see no tackle either 'cos you found Sailmaker east of 'ere."

"But what about these dead blokes?"

"What dead blokes? You couldn't 'ave seen no dead blokes. You didn't come far enough west, did you?"

Sully and his brother Fred exchanged anxious glances. Uncomfortable with this unexpected, traumatic situation, they were not being given time to get their head around it. Bannerman spread his arms wide. "Come on, lads. I'm not askin' you to get involved in the death of these blokes. I'll look after that. I just need you to get Sailmaker to Doc for some needlework. I promise to bring you up to date as soon as I get back to Ryeport. Meantime, I'll be lookin' after all our interests regardin' the trade goods."

"What's that all about then?" Sully asked. The brothers' faces showed their anxiety.

"Come on, Sully, I don't know myself right now. I 'ave to sort that out with people who do know. What I do know is – we're bein' 'kept in the dark'. Remember the blokes we met t'day, that told us goods were bein' brought ashore, secret like. Why ain't we involved in that?" Sully and Fred shuffled their feet, looking very unsettled. But, finally, with a shrug, Sully gave in. "Alright, Bannerman. We'll take Sailmaker back. We'll trust you. But don't you let us down! And make sure you get back to us as soon as you get back. Meantime, we 'av'nt seen you at all. Is that right?"

"That's right. When I get back, I'll just say: I couldn't find Sailmaker."

"Aye. Come on then, Sailmaker. Let's get you 'ome. You can tell us 'ow you were fallin' about, delirious like, on the way back. Then we'll make a story of it." They helped Sailmaker aboard and pushed off. "See you later, Bannerman. Good luck." Bannerman waved. "Thanks, lads. You too."

Dusk was falling as Bannerman rejoined the group at Pringle's. Prudence had finally persuaded the inebriated Jed that food would be better medicine than brandy. She was shown the pantry with a flourish that all but cost the farmer what little was left of his balance. Homemade bread and butter, some fried sausage, and eggs and bacon soon sat before the conspirators. All was quiet while they satisfied a hunger that had been ignored until the tantalising aroma of the food had invaded their senses. Bannerman was the first to break the silence. "I think we should take friend Goodman back to Nextwest. In fact, I think we should leave him at Godfrey's place."

Prudence and the vicar turned from their meal and looked at Bannerman as though he'd lost his mind. Pru's response was quite emphatic. "Why on earth would we do that? Godfrey is the most dangerous enemy we have right now. And he'll know he's in danger as soon as he knows Goodman is dead. He'll suspect Sailmaker must be alive and that the tables have turned somehow. He and his thugs will have no compunction about killing us. They'd dump our bodies where they'd never be found, and that would be the end of it." Bannerman smiled. "Like they did away with me, you mean?"

"Oh, come on, Bannerman," responded Prudence, sarcastically. "Those two that you settled for were not following one of Godfrey's assassination plans. That was a fair fight compared to what he'd set up for us."

"Hear me out, Miss. Godfrey doesn't know what happened here this afternoon. 'e'd already left before you revealed yourselves, remember? Besides, I don't intend to just dump Goodman on his doorstep. I know Godfrey's dangerous. I want him out of the way for good. Once 'e's gone, I think we'll be safe from all sorts of danger from Revenue officers and old guard smugglers alike, but only if we 'andle this proper. Besides, 'ow will 'e know we're involved? 'is two thugs from the cliff-top are dead. Goodman too. An', if we're careful, it's likely no one will see us dump Goodman at 'is place either." Prudence had to concede the first two points, so Bannerman continued. "Now I know Godfrey lives over 'is shop, somewhere in Nextwest, but I don't know where that is." He raised his eyebrows questioningly as he looked around the table for an answer. Prudence obliged: "It's a scruffy, converted stable at the bottom of Church Street hill. As you said, he lives upstairs and has a carpentry shop on the ground floor."

" 'as 'e got a woman?"

"Are you joking?" The expression on Prudence's face left no doubt as to her opinion of Godfrey's appeal to the fair sex. "Who would own up to that? If he needs female company, he'd have to pay for it. And even then the woman would have to be drunk or desperate." Bannerman gave a satisfied smile. "So, after 'is workin' day is finished, where does 'e go? What does 'e do?" Bannerman spread his arms again, inviting comment. Jed's head was resting on the table, and everyone believed he'd finally succumbed to the brandy, but, without raising his head, he mumbled: "Sometimes 'e goes to The Coach 'n' 'orses to eat, an' ave a couple. Other times, 'e'll fry up somethin' for 'imself or maybe just scoff some bread n' cheese. If 'e's been on a job for Goodman though, 'e usually gets treated to a couple o' pints at The 'Coach'. Gets real narked if Goodman don't 'come across' too. Our Godfrey is a very sensitive man, 'specially if 'e's shown no 'appreciation', as 'e calls it. He's got no friends. Goodman's the only one that'll talk to 'im, as a rule."

"Thanks, Jed. That's valuable information." Bannerman brightened up and started ticking off points on his fingers: " 'e's got a reputation for a nasty temper, gets upset if 'e feels 'e's been slighted, 'e likes 'is ale and I've 'eard, that 'e's a mean drunk. Is that right?"

" 's right," responded Jed.

"Well, we know Godfrey's been on a big job for Goodman t'day. And we've already 'ad our supper. I wonder if Godfrey's 'ad 'is. If 'e 'as, we know for sure that Goodman ain't shown 'im no appreciation, don't we?" He spread his arms wide again. "Odds are: Godfrey's at The Coach right now, tyin' one on. So, let's suppose that after 'e goes 'ome t'night, we all slip into town, quiet like. I'll take Goodman in 'is buggy – we can prop 'im up beside me, so 'e won't look suspicious by floppin' about all over the place. Then we'll carry him into Godfrey's shop, sit 'im down and take off. Vicar, you gotta put 'is money an' watch back. This ain't meant to be no robbery."

"What is it meant to be then? I was only trying to get some of the money that was owed to Sailmaker."

"It's meant to be a murder. That's what – by Godfrey. Look, 'e's a known associate of Goodman. No one would expect someone would go to Godfrey's shop to kill Goodman. But because Godfrey's a mean kind of bloke, an' people are scared of 'im, they'll think Godfrey did Goodman in. I'd bet good money on it. Who else would 'ave cause to kill 'im? 'specially right there in Godfrey's shop? I'll knock a few things over. Make it look like they 'ad a fight."

Jed was more awake than they thought and he piped up. "What 'appens if Godfrey's 'ome? What if 'e's entertainin'?"

"Well then, we 'ave to wait for 'is company to go. Then I'll find a way to slip in, knock Godfrey on the noggin an' put 'im downstairs with Goodman. Maybe 'ave 'im 'oldin' one of them long turnin' chisels that carpenters use on their lathes. Make sure it fits the wound first and put a spot of blood on it for good measure. He 'as got a lathe, I s'pose?"

"Aye, 'e's got a lathe. Made it 'imself. Quite proud of it, so 'e is." Jed was still contributing. Suddenly, the farmer jerked upright in his chair. "My Gawd! The wagon! I forgot to return the bloody wagon." Suddenly, he was very sober – sober but shaky. Prudence too was quick on her feet. "He's right, Bannerman. Jed borrowed a wagon from the church. If it's missed by Tubby or the bishop, Fletcher would be in big trouble, and it's bound to throw suspicion on our whereabouts too. Can you drive, Jed, or shall I? Bob will be worried about you too. That could cause more problems; he might have people looking for you."

Bannerman was quickly on his feet. "Steady, Miss. We'll take all three carriages to Nextwest in a few minutes." Bannerman moved to block passage to the door, as though to prevent any mass exodus. "One more thing before we go. It looks as though Goodman was planning to cut out the Ryeport boats and maybe sell us out to the Revenuers. Maybe because I referred Sailmaker to 'em for the tackle job, 'e might 'ave thought I was in on the informin'. Why else would he leave us in the dark an' our goods still in the water? To me, that means that our goods – 'specially with Goodman dead and, hopefully, Godfrey arrested – should really become 'our goods'. That's the only way we'll get paid now. That's where we'll get Sailmaker's money from too, Vicar. Hey! With those two blokes gone, what's to stop us runnin' our own ring? Not so big o' course, but with people we can trust. No violence, nothing greedy either, just a safe little money-maker. We'd need people with experience, an' some contacts. 'ow about it, Miss Prudence? Jed? Are you two game?"

"Not me," said Jed. "The Revenuers are on our backs already. It's like I told Goodman: our families are our first concern. We'd be no use to them if we're in the jug or danglin' from a rope." Jed moved to pass Bannerman, but the fisherman held up a hand to detain the farmer. "But what if the smugglin' ring is seen to be broken up, the ringleaders dead, their equipment seized and publicly cut up? Like they do with seized smugglers boats.

Don't you think the Revenuers might pat themselves on the back, take all the credit an' get lazy? Bannerman spread his arms wide as if it was a foregone conclusion that he was right. "What equipment are we talkin' about?" said Jed.

"The tackle on the cliff-top," replied Bannerman. "But Sailmaker hasn't been paid for that," objected the vicar. "Never will be, Vicar. Not by Goodman anyway. But we can pay 'im from the proceeds of our trade goods. An', if losin' the tackle to the Revenuers gets 'em off our backs, an' their reinforcements leavin' the area, won't that be a good deal?" The vicar stood up. "I don't agree with setting up Godfrey for Goodman's murder. I'm to blame for that. It's not right that some innocent should pay for my actions, no matter how bad a person he may be. And I want no part of any smuggling." Bannerman shook his head. "Innocent, you say? I don't know anyone who would describe Godfrey as innocent. Not even 'is mother. Look, Vicar – should you pay for it? You were savin' three other people's lives when you killed Goodman, an' remember, 'e was tryin' to kill you at the time. That wasn't murder, just self-defence. Yet by your standards, you're the only person who should be punished. Remember, it was Godfrey who set up Sailmaker for murder and the rest of you too as a consequence of that. Besides, there's no way you could tell Whitestone about this afternoon's troubles without putting all our lives at risk. As for Godfrey, e's killed a few people before. Boasts about it too at times. Relives some of 'is escapades, 'e does too, when he's had a few ales, an' forgets that people might be listenin'. You'd be surprised what you can learn if you pretend t' be asleep when 'e's 'avin' a little chat to 'imself. Like I say – 'e's got away with a few murders in 'is time', so it won't be no injustice if 'e 'angs for one 'e didn't commit. Seems only fittin' if you ask me."

Jed was very much awake now. "But 'ow do we tell the Revenuers about all this business, the tackle, an' Goodman, without being caught ourselves?" Bannerman smiled. "They'll find out for themselves, the next time one of their cutters goes by the beach. Then when they land, they'll find the two bodies at the foot of the cliff. Most likely, they'll think they installed the gear, then got drunk celebratin' and fell off the cliff. Which they did, o' course!" He smiled a happy, confident smile.

CHAPTER 4

Convoluted justice

The beacons were blazing brightly when Sully's boat reached Ryeport. On the way home, they had met Carter's and Joshua Cobbe's boats and lost some time telling them their fabricated story of Sailmaker's alleged fall whilst trying to recover some flotsam that he'd thought worth salvaging. The fishermen were happy that he was safe and very understanding of the need to rush him to Doc Hudson for some speedy repair work.

A small group of villagers were at the jetty, and runners were soon on their way to spread the news that Sailmaker had been found. When Ernie and Meg arrived, they had to help Sully clear a path through the swelling crowd to get him to Doc Hudson; they thought they would never get him there. Finally, Ernie bellowed: "Quiet now! Can't you see he's hurt? Let's get him to Doc's cottage. Fred here will give you the news. You can talk to Sailmaker later when Doc says so." Meg was a little teary, but her tears were of relief rather than concern over his injury. She had feared he was lost forever. The doctor was sleeping in his fireside chair when they hammered on his door. He awoke with a start and yelled: "Stop the damned noise and wait." It took a minute or two before he recovered his composure well enough to present himself at the door as the calm and collected doctor they had all come to know and trust. "So! What have we here? Half the village, by the look of things; are you all sick or just this bandaged young man I see before me?"

"Just Sailmaker, Doctor," Meg replied. "He's hurt his head."

"That appears to be a very credible diagnosis, young Meg. Come on in then, young Sailmaker. Is there anyone here who can throw some light on our young friend's injury?"

"I can, Doc," responded Sully, Meg and Ernie in almost perfect unison.

"Well, I only need one, so I think I'd best take the patient's word for it. The rest of you can go home." Meg looked ready to burst into tears. "Except for you, Meg. The insights of a person as competent in diagnosis as you could prove invaluable." Doc took Sailmaker by the elbow and led him into the living room. "Close the door please, Meg. Bid the good folks outside good-bye before you do. Tell them: we will post bulletins every hour, on the hour." He gave the young girl a comforting smile. "I'm sure this strong young man of yours will be quite safe, Meg. Don't worry." Doc positioned a chair close to the table, to gather as much light as he could from the lamp, and perched his silver-rimmed spectacles on his nose. "Sit here, young Sailmaker. When I brought you into this world, I didn't expect you to be so careless with the good body I delivered. Whatever have you been doing to yourself?"

"Well, Doc, I was climbing over some rocks, looking for some salvage I'd spotted a couple of days ago, but I slipped and bashed my head real bad when I fell. Must've knocked myself out. I think I was delirious or some-thing because I'd wandered quite a way before Sully and Fred found me. I forgot where I left my boat too."

"Really! And who bandaged you up like this?" said Doc as he carefully loosened the bandage and lifted it away from Sailmaker's skull. "Oh, Sully and Fred worked on me as they brought me home."

"Really! They are much more capable than I would have given them credit for. I must watch out, or they may be stealing my position here as village doctor."

"Oh, you've not got anythin' to worry about there, Doc. No one in this village would trust anyone other than you."

"Well, that at least is comforting to know, Sailmaker. Meg: would you please bring me some fresh water from the well? I'll need to clean the wound, and I have spilled some chemicals in the water I have here."

"Certainly, Doc," replied Meg. "I'll not be long. I'll run all the way."

"Don't rush, lass. I don't need you to fall and present me with another patient. One of these is quite enough." When Meg had closed the door behind her, Doc moved around to face Sailmaker. Holding up one finger, he had him follow it with his eyes as he moved it around. "Now, young man, this is quite a nasty wound. I'm afraid it will hurt when I stitch it up. It would have been easier had I got to it earlier."

"Yes, Sir. I understand."

"Do you also understand, Sailmaker, that I am old – not senile – just old. Through those many years that I have lived, I have seen and experienced many strange things. But I've never known men like Sully or Fred – or their good ladies come to that – to wear fine petticoats such as the one that provided your bandage. I'm also sure that those excellent fishermen could never have cleaned your wound as thoroughly as this has been." He picked up a pair of tweezers from a tray on the table. "And I've never yet seen a rock yet that would leave slivers of wood in the flesh that it damaged. Hold out your hand and be quite still."

"Ouch!" yelled Sailmaker as the doctor removed a broad, one inch long sliver and placed it in Sailmaker's outstretched palm. "That hurt, Doc!"

"I'm sure it did. It was almost completely buried in your scalp. Hold still now; there's at least one more like that, buried just as deep too. I can barely see the end of it. No, actually there are two more. That piece of rock must have been made of badly shattered wood. Care to tell me what really happened before Meg gets back? I promise to respect your confidence and even support your story in public. We are friends, are we not? And I seem to recall that I have proven that on more than one occasion." And so Doc Hudson became a party to the details of what Sailmaker had really been doing before he was laid low and how Bannerman had handed him over to Sully whilst he went back to look for answers on the cliff-top. Sailmaker made no mention of the death of the Spotsman or the two men that had lost their lives whilst trying to end Bannerman's. "Mmm! I see. So, you are still involved with the smugglers. I'm not sure your father, Ernie or even Meg would approve of that."

"No, Doc. I'm not really involved. I just rigged the tackle on the cliff top. That's all. I needed the money to help Meg and me get started when we get married. My involvement was meant to end right there with the rigging of the tackle."

"And did you get the money?"

"No, Sir."

"Do you think you will ever get the money?"

"No, Sir."

"Well, my friend, experience is a wonderful thing. We must make sure to learn its lessons or we will be doomed to repeat our mistakes and possibly suffer more wounds like this, with possibly even more disastrous consequences. You are a lucky man to have such a hard head. Otherwise, your experiences might have ended today. Uh oh! Here comes Meg. We never had this conversation."

"No, Sir. Thank you, Sir."

"Don't thank me yet, young man. I'm afraid I shall have to hurt you quite a bit more before I'm finished here. Also, I shall take this piece of petticoat, that smells so of brandy, and throw it in the fire before Meg gets a chance to examine it. I wouldn't want her to get the wrong impression of the Sullivan boys. Quite an expensive petticoat I would think. Good brandy too, by the aroma. Maybe you will have more to tell me later when I change your dressing perhaps. By then you should be feeling better and your memory should have improved."

Meg was a little breathless as she offered the fresh water to the doctor and looked anxiously at Sailmaker. "Thank you, my dear," said Doc. "Would you please heat some of that for me? That clean kettle over by the fire will do just fine. Then perhaps I'll get you to hold this young man's hand whilst I stitch up that nasty cut. I'll also need another lamp, I'm afraid, although they are a poor substitute for daylight."

• • •

Dark clouds were beginning to obscure a crescent moon as the three carriages prepared to leave Pringle's farm for Nextwest. Bannerman had scouted the Coach Road for unwanted observers and insisted on a respectable distance between each carriage to avoid any appearance of a convoy. The conspirators badly needed this night to be as quiet and uneventful as possible, so they waited patiently for Bannerman to signal their individual departures. Goodman had been a big problem. The dead man's size and weight had made it difficult to position him so that he looked natural in the buggy whilst ensuring that he wouldn't collapse in his seat at the first bump in the road. That had taken about half an hour. Bannerman had grumbled all through their struggles as his mind raced ahead to the uncertain problems they would face once they got to Godfrey's shop in Church Street. Goodman had arrived at the farm in Whatson's buggy, and they planned to leave that tied up beside Godfrey's shop, giving the impression that Goodman had gone there for a visit. Prudence would ride with Roddy in his wagon, and he would take her directly to The White Hart. Hopefully, she would be able to slip into the inn by the back staircase, unobserved, so as not to provoke questions about her badly bruised face. After that, the vicar would go directly to the carpenter's shop on Church Street to help Bannerman and Pringle with Goodman's body.

Pringle's first job was to return Betsy and the borrowed wagon to Fletcher at the church. They were desperately hoping that no one had needed the wagon during the unintentionally long loan. Jed would then walk to Godfrey's, briefly pausing on the way at The Coach and Horses, in the hope of seeing his brother. He badly needed to bring him up to date on the afternoon's events, but he did not want to be seen by anyone else at the inn, in case his injuries drew too many questions.

Jed led the way, with the vicar's wagon second in line. Bannerman and Goodman, in the buggy, would bring up the rear. They were less than a mile from Nextwest when the first smattering of rain added an uncomfortable dampness to the already cool night. Bannerman cursed. He didn't want Goodman to be wet when discovered in the dryness of the carpenter's shop. Someone might remember what time the rain had started, and his wet clothes and his stiffening body might raise suspicion about the scenario that Bannerman intended to set up. Leaving his horse free rein, Bannerman fastened the cape across the front of the buggy as they travelled, cursing Goodman all the while for not helping. The rain got heavier and, as much as Bannerman worried about its effect on Goodman's condition, it did benefit the conspirators by causing most people to stay indoors, and their journey was unobserved. "So far so good," muttered Bannerman, as he saw Jed's wagon turn right, into the church driveway. The lanterns of the vicar's wagon up ahead continued on, across the Church Street intersection. Bannerman turned Whatson's buggy left, off the Coach Road, and proceeded downhill on Church Street. Godfrey's place would have been hard to miss, even without Pru's clear directions. It was the last building on the right-hand side as he descended the hill from the church, and he soon spotted the rutted lane that ran off to the right at the far side of the carpenter's shop and at right angles to Church Street.

Unwittingly, the vicar echoed Bannerman's remark: "So far, so good," as he crossed Church Street, following that with a long sigh as the carriages parted company. Prudence looked at his tense, rain-spattered features and said, "Try not to worry, Roddy. I think Bannerman has found a way to turn this situation in our favour. I know the idea of laying Goodman's death in Godfrey's lap doesn't sit well with you. But it's just a crooked way of achieving a just result. Just think of how this day would have ended had Goodman and Godfrey had their way. If you hadn't turned up when you did, three of us would be dead, and Godfrey and Goodman would be celebrating right now."

"That's hardly the point, Pru. Two wrongs don't make a right. Without saying a word, we are lying a man all the way to the gallows for something he didn't do. Even if I weren't in the church – and you know how much I wish I weren't – it's still an unjust thing to do. How can we expect any good to come of it?"

"Well, Roddy, it's far better for us, and certainly more just than the alternative. Anyway, we're committed now. So, make the best of it!" Her tone was impatient and the last words were harshly spoken. Roddy turned to look at her as if she were a stranger. "Pru, there is an underlying hardness about you that I would never have believed possible."

"Well, if you had shared my experiences with the likes of the Godfreys and Goodmans of this world, you would understand." Then they were past the built-up streets of Nextwest, and the road now ran between scattered cottages that lined the last mile to The White Hart. The windows of those homes glowed warmly, making them look most cosy and inviting to the damp and troubled pair, and they both fell silent, each occupied by their own thoughts about this dangerous venture and its possible outcomes.

• • •

Jed Pringle was apprehensive as he drove the wagon into the stable yard behind the church, muttering an improvised prayer as he went. "Oh, dear God! Please let us get away with this one. I know we've been bad...but not really that bad. Not really." His tone brightened a little. "More good than bad if you consider our intentions. Please Lord; we don't need no bishop or reverend to jump all over us and 'and us over to the constable for stealin' this 'ere wagon or any other bad thing neither. Not now. Please, Lord. Please." Jed had become much more of a believer since perceiving the vicar as an avenging angel, and he was hoping for a modest reward for that as he drove the wagon close to the door that led to Fletcher's flat, above the stables. Tentatively, he knocked on the door. No response. He knocked again, louder this time, as he called softly: "Fletch. Fletch." But there was still no answer.

Suddenly, he was seized from behind by strong hands that grabbed his upper arms. Startled, he let out a frightened: "Ooooh!"

"What's the meaning of this then?" The unfamiliar voice was deep, stern, and assertive. "What are you doin' with this 'ere wagon? Stealin' it, were ye?" Jed tried to turn and face his captor, but the strong grip wouldn't allow it. "Who are you?" he said. "Who were you expecting?" responded the gruff voice. "I...I was looking for Fletcher, Sir," said Jed, in a shaky voice. "Well! You've bloody well found 'im then, 'aven't ye?" Fletcher responded in his normal voice and followed that with a deep chuckle. The stableman relaxed his grip on Jed's arms, allowing the shaken farmer to turn and face him. Then he resumed the deep, assertive voice: "An' what's the meanin' of you bein' so bloody late back, with this 'ere wagon then?" He gave another chuckle, obviously enjoying his play-acting and the scare he'd given Jed.

Jed, however, was not amused. "You silly old sod, Fletch; you scared the shit out of me! 'ere was I, worried that I might be gettin' you in trouble by bein' late back with the wagon, an' you sneak up on me like that." He took off his wet hat and swatted the stableman with it. Fletcher laughed, and Jed realised that this was the first time he'd ever heard this melancholy man laugh out loud. Then he caught a whiff of rum. "You drunken old bugger!" he said in a surprised voice. " 'ere's me, worryin' about you gettin' in trouble and all the while you're gettin' pissed up, an' 'avin' a great time. I'll remember this, I will."

"Stop your blatherin', you old fool. You're very late back, and it's no credit to you that I'm not in deep trouble," responded Fletch. "I don't owe you any more favours, Pringle. We're all square after this!" He pulled a bottle from his coat pocket. "Wanna drink?"

"No thanks, Fletch," Jed responded. "Thanks, but I've gotta find me brother, Bob. 'e must be wonderin' where the 'ell I am. Can I leave the wagon 'ere – like this – Fletch? I'm really in trouble and a bad 'urry."

"Oh, sure! Borry the wagon, by all means, Pringle. Return it late with the 'orse all wet and the wagon dirty, an' then piss off. No time to share a drink with the good friend that 'elped you out when you came cryin'. Just leave me to clean up your mess an' put the 'orse away. I'm only a lowly stableman after all. Well then, you can piss off if that's what you want." Fletch put on his best 'poor-me' expression, but in the dim light of the carriage lantern, it was wasted on Jed. He had never seen Fletcher in such a playful mood before, but it certainly made him more interesting.

"Oh, alright. But just one swig, Fletch. I really am in trouble, 'specially if I can't find Bob quickly. 'e'll likely 'ave people out lookin' for me right now." He grabbed the bottle from Fletch's hand, took a quick swig and handed it back. "Good 'ealth, mate. I owe ye' one. I'm sorry I must rush away. I'll make it up to ye' later." As Jed turned to leave, the light from the lantern fell on his bandaged head and bruised face. "My God, Pringle! What the 'ell 'appened to you? Looks like you been in a bloody war."

"I fell, Fletch. I went back to the farm to get me dad's old musket…'cos some bloke at the market was int'rested in buyin' it. Thought I might make a shillin' or two. Then I went into the barn to check on somethin'. I fell off the bloody ladder an' banged me noggin on a shovel when I landed. Knocked me out, so it did. That's why I'm so late! Bob'll be mad as 'ell. "

Jed grabbed the musket from the back of the wagon and waved it at Fletcher, saying: "The bloke that wanted the musket is likely gone by now too." The stableman jumped back, startled. "Is that thing loaded?" "Nah! You're the only thing that's loaded around 'ere. This is broke. Gotta run. Thanks, Fletch." Jed took off at a slow trot, aware that time was valuable and worried that Bannerman might badly need his help.

• • •

After turning onto Church Street, Bannerman had slowed the buggy to quieten his approach to Godfrey's shop. He was grateful that the rain was keeping casual strollers indoors and that the street was deserted. "Easy now," he called softly to the walking horse, dreading that the animal might whinny at the sight of a familiar resting place. "Easy!" He turned right into the lane, hiding the buggy behind the mature trees alongside the shop before getting down. He looked up the street, to reassure himself that he'd not aroused any attention, before looping the reins over a broken piece of fence. "Good girl. Good girl," he said softly, as he patted the animal's wet neck.

There were no signs of life around the building, so he peered through a window into the dark interior, wondering if Godfrey was home. The place appeared deserted, and it was too dark to see anything other than vague shapes inside, but Godfrey might possibly be upstairs, sleeping. "Might even have some paid company," he muttered. He was concerned that the door might have a bell attached and needed to find a quiet way in. The first window was immoveable, so he moved cautiously around the back of the building where he found two more secure windows. Those on the other side of the building were secure too. That left only the exposed front of the building. "Damn!" He took a quick look around before moving through puddles in the pathway to try the window. That too was immoveable, and he felt the tension beginning to build. "What if I can't get in?" he muttered. He grasped the door handle but fearing that it might be fitted with a bell, tentatively lifted the latch and eased the door open a little so that he could feel for a spring hung bell overhead. The hinges squeaked but, finding no bell, he walked in. "Well, I'll be buggered!" he said, " 'e locks all the winda's and leaves the door unlocked." Standing in the shop, he tried to collect his thoughts whilst his eyes grew accustomed to the darkness. He was damp and uncomfortable despite the topcoat that Jed had lent him at the farm. The rattling noise of rain on the windows reminded him that Goodman could be getting very wet right now. He fumbled around in the dark, trying to familiarise himself with the layout and find the stairs to check the bedrooms. He wanted to light a lamp, but that could invite trouble. He was still fumbling around the cluttered bench, his back to the door, when he heard the latch lift.

• • •

The vicar and Prudence pulled into the rear yard of The White Hart Inn without attracting any attention. Apart from a single buggy in the front yard of the inn, it appeared that the place was devoid of customers tonight. Apparently, busy market day activities, plus the rain, had dampened the socialising spirits of the usual patrons of this country inn. "Thank God for a quiet night," said the vicar. "Let's hope our luck holds." He helped Prudence down from the wagon, then climbed the stairway to check that the way was clear for her. "All clear, Pru," he said. "I'll see you to your door."

"No need. I can manage."

"I'm sure you can. But I will see you safe before I leave anyway." His tone was more assertive now, and she sensed that he had been hurt by her earlier intolerance. "Very well, kind Sir, but you should consider that it could compromise your reputation if you were seen escorting a lady to a room at an inn in such a furtive manner. On the other hand, I could scream and claim that you attacked me. I do have these bruises, you know."

"Oh, Pru! For God's sake, stop playing around. This is a serious situation."

"Roddy, I don't need to be serious. You're serious enough for both of us. We can't turn back the clock. We must make the most of what we have. We'll get over this, and later, we'll be able to look back on this day and laugh about it."

"I hope you're right. I've never killed a man before, and I don't find it funny. And don't forget, the hard part is still to come. I now have to put the blame for that on someone else. Pru, I must hurry away and see how Bannerman and Pringle are getting on." Prudence managed to open her door without appearing to alert anyone, and she quickly pulled him inside before closing the door. "Thank you for saving me today, Roddy." Then she wrinkled her nose and, looking very disappointed, added: "I'd always hoped it would be a knight in shining armour that would ride to my rescue. But the gallant that rode to my rescue arrived in a church wagon and wore dowdy black." Then she smiled, put one hand behind his head, pulled him close and kissed him. "I would be dead today if it weren't for you, Roddy. You are the only man who has ever come to my rescue, except for Grandfather, of course, and gallant though he was, he was too old to be the knight in shining armour that girls dream of." She stared into his worried face and said: "But you must be going now," and turned him towards the door. "Be careful, Roddy; try to think of the just reasons for what we are doing rather than the rights and wrongs of some legal code. Just do what has to be done. Go, quietly now."

Roddy gently touched her bruised face. "I'm so sorry you were hurt like this."

"Don't worry about it. Once he'd spent all my money, my husband did more damage than this. I will heal." She looked out the door. "All clear, away you go," she whispered, and pushed him through the door, blowing him a kiss as he tiptoed down the stairs. She hadn't noticed that the next door, across the hall, was open just a crack or the eye that was pressed to that crack.

• • •

Bannerman's senses seemed unnaturally heightened and muscles that he didn't know he had tensed like coiled springs in response to the quiet squeak of the doors hinges. Curled wood shavings that littered the floor crunched underfoot, and he turned his head towards the sound. A shadowy figure was briefly framed in the doorway before it closed. Bannerman's searching fingers found a chair leg on the bench. He gripped it and froze, waiting for an opportunity to deliver the first blow in this confrontation with Godfrey.

"Bannerman?" The voice was low and hesitant.

Bannerman's shoulders relaxed, and he felt the tension slip from his cold muscles. "Pringle, you silly arse. You scared the wits out of me. I thought you was Godfrey."

"No worries there," the hushed voice responded. "'e's passed out in the side yard at The 'Coach.' Soakin' wet 'e is. Inside an' out, by the looks of 'im. What're you up to then?"

"We've got to get Goodman in 'ere. Wish we could 'ave a light."

"Let's put the front shutters up. There's an oil lamp by the door 'ere."

" 'ow come you know so much about this place, Pringle? An' 'ow did ye get on with the wagon?"

"Wagon's alright. Fletch scared the hell out of me though. 'e's pissed too. Thought 'e'd 'ave some fun with me, so 'e did. I'll tell you about that later. I've been in 'ere a few times. Carryin' messages for Goodman an' things like that. Give me a 'and with the shutters. You get over to the right side of the winda." The loose shutters were soon hooked in place, and they lit the lamp and placed it on the floor to minimise any light that might show through cracks in the dilapidated wooden shutters. They had just finished this when the sound of the latch lifting startled them both. The door squeaked, and someone slipped quickly through the door and closed it behind him. Bannerman was positioned just inside the door, with the chair leg raised over his head. Pringle too was crouched and ready to do battle. Roddy hurriedly raised his left arm to shield his face. "Steady, Bannerman. It's me!"

"I can see that now, you silly sod. Why didn't you let us know you were there before you opened the door?"

"Because I knew you were expecting me, Bannerman. I parked my wagon just ahead of your buggy, so I knew you were here."

"We weren't expectin' you yet. You made good time."

"What's first then? Let's get this ugly business over with."

• • •

Back at The 'Coach,' Godfrey was stirring. He groaned and rolled on his side as he felt a sudden compulsive heaving in his stomach. Raising himself to his hands and knees, he parted company with most of his supper. He was soaked through and freezing cold from lying in the rain. Miserable and disoriented from the effect of the alcohol, he struggled to his feet and found, to his surprise, that there was still something in his stomach that he would not be allowed to keep. He collapsed against the gatepost of the side yard until his stomach muscles had finished pumping him dry, and he had to cling there for a while longer whilst those same muscles checked and re-checked to make absolutely sure he was holding nothing back. Eventually, he staggered around the fence and stumbled off towards Church Street and his shop.

Back at Godfrey's shop, Bannerman was rummaging through his tools. Eventually, he found what he had been looking for: the long, narrow-bladed, turning tool. "Jed says Godfrey is passed out in the side yard of The 'Coach,'" he said. "That should give us enough time to make the little scene that we're settin' up look more realistic." He held up the wood turning tool. "This chisel's long narrow blade is about the same thickness as the tines on your pitchfork, Vicar. I'll stuff it into the wounds in Goodman's chest, just so's they match 'cos, unlike them tines, this chisel 'as a square blade. I'll leave it in Goodman when we go. Now let's see if we can get the big fella in 'ere." The three conspirators positioned some boxes to shield the lamplight from the door and slipped out to the buggy. Bannerman removed the cape from around Goodman's lower half and also the board that he had tied him to. Then he took the chisel and pushed it into the wounds on the dead man's chest, finally leaving it in the one that had penetrated his heart. The vicar had to turn away, fearing that he would vomit. "My God, man; that is sickening," he said.

"It's just a necessary part of the plan," responded the fisherman.

"Oh, my Lord – Godfrey's comin'!" exclaimed Pringle hoarsely. The vicar was quickly at his side at the corner of the shop. "Where?"

"There," Pringle pointed, "about four 'ouses from the top o' the street. Oops! Looks like 'e's stopped to water someone's garden." Sure enough, Godfrey had decided that he didn't need to be as wet inside as he was out and was relieving himself in a neighbour's flowerbed. Suddenly, the door of the house opened, and a deep threatening voice could be heard yelling at Godfrey. "We've got to 'urry up, matey," Jed called to Bannerman. " 'e'll be 'ere in a couple 'o minutes unless 'e passes out again."

Bannerman had turned the stiffening Goodman sideways in the seat so that he faced towards them. "You two will 'ave to take 'is legs, an' I'll take 'is shoulders," he said as he climbed up into the buggy. "We'll get 'im inside an' prop 'im up on one o' them boxes. Ready?"

"Ready," Jed responded and, moving to the side of the buggy, grabbed Goodman's right leg as the vicar took the other leg. They lowered Goodman down from the bench seat, onto the footboard. "I don't like this," said the vicar. "Godfrey will be here before we can get Goodman inside." Leaving Goodman sitting on the footboard, with his back propped against the seat, he and Jed ran to the corner of the shop for another look. "The man that was yelling at him has just thrown a bucket of water over Godfrey," said the vicar. "Very soon this place is going to be too public. There'll be a fight by the look of things; then we'll have an audience to contend with. Someone might go in the shop and find Goodman sitting there, already dead. Then it'll be obvious that Godfrey didn't kill him." Goodman was left sitting on the footboard of the buggy, with one foot on the iron step and the other dangling alongside as Bannerman hurriedly joined the vicar and Jed at the corner of the shop.

Godfrey had fallen over when the water hit him. Now he staggered to his feet and moved towards his antagonist. The man then threw the bucket at Godfrey, who promptly fell over it. The three conspirators looked at each other in alarm, realising that their plans were about to be shattered. "Looks like we'll 'ave to take Goodman away with us after all," said Bannerman despondently. "There's no point in trying to set up this scene with people watchin'. An' Goodman's gettin' wetter all the time."

Godfrey had staggered to his feet again. "I've got yer bloody bucket!" They heard him yell at the water-chucker, and then he turned and stumbled in their direction. Then he dropped the bucket and fell over it. The 'water-chucker' followed him just far enough to retrieve his bucket and then made some comments to a neighbour who had stepped out to see what all the commotion was about. Then 'water-chucker' went indoors; the neighbour remained long enough to watch Godfrey until he stepped inside his shop. Then he also went indoors.

"Too late! We're done for now," said Pringle as he waved his hand despairingly. "Now what do we do?" said the vicar. "Let me think," responded Bannerman impatiently. Suddenly, Godfrey was back in the doorway of his shop, holding the chair leg that Bannerman had been about to brain the vicar with only minutes before. "Who's 'ere? Where are ye? I know yer 'ere, ye thievin' bastard." Godfrey yelled as he staggered out of the shop towards the laneway – looking for a fight. "Look out; 'ere 'e comes," Pringle called in a hushed voice. "Does this lane lead anywhere?" Bannerman asked Pringle. "Aye! It's rough and twisty – 'ardly ever used, but it leads back to the Coach Road, about 'alf-way between Church Street and The White 'art." Bannerman turned to the vicar. "Vicar, take your wagon and go out that way. Take the Coach Road and get back to Ryeport. Pringle an' me'll take care of this matter now. We've got to change plans."

"I can't leave you two alone with all this trouble," said the vicar.

"Go, Vicar. Go now! Or you'll get us into more trouble. How could we explain you being 'ere as well as a buggy with a dead man in it? Go, quickly. Quickly but quietly. Get your wagon out of sight before the locals come to see what this commotion's all about." Roddy reluctantly backed away. Then taking Slondosh's bridle, he led the animal quietly down the lane, struggling with conflicting emotions over deserting his friends. Bannerman pulled Pringle around behind the buggy as Godfrey rounded the corner of his shop. The drunken man paused there to retch painfully one more time and then focused on the buggy. "Goodman? Is that you? You miserable bastard, where was you earlier? After all I did for ye t'day, you could've bought me a few drinks, at least." He staggered the last few steps to the buggy and held on to the dashboard, looking uncomprehendingly at the wet figure of the Spotsman. "Goodman! Goodman! Answer me. What's wrong with ye?" He dropped the chair leg, grabbed Goodman's coat with both hands and started to shake him. Then in the dim light of the coach lantern, he saw the chisel handle protruding from the dead man's chest.

"My Gawd! Who did this? Are you alright?" He gingerly touched the chisel's handle, then stumbled and had to grab Goodman's coat to recover his balance. Goodman's body shifted a little. "Talk to me, Goodman. Talk t' me!" Then the stupefied Godfrey gave Goodman another shake, and the body suddenly lurched and tumbled from its precarious perch, knocking the drunken Godfrey down and pinning him to the ground. Godfrey tried to wriggle out from under Goodman's dead weight, but in his drunken state, it was too much for him. He was pinned, face up, beside the buggy, in the puddle-filled laneway. Bannerman and Pringle looked between the wheels of the buggy at the two prostrate figures until Godfrey gave up struggling. "Quick, Jed. Go after the vicar," whispered Bannerman. "Don't let Godfrey see you. The vicar was leadin' 'is 'orse, so you'll catch 'im if you run. Tell 'im to wait for me. I'll see 'ow this works out. Then I'll follow ye."

• • •

The landlord at The Coach and Horses decided to check on Godfrey. The barmaid, guessing his intentions, went as far as the door with him. "No point in us both gettin' wet," she said with a smile, as she handed her employer an oilskin cape. Shields slipped the cape over his shoulders and left the shelter of the porch, carrying a candle lantern. The rain had been falling heavily for an hour now. "No sign of 'im 'ere," Shields called back to Ada as he looked into the side yard. "Oh, that dirty bugger!" he yelled suddenly. "What's up?" called Ada. Shields turned to face her, looking disgusted. "'e's spewed up all over the path, the bushes, and the bloody fence. And I've gone an' trod in it." He quickly left the side yard and cleaned his shoes on a patch of grass, before stepping past the barmaid and back into the inn. "With any luck, the rain will clean most of that away," he said as he removed the cape. Ada gave him a clean bar towel to dry his face. " 'ave a word with Jack tonight, Ada. Tell 'im to make sure that's all cleaned up first thing tomorrow. Y' know, I'd like to ban your Mr. Godfrey from the inn, Ada. But I'm not sure 'ow well that would sit with Goodman. He seems to be the only bloke that can control that maggot." Ada pulled a face. "'e's not my Mr. Godfrey, Guv'nor, but at least 'e's gone from 'ere. D'ye think 'e made it 'ome?"

"Who cares? It would do this whole town a favour if 'e never made it 'ome again. I wonder what friend Goodman would've said if 'e'd 'eard Godfrey cussin' 'im earlier t'night. One thing Godfrey's good at is makin' enemies. It sounded like they'd 'ad a fallin' out, didn't it? Trouble is, no one's got the guts to sort Godfrey out. Too scared of 'ow many of 'is thugs might be waitin' for ye one dark night when ye least expect it."

Bob Pringle was waiting at the bar as they returned. "Evenin', Guv', Ada. I wondered if either of ye 'ave seen or 'eard anythin' of my brother Jed. 'e should've been 'ere for supper, but no one's seen 'ide nor 'air of 'im since this mornin'."

"Sorry, Bob," said Ada. "Last I 'eard, 'e was drivin' a wagon through the market around noon time. Not seen 'im since." Shields nodded his agreement. "Where was 'e goin', Bob?"

"I think 'e may 'ave gone back to the farm. But he's been gone a long time. I'm concerned 'e might 'ave 'ad an accident." Shields looked sympathetic: "Look, Bob, if you're worried about 'im – my buggy's out back in the stable if ye' want it. Be a job gettin' your 'eavy wagon on the road tonight, wouldn't it? And no protection from the rain either. You'd be soaked through in a couple of minutes. Tell Jack I said it's alright. No charge t' you. I must be off t' bed myself. Got an early start tomorrow'". He gave Bob a consoling slap on the shoulder and left. "Why would Jed go back to the farm, Bob?" asked Ada.

"Maybe he forgot something, Ada. It's always a problem leavin' livestock unattended an' we left in a bit of a rush this mornin'. I think I will borrow that buggy. Maybe Jack'll come with me. Just in case I need a hand."

"Of course 'e would. Good lad is our Jack. You be careful now."

"I'll do that, Ada. I'll be away then. Please let my wife know I'm goin' back to the farm just to check on Jed. I'll be as quick as I can."

"Sure, Bob, right now," and Ada headed for the staircase leading to the rented rooms. Half an hour later, Bob and Jack were headed east in Shields' buggy.

. . .

Godfrey hadn't moved for almost five minutes, but it seemed more like an hour to the rain-soaked Bannerman as he lay in the rain beside the buggy, listening to the man's irregular and laboured breathing. Bannerman crawled further under the buggy, hoping for some protection from the pouring rain, whilst he fathomed out a way to change his badly shattered plan. Unfortunately for him, the run-off from the laneway was draining into a low area under the buggy, and he found himself lying in a deep, muddy puddle under the buggy.

Godfrey's outstretched arm was trapped by Goodman's weight. Bannerman tickled the palm of Godfrey's hand, but there was no response, so he crawled out from under the buggy to get a look at Godfrey's face. His eyes were closed, and his breathing had become a weak, irregular struggle for air. Every so often, he would give a great gasp and then seem to stop breathing completely until the next great gasp. Goodman's weight was crushing his chest and stomach, making his breathing difficult. His flesh was icy cold to Bannerman's touch, and feeling a sudden surge of compassion, he stood up, grabbed Goodman's arm and started to pull him off the distressed Godfrey.

Godfrey's eyes opened, and his head jerked around. "Get...off...me... Goodman. You-ou... bastard!" he gasped. "Get...off...me!" Bannerman jumped back, startled, dropping Goodman's full weight back on the prostrate man. That had the effect of squeezing any remaining air out of Godfrey's lungs in one painful wheeze. He hadn't been able to raise his head far enough to see over Goodman, and his head now dropped back to the ground. The two men were completely saturated, as was Bannerman, but at least he was no longer lying in a puddle.

Bannerman was considering what to do next when he heard voices, but the words were inaudible because of the noise of the rain falling on the roof of the buggy and the shop. He looked up the lane in the direction taken by the vicar and Jed, but there was no sign of them. The voices were closer now, coming from the street beyond Godfrey's shop. He backed quietly up the lane and hid behind the shop, where because of the lantern inside, he now had a clear view of the shop's interior through a back window. The man that had thrown the water over Godfrey – the 'water-chucker' and his neighbour were entering the shop.

"Not like 'im to leave a lantern on the floor," the neighbour said. "I always remember 'im bein' worried about startin' a fire with all these shavin's an' sawdust. Where is 'e, d'ye think?"

"I'll check upstairs," said the water-chucker. "Real pissed 'e was. He's most likely passed out up there."

"Aye, that 'e was." A minute later, the water-chucker called down. "Not up 'ere. My God, this place is like a pigsty an' it stinks even worse. Makes ye wonder 'ow anyone could bear to live like this. 'e's got a bucket up 'ere. Don't look like e's ever emptied it. What a stink."

Bannerman moved closer to get a wider view through the window. He didn't know what he would do if the men looked into the lane and saw Godfrey pinned under Goodman. Everything was going badly, and he'd not been able to form a plan that would respond to the changed situation. He was moving to the next window, treading very carefully, when he was suddenly grabbed from behind. His heart skipped a beat, and he whirled around, fist raised, to confront – Jed Pringle. "By Jesus, Jed," he grated in a hushed voice. "You scared the shit out of me! That's twice in one bloody night, you silly sod. Be still now!" He took a quick look through the window. The two men had moved the boxes surrounding the lamp, which they now hung on a ceiling hook. "Safer there!" the water-chucker said.

"Aye. We'd best look around, don't ye think? Daft bastard's most likely passed out outside somewhere."

"Aye. Be fine by me if 'e'd passed out with 'is 'ead in a ditch full o' water. Be an end to all sorts of trouble 'round 'ere." They moved outside. "I'll go left; you go right," said the water-chucker.

Bannerman turned to Jed, put a finger to his lips and motioned him back towards a thicket. They quickly tiptoed to deeper cover. Suddenly, there was a shout from the man that had gone to the laneway. "Bill! Over 'ere, quick." The water-chucker ran from the other side of the shop and froze at the sight of the two sodden figures on the ground.

"Oh, my God!" he said as he hurried to join his neighbour. The two men pulled Goodman off Godfrey, and as they rolled Goodman over, Bill spotted the chisel in his chest. "By Jesus, Jonesy, Godfrey's killed the big fella an' then got trapped under 'im when 'e fell. 'ow is 'e? Godfrey, I mean."

"He looks bad, Bill. You might get your wish yet. 'e's 'ardly breathin'. The big guy's dead as a doornail. Judgin' by the angle of the chisel, looks like Godfrey stabbed 'im as 'e was gettin' down from the buggy. We'd best get the constable." The two men started to run up the street. Suddenly, Bill stopped – panting heavily. "We're bloody mad," he said. "Let's take the buggy. It's a long way to the constable's 'ouse." And so, they took Goodman's buggy, pausing only long enough to tell their wives what they'd discovered. "Where's the vicar? We've got to go now and fast," said Bannerman, as he grabbed Pringle's arm.

" 'bout a quarter-mile up the road." They both trotted off quietly, taking an occasional look over their shoulders as the noise of the gathering crowd grew louder.

• • •

Prudence had changed into her nightdress and was at the washstand bathing her bruised cheek when the knock came at her door. She stood silently for a few seconds, deciding whether or not to answer it and preferring not to let anyone see her bruises. The knock came again, more insistent this time –

then again, louder still. Finally, she went to the door. "Who is it?" she called softly.

"Your benefactor," was the reply, and she recognised Whitestone's voice. "I'm just going to bed. Can't this wait until tomorrow?"

"No. I need to see you now." Reluctantly she opened the door, as her mind raced, seeking a plausible but innocent reason for her bruises. Whitestone quickly slipped through the doorway. "Well, well, my dear. Is this the vicar's handiwork? Did you have a falling out?" He put one hand under her chin, turning her head so that he could get a better look at her swollen cheek.

"What makes you think the vicar had anything to do with it?" Prudence still hadn't fashioned a reasonable explanation for the bruises and was trying to delay the inevitable questions.

"Well, my dear," said Whitestone. "I've taken the room across the hall. Just to be close to you. I saw the vicar of Ryeport leave just minutes ago. I was wondering if you had any news for me. He is in on the smuggling after all, isn't he?"

"Not to my knowledge. In fact, I'm certain that he wouldn't have the stomach for it."

"Then what are you doing associating with him? And where did the bruises come from?"

"Actually, I met the vicar after my grandfather's funeral. He initiated clothing donations from this parish for the villagers of Ryeport. I had some clothes I didn't need, so I participated. It so happens I enjoy his company. I find him entertaining and respectful, something I rarely experience with my other male acquaintances."

"Oh, dear! Was that a dig at me?" Whitestone put his hand on his heart and adopted a theatrically hurt expression. "If the shoe fits," Prudence responded.

"Oh, well, enough of this playful banter. Let's get down to business. You owe me some information."

"I already gave you information. You wanted a timely warning of a run. I gave it to you, and you made a mess of it. I owe you nothing."

"Don't try me on, young lady." Whitestone's jaw tightened, and he leaned belligerently towards her. "Your pardon can be revoked. I dealt with you in good faith. You need to do the same." Prudence looked at him scornfully.

"So, what do you want from me now?"

"Just as before, the details of the next run and information on how smugglers plan to bring their sunken trade goods ashore. The goods from the failed ambush, which they either had to sink or hide. And where did you get the bruise, from a smuggler or a lover?"

"My private life is none of your affair!"

Whitestone sneered as he said: "You know that any part of your life can be my affair if I choose to make it so." Prudence fell silent, but Whitestone was not prepared to accept stalling tactics any longer. "You were seen leaving Nextwest this morning in a wagon driven by a man. Who was it?" Prudence realised that whoever had tipped Whitestone off about her departure didn't know Jed Pringle. But she needed time to consider how much she could safely involve Jed. She had no way to advise him of what she would tell Whitestone, who was bound to have it corroborated. So, she changed tack. "Who's Corby?" she said. Whitestone visibly stiffened. "What did you say?" he said.

"Corby! Who's Corby? One of yours?"

"Where did you hear that name?" Whitestone stared intently into her face as though trying to read her mind. "From Goodman; he asked me to have dinner with him downstairs about a week ago to talk business. *Business*," she emphasised. "I have no more romantic interest in him than I have in you, despite your insinuations." Whitestone's expression was angry. "Get on with it."

Prudence improvised. "We'd arranged that he would wait for me in the bar, but when I arrived, he was standing at the bar talking to Godfrey. You know Godfrey?" Whitestone nodded. "I thought I might learn something if I didn't interrupt them, so I sat and waited at a table with my back to them. I was close enough to hear them, but I had missed some of the conversation. However, I did hear the name Corby mentioned a couple of times. What made it seem significant was the way they lowered their voices when they said it, as though they were talking secrets. I couldn't make out what Corby was supposed to have done, but I'd not heard the name before. I got the impression that he's not a smuggler but that they'd been able to get information from him about your ambush. They seemed to think he could be a future source of information. Who is he?"

"Never mind. There's no need for you to know. What did they say, exactly?"

"I don't remember, *exactly*. Remember, I was not meant to be party to the conversation. Also, I came in part way through it. I do remember Goodman saying: "Thank God for Corby. We'd have been finished but for him! So, is he one of yours?"

"Just answer the questions. The rest is none of your business."

"Well, thank you, kind Sir, for your gentle manners," she said, with a coy smile and a batting of her eyelids. Whitestone got very angry. "Don't play smart with me, woman. You don't know how dangerous it can be."

"Oh! Might you be more dangerous than extreme torture followed by hanging? If I recall correctly, that was an earlier promise that you made to me. But be aware that I have already given my 'pardon' to a reliable and highly placed advocate in the government – together with a full account of our agreement – for full disclosure in the event of my untimely death or imprisonment." Whitestone was furious, and his jaw muscles were clenching and releasing as he struggled to control his temper. "How did you come by the bruise?" he demanded. "Or would you like a matching one, on the other side of your face?"

"Well! How could I possibly refuse such a brave and chivalrous offer?" Prudence turned her face to present her undamaged cheek. Whitestone looked embarrassed and confused. "Answer me! Where did you get the bruise?"

"Well, since you claim to own every breath I take, how can I possibly refuse to answer? I happen to be enamoured of the vicar of Ryeport. As I said earlier, he has more charm and grace than most men of my acquaintance. I have a connection with him in regard to donations of clothing, and I sought the help of a friend to drive me to Ryeport on the pretext of arranging more donations for the villagers. We never made it that far, however, because my friend Jed Pringle, who had borrowed a wagon from the church, had an accident at his farm when he made a brief stop there to attend to a forgotten chore. As I got down from the wagon, my foot slipped on the step. Jed hurriedly raised his hand to catch me but struck me on the cheek instead. That's not a story I want publicised, as I'm sure you would understand. The vicar has no knowledge of my feelings; neither does Jed Pringle, and I'd prefer things to stay that way. I'd rather that the vicar declared first. Would that surprise you?"

Whitestone's expression was impassive. Prudence could not read any acceptance or refusal of her story and gambled on a little embellishment.

"Unfortunately, Mr. Pringle fell whilst attending to his chore in the barn and struck his head. He was gone for such a long time that I went looking for him. I helped him to the house to clean and bandage his head. Whilst I was doing that, the vicar arrived. Apparently, there had been some mix up concerning bedding hay purchased from Pringle. He needed more hay and of a better quality. Anyway, the vicar took over the chore of cleaning Jed's wound and, after a rest, he brought me back to the inn. We never did discuss the clothing. I suppose I can use that excuse for a later visit. There! Now you have all the sordid details. Can I take it that you will let me attempt to unravel the problems that this Corby fellow has started for you, or are you more intent on publicising some lurid story of my personal desire for a meaningful relationship?" Whitestone remained impassive. He had regained his composure. "That's not much of a story. Certainly not much help. I need more substantial information if we are to destroy this smuggling ring. And you won't be off the hook until we do!" He pointed his finger at her in an accusatory manner.

"I'm sorry to disappoint you. But you can be sure that I'm just as anxious to be rid of you as you are to catch the smugglers. However, you are not interested in rumours, so I shall bid you goodnight."

"Not so fast, my girl. You can tell me the rumours now. But I shall need more substantial information and soon. What rumours have you heard and where from?"

"Well, from snatches of conversation that I overheard between Goodman and Godfrey, I believe that the goods are already ashore. That seemed to be confirmed by a loose-mouthed fisherman at The Coach and Horses, who whispered – rather too loudly – to a drinking companion that boats from the west had been creeping up goods over the last few days and bringing them ashore in small amounts, along with their catch."

"What is the name of this fisherman?"

"Oh! How the hell would I know? I heard that rumour in the market, just as I gave it to you. For all I know, it could be pure fantasy. Would you suggest that I go to the inn and ask who knows about this business? Or do you think that might arouse the suspicions of any smuggler that happened to be there?"

"It's strange how you never give me anything I can corroborate."

"Well, believe it or not, I'm not a smuggler's confidant, just a delivery girl with big ears who works on commission. However, Godfrey did start to talk about preparing for the next run. But then Goodman spotted me, silenced Godfrey, and he left. Do you think that Corby might have tipped them off that I'm working with you? That would guarantee a sudden fatal accident for me. You need to check that man out, and quickly, or I may not live long enough to earn my release from your gallant attentions." Whitestone's expression was grim. "Don't ever mention the name Corby again, except to me. Understand? This is a dangerous situation for you. Better to forget you ever heard that name."

"Well, well. Touched a nerve, have I? Surely, if my life is threatened by the mere knowledge of a name, I should know who he is. How else will I know how to react if I'm confronted with it again?"

"You won't be. Just keep your ears and eyes open for news of the next run and any other relevant details. Keep me informed. I'm in room 6, across the hall. If you have any information, just slide a plain piece of paper under my door, and I will contact you. Any questions?" Prudence shook her head. "No." Whitestone went to the door. "Then I'll bid you goodnight."

"You have a good night," replied Prudence. "You've already ruined mine." As Whitestone was leaving, she said, softly: "Oh, one more piece of gossip. It appears that Goodman and Godfrey are having some differences of opinion regarding who should be the Spotsman. Rumour has it that Godfrey thinks it should be him. It's only barroom gossip, but it seems to support your suspicion that Goodman is the Spotsman." Whitestone nodded and then closed her door behind him; Prudence promptly locked it. "Now, she muttered. "How do I get this information to our little band of conspirators before Whitestone gets to them?"

CHAPTER 5

Escape from Nextwest

When Bannerman and Pringle reached the vicar's wagon, they found him stretching a canvas cover over frames that he'd found in the storage boxes under the seats. He was relieved to see them but seemed more enthusiastic over his discovery of the cover for the wagon. "Oh, how nice," said the sodden Bannerman. "Now we won't get wet."

"What happened back there?" asked the vicar.

"Let's get goin', Vicar. I'll tell you on the way," responded Bannerman as they hauled their wet bodies under the shelter of the wagon's roof and, once underway, Bannerman gave the anxious cleric full account of the events at Godfrey's shop. "Good thing you left when you did, Vicar. If those two blokes that discovered Goodman 'ad seen your wagon, we'd 'ave been in deep trouble. It would be real 'ard to come up with a believable excuse for all of us bein' at the scene. 'specially as Whitestone already fancies us as smugglers. Bet your sweet life – he'd 'ave found ways to involve us in Goodman's death. We 'ad no logical reason to be there, did we? Unless, of course, Godfrey 'ad invited us over for one of 'is fancy dinners an' a booze-up. No, we would've been done for. The way things turned out though, I think the two blokes that found that miserable pair will likely convince the constable that their version of Goodman's death is the right one. I couldn't tell just 'ow bad Godfrey is, but 'e looks and sounds real bad. It'll be a while yet before they can get 'im to a doctor. I think Goodman's weight was suffocating 'im. An 'e was cold as ice. Actually, it might be better for 'im if 'e doesn't make it to trial. I'm sure he's bound for the gallows. But they're real compassionate people in them gaols. They'll most likely get 'im well again before they 'ang 'im. Just so 'e can enjoy the full benefit of the experience. This cold rain's done a lot to stiffen 'em up too. Maybe they'll blame the cold rain for Goodman bein' stiffer than Godfrey. Would've been better for us a' course, if they 'adn't been found 'til mornin'".

"My God, man; that sort of talk doesn't show much humanity," said the vicar.

Bannerman gave a derisive snort. "Godfrey wouldn't have shown us any 'umanity if 'e'd been given the chance. Don't waste your pity on 'im, Vicar. At least, it'll be warm where 'e's goin'". Slondosh was moving slowly over the rough laneway. "Can't this old nag go any faster, Vicar?" said Bannerman, through chattering teeth. "I'm soakin' wet an' freezin' cold back 'ere. I'd like to get somewhere where I can dry out and maybe somethin' to warm me up."

"Me too, Father," said Jed. "Where do we go from 'ere?"

"I think we'd best go home, don't you?" replied the vicar. If we were to stop at an inn, people would remember us being together, in this area, and at this time. That would be good reason for investigators to dig deeper. Don't forget, Bannerman, you and I were suspects in the recent smuggling investigation. Goodman too. They would consider this whole business related. I'd rather that they accepted the water-chucker's version, wouldn't you? Could you hold on until we get to Jed's place?"

"Aye! If we have to," said the shivering Bannerman. "But see if this old nag of yours can step it out a bit, will ye?" The vicar shook his head. "This is a rough track. The last thing we need now is for the horse to come up lame." Nevertheless, he slapped the reins on Slondosh's back, and the animal increased the pace a little. Then Jed added his concerns to the discussion. "I'm worried that Bob may 'ave people out looking for me," he said. "That could cause real problems too. There might be a crowd of people waiting for us at the farm or searchin' around. We need to get our stories straight. Just in case we're questioned."

"I've got an idea!" said the vicar. "Bessie Drew's sister, Marie, lives a couple of streets past the church. I'm sure she'd give us a place to dry out and something hot to warm us up. She makes pies and sells them locally." Bannerman's response was sarcastic: "And what are we to say to 'er, Vicar? 'Would you kindly give food and shelter to three murdering smugglers who are trying to 'ide their tracks?'" At this point in the conversation, the rutted lane intersected with the Coach Road and they turned right and headed east on the better-surfaced road. Slondosh picked up the pace, possibly sensing that they were heading home. "Can I trust you boys with a secret?" said the vicar, looking over his shoulder at his shivering accomplices. They both shrugged and nodded. "Could it be a bigger secret than we've already shared t'day?" asked Bannerman. "No, but it's not really my secret to share. That makes it more sensitive," replied the vicar.

"Well, I'm a very sensitive person," said the fisherman, with a smile, "and cold enough to swear my way out of 'eaven and into the other place."

"Me too," agreed Jed.

"Bessie's sister is involved in the trade," said the vicar. "But it must go no further than us."

"Oh, hell, I knew that," said Bannerman. "Me too," added Jed. "I arrange 'er deliveries." The vicar turned to look at the dim faces in the back of the wagon. "Are there no secrets in this place? How did you know, Bannerman?"

"Bessie told me after she came back from selling those pies, door to door, in Nextwest. She was quite excited about that. Used this wagon as I recall. I think she would have liked to get involved too. She needs the money, you know; you don't pay 'er enough to live on. She was real worried about 'er sister though. Marie keeps trade goods in a secret cupboard. Customers pick up trade goods from 'er as they make out they're buyin' pies or pickin' up Godfrey's used furniture. Bessie is scared that the cupboard ain't secret enough." The vicar was flabbergasted. "Well, I guess we can call on Marie after all since you're all pals together."

"Oh, I wouldn't say that, Vicar. Marie don't know about us," said Jed. "I arranged 'er deliveries', but Godfrey did the deliverin'. 'e used to 'ide the trade goods amongst chairs and things on 'is 'and cart' just to make it look like 'e was deliverin' furniture, to store in 'er back room. He would go back and forth pickin' up broken bits of furniture and then take some repaired stuff to Marie's for customers to pick up. Just as a cover. Marie would 'and over goods to people that 'ad a chit from Godfrey. There would be a code of some sort if the 'trade' goods were involved. 'e paid Marie a bit of commission, plus some rent for the back room. 'e won't 'ave no trade goods at his place. 'e's too canny for that."

"That's right," agreed Bannerman. Marie don't know about me neither. An' Bessie told me I was never to repeat anythin' about 'er sister – except that she made good pies and preserves that is – an' that they was thinkin' of goin' into business together. You wouldn't know, Vicar, but 'er son, Mick, was like a kid brother to me. I tried to make up for some of 'is loss when 'is dad died. I was real close to the Drew fam'ly. Mick's dad an' me fished together for years."

They were approaching Church Street now, and Bannerman raised the canvas cover just enough to peer down the street. The crowd was larger than ever now but quieter. Then, from up ahead, a buggy appeared, trotting fast, heading their way and closely followed by a second buggy.

"That first one is Goodman's buggy," said Jed in a hushed voice. "You can see Whatson's big fancy brass 'W' on the dashboard. That's the Whatson's badge, so it is." The second buggy also had a badge on the dashboard, but that was unrecognisable in the poor light. "I'd bet that second buggy is the constable," said Bannerman, as the two carriages turned into Church Street. "No takers," responded the shivering farmer. "We're almost at Marie's," said the vicar. "I'll have a word with Marie before she sees you. My story is that I drove Prudence home from Jed's farm and thought that Bessie would want me to stop by and check on her sister. Then I'll say: 'By the way, Marie, can I buy a hot pie or two and maybe some mugs of hot tea?' And, if things look favourable, I might say: 'Would you mind if my friends had a little warm-up by your fireplace?' What do you think lads?"

"What if the constable stops by and wants to know what your wagon's doin' 'ere at this time of night?"

"Same story. Just leave out the part about you two. You'll have to skip out the back door if they want to come inside. Make your way to the back of The Coach and Horses, and I'll pick you up later."

"I'm so bloody cold, I'd agree to anythin'," replied Bannerman. "Aye, me too," added Jed. And so it was that at a quarter to ten on that miserable, rainy night, Marie opened her door to a very damp and dishevelled vicar from Ryeport.

. . .

Jed's brother, Bob, and Jack, the stableman, were grateful for the oilskin apron that partially protected them from the driving rain on their miserable drive to Pringle's farm. Because of the poor visibility, Jack had been pleased to allow the horse to choose its own path most of the time. Bob was worried sick as he speculated about what might have happened to Jed. He thought he might find him dead, alongside Sailmaker and then, what about Miss Prudence? He didn't want to think about what might have happened to her. Their journey had been made without conversation, but even in the weak light of the coach lanterns, Jack could read the anxiety on Bob's face, but he asked no questions. Eventually, they pulled into the farm's driveway, and Bob unfastened the apron, jumped down, ran into the house and lit a lamp. He was shaken as the light revealed a table covered with dirty dishes, glasses, and an empty brandy bottle. "What the 'ell's been goin' on 'ere!" he exclaimed. Jack, who had tethered the horse before following Bob into the house, paused at the doorway. "What's up, Bob? Trouble?"

 "Don't know yet, Jack. Looks like someone's 'ad a party 'ere." The two men went through the house, calling Jed's name but got no response. As they left to search the barns, Jack noticed the bucket of blood-stained cloths near the kitchen door and called Bob. "My God," exclaimed the worried farmer. "Looks like someone's 'urt real bad. Let's check the barn. Maybe Jed's passed out somewhere."

The livestock barn produced no clues. "Nothing out of place 'ere," said Bob and they left for the storage barn. The hole at the edge of the manure pile was now filled with water that had run off the pile and, in the darkness, was no longer visible. Jack stepped into the shallow grave that had been dug for Sailmaker and cried out as his lantern went flying. Bob caught his arm, saving him from falling into the pit, but his left leg was soaked from the thigh down in stinky water. Then Bob saw that the edge of the manure pile was farther back than when he had left this morning and the crudely rectangular shape of the hole that had been dug in its place. He grabbed the spade lying nearby and frantically tried to search the bottom of the hole. Jack stopped him. "There's nothing in there, Bob. It's just a hole. Let's try the barn."

Bob ran to the storage barn, still carrying the spade, but there was no sign of Jed there either. But the lantern did reveal a small patch of dried blood and some cut pieces of rope. Bob poked at the blood with the spade, trying to estimate how long it had been lying there. Then he went to the foot of the hayloft ladder, dropped the spade and scrambled to the top, calling his brother's name. "No sign of anyone up 'ere," he called to Jack. The blood and cut ropes had raised Bob's state of panic even higher. He ran around outside, calling Jed's name. Jack had relit his lantern and was searching more methodically than the frantic farmer and spotted some tracks where the buggy and wagon had stood. "Bob!" he called and pointed to the tracks when the farmer joined him. "This is slightly higher ground, Bob, so most of the rain ran off. Looks like a buggy and a slightly bigger carriage. A small wagon most likely." Bob threw his hands in the air. "Let's go back to the house and get dried off, Jack. We'll take a rest, 'ave a drink – if there's anything left that is – then I think we'd best 'ead back to Nextwest. I can't think what else to do. We'll just 'ave to hope Jed turns up. I can't make out why there are five dirty plates up at the 'ouse. Who on earth was 'ere? And what about all that blood in the barn?"

• • •

Back in Nextwest, Marie was shaken by the vicar's visit and bedraggled appearance. "Oh, Father! Whatever are you doin' out on such a bad night? Is Bessie alright? Is she with you?" She peered around the vicar, trying to see if her sister might be sheltering in the wagon. "Bessie is fine, Marie, but she's not with me. Sorry. I just happened to be in Nextwest and thought I had better stop and see how you were – or Bessie would never forgive me." He gave a short, apologetic laugh. "Come in. Come in. Sit by the fire," said Marie. "You must be frozen; you're soaked through."

"Well, I really can't come in, Marie. I have two friends with me, and they too are soaked through. I must get them home as soon as possible."

"Well, bring them in too." Marie re-opened the door and called to the wagon. "Come on in, you two! Quickly now! I'll get you all some 'ot stew."

"But, Marie," stammered the vicar.

"No 'buts', young Sir. Get yourself around the fire."

Jed Pringle and Bannerman shuffled in and closed the door. They stood hats in hand, just inside the door, water dripping from their sodden clothing and looking rather like two youngsters that had been caught in some mischief. "My goodness, whatever have you done to your head?" Marie asked Jed.

"Nothing serious, Ma'am. It's all looked after, thank you."

"Get those wet coats off then," said Marie, still keeping an anxious eye on Jed's bloody bandage. " 'ang your coats on the chair backs in front of the fire. Try and leave room for me to get by so I can reach the stew pot. Then I'll get you somethin' 'ot and tasty to drive out the cold."

"Thank you, Ma'am," they chorused and hastened to comply. Marie soon filled three bowls from the pot on the back of the stove, placing them on the table together with some bread and butter. "Would one of you lads 'elp me get more chairs from the back room?" she asked. Bannerman was there in a flash. He brought in extra chairs and set them at the table. "Expectin' company, were you, Ma'am? You've enough furniture in that room for a small village."

"Oh, that's not mine. A bloke I know repairs and sells broken furniture. 'e stores it 'ere, an' pays me a little rent for the space. A little 'elp is worth more than a lot of pity, me old mum used to say. I got no 'usband, ye see. Passed away a few years ago, 'e did. So I bakes pies, an' make jams an' pickles an' the like. It makes me a little extra money. I get by quite well really." The vicar interjected, pausing after a mouthful of hot, and much appreciated, stew. "I'm so sorry, Marie. This tall man is Jack Bannerman, from Ryeport, and our wounded hero is a local farmer, Jed Pringle. Jed fell in his barn earlier and struck his head. They both know Bessie quite well." Marie stood dumbstruck for a few seconds. "Pleased to meet ye both, I'm sure," she said. "But I know about both of ye. Bessie 'as told me..." and her voice trailed off as she realised she may have said more than she should. "Well, any friends of yours, Father, are welcome in this 'ouse. That's for sure."

"You're a fine cook, Ma'am. This is really good stew. Very kind of you. Very 'ospitable! Thank you." Bannerman was on his best manners. Jed quickly added his compliments. "Where are you boys off to now?" Marie questioned. "Are you staying at the inn?"

"No, Ma'am. The vicar an' me 'ave to get back to Ryeport," Bannerman replied.

"And you, Jed?" asked Marie, with another concerned look at Jed's bandaged head.

"Er. Well, me an' the wife do 'ave a room at The 'Coach' t'night, Ma'am. My brother and our wives are there now. We run a stall at the market, ye see. Veg'tables mainly. But I thought that p'raps I'd better go back to the farm. The vicar could drop me off there on 'is way 'ome. Might scare folk if I turn up lookin' like this."

"Scare them a damned sight more – oops – sorry, Father – if you don't show up. They're likely worried sick right now, 'specially if they've been expectin' ye. The vicar will take you by. Won't you, Father?"

"Certainly, Marie, if that's what Jed wants. But I can't tell him what to do. He's a grown man after all."

"You men; I don't know what you use to think with, but it don't work very well. Once you've got that stew down ye, ye'd best be off to The 'Coach,' Jed. 'Ow long you bin gone? If I was yer wife, I'd give ye another smack for makin' me worry so. Keep yer 'at on when you see 'em first. Only take it off after they can see you're alright, ye daft 'a'porth!" The three men were a little drier and warmer when they left Marie's. After they climbed back into the wagon, the vicar said: "Bannerman. You'd best lie on the floor in the back of the wagon. Stay out of sight whatever you do. I'll go into the inn with Jed and make sure that all's well there. Maybe get a little bit of news. Then we'll hurry back to Ryeport."

"I can't do that, Vicar. Go back to Ryeport I mean. I've got to get Sailmaker's dinghy an' sail it back to the village."

"Oh, yes; I'd forgotten about that. But can you sail it back on a night like this, alone?"

"Well, I suppose I could. But I'd rather not. Getting down the cliff could be real tricky in the dark, 'specially with all this rain. Be as slippery as a pile o' fish guts," replied Bannerman. He turned to the farmer. "Could I stay at your place tonight, Jed? I'll kip on the floor and be gone at first light."

"Of course," said the farmer. "There's food and drink there. Just 'elp your-self, Bannerman. Grab a blanket from the cupboard in the back room. You can sleep on the couch. We'll not be gettin back there 'til about noontime, I reckon."

"Well, that should fit very well with our story then," said the vicar, as he reviewed their situation and their need for alibis. "Let's see: Jed and Prudence left Nextwest, in a borrowed wagon, to get Jed's musket from the farm." Then, puzzled, he asked: But why was Prudence with you, Jed?"

"To try and save Sailmaker, you silly sod," said the farmer. "Oops! Sorry, Father. Forgot me'self for a minute."

"Don't worry about it," smiled the vicar. "No, what I really meant was: What do we say to the Revenuers, as to why she went with you?"

"Search me!" said Jed.

"Do you think we could say you intended to take her to Ryeport, to see Bessie about the donated clothes for the villagers?"

"Only if she knows that's what we're goin' t'say. Don't want us sayin' one thing and 'er sayin' somethin' else now, do we? We'd be caught out in a lie. That'd cook our goose for sure."

"Well, Jed, is there some way you could get out to The White Hart tomorrow before you leave for the farm? Have a word with Prudence and then maybe get word to me somehow? You can always say that you 'thought' that was why she wanted to go to Ryeport. You only need to let me know if that story isn't acceptable to her. Otherwise, I'll assume she agrees."

"Aye. I could do that." Jed was thoughtful for a moment, before saying: "Could even try to sell some veggies to the landlord there. That'll give us a reason to go there. Aye! That's what we'll do."

"What about me?" said Bannerman. "What's my story?"

"You didn't see any of us," said the vicar. "You were searching for Sailmaker. You spent all the time looking for him. You didn't go to Jed's place. Didn't climb the cliff. Didn't see the tackle."

"Didn't go to Marie's either?" Bannerman raised his arms despairingly. "If your wagon was spotted there and they question Marie, she's bound to say there were three of us." The vicar fell silent. "Marie's one of us," said Jed. "She don't know that we know that, but I'm sure that if Bessie or the vicar 'ere were to tell 'er that it was only me an 'im at 'er place tonight, she'd go along with that." They stopped in front of The Coach and Horses. "Good idea, Jed," said the vicar. "I'll have a word with her on the way back. Now, Jed, I need a reason to have been at your farm today."

"Er, le' me see. You were out for a drive you said. 'ad a 'eadache as I recall. Alright, you were out for a drive, saw my place, and decided to come in an' order some 'ay. Good stuff this time. Not beddin'. Just a stroke of luck that I was there really; I should'a been at the market."

"Good! So you went back for the musket, Jed. I dropped in, casually, to order hay. Prudence was hoping you'd take her on to Ryeport to see Bessie about donating clothes. Sailmaker was never there. Neither was Bannerman, Goodman, Godfrey, or his thugs. Not to your knowledge anyway. If someone else says they were there – you never saw them and wouldn't be able to guess why they were there."

"Well, there ain't too many villains left to argue that they were there," said Bannerman with a quick laugh. "That's one thing we can be sure about.

Godfrey could be the only fly in the ointment." The three men went over their stories a few more times before Jed and the vicar entered the inn. Bannerman hid in the back of the wagon again. The barmaid, Ada, gasped and clapped a hand over her mouth as Jed entered the bar with the vicar. Jed had kept his hat on, but a loose piece of bloodstained bandage was dangling over his ear. It was almost half an hour later before the vicar climbed back aboard the wagon. "Where the bloody 'ell 'ave you been, Vicar?" said the shivering fisherman. "I thought this was goin' to be a quick stop, so's I could get back to Pringle's an' you back to Ryeport. I'm frozen bloody stiff, I am. Been 'avin' a party an' a couple of drinks, 'ave ye?"

"Sorry, Bannerman. I had a job to get away. There's a lot to tell you when we get on the road again. Looks like the rain's easing off at last," responded the vicar as he slapped the reins on Slondosh's back. "Giddap, boy!" Bannerman started to climb into the front seat. "No, Bannerman. Not yet. We have to stop at Marie's for a minute to tell her that you weren't here tonight. Not much point in doing that if you're going to ride up front for all to see."

"Well, I'm cramped and bloody cold. It's not very comfortable 'idin' in the back of the wagon, Vicar, an' that coat that Jed lent me at the farm is soaked through. This quick visit ain't goin' to turn into another 'alf-hour long, 'couldn't-get-away' thing, is it?"

"Sorry, my friend. We're almost at Marie's now." Marie was more shocked by the vicar's second visit than the first. "I was just goin' t'bed, Father. 'ow's Jed? Is ev'rythin' alright?"

"He's fine, Marie. We did as you suggested and his family was relieved, just as you said they would be."

"Told ye! You men! Got no idea!"

"Yes, Marie. You were right. But I have another favour to ask of you. May I step inside?"

"Certainly, Father. Let's get Bannerman in 'ere too."

"No, Marie. Not Bannerman. Not this time. In fact, I need you to forget that you ever met him tonight. Do you think you could do that for me? Us?"

"Why, Father? What's up?" Marie's hand was at her mouth, and she was looking scared.

"Well, Marie, this is smugglers' business. Today, Bannerman was looking for a fisherman friend they believed was lost at sea. You see, his friend's boat was found empty, some distance east of Ryeport. The villagers searched the coast, almost as far as Pringle's farm without success. Bannerman decided to go farther and ended up climbing the cliff to see if his friend had gone to Pringle's for help. He didn't find him, but he did find Jed and me, and Jed was hurt. Now, this wouldn't be a problem normally, Marie, but it seems that there's been some trouble amongst the smugglers. One of them is dead and another one close to it. Apparently, they had a 'falling out' and a fight of some sort. If it was known that Bannerman was in the area, he might be suspected of some involvement because the Revenue men already suspect that he and his lost friend are smugglers." He pulled a face: "Me too actually. If the Revenuers knew that we were all here, at the same time, and in a place where one of the smugglers was killed, they might think we had a hand in it. So, it's better if Bannerman was never here. Jed and I had good, honest reasons to be here together. But if Bannerman were here too, that would be too much of a coincidence. The Revenuers would try to tie us all in for sure. So, if it's alright with you, Marie, we'd like you to forget you ever saw Bannerman tonight. Everything else stays the same: Jed and me, you taking us in for some hot stew – everything."

"I didn't realise you were in the 'trade,' Father."

"I'm not, Marie, honestly. But some people that I care about, you for one, are. Yes, I know you have a small part in the trade, and I sympathise with your reasons. Remember, you were all at risk during that failed Custom's ambush. I'm just trying to keep people like you above suspicion." Marie was looking really anxious now, both hands clasped over her mouth. But she quickly recovered from that shock. "Alright, Father. So, it's okay for me t'say that I met you an' Jed t'night but not Bannerman. It's alright that I 'elped you dry out an' that? Did I see you twice or just the once?"

"Twice, Marie, but on the second time, I just stopped by to let you know Jed met his family at The 'Coach,' and everything was alright. Everything just as it happened but forget that you saw Bannerman. If anyone should ask: He was never here. Alright?"

"Alright, Father. 'ere' who is it that's dead? Do I know 'im?"

"The dead man's name is Goodman, Marie. The one close to death is named Godfrey. His neighbours believe that he killed Goodman."

Marie's hands flew to her mouth again. This was a night of shocks for the widow. "My Gawd! I know 'em both. Goodman's a real big fella, a toffee-nosed butler to a posh 'ouse." She pointed to the back room. An' Godfrey, 'e's the man that stores furniture in me back room. Delivers other stuff too, sometimes. Where did ye 'ear all this, Father?"

"At The 'Coach,' Marie. Godfrey was drunk apparently and causing such a disturbance that the innkeeper threw him out. He went on home to his shop, but his neighbours got involved and found him lying on the ground, outside his shop with Goodman lying on top of him. A long chisel was stuck in Goodman's chest. They believed Godfrey stabbed Goodman as he was getting down from his buggy and that when he fell, he landed on top of him on the ground. Goodman was a big man, and Godfrey was too drunk to get out from under his weight. They must have lain there, in the cold rain, for a long time. The constable had Godfrey taken to the infirmary, and a doctor and a guard are watching over him. They believe he's a smuggler and want him to name his accomplices. We know Goodman and Godfrey are smugglers, that's why we're so concerned. I know Bessie told you about Captain Whitestone, the Customs officer in charge down here. That's why Bessie started delivering your pies door to door. It was to warn Goodman, remember? Whitestone was furious about failing to catch the smugglers. If they'd been arrested, you might have been named by them too. All of this could unravel if Whitestone knew we were all here tonight. He believes that someone from Ryeport was responsible for warning-off the run. He'll use this incident to re-investigate all previous suspects. It was one of Godfrey's neighbours that ran back to The Coach with the news. There's quite a crowd down there now, Marie. The whole town is talking about it. Marie, I'm sorry, but I must go now. Bannerman is soaking wet and hiding in the back of my wagon. I'll talk to you again later. Are you going to be alright?"

"Yes, Father. I'm alright. You go. Hurry now. I'll be fine. Is it alright to say you told me all this?"

"Yes, Marie. Everything as it happened. Just forget that you ever saw Bannerman. If you should ever see him again, act as though it was a first meeting. Okay?" Marie nodded silently and looked very downcast.

"What's the matter, Marie? You look really sad. Were you fond of this man Godfrey?"

"Oh no, Father. 'orrible bloke, 'e was really. Good riddance, I say. But I will miss me rent money that's for sure. An' that little bit o' 'trade' money too, by the looks o' things." She gave him a rueful smile. "I'll be alright. Just 'ave to sell more pies, that's all."

As a parting favour, Marie gave the vicar a heavy topcoat. "Belonged to me 'usband," she said. "Don't know why I kept it really. Not like 'e's comin' back, is it? But it might keep that bloke that wasn't 'ere t'night a bit warmer than the wet rag 'e's wearin' now. Good luck to ye both. Tell 'im 'e can keep the coat."

"Good lady, that Marie," said the grateful Bannerman, as he stripped to the waist and struggled into the dry coat in the confined space of the covered wagon. "God, that feels better. I'm still bloody cold and wet, 'specially me legs, but at least I've got rid of the cold, soggy weight of that water-logged topcoat."

Once they were out of the town and safe from prying eyes, Bannerman climbed into the seat alongside the vicar, who soon apprised him of the information gleaned from the patrons at The 'Coach', as well as his agreement with Marie. Bannerman listened quietly, nodding his understanding until the vicar had finished. Then he added his comments. "Well, at least we'll all be telling the same story – provided o' course that Jed manages to get the information to Miss Prudence. Things are goin' to be rough for Marie though, Vicar. No 'usband an' now the loss of the rent an' trade money. She'll miss that. Maybe I can 'elp out there."

"We'll all try to help, Bannerman. But a lot will depend on what Whitestone decides to do about this business with Goodman and Godfrey. We should live our lives as innocently as possible, and you should know nothing about Goodman and Godfrey until the rest of the village does. Be ignorant of all this, and play it carefully, my friend."

"Aye, I agree. I can arrange to get a little money to Marie though. Not a lot but enough to 'elp out 'til we can sort somethin' out. Oh, by the way, Vicar, I ain't your friend! Not in public anyway. You can count on me, that's for sure. But it'll be safer if the villagers still think we don't like each other. Let's keep the old animosity goin' until we 'ave good public reason for change, if ever. After all, we don't want Whitestone to think we're mates, do we? I'll still call you 'vicar.' None of this Father stuff. People think I don't respect you. But you know better – right?" The vicar laughed. "Alright, Bannerman, our friendship shall remain our secret. Here's my hand on it." The two men shook hands, and the strength of the fisherman's grip reminded the vicar how fortunate he'd been to have Ernie's protection in his early days in Ryeport.

They were almost at the farm when the vicar spotted carriage lights coming towards them. "This might be Bob Pringle. He borrowed a buggy from The Coach and Horses to look for Jed back at the farm. He's got someone with him. We'll have to stick to our public story, Bannerman. I'll tell him that Jed's safe and that he'll get all the news from him. You, my friend, will have to hide in the back again."

Bannerman groaned: "Oh, sod this business, Vicar. Don't you take too long then! I want to get to the farm, get a bite to eat, some o' Jed's brandy and some shut-eye. I've got to get away early to-morro' mornin'. The villagers will be out lookin' for me at first light. I just hope I can get home before Whitestone sends some of 'is blokes after me." The two carriages reined in alongside each other, and Bob Pringle began plying the vicar with questions. Bob was relieved to hear that his brother was safe but alarmed at the news of Goodman's death and Godfrey's apparent part in it. He made no mention of Sailmaker. Roddy guessed that he might be unsure of his companion's reactions. But Jack spoke up too, telling the vicar of their problems with Godfrey in the inn earlier that evening. The vicar gave them the basic outline of the evening's events, explaining that he'd gathered his information from the people at The Coach and Horses and then asked that Bob get the rest of the details from his brother because he was long overdue in Ryeport.

Once at the farm, Bannerman relit the kitchen fire, stripped and towelled himself dry. He hung his clothes to dry on chair backs in front of the fire and wrapped himself in a blanket before munching on a thick crust of bread and cheese. The vicar poured them both a generous sized brandy and shared the warmth of the fire with Bannerman, whilst he too enjoyed a sandwich. "I don't know when I've eaten so much in one evening," he said. "Is that because of the cold rain or the excitement, I wonder? But I must be leaving soon, Bannerman. What shall I tell the villagers if they ask about you?"

The startled Bannerman looked nervously at the vicar. "Nothin', Vicar. You never saw me, remember?"

Roddy laughed. "Just testing. I'll wait for you to show up tomorrow. If the villagers start a search for you, I'll offer help."

"That's right. I'll stick a pebble in me shoe an' limp in, with a story about fallin' on some rocks east of 'ere an' sprainin' me ankle too bad to climb back down. It'll be a lot better by then, o' course. Just tender, is all. Good luck, Vicar. By the way, take Marie's topcoat with ye. I didn't 'ave it when I left an' people might wonder where I got it while I was searchin' for

Sailmaker. I'll 'ang up the one Jed lent me. Should be dry by mornin'. Good night! I'm goin' to get me 'ead down."

It was past midnight when the vicar pulled his wagon up to The Harbour Light. Lamps were still burning in village windows, and people had quickly gathered in their doorways at the sound of the approaching wagon. Bessie and Ernie led the flurry of questions. "Where've you been? Are you alright? Why are you so late?" The vicar held up his hand. "Whoa, just a minute, my friends! Allow me to get myself warm, and a drink and a snack. Then I'll give you the news. I'm alright but cold and damp. I had an unexpected trip into Nextwest, that's all. Would you be kind enough to look after Slondosh, Tom? I'm dead beat. Give him some extra oats. He deserves a treat." He retrieved the topcoat from the wagon and headed into the inn. Bessie stepped alongside him, took the topcoat from him, looked it over and was about to say something, but when he shook his head, she kept silent. Inside the inn, and nursing a generous measure of rum, Roddy told their carefully fabricated story to the villagers. They listened to the news of Goodman and Godfrey with apprehension.

"This is likely to bring the Revenuers back in here again with more questions," commented Ernie. "By the way, Father, we've got another problem now; Bannerman's missing." And the vicar, looking appropriately concerned, was given the news as the village knew it of Bannerman's hasty solo effort to find Sailmaker. The Sullivan brothers stood in the background, nodding their heads as Ernie told the story, and the vicar sensed that they were concerned about saying something that Bannerman wouldn't approve of, so they said as little as possible. He hoped that all these adulterated versions of the truth would hang together under Whitestone's incisive questioning.

"Well, this has been quite a day," he finally said. "I'm for bed. Please excuse me. If I can be of any help looking for Bannerman, please let me know." He and Bessie left the inn together, leaving the villagers speculating on Bannerman's whereabouts and the probability of Whitestone paying them another visit. Walking back to the vicar's cottage, Bessie asked the question that she had suppressed at the inn. "Why did you go to Marie's? Is she alright? Is she in any danger because of this?" Roddy paused in mid-stride and turned to face her. "You knew I'd been to Marie's before I said anything. How was that?"

"This is 'er 'usband's coat. I recognise the braiding at the collar. I've been tellin' 'er to sell it for years. Bit big for you, Father. You'd be treadin' on it as you walked." He laughed. "You certainly don't miss much, Bessie. But Marie's fine, and no, she's not involved. Let's get indoors, and I'll tell you the true story of the day's events. Provided that you keep it strictly – very, very strictly – between us."

"Of course, Father. We share quite a few secrets between us already, don't we? One more won't 'urt." Bessie spent most of the next half-hour with one hand clamped over her mouth as the vicar gave her the unadulterated version of the day's events.

· · ·

At the first hint of daybreak, several boats were already heading for the sea. Roddy was at the landing and offering his help as the men shoved off. Ben Cobbe had assigned search areas to each boat the night before, with his being the farthest west. Archer was at his beacon hut, the best lookout position, armed with Ernie's spyglass. He would signal the first sighting of a returning boat by raising a pennant to the yardarm on his flagstaff. Bannerman was already leaving Pringle's farm. He had been up well before dawn and had washed the dishes and cleaned the table at the farmhouse before burning the bloody rags from the bucket by the door. He wanted to remove any evidence that would cause the ladies of the house to ask awkward questions concerning Jed's version of the previous day's events. Bob and Jack had already seen the mess, but he hoped that they would not have mentioned it to their wives. Dawn was breaking, and it was cold and breezy as he made his way to Sailmaker's dinghy. He began his descent of the cliff at first light, pausing every few feet to listen and look for watchers or Revenue cutters. He was about 20 feet above the beach when he caught his first glimpse of the dead smugglers. "No one's found 'em yet. That's good," he muttered. "The longer they stay like that, the better for us." The two bodies were lying in shallow water, within the confines of a rocky basin.

He was only three feet above beach level when the ledge beneath him collapsed, causing him to fall the rest of the way. He ended up on all fours, amongst scattered rocks and in a shallow puddle, just a few feet away from the closest corpse. His shirt and the flesh beneath it were torn, and he had cut his right knee. Shaken, he remained on all fours for a few moments. "Bloody good job I didn't see 'em from the top o' the cliff. Might 'ave ended up as a 'floater' meself." He wagged a finger at a dead smuggler. "You should have warned me about that last step, matey," he said. "People might think you don't like me." He laughed quietly. "Never known a coupl'a days like this in me whole life." When he tried to stand up, his right ankle gave way, and he had to use an outstretched arm to save himself from further damage. "Won't need no bloody pebble in me shoe now," he said, as he tested the damaged ankle. It held, provided he didn't put full weight on it. Painfully he clambered over a rocky ledge to the concealed dinghy. It was floating, securely tied, but he had to spend about 20 minutes bailing it out before clambering in and pushing it clear of the rocks. He rowed out for about a hundred yards, watching carefully for other vessels or people on the cliff top. Then, seeing none, he hoisted the sail. Less than half an hour later, he spotted Cobbe's boat. He was soon aboard the larger boat and headed for Ryeport with the dinghy in tow. Ben was concerned about his cuts and bruises but soon convinced that they were not serious.

A pair of dry trousers, and a heavy jersey from Ben's waterproof locker, quickly improved his comfort level and a cold Cornish pastie and some rum did wonders for his morale. He had been spotted slightly closer to Ryeport than the Sullivans claimed to have found Sailmaker. That would fit quite well with his story. "I never did see any of that flotsam that Sailmaker thought was so interesting," remarked Ben Cobbe. "Nor did anyone else; do ye think the lad's been dreamin' a bit?" He raised his eyebrows as he looked to Bannerman for a comment. "Most likely someone beat 'im to it, Ben," replied Bannerman. "Plenty o' people combin' the beaches these days. You need to collect anythin' worthwhile as soon as ye see it or someone else will beat you to it."

"Aye, that's true enough," agreed Ben. Shortly after that, Archer hoisted Cobbe's pennant to his yardarm. He soon followed that with those of others in the search party that Cobbe met on the way in. Archer always denied it, but the villagers all knew he enjoyed 'tossing-the-bundle-aloft', as he called it. It added a little colour to his otherwise monotonous routine. He didn't get to do it very often these days. Not much sense putting up pennants in the dark.

Sailmaker was in Doc's cottage waiting for a change of dressing when Bannerman was ushered in to join him. "My, my, what a sad pair of wounded mariners we have here," said the doctor, after shooing away the curious villagers once again. Although there was a genuine concern for their two neighbours, many would confess that these past two days had been more interesting than a visit from the coachmen. "I hope you didn't encounter any splintered wooden rocks on your fall down the cliff, Bannerman," said the doctor. Bannerman turned his puzzled expression to Sailmaker, hoping for an explanation. "Doc had to remove some wooden slivers from the cuts in my head," explained Sailmaker. "He says I must have hit my head on some splintered wooden rocks."

"There is a lot of shattered wood amongst those rocks, Doctor," said Bannerman. "Reckon I was lucky not to get speared by some me'self." Doc smiled. "Well, yes, I can appreciate that," responded the old man patiently as he finished their dressings. "Never mind, it's none of my business. You two boys run along and play now. It's time for my nap," and he opened his back door as an invitation to escape the villagers' questions. They sat quietly in his backyard, whilst Bannerman explained all that had transpired since he last saw Sailmaker. But Doc wasn't able to sleep; their conversation was too interesting.

• • •

It was shortly after nine a.m. that morning when the Pringles drove their produce wagon into the yard of The White Hart. Bob went to see the landlord in what he already knew would be a fruitless endeavour to sell some leftover produce from market day. As Bob anticipated, the landlord was not at all receptive. "All our vegetables are fresh from our own garden. Fresh, you understand. We need nothing from you. Just leave. I don't want you annoying my customers with your peddling."

Jed was in the bar, hoping to see Prudence at breakfast, but she wasn't there. However, he was alarmed to see Whitestone, watching their wives with obvious contempt as they handed out samples of their homemade toffee. Jed quickly turned his back, hoping that Whitestone hadn't seen him, for he would surely have recognised him from the hay cart incident.

Jed didn't know which room Prudence would be in and was concerned that enquiring might cause Whitestone to notice him. So, he steered Bob to a distant table and muttered: "Revenuer," indicating Whitestone with a furtive backwards jerk of his head. "Let's 'ave a drink and decide what to do." Bob waved for their wives to join them and Jed sat with his back to Whitestone. They ordered ales and a snack and tried to relax as they considered how they might contact Prudence without attracting Whitestone's attention. As they were talking, a horseman rode up, hurried into the bar and whispered something to Whitestone. The Revenue officer jumped to his feet saying: "Get my horse." The rider left the bar but soon reappeared outside with Whitestone's saddled mount. The two men galloped off in the direction of Nextwest. Now Jed was free to enquire about Prudence from the barmaid. "I'd 'oped to see a friend of ours 'ere t'day, dear. Prudence Mercer is 'er name. I know she lives upstairs and I thought she might be at breakfast. 'as she eaten yet?"

"Miss Prudence 'ad breakfast in 'er room this morning," the girl replied. "She had an accident yesterday, and bruised her face. It's quite swollen, and she didn't want to come into the bar looking like that. She's in Room 3, if you wanted to see her."

Jed used the outside staircase to climb to the first floor and knocked on Pru's door. "Go away!" came her stern reply. "That's no way to treat a friend, Missy," said Jed quietly, through the keyhole. "Jed! Is that you?" Prudence sounded startled. "Aye, it's me. Are ye decent? I'd like to 'ave a word with ye, in private." The door opened, and Prudence almost dragged him into the room, closing the door swiftly. "Jed. There's a Revenue officer at the inn. Whitestone is staying across the hall. This could be dangerous."

"Aye, Miss, but I just watched 'im gallop off with one of 'is men, only a few minutes ago. Why would 'e be staying here, d' ye think?"

"I've no idea, Jed!"

"Well, 'e just took off in a real 'urry, towards Nextwest. D'ye think something might've 'appened to Godfrey? D'ye think 'e may be talkin?" Oops! I forgot. You don't know the latest news. That's why I'm 'ere."

"What's wrong? And why are you here? How did things go with Goodman?"

"Well, Miss, not accordin' t' plan, that's for sure," and Jed brought Pru up to date with the happenings at Godfrey's shop and the resulting clamour when Goodman was found dead, lying on top of a sick and drunken Godfrey. She was shocked. "How's Roddy? The vicar, I mean."

" 'e's fine, but we 'ave to make a few changes to our stories, Miss. It doesn't 'ave to be word for word, mind ye, but the gist of it all 'as to tie-in like." And so Prudence and Jed synchronised the details of how she received the bruises, etcetera. Prudence nodded, relieved that she had given Whitestone a story that Jed would now corroborate. "What shall I say if the landlord tells Whitestone that you came to see me?" she asked.

"That's alright, Miss. I gave ye the bruises, remember, accidental like, an' I felt badly about that, an' just came to see 'ow you were. Then Bob an' me thought we'd try and sell some veg'tables while we were 'ere." He gave a little laugh and a shrug. "No point in tryin' that again. Landlord made it clear 'e don't want nothin' from us – except our money, o' course."

"What about Marie?"

"She's alright. She can tell everything just the way it 'appened. No need t' lie. She just 'as to forget she ever saw Bannerman."

"I see. So my story is: It was just you and me at the farm. You were going home for your musket and agreed to drive me to Ryeport because I wanted to talk to Mrs. Drew about the clothing donations. But we had a job getting a wagon and started late. I slipped getting down from the wagon at the farm and you gave me the bruises whilst trying to save me. Then you fell in your barn, doing a forgotten chore, and cut your head. The vicar stopped by to order more hay and, after helping us, drove me back here."

"That's it! No mention of Bannerman, Goodman, Sailmaker or Godfrey. Alright? As far as we know: they were never there." Prudence nodded her understanding. "That's fine, Jed."

"Right you are then, Miss. I'd best be off now. We'll stop at The 'Coach' to see if we can get any more news about Godfrey and the Revenuers. Then we're all off 'ome to our chores and bloody glad to be so. Oops. Sorry, Miss."

"No problem, Jed. Oh! By the way, whatever happened to Bannerman's idea about leaking the information about the cliff-top tackle?"

"Well, we all thought that would be a good idea but couldn't think how to get the information to the Revenuers. Bannerman was relying on a passing cutter spotting it."

Prudence was thoughtful for a while before saying: "Leave that to me. Whitestone has a room right across the hall. When he goes downstairs for a meal, I could follow him, sit close by and chat to a barmaid or potman – tell them you came to see me because of this" – she pointed to her bruised face – "and told me what you'd heard about the Goodman incident at The 'Coach' and that someone at the inn had heard Godfrey say something about tackle being rigged and ready. What tackle? And where, or when, you didn't hear. But Whitestone will know. He knows he's smarter than a bunch of smugglers," she smiled.

"But Whitestone will be on you like a ton of wet fish, Miss. An' 'e'll question me too."

"Well, he'll do that anyway, Jed. He'll want to get as much information as possible. But if all we know is gossip – from a crowd of drinkers at The 'Coach', all excited and talking at once – and me, telling him only what you remembered. Where's our connection? How could you remember who told you what, with all that excited chatter going on? And we've already got our earlier stories set up."

"Alright, Miss. Let's do that. I'll get this information to the vicar some'ow. Good luck then, Miss, and thank ye." Prudence leaned over and kissed Jed on the cheek. "Thank you, Jed. You are a good and true friend. After yesterday, I feel we really are all comrades-in-arms." As he was about to leave, she reached out and held his arm. "Jed, I've an idea. It would be in keeping with our stories if I were to try and go to Ryeport today to see if we can get more clothing organised. After all, that's what I was supposed to be doing yesterday before you had your accident. Could you give me a ride to the church? I'm pretty sure Reverend Tubbs would take me to Ryeport if he's not busy." She smiled. "Knowing Tubby, I think he would take me even if he is busy. He has a hard time refusing anyone a favour. I also know that he has another donation of clothing at the church."

"Good idea, Miss. I was goin' to try an' rustle up some fresh 'ay and use that as an excuse to go see the vicar. But, to be truthful, we're a bit short ourselves. And now, after all that rain, we'll 'ave to wait until the weather dries up our field before we can take some off. You could tell the vicar that too. Tell 'im that I told 'im that yesterday, an' that 'e could 'ave some of the fresh crop once we cut it. Delivery will depend on the weather." Prudence smiled. "I'll meet you outside then, Jed. Just give me a couple of minutes to freshen up." So, Jed joined his family downstairs, and they waited at the back staircase so Prudence would not have to show her face in the bar. The two men sat on the floor of the wagon with their backs to the driver's seat, leaving the three ladies to chat in comfort on the cushioned bench. Their first stop was the church. But, as soon as Prudence signalled that Tubby was going to take her to Ryeport, the Pringles left for The Coach and Horses. The landlord, Shields, had learned that Whitestone had tried to question Godfrey last night, but he'd been delirious and making no sense. Then, this morning, one of his officers who had gone to see the prisoner, got very excited and sent a rider to get Whitestone from The White Hart. "Why the bloody 'ell 'e would stay at the 'art rather than 'ere, God only knows," Shields grumbled. "Ain't we good enough for 'im?" "What made the officer so excited then?" Bob asked.

" 'e wouldn't say. When I asked 'im a second time, 'e told me to mind me own business. Nice, eh! You'd expect officers would 'ave better manners." The Pringles were about to leave when Fletcher arrived. He walked directly to their table, doffed his hat to the ladies and wished them all a good morning. Then he asked if he might have a private word with Jed and sat at an empty table. Jed gave his family a puzzled look, shrugged and joined Fletcher.

"What's up, Fletch?" he asked. "Trouble with the wagon, is it?"

"No. That's no problem, but I expect you've 'eard about all the goin's on at the carpenter's shop on Church Street," he said, grinning.

"Aye. What about it?" Jed responded. "Well, I used to own that shop, ye know. Left to me by my father, it was. I couldn't make a go of it though, so I sold it – to Godfrey."

"Aye. I knew that too."

"Well, just like Godfrey, my dad also used Marie's back room to store stuff that he'd repaired. I know you know Marie, the lady that bakes pies for the shop in the marketplace."

"Aye, get on with it, man. Spit it out."

"Well, I know she's got a secret cupboard!" He raised his eyebrows and gave Jed a little smile. "My father built it. What's more, I also know what's in that cupboard. Now, here's the problem: Godfrey keeps a book in 'is shop that lists all 'is stuff at Marie's and other places besides. 'e doesn't list the trade goods by name, mind ye, just the furniture. But 'e also marks in a 'code'. That tells 'im what trade goods are there. That's 'is only record, ye see. I don't understand the code mind ye, but some smart Customs man might work it out."

"And?" Jed was waving one hand in a circular motion trying to get the dour looking Fletch to hurry his story. "Well, the constable called for a reverend to go an' see Godfrey this mornin'; it seems like 'e's dyin'. So, Reverend Tubbs went to see 'im. Godfrey was only conscious for a coupl'a minutes, the reverend says. But when Tubbs tried to talk to Godfrey, 'e cussed poor ol' Tubby so bad, 'e backed up all the way out the door." Fletch laughed, and for a moment Jed caught a glimpse of the playful drunk that he'd seen last night. "Is that it?" he said.

"Impatient little sod, ain't ye? responded Fletch. "No. That's not it. The constable and the Revenue officers will be searching Godfrey's an' Goodman's places today, for sure. They'll find the book, and then they're bound to search all those places listed in Godfrey's book, so Marie will be in trouble. Now I like Marie – but she don't know that." He touched a forefinger to the side of his nose as he gave Jed a fixed stare, intending to ensure his silence on that matter before he continued. "I thought you could put in a good word for me with Marie, just so as I could shift them trade goods for 'er, before 'er place gets searched. I could buy a pie or two. Just to make things look like they're on the up-n-up." His expression went blank, and he raised a hand, in a questioning gesture. Jed was looking at him in amazement. "What makes you think I want to get involved in any of this smugglin' business? I'd like to 'elp Marie', but I've got a family to consider."

"Aye! But I ain't as green as I am 'cabbage-lookin', Jed. I knows 'ow many beans make five."

"You silly old sod! You're not makin' sense," said the farmer.

"Come on now. Last night you said you owed me one. It's time for you to come across. We're on the same team. I'm just in a different part of the organisation, but we've got the same goal after all. Come on, Jed. Do I look like a Revenuer to you? Where d' you think that rum came from last night? There's no King's mark on that cask. Look, I can 'ide Marie's trade goods safely. Godfrey ain't gonna claim 'em, is 'e? It's gonna be 'ard for Marie to manage for money, now she' lost that little bit-o-rent an' the trade money. I've never let on that I was in on the trade, but I know you are. Never said anythin' about that neither. All I want is for you to tell 'er she can trust me. That I've 'elped you out before an' that I'd like to empty 'er cupboard before the Revenuers do it for 'er. Then she can claim she never knew about the cupboard. You could stop at 'er place on the way 'ome. Tell 'er you want me to come by and make things safe for 'er. She trusts you because of the vicar."

Jed's face betrayed his shock. "Yes, I know about the vicar too," Fletch added, impatiently. Jed sat with a shocked look on his face for a few moments before agreeing. "Alright, I'll stop by on the way 'ome an' 'ave a little chat with Marie." Fletch thrust out his hand. Jed grasped it and smiled. "You're a dark 'orse, Fletch. Do ye know that?"

"Aye. But now you can buy me a pint before ye go. After all, you did leave me with a messy wagon and a wet 'orse to look after."

CHAPTER 6

Beware the constable

Whitestone and his lieutenant had ridden hard from The White Hart to the ugly stone building that housed the gaol and the constable's office. During that ride, Whitestone had mentally chastised himself for not staying at Godfrey's side the night before and worrying that he might have lost the opportunity to glean something meaningful from his infrequent and disjointed ramblings. However, he had been desperate for any news that Prudence might have gathered concerning the recovery of the hidden contraband. Analysing such scraps of seemingly irrelevant and disjointed information was an essential part of his job. He tethered his horse and shuddered at the sight of the menacing stone structure that housed Godfrey and Goodman's dead body. He had blamed the depression that he felt last evening on the miserable weather. Today, however, was bright and sunny, and yet this building still infused him with a disquieting unease. "A couple of days in here would convert most villains to law-abiding citizens," he remarked to his lieutenant. "Aye, Sir!" responded his smiling companion. "But the cells do have all the comforts of home: a wooden bench and a bucket. What more could a man want?"

Godfrey was upstairs, in a cell designated the 'infirmary' and had the added luxury of two heavy blankets. Whitestone wanted him kept alive, at least until he had given up some information. A shivering doctor had occupied a chair beside the ailing man all night. Goodman had been the first off the wagon that brought him and Godfrey here, and the officers had no intention of struggling up the stairs with his heavy body, so they moved their regular client instead. The doctor had begun examining Goodman as Godfrey was being carried upstairs. He noted that Goodman's second wound had penetrated his ribcage left of, and about three inches lower than, the one that had pierced his heart. But that examination was halted by Whitestone, who insisted that bringing Godfrey back to consciousness was to be his only priority. So the doctor had left the bloodstained chisel on the Spotsman's exposed chest and climbed the stairs to the infirmary.

Goodman and Godfrey, of course, were prime suspects in the smuggling, but only Godfrey could identify other smugglers to Whitestone now, and he was drifting between delirium and unconsciousness. Goodman's contribution would be limited to what could be gleaned from his wounds, but that brief examination had troubled the doctor. He told Whitestone that Goodman was in the early stages of rigor-mortis and that was unusual, given the time of the murder and he quickly dismissed Whitestone's suggestion that the cold rain could have been responsible for that. There was also something about Goodman's wounds that troubled him. The angle of penetration for both wounds appeared to be parallel. That was an unlikely coincidence for two independent thrusts from the same weapon. He said the blood on the chisel was also inconsistent with the theory that Godfrey had stabbed the man as he was alighting from the buggy. The blood hadn't flowed down the upwardly angled chisel and had a smeared appearance. It seemed irrelevant, but he also claimed to smell a faint odour of manure around the wound. However, he couldn't offer a reason for these strange findings. Whitestone, who couldn't smell the manure, and only liked decisive statements, concluded that the doctor was merely incompetent.

The brief improvement in Godfrey's consciousness that had sent the horseman racing to fetch Whitestone had passed, and for the next half-hour, Whitestone stood beside the doctor whilst he tried to bring the prisoner to consciousness. His patience had all but run out when Constable Joshua Cooper made his appearance. The constable was a six-foot-tall, rugged and heavily built man, with a ruddy complexion and cheerful countenance. "How goes it, Whitestone? Any luck?"

"Nothing! Nothing at all! The doctor seems incapable of rousing him." His phrasing and tone of voice strongly reflected Whitestone's impatience, and he gave the doctor a despairing look. The weary physician took exception to his manner and snapped: "If you think you can do any better, Whitestone, you're most welcome to try. I resent the implication that I'm not doing everything possible." The constable interjected: "Come now, Doctor.

I'm sure that Whitestone meant nothing derogatory. All of us are just weary of this frustrating situation. Isn't that so, Whitestone?"

"Yes, Constable. My apologies, Doctor. No slight intended."

"Good man," said the constable. "Now, Doctor, how about we leave you in peace to attend the prisoner, whilst Whitestone and I discuss the other aspects of this case in my office. Agreed?"

"Go ahead," replied the doctor.

"Come then, Whitestone. I'd like you to bring me up to date with your investigations. Perhaps I can be of some assistance." The constable's office, in stark contrast to the miserable dampness of the rest of the building, was comfortably furnished and warm. Dark oak wainscoting covered the lower sections of the walls, with decorated plastered sections above. Heavy brown beams spanned the plastered ceiling and a wrought iron chandelier carrying 20 candles was suspended in the centre of the room. Large area carpets adorned the floor, and landscape paintings decorated walls above the fireplace and behind an elegant desk. Well-stocked bookcases were set on the walls behind the desk, and comfortable looking wing chairs sat on either side of a cheerily blazing fire. In the wall opposite the fireplace, a large window was framed by red velvet curtains with decorative gold trim; a comfortable couch and a low table were set below that, on another large carpet. Whitestone paused as he entered the room, shocked by the unexpected luxury. "What a pleasant room, and what a stark contrast to the accommodations upstairs."

The constable laughed. "Would you have me change places with the villains then, Whitestone?"

"Obviously not, Sir, but I must say I've never seen an office so well appointed. This is very comfortable indeed."

"Well, I spend a lot of time here, Whitestone. The furnishings are my own. Not taxpayer's money, you understand. Please, take a seat by the fire whilst I pour you a glass of sherry." Both men retired to wing chairs beside the fireplace with their sherries. Whitestone said: "I hope the doctor will inform us immediately if Godfrey shows any sign of consciousness or starts to babble?" He leaned forward, emphasising his concern. "I can't afford to lose any chance of questioning him simply because of concerns for his health. Time is of the essence here." The constable had raised his glass towards the sunlit window, studying the clarity of the amber liquid.

He gently swirled the sherry in the glass and inhaled the aroma before answering. "Have no fear, Whitestone. I've made it clear to the good doctor that we must take advantage of even the smallest opportunity to question Godfrey. He'll not prejudice our lawful need to question a criminal simply out of concern for his health. He's with us. I can assure you." Whitestone slumped despairingly in the wing chair. "My biggest fear is that he'll not recover at all. All I have at this point is hearsay and Godfrey's delirious ramblings. Goodman was my main suspect for Spotsman, and Godfrey appears to have been his second in command and enforcer. I've been told that they had some sort of a falling out over leadership and discipline." He snorted derisively. "Discipline hardly seems an appropriate word to apply to such rabble. I've no way of knowing how accurate my information is, but such a rift might have set the scene for last night's murder."

"Well, that information corroborates what I've heard," responded the constable. "I'm told that Godfrey was voicing threats against Goodman at The Coach and Horses last night. Several patrons attest to that. Mind you, he was addressing no one in particular. Apparently, he has a habit of talking to himself when he's been drinking and, as you know, the man was very drunk. Given his condition, it's hard to say how much was bluster and how much was intent. But however it goes now – with the Spotsman dead and Godfrey close to it – even if he were to die, surely it would still be a victory for law and order. I imagine you would have been well satisfied had they been caught smuggling and shot by your officers?"

"Not really. My orders are to apprehend the whole ring: the distribution network and the funding parties, buyers too if possible. Have you heard how we are faring with the search of Goodman's rooms and the carpenter's shop, Constable? Has that yielded clues to others in the ring? I really wanted to be in on that search. But Godfrey had to be my first priority." Whitestone was fidgeting on the edge of his seat.

"Calm yourself, Whitestone. You told me that the officers that you've assigned to that job are competent and ambitious. My men are equally so. I'm sure that such teamwork, from two different perspectives, should provide a more complex and penetrating picture. Or wouldn't you agree?"

"Possibly, possibly!"

Just then, there was a knock at the door, and the gaoler entered. "Beggin' ye pardon, Sirs, but the doctor says the prisoner is stirrin' an' makin' attempts to speak." Both men set their glasses aside and hurried to the infirmary. Godfrey was rolling about on the narrow bench and mumbling incoherently. Every so often, he would utter a recognisable word or two but nothing structured. "Can't you give him something to bring him out of this?" Whitestone snapped impatiently. "I'm afraid this might be as good as it gets," responded the weary doctor. "I've tried everything I know. I doubt he will last much longer; he is very weak, and his lungs are flooding."

"Rouse him then! Rouse him, man! Slap him; give him brandy or something that might stimulate him, if only for a few minutes." The doctor took a flask from his bag and trickled some of the contents into Godfrey's mouth. Godfrey coughed as the fiery liquid burned his throat and his eyelids fluttered open. He appeared to be struggling to focus on his surroundings. Whitestone pushed the doctor aside and took his place on the chair. "Godfrey! Godfrey! This is your last chance to punish those who have wronged you. Tell me, who is the Spotsman?" Godfrey managed a weak smile. "Brandy," he murmured. Whitestone took the flask from the doctor's hand and cradled Godfrey's head with his left hand, as he poured more brandy into the man's mouth. Godfrey gasped and sputtered, and his eyes rolled back a little. "Who is the Spotsman?" Whitestone demanded.

"Shpotsma', dirty bah . . .bah . . . bastard," mumbled Godfrey. "Run th' goods ashore. Spotsmannnn."

"Where will the run come ashore?" Whitestone demanded. "Tackle… works… tackle works good. Rotten bast'd, no 'pre-see-a-shun… Drink." Godfrey's eyes rolled back, and his head grew heavier in Whitestone's hand. The doctor felt for the pulse in Godfrey's neck, looking at Whitestone with a grim expression. Suddenly, Godfrey lifted his head. "Me… I'd kill 'im. Sail… Sails… Spotsman. I should be…." The rest of his words were lost in a gurgling noise as he collapsed. The doctor examined the prisoner. "He's gone," he said. Whitestone poured more brandy into the man's mouth. No response. He slapped his face again, harder this time. But there was still no response. "He's gone, Whitestone!" The doctor's impatience was open and hostile. Whitestone hung his head for a moment. When he looked up, he said: "Keep him here. No one but us knows he's dead. I can use that to pry information from suspects if they think he's alive and talking. I can offer leniency in exchange for information." He looked to the constable. "The gaoler must go along with this. His relief too; they must be reliable and tight-lipped. Agreed?" The constable nodded. "Did he say anything meaningful?"

"Maybe. Tackle suggests that they may be planning to lift the goods from the beach, as opposed to carrying it ashore. That's how they intended to do it last time. Might even be the same beach; we never found any tackle that time though. But he might have been talking about that last time. We know they found a way to use that difficult beach, but because of the failed ambush, they know we are aware of that." Then, abruptly: "I must go. There is nothing to be gained by staying here now. I have to go to Goodman's and Godfrey's places. Can I leave the details here to you, Constable?" The constable nodded. "Then I'll bid you good-day, Sir. First I'll go to Goodman's, then Godfrey's. I'll keep you informed." With that, Whitestone hurried out to his horse. The constable, looking pensive, returned to his office and retrieved his sherry. Standing in front of the fireplace, he kicked at a protruding log in a distracted manner. "Damn! I wonder what the hell happened out there," he muttered. "Something doesn't smell right. The doctor knows it too but can't put his finger on it. What the hell are we missing?" He picked up Whitestone's glass and poured the remaining sherry into his own glass before sitting in his chair. "This could be dangerous," he muttered. "Bloody dangerous!" He sat quietly for a few minutes before he arose from his chair and opened the door to the stable yard. "Chalmers! Chalmers!" he called, "Get in here." Two minutes later, his young, ginger-headed groom was standing, cap in hand, watching the constable write.

"Chalmers, I want you to take this message to the church. Harness up the buggy and go straight away. The message is for Reverend Tubbs; I need his advice on what preparations we should make for the two prisoner's funerals. Time is short. This must be attended to without delay. What's that old saying: 'A fix in time saves nine'?"

"No, Sir," smiled Chalmers. "A *STITCH* in time saves nine!"

"No, Chalmers, I'm sure it's 'A *FIX* in time'. It makes more sense; it wouldn't need to apply only to needlework."

"No, Sir," smiled the young groom. "It's definitely *STITCH*."

The constable returned his smile. "Sure of yourself, are you? Well then, young man, let's make a wager. I'll bet you a shilling that I'm right, and you're wrong. Tell you what. You ask Fletcher, at the church, which is correct. He's an expert on these old sayings. I'd take his word for it any day. If you come back and tell me he agrees with you, I'll give you a shilling. If he agrees with me, you can cut me some kindling for my fireplace at home.

Enough kindling for a month, how's that?"

"You're on, Sir. That's an easy shilling." The groom knuckled his forehead and turned to leave, carrying the constable's sealed message and wearing a big smile on his freckled face. "Oh, by the way, Chalmers," said the constable. "The reverend could be busy, so give my letter to Fletcher. He's to make sure the reverend gets it as soon as possible. If Fletcher's not at the church when you arrive, you must find him, even if you have to drive all over town. Don't leave it with anyone but Fletcher. Understand! Tell him it's urgent." He pointed a finger at Chalmers. "You can tell Fletcher – but no one else, mind you, and he's not to mention to anyone – anyone at all – that Godfrey is dead. Understand? No one is to know that until Captain Whitestone releases that information. Be sure that Fletcher understands that. Now, Chalmers, I could really use that box of kindling. Be sure to let me know whether Fletcher agrees with you or me."

"Aye, Sir, Mum's the word about the prisoner bein' dead. I'm lookin' forward to that shillin', Sir."

"Good lad." The door closed behind the groom, leaving the constable at his desk, smiling. After he heard the buggy leave, he went to see the gaoler. "How's our regular customer? Awake, is he?"

"Aye, Sir. As usual, 'e's got a few bumps an' bruises an' a real bad 'eadache; apart from that 'e's 'is usual charmin' self."

"Well then, turn him loose. You don't think he heard the doctor pronounce Godfrey dead, do you? We wouldn't want him blabbing that news at the inn before Whitestone approves. No one is to mention that outside of this building. Make sure your relief is aware of that too."

"I'll do that, Sir. I don't imagine the prisoner 'eard. I think 'is 'ead would be 'urtin' too bad for 'im to even listen."

"Turn him loose then, after he's cleaned his cell, of course, and emptied his bucket."

"Aye, Sir," responded the gaoler, smiling. "Makes ye' wonder what life must be like at 'ome, Sir, when 'e prefers to spend so much time in 'ere."

"That it does, my friend. Maybe we're running too pleasant a refuge here. Perhaps we should charge rent." And both men laughed.

About half an hour later, a knock came at the constable's office door. It was one of his officers – Winters. He was accompanied by Scrivener, one of Whitestone's men. "Sir, we have a problem at the Whatson house," said Winters. "Mrs. Whatson slammed the door on us when we asked permission to search Goodman's room. I got the impression that the lady was unaware of Goodman's death until Scrivener mentioned it. She promptly slammed the door in our faces and became hysterical. We could hear her screaming and carrying on through the door. Captain Whitestone came by shortly after, and when we explained the situation, he asked if you would be kind enough to use your influence to pacify the lady. He then left for Godfrey's shop, asking that you let him know the outcome at the Whatsons, Sir." Winters then took a half step back, so that he was behind Scrivener and out of his line of sight. Then after indicating Scrivener with a nod, he shook his head. The constable looked from one to the other of the two officers and Winters repeated his little mime. The constable thought for a few seconds before saying: "Well, it seems I shall have to go and apologise and try to calm this influential lady. But Chalmers has just taken my buggy on an errand."

"Shall I saddle your horse, Sir?"

"Aye! Please do that, Winters."

"Shall we come with you, Sir?"

"Just you, Winters. Scrivener: I think you had best find the captain and report that we are on the case as he requested. Time is of the essence, so you'd best leave right away."

"But, Sir, there should be a Customs officer present to search Goodman's rooms," protested Scrivener. "I would be more familiar with clues that might indicate smuggling."

"Aye, that's true, and as soon as you've spoken with the captain, you may join us there. Hopefully, that'll give me time to calm Mrs. Whatson to the point where she will consider letting us enter her house. Don't fret, Scrivener; we'll not disturb anything. We may still be locked out when you return." Obviously annoyed, Scrivener left the building.

Winters then told the constable that when the maid had answered Whatson's door, Scrivener had declared, in a very officious manner, that they were there to search Goodman's room by order of the constable. The nervous maid had asked them to wait outside whilst she summoned Mrs. Whatson. They had made no mention of Goodman's death to the maid, believing that the household had been notified the night before. Mrs.

Whatson had stamped her way to the front door ready for battle and opened her attack on the officers as soon as she opened the door. "Goodman's not home," she had declared, "and I have no idea where you get the gall to demand to search his room, but if and when Goodman says you may, and provided that you show better manners, I may consider allowing you into my house but not a moment before," and she moved to close the door. "I realised immediately, Sir, that Mrs. Whatson was unaware of her butler's death, but before I could speak, Scrivener stuck his foot in the door and said, very sarcastically: "Well, Ma'am, since he was murdered last night, that's not likely to happen, is it? We're here on King's business, investigating his murder and related crimes, Ma'am. You'd better let us in; there are severe penalties for obstructing King's officers in pursuit of their duties."

Whitestone was aware of Scrivener's lack of tact but considered that his ruthless thoroughness more than compensated for a few ruffled feathers. However, Scrivener's tactics were not appropriate for this situation, and the shocked Mrs. Whatson slammed the door hard on his foot. Scrivener screamed and quickly removed his injured foot, and Mrs. Whatson swiftly closed and bolted the door.

"We heard the lady scream and burst into tears; she sounded hysterical, Sir," said Winters, "so we backed off." Winters had trouble suppressing a smile as he said: "Scrivener was sitting on the grass, holding his foot and groaning in pain." He seemed to enjoy the fact that the 'cocky' Scrivener had got his comeuppance, but he managed to continue: "Captain Whitestone arrived a few minutes later, Sir, and I advised him of the situation. He was reluctant to confront the hysterical lady and asked for you to use your influence to placate the lady, Sir. The captain then went on to Godfrey's shop."

• • •

Reverend Tubbs was shocked at the sight of Prudence's bruised face, but once she had assured him that she was well, he quickly assigned his priority tasks to others, thereby freeing himself up to take her to Ryeport. His biggest concern was Godfrey. Someone would need to assume responsibilities for the prisoner's last spiritual needs when that request came from the constable. However, Reverend Watkins, who was fully aware of the situation at the gaol, was quite unconcerned about Tubby's warnings of the man's offensive language and willingly undertook that responsibility. Half an hour later, Prudence and the nervous cleric were on the road to Ryeport. Tubby told Prudence: "I'm so happy to do this errand for you, my dear.

You see, I was to provide a prisoner in the gaol the opportunity to repent his sins, but he was incoherent most of the time that I was there, and his rare lucid words were so vulgar that I was glad when he finally passed out providing me an opportunity to leave. I hope you won't think too badly of me for running away from that responsibility."

"Oh, Reverend Tubbs, I'm hardly likely to think badly of someone as generous and kind as you. I'm sure you only acted as you thought best."

"I was first called to the gaol, in the early hours this morning. The prisoner's name is Godfrey; they say he was the man who murdered Whatson's butler." He paused, searching her face for signs of distress. "I'm sure you must have heard of the murder. The whole town is talking about it."

"Well, yes, I did hear something about it, but as you know, I'm not welcome in Mrs. Whatson's house. I'm sure you remember the situation at Grandfather's funeral. Perhaps you could tell me what happened. Otherwise, I will only have rumour and gossip to depend on."

"Yes, of course, my dear. I understand. Well, it appears that the man Godfrey was part of a smuggling ring, apparently led by Goodman, the butler." He looked for her reaction.

"Really!" Prudence clapped a gloved hand over her mouth in feigned shock.

"I'm sorry, my dear, this must be quite a shock for you. Forgive me. I'll say no more."

"No, no! Please go on. I must learn to face these things."

"Very well then, provided you are sure?" Prudence nodded. "Well, it appears that these two had a falling out and that Godfrey killed Goodman, during some sort of drunken rage. This happened right outside his carpenter's shop on Church Street, at the bottom of the very hill that our church sits on. Isn't that shocking?"

"Oh my; that is terrible. Whatever did the bishop say?"

"Oh, he is still away at a conference. I had the task of recording the incident and, even worse, visiting the murderer in his cell."

"How terrible, Reverend. How could you possibly help such a sinner?"

"Well, frankly, my dear, I don't think I can. But, of course, he must have the opportunity to repent his sins before he meets his Maker. I should have asked Fletcher to take you to Ryeport so that I could handle that unpleasant task myself. Instead, I'm embarrassed to say, I persuaded myself that my more experienced colleague would be better able to help this sinner than I. I would like to believe that I was not acting out of cowardice alone." He looked at Prudence imploringly, as though dreading an unfavourable response. "Oh no, your reasoning appears very sound, Reverend Tubbs. You left the man in more experienced hands. I think that was unselfish of you. Some people would have sought the glory of the encounter rather than the best interests of the sinner. Tell me, how sick is the prisoner? Is it true that he might die?"

"Oh, I'll be surprised if he sees tomorrow, my dear. The doctor told me his lungs are filling with fluid. He was lying in the street, soaking wet and pinned there by the butler's suffocating weight, for an hour or so. And he'd already spent a similar time lying in the rain in the side yard of The Coach and Horses, drunk of course. Then, when he came to, he walked to his shop on Church Street, where he killed Goodman. It appears that he stabbed Goodman twice, as he was getting down from his buggy. Mortally wounded, Goodman fell from the buggy and landed on top of Godfrey. They would have both lain there all night but were discovered by neighbours who had decided to check on Godfrey. The constable had both men taken to the infirmary." "Infirmary," he repeated derisively. "Anyone who enters there is unlikely to leave alive. Barbaric place."

"Were they able to get any information from Godfrey?"

"Oh no; as I said, he is either delirious or unconscious most of the time, and his coherent words are foul and abusive. Nothing structured, you understand. The doctor thinks he will be dead before the day is out, Miss."

"How terrible! Oh, look, Father! There is Pringle's cart. You have made excellent time, Father. Do you think we could spend a moment or two to give the Pringles your news? They were very concerned about this affair." The Pringles were quickly updated, and Prudence and Tubby left arriving in Ryeport around noon. The vicar was pleasantly surprised to see them and suggested that they retire to the inn for a meal. Tubby's news quickly made him the centre of attention there as he told Ernie's patrons of the events in Nextwest. He was bombarded with questions, most of which he could not answer, and Prudence managed to hide her bruises by keeping her bonnet pulled close to her cheek.

Hawksworth arrived shortly before the coach delivered his mail pouch.

Then more villagers arrived, responding to the post horn, and Tubby was persuaded to re-tell the story for the benefit of the newcomers. Prudence and the vicar seized that opportunity to leave for his cottage. A more detailed and private discussion of yesterday's events followed that would enable the vicar to bring Sailmaker and Bannerman up to date after his visitors had left. "Now, the circle of information is complete, and we'll all be 'singing the same song,'" said Pru, smiling. "Or should I say praying the same prayer?" Reverend Tubbs was enjoying his celebrity. He had the rapt attention of all the villagers, plus the coachmen. They would obviously carry news of this meeting back to Nextwest. "That won't be a bad thing," said Roddy to Prudence. "An uninvolved party will establish our source of this information. How could anyone suspect collusion?" Tubby and Prudence left a couple of hours later, but Bessie noticed that Prudence seemed reluctant to part from the vicar. On arrival at The White Hart, Prudence slipped a plain sheet of white paper under the door of Whitestone's room.

• • •

Whitestone had found the situation at Godfrey's shop far more rewarding than that at Whatson's. His officers had pretty well stripped the shop and the upstairs apartment. All papers and suspicious materials, including the rest of the turning chisels, were laid out on a freshly cleared work bench. They had also paid a curious neighbour to empty the bucket that had so dominated the atmosphere upstairs. Fortunately, that neighbour proved to be a strong man with an excellent sense of balance and a poor sense of smell. They had him leave the emptied bucket amongst the trees outside.

Whitestone's officers had discovered a tattered book containing references to what appeared to be storage places. Several suspicious and unexplained symbols were ascribed to each reference, but there was no legend for these symbols. On the face of things, it appeared that these were locations where repaired or broken furniture was stored. But the unexplained symbols had Whitestone's mind working overtime, and why were there so many diverse storage locations? Most of those places listed were sheds or barns, but one stood out because it was a residence and that was Marie's home. "We'll start right here," said Whitestone, pointing to the address. "From this sketch, it appears there is an unaccounted for space within the normal confines of the building. Bennet, you come with me. Baxter, you remain here and continue your search. We'll be back as soon as we've investigated these locations."

Whitestone stationed two officers at the rear of Marie's house before he and Bennett went to the front door. A handwritten sign in her window advertised pies, preserves, and pickles for sale. Marie smiled at the officers when she opened the door. "Good Mornin', Gentlemen! What can I do for ye? Some pies per'aps?"

"No, Ma'am. We are Customs officers, and we have good reason to believe that there are smuggled goods on these premises, and we're here to search for them." With that, Whitestone pushed past the startled Marie, into her living room. "Why don't you come in?" she asked sarcastically, as she followed the officers. "There ain't no smuggled goods in 'ere. I'm just a widda'. Do I look like I can carry casks o' rum up cliffs?" Whitestone ignored her. "Bennet, go into the back room. Look for a secret door."

Marie laughed. "Started drinkin' early t'day, did ye? Ain't you supposed to wait 'til the sun's over the yardarm? There's nothin' but stored furniture in the back room. B'longs to that bloke Godfrey wot's in gaol. Still owes me last week's rent, so 'e does."

Minutes later, Bennett called to Whitestone: "Scrape marks on the floor, Sir. I think I've found it." The two officers quickly moved enough furniture to clear the tell-tale scrapings that betrayed the travelled radius of the disguised door. Bennett found and released a concealed catch at the top of the fake beam and plaster wall. "It looks as though your worries about overdue rent are over, Madam," said Whitestone. "You won't have to worry about rent where you're going. Detained at the King's pleasure may not offer luxurious accommodation, but it is free." He permitted himself a self-satisfied smirk.

Bennett swung the false wall open, revealing the shelved cavity behind it. Marie was putting on a splendid performance as the shocked and surprised housewife, but Whitestone wasn't buying it. When they entered the closet though, they found it empty. Empty that is except for one dusty bottle, almost half full and sitting alone on the middle shelf. The shelves were covered with a layer of dust, as was the bottle, and a cobweb was stretched between the cork in the bottle's neck, a corkscrew lying nearby.

"So that's where the cunning bugger 'id 'is bottles," said Marie. "I never could find 'em. An 'e swore 'e wasn't drinkin' no more. I knew 'e was lyin' o-course. Just couldn't catch 'im at it." Whitestone's expression was grim. Still clutching Godfrey's book, he walked into the closet to examine the shelves for 'footprints' that might have been left in the dust by removed items, but there were none; the carpet of dust was evenly spread. "So whose bottle is this?" he said to Marie. "Well, I s'pose it's mine now," she replied. "That's more than 'e bloody well left me when 'e up an' died. An' 'e didn't even tell me about that."

"And who is 'he?"

"Me 'usband, that's who. Died near on seven years ago. There's been plenty o' times I'd 'ave been glad of a little nip of somethin', 'specially on them bad days. But I didn't even know it was there." She reached into the cupboard and took the bottle from the shelf, leaving a clear 'footprint' on the shelf. "What is it, I wonder?" She said, wiping the dust off the bottle with her apron. She pulled the protruding cork with her teeth, sniffed the bottle and took a sip. "Ooh! That's good stuff!" She offered Whitestone the bottle. "Wann'a drop?" The officers ignored her and carried on searching the house. They even searched the chimney whilst the officers at the rear of the house checked the yard. "No signs of freshly turned earth or any other clues," reported his officers. Marie just sat and watched taking occasional swigs from her bottle. Whitestone assumed that the badly depleted bottle was responsible for the smile on Marie's face when they left. However, once she was alone, Marie raised the bottle in a toasting fashion and took a longer drink. "God Bless ye, Fletcher!" she said. "Oops, maybe I should leave some, for 'manners'. Or maybe for you, Fletch. It is your bottle after all. Got a real delicate touch 'as Fletch,'" she murmured thoughtfully. "I must tell Bessie about that. About the way 'e cleaned them shelves after 'e took the goods away. Then 'ow 'e put 'is bottle there – just so." She reached out and gently placed the bottle on the table, imitating Fletcher's careful action. "Then 'e collected dust from all over the 'ouse, put it on a sheet o' paper and gently blew it off the paper – nice an even like – all over ev'rythin' in the cupboard, includin' the bottle." She held her two hands together palms up, in front of her, and blew gently as she moved her hands slowly from left to right. "Real delicate, 'e was." Her expression was blank with admiration as she reflected on the care that the stableman had used in preparing the closet. "Best of all was the cobweb! Unbelievable!" she muttered. "Carried it safely from the porch, so 'e did. Then 'e transfers one end to the bottle an' the other to the corkscrew. What a touch! Real delicate! 'ere's to you, Fletch," she said, taking another drink from the bottle. "I likes a man with a gentle touch, I do," she said, smiling mischievously and promptly burst out laughing; all the tension that had been building in her since hearing the coachman's story floated away on her laughter. Finally, she felt free to relax. Marie raised the bottle to her lips, but this time she drained it. "Plenty more where that came from, Fletch," she said before she dozed off.

• • •

Chalmers turned the constable's buggy into the church driveway and eased up to the stables. "Whoa, girl!" Fletcher had seen him coming, and was at his side as soon as he stepped down. " 'ello there, young carrot top! What are you doin' 'ere? I don't recall you attendin' church on Sundays, much less on a weekday."

"I've got an urgent message from the constable, Mister Fletcher. It's for Reverend Tubbs – urgent, sez the constable. But give it to Fletcher, an' tell 'im to make sure Reverend Tubbs gets it as soon as possible. It's about funeral arrangements for the prisoners, 'e sez. Not to give it to anyone but you, 'e sez. An' to tell you, you're not to mention Godfrey is dead until Cap'n Whitestone sez it's alright. So, 'ere I am. Why would 'e want me to give the reverend's message to you, not 'im?" He handed the sealed message to Fletcher. "Well done! You certainly 'andled that job very well," responded Fletcher, ignoring Chalmer's question. "Anythin' else keepin' you 'ere? Or do you just enjoy makin' the place look untidy?"

"Well, yes, Sir. The constable told me to get that message to you right away b'cos it's urgent, an' urgent things 'ave to be done right away." Chalmers grinned. "The constable sez: 'A fix in time saves nine.' I sez: "Beggin' ye pardon, Sir. The proper sayin' is: 'A *STITCH* in time saves nine.' 'Oh, no' 'e sez. 'A *FIX* in time saves nine makes more sense.' So I sez: ' No…"

"Whoa, boy! I get it. You say *stitch* an' 'e says *fix*. I get it! What about it?" Chalmers grin grew larger. " 'e bet me a shillin' to a box o' kindlin' that 'e was right an' I was wrong. Fletcher shall be the judge, 'e sez. So, who's right, Mr. Fletcher, me or 'im?"

"Well, it seems that you are, my carrot-topped friend. Stitch is right, fix is wrong."

"Aha! I knew I was right! Bye, Sir. Got to rush back an' get my shillin'".

"Our shillin', you mean," said Fletcher.

"No! My shillin'," said the confused looking Chalmers.

"Well, without me you wouldn't be gettin' the shillin', would you?"

"Well, no, but…"

"No buts about it, young fella. It took two to earn it, so two should share it. We should be equal partners. I look forward to gettin' my sixpence real soon. Buy me couple'a pints, that will." Chalmers looked downcast. "Constable didn't say I 'ad to share it." Fletcher's face cracked into a smile. "I'm just teasin', young fella. But you be sure to tell the constable that I've already taken care of that little job 'e wanted done. If you don't do that, I'll be after you for my share of the shillin'. Understand?"

"What job was that then?"

"Never you mind! The constable will know. Just make sure and tell 'im as soon as you get back, alright?"

"Alright, Mr. Fletcher, Sir. You've already done the job 'e wanted done, right?"

"That's right," confirmed Fletcher, and the grinning Chalmers climbed back in the buggy and headed for the gaol and his shilling. Fletcher smiled as he waved him goodbye.

• • •

The constable dismounted at the Whatson house and handed Winters the reins of his horse. "Stay with the 'nags' for a while, Winters. I'll check the lay of the land and call you in if I manage to calm Mrs. Whatson down."

"Aye, Sir. Good luck." The constable knocked at the tradesman's door and smiled as he introduced himself to the cook when she answered the door. "Aye, Sir. I know who you are," she said. The constable said: "I would appreciate your help, Mrs.…?"

"Stone, Sir. Emma Stone. Certainly, Sir."

"Thank you, Mrs. Stone: It seems that my office failed to notify Mrs. Whatson, or anyone else in the house, of Mr. Goodman's death last night. That was a terrible affair!"

"Yes, Sir, a real shock, that was."

"I also learned from my officer that Mrs. Whatson was terribly upset when the Customs officer arrived here this morning and asked leave to search Goodman's room. That officer was under the impression that Mrs. Whatson knew of her butler's death. When I learned of this situation, I was anxious to come and apologise. Do you think that Mrs. Whatson would be recovered sufficiently to receive me now, Mrs. Stone? I understand that she was crying hysterically when the officers left."

"Oh, no, Sir! That wasn't 'er. That must 'ave been the maid they 'eard. She's still upstairs in 'er room an' still cryin'. Mrs. Whatson was shocked, of course. We all were. But she's made of sterner stuff than that. I'll go and see, Sir. If she'll receive you, I mean." A short time later, Mrs. Whatson and the constable were in the parlour, and Emma Stone was pouring tea. Winters remained with the horses, and the constable was apologising most profusely, blaming the lateness of the hour, confusion between his staff and the stress of trying to save the life of the seriously ill Godfrey. "An officer was sent here, Ma'am, and we believed that you had been notified. In retrospect though, I feel I should have visited you personally. However, I do hope that you will understand. We really had our hands full. I appreciate that this must be a most shocking and difficult time for you. A distressing event such as this has never occurred in Nextwest before. A murder, compounded by a smuggling investigation, and with Customs officers swarming all over our investigations. Even the terrible weather seemed determined to make our task more difficult."

Mrs. Whatson did her best to appear offended. "Well, it certainly would have been more acceptable for you to attend, rather than the lout that threatened me with dire consequences on my own doorstep this morning. I would have thought, Constable, that a man of your reputation would have shown better judgement in selecting your officers."

"Actually, Ma'am, he is not one of mine. He is a Customs officer, responsible to Captain Whitestone. I'm sure the captain will offer his apology as soon as he can get here. Time is of the essence here, Ma'am, because Goodman and his murderer are both suspects in the captain's smuggling investigation. Goodman's death has been common knowledge since last evening, and the smugglers will have been scrambling to conceal evidence ever since, leaving us struggling to catch up."

"That is no reason for the affront that I was offered this morning, I'm sure." Mrs. Whatson was pouting. "No, Ma'am; I agree. And as I said, I'm sure the captain will have his officer apologise once he is aware of the circumstances. By the way, we do need to inform Goodman's next of kin. They will need to be apprised of the situation. Possibly they may want to arrange the funeral."

"He has no family. There is no next of kin."

"Ah! Then would you know who we could turn to for some insight regarding funeral arrangements? Was he a religious man? Did he confide any such details to you?"

"He was my butler, Constable, not my husband. How would I know?" she responded tersely.

"Of course, Ma'am. I only asked on the off chance. After all, we failed to communicate effectively last night. I wouldn't want to repeat that error." The constable declined more tea. "Actually, I did not get home until late last night," Mrs. Whatson said. "It was after midnight when my friend Mr. Corby brought me home. I wondered why Goodman did not greet us. Then I remembered that I'd allowed him the day off and the use of my buggy for some personal business. I assumed his business had taken him longer than expected." The constable nodded. "That could explain why my officer was unable to reach you last night. I understand that the cook doesn't live in, and since you were not home, that only leaves the maid. Was she home?"

"She was most likely sleeping. Her room is at the back of the house on the top floor. She sleeps a lot and is difficult to wake."

"Did Goodman advise you of the nature of his personal business of yesterday?"

"Really, Constable! Personal business is just that – personal."

"Yes, Ma'am. Forgive me. It is my duty to ask, you understand. Would you mind then, Ma'am, because of these unusual circumstances, if I took a quick look in Goodman's room for the address of a friend or associate that may be able to guide us regarding his interment wishes? Or perhaps there might be a copy of his Will. I would be pleased to do this together if you would allow it." Mrs. Whatson led the way upstairs, pushed open the door of Goodman's room and ushered the constable into a large, comfortably furnished, bed/sitting room with a desk and bookcase. He began to go through the papers on the desk, taking great care not to disarrange anything. Mrs. Whatson soon grew tired of watching him. "I'll leave you to it, Constable. I cannot believe that Goodman would be involved in smuggling. This accusation is almost as disturbing as his murder. By the way, there is a man outside with two horses. Is he with you?"

"Yes, Ma'am."

"Would you prefer he come in and help you?"

"Not yet, Ma'am. We are expecting Captain Whitestone. My officer, Winters, will advise me of his arrival so that I can introduce him."

"Very well," she said and left the room. Once he was alone, the constable started frantically scrambling through drawers and bookshelves, looking behind pictures and under chair seats – anywhere that might have provided a hiding place for secret information. He had all but given up when he noticed a circumferential scuff mark part way down one of the turned wooden bedposts, just below some decorative turning. Taking hold of the post's upper section, he twisted and gently lifted. The upper section separated from the lower part of the post, revealing a roll of papers concealed in a tubular hollow. He quickly scanned through them. "Aha!" He took two lists from the roll and returned the rest to their hiding place. He folded one of the retained lists and put it in his pocket; the second seemed to demand more attention.

He listened carefully at the door, checking that no one was close by before spreading it on the desk. Then he took a fresh sheet of paper from the desk and began to copy the list except that he substituted the names of trees for the family names on the original list. He didn't try to match the handwriting but did ensure that it differed from his own natural hand. The constable then wrote the tree names alongside the family names on the original list and put that back in his pocket, anxiously listening all the while for footsteps on the stairs. He blotted the sheet, containing only tree names and placed that with the others in the bedpost. He then refitted the top of the post and left the room.

"No luck, I'm sorry to say, Mrs. Whatson. I found no reference to a Will or to any kin. I fear I shall have to leave this matter to the church. Would you mind if I have Reverend Tubbs look after those arrangements? I imagine Goodman would have sufficient funds to cover any final expenses. If that is not the case, I will arrange burial. Winters, my man outside, would need to have a more thorough look around for some clue as to why Goodman was murdered. Whitestone too will need access because of the alleged smuggling. With your permission, Ma'am, I will have them introduce themselves and arrange a convenient time with you. Time is our enemy in this investigation." Mrs. Whatson sighed heavily. "I shall cooperate, provided they are respectful, but I shall be glad when this affair is behind me."

"Me too, Ma'am! Me too!" Winters seemed relieved to see the constable. "How did things go, Sir?'

"Well enough, Winters, provided we walk around this lady as if we were on eggshells. We all need to be extremely polite and considerate. I know that will be no problem for you, but I believe Captain Whitestone should send Scrivener about some other business. Mrs. Whatson is prepared to allow us access to Goodman's room – provided we treat her with respect. Now, I have urgent business to attend to and will need you to stay and advise the captain of what has happened. The constable gave Winters details of his search of Goodman's room but made no mention of the hollow bedpost. "I found nothing of interest," he said. "Perhaps sharper eyes might spot something I missed. I want you to assume the investigative role for our office, Winters. Whitestone can look after the smuggling end of things. One more thing: Mrs. Whatson was the guest of a Mr. Corby last evening, and he brought her home around midnight. Ask Whitestone if he wants us to investigate Corby. I've never heard that name before." Winters nodded. "Aye, Sir."

Whitestone called at the Whatson's house on his return from Marie's. Winters was relieved to see that Scrivener had been replaced by Bennett. "You've missed the constable, Sir," he said. He had to leave to attend to other urgent business. I thought that Scrivener would be with you, Sir."

"No. I've sent him to the Customs house. I want the cutter to investigate the beach where the last run was to have come ashore. There's a possibility that the smugglers may be using that same beach to bring ashore the goods they concealed during the failed ambush. There's nerve for you. Apparently, they believe we wouldn't expect them to go back to that site, knowing it had been discovered. By the way, Godfrey is dead – but no one other than us is to know that – until I say so. Is that clear?"

"Aye, Sir. The constable has already informed me of that."

"Have you discovered anything about a run?"

"No, Sir. Not a thing. I've been waiting here for you since the constable left. Any luck at Godfrey's place?"

"Nothing of any consequence! We did find a record book of sorts and searched a number of premises where it recorded stored or repaired furniture, but that was all we found – furniture. It seems they've had sufficient time to remove and conceal any contraband. How goes it inside?" Winters quickly brought Whitestone up to date before knocking on Whatson's front door. Before the door was answered, Winters managed to draw Whitestone aside and quietly inform him of the constable's suggestions regarding Scrivener. "No problem there," said the captain. "After ordering the cutter away, he has to take some men and secure the suspected landing site from the shore side. Please inform the constable that I will also be visiting some farmers close by there. Their name is Pringle. It seems there was some unusual activity at that farm on the day of the murder. Their names were also mentioned at The Coach and Horses. Apparently, one of them went missing for several hours and returned with his head bandaged up. I'd like to know what that was all about."

"Aye, Sir. We'll make enquiries too, as a cross-reference. Oh, one other point. Mrs. Whatson was brought home after midnight last night by her host for the evening. Not a local man. The constable wanted to know if you would like us to investigate that, seeing that the man is a stranger to the area. We wondered if he might have some connection to Goodman or the smugglers. His name is Corby." Whitestone's head jerked up in surprise. "Corby, you say?"

"Aye, Sir, Corby!"

Mrs. Whatson opened the door just in time to hear the last few words. "What about Mr. Corby? She demanded haughtily. "I trust you will not be bothering my friend with this business. Isn't it enough that I have to endure all these questions, in addition to the horror of having a member of my household murdered? Do you now intend to drag my friends into this matter too?" Whitestone was a little taken aback by her sudden appearance and speed of attack. "Begging your pardon, Ma'am, Winters here was just advising me of the situation last evening and our failure to find and notify you of your butler's demise. He was explaining that you did not arrive home until around midnight and that your host for the evening had brought you home. We had no intention of questioning Mr. Corby. If I may introduce myself, Ma'am, my name is Whitestone; Captain Whitestone of the Customs and Revenue Service. My associate here is Lieutenant Bennett, and I believe you already know Mr. Winters, of the constable's office." Mrs. Whatson nodded. "Madam, I would be grateful if you would accept my most sincere apologies for any affront and inconvenience that you may have suffered as the result of our inability to contact you last evening. I also extend the sincere apology of Lieutenant Scrivener whom, I'm given to understand, was most inconsiderate in his approach to you earlier this morning. I have removed him from this investigation. In his defence though, Ma'am, I feel honour bound to inform you that he believed you had been notified of Goodman's death."

"Very well then. Apologies accepted," she responded impatiently. "You had best come in. The constable has already looked over my butler's room, searching for a Will or some indication of religious preference for his funeral arrangements. I told him you could have access to Goodman's things, provided that I am given my due respect." Mrs. Whatson made direct eye contact with each man individually until they each indicated acceptance of her terms.

It was Bennett that found the hollow bedpost and its contents. There was much excitement as Whitestone studied the pages and handed them in turn to the two officers. "This certainly confirms Goodman as the Spotsman. But it does precious little else for us. These tree names are obviously code names for contacts or clients of the smugglers. The numbers could be quantities, but of what? These symbols might indicate the contraband. Can either of you see a way to break this code?" Both men studied the documents intently, eventually shaking their heads before conceding: "No, Sir."

"Well then, Bennett, please ask Mrs. Whatson if she would be so good as to join us for a few minutes. Maybe the lady has heard an acquaintance referred to by a tree name, a nickname, perhaps." Mrs. Whatson was genuinely shocked when shown the secret hiding place and the documents but could offer no help in solving the code names. The officers left the house an hour or so later, having found nothing more of interest. The Customs cutter arrived at the smugglers' beach late that afternoon and found the bloated, rock damaged bodies of the two smugglers and the tackle. Scrivener and his men spread out along the Coach Road and worked their way down to the cliff top. They found no smugglers in the area or clues from the tackle.

Whitestone questioned the patrons at The Coach and Horses before visiting Pringle's farm. All the stories supported what Prudence had already told him. He visited the barn and discovered the bloodstained shovel at the foot of the hayloft ladder, where Bob had dropped it. This seemed to corroborate Jed's story of a fall from the ladder. Later, at The Harbour Light, Whitestone questioned the vicar and Bessie Drew, but their stories all served to corroborate statements he had already gathered.

• • •

The following week, Whitestone had the cliff-top tackle, cart, and capstan dragged into the market square at Nextwest and publicly broken up. The rope was sold for oakum and the pulley blocks purchased by a local boat builder. The broken cart and capstan were left for the townspeople to gather up as firewood. This was not as commanding a spectacle as the customary public breakup of a smugglers' boat, but it did set the stage for a speech from Whitestone, who read aloud from a news sheet that was later posted around the town, declaring that Goodman had been positively identified as the smugglers' ringleader and that he'd been murdered by his accomplice, Godfrey, during a dispute over leadership. Two other smugglers had also met their deaths as a result of the local Customs officer's investigations. Actually, Whitestone suspected that the loose shale and an empty rum bottle were likely the cause of the smugglers' deaths. However, since no one knew better, he took credit for their deaths anyway. It would look more impressive in his report. So, Bannerman was off the hook. Whitestone went on to warn the gathering crowd of the dangers of smuggling. "Be assured that if you participate in any area of smuggling, you will be caught, and the punishment will be as severe as it was for these men who died because they sought to rob the King of his legal dues."

The coachman had 'acted' a dramatic imitation of Whitestone's speech, in The Harbour Light, holding aloft a copy of the news sheet. His performance was well worth his free ale and a hearty lunch. Ernie surveyed the faces of the villagers soaking up the entertainment, eventually making eye contact with a trio by the window. He shook his head as he gave them a grim smile as if to concur that smuggling was indeed a dangerous and foolish game. Bessie, Sailmaker and the vicar smiled back. Sailmaker held his head as he gave a nod of agreement. The significance of this little performance was lost on all patrons except Doc Hudson, who had the benefit of inside knowledge. He just smiled his weary smile and kept his secrets. Bannerman heard all about the coachman's performance when he returned from fishing later that day. They had brought home a most satisfying catch, plus a couple of ankers of retrieved brandy, concealed beneath the fish. Bannerman was happy to learn that Whitestone had claimed the dead smugglers at the base of the cliff.

Two weeks later, the coachman provided fresh news of Corby. Looking furtively over his shoulder, he whispered – loud enough for all to hear: "We took that bloke Corby back to London last week, so we did. Not all the way, o' course, just our stage. We 'eard it was 'im who warned the smugglers! Can't trust no one these days, can ye?" Whitestone had questioned Corby regarding his relationship with Mrs. Whatson, and Corby declared that he was unaware that it was her butler who was suspected of being the Spotsman.

In a report to his superiors in London, Whitestone sarcastically wrote: "Since Corby claims that he said nothing to Mrs. Whatson regarding either his position with the Customs Service or any detail of our business, I have to wonder if perhaps he talks in his sleep. Isn't it strange that just when we had these villains in our grasp, Corby arrives – anxious to assume full credit for our long and exhaustive investigation – and that is the very moment that the smugglers learn of our ambush and slip through our fingers?"

Meanwhile, Bannerman and the Sullivan boys, with Carter's help, gradually 'crept-up' the remainder of the goods they'd sunk on the night of the fire-boat and sold them in discreet amounts, through Pringle's resurrected distribution network. Fletcher also blended Marie's 'inherited' share of the contraband into this quiet network of buyers. The alarm code of misspoken sayings had also changed. Young Chalmers grinned and touched his cap every time he saw Fletcher, still grateful for his shilling.

From the proceeds of the aborted run, Bannerman gradually compensated Sailmaker for his lost fee, and Marie was finding her discreet, extra income very acceptable. Fletch too was proving a great friend and justified his newfound reputation for a delicate touch, in many ways. In appreciation, he was treated to supper at Marie's on a fairly regular basis. Breakfast was soon to follow. They obviously enjoyed each other's company. Fletch was displaying more of his playful side these days, and Bessie was pleased to see how much happier her sister was.

A study of the bill-of-sales revealed that the inventory of the carpenters shop had not been listed in Fletcher's original sale to Godfrey. The constable said: "I will seize the shop but have no legal right to seize the inventory since it didn't belong to Godfrey." No one had shown an interest in the run-down carpenter's shop, so the sale price fell very low. The constable, therefore, told Fletcher that, should he wish to repurchase the shop, he would be willing to accept his rediscovered stock as collateral, in a purchase offer. Fletcher could then buy the place with small monthly payments made directly to the constable's office. So, Fletcher and Marie decided to fix the place up. Once that was done, Marie would operate her little bakery and preserves business from that new location, and Fletch would start a handy-man business from there. However, he would not quit his job at the church until his new job proved fiscally viable. Marie had learned to appreciate regular income. The vicar was content that he and his friends had escaped this business with whole skins. Prudence, though, was bored and restless.

CHAPTER 7

Trouble with the ladies

Two months had elapsed since Goodman's death, and there had been no evidence of smuggling in the area. Whitestone and his men had relaxed and become complacent, and the wounds Roddy's friends had suffered at Goodman's hands had all healed. It was as though the dramatic events at Pringle's farm had never happened. Bannerman had even abandoned his idea of buying a boat, and instead, had bought a one-third share in Sullivan's boat. There were no longer any problems to distract Roddy from his role as the Vicar of Ryeport, and once again, the coachmen had become the village's most consistent source of entertainment.

Much to the chagrin of Mrs. Whatson, Pru's grandfather had been thoughtful enough to leave his granddaughter a small income through a trust and three cottages that he owned in Nextwest. Pru decided to set up house in the nicest of the cottages on the Coach Road.

From that moment on, Roddy's highlight of the week was no longer the arrival of the stagecoach, but instead, he anxiously awaited his visit with Pru. That visit was made under the pretext of his taking Bessie for a regular overnight stay with her sister – when they could work on their new business. Just another secret that Bessie and he would share. He would drive to Pru's. Then Bessie would take the wagon and deliver pies and preserves to her growing clientele – their trade was building nicely. On this visit to the manse, however, Tubby had some startling news.

"Roddy, old chap. It's so good to see you." But somehow Tubby's usual spontaneous smile appeared a little contrived this time. "I've some good news," he said. "I hope you will join me in celebrating my good fortune. But first, let me get you a glass of our very best wine for the celebration." Tubby's display of good humour seemed overdone somehow, and Roddy sensed that there would be some downside to his good news. Once they were seated, glasses in hand, Tubby blushed, cleared his throat and blurted out: "Roddy, I am to be married!" Roddy was shocked. "Really, Tubby? This is certainly unexpected news. Who is the fortunate lady? Do I know her?" Tubby broke eye contact and then almost defiantly restored it. "Yes, indeed you do, Roddy. It's Mrs. Whatson." He paused, anxiously searching Roddy's face for a reaction. Despite himself, Roddy's jaw dropped, and there were a few moments of awkward silence before he recovered his composure. Then he raised his glass to his anxious friend. "Well, Tubby, you really are a dark horse. My congratulations, of course! I knew that you greatly admired the lady but had no idea that you had so actively pursued the relationship. I can't wait to hear how this all came about." They clinked glasses, as he repeated: "My most hearty congratulations, my friend, and all my best wishes for your future happiness." Tubby smiled, a tentative, embarrassed smile, obviously ill at ease. "There's more news, I'm afraid. The lady is.… with child." Again Roddy was unable to conceal his shocked surprise. It was so unlike Tubby to be so direct. "You sly old dog, Tubby. I would never have thought…"

"Oh, no, the child isn't mine, Roddy."

Now it was Roddy's turn to be embarrassed. "Forgive me, Tubby. You are full of surprises today. Why don't I just be quiet whilst you finish telling your news?"

"I hope you'll not think badly of me, Roddy. After all, our calling demands a certain code of conduct, and I'm not sure that this affair fits well with that."

"Tubby! I know you well enough to know where your heart is. Have no fear on my account. I am here to help and support you, as a friend." Tubby swallowed the rest of his wine in one gulp, seeming to have difficulty in framing what he had to say. "Well, as you know, Roddy, the lady's deceased husband was an older gentleman and, as men of the world," said Tubby as he straightened his back and squared his shoulders as if to underscore his membership in that club, "we know that the passing of time depreciates one's physical capabilities." He paused, blinking, as though trying to recall a practised speech, then cleared his throat. "Hmmph! Er. One's physical abilities decline. It seems that Mr. Whatson's had declined to the point where he could not adequately meet his wife's more youthful needs." He blushed like a schoolboy caught in an indecent act, and Roddy hoped he interpreted his smile as one of understanding. Tubby continued: "It seems that they – the Whatsons – had made an arrangement because of this. Provided that due discretion was observed, Mrs. Whatson was permitted to enjoy the company of another male friend." Roddy was intrigued. "Really? I find that hard to believe. Who might that be?" Tubby hung his head for a few moments. "It appears that it was the butler… Goodman." He looked into Roddy's startled face, as though dreading what he might read there.

"My God, Tubby, she is carrying Goodman's child?"

"It would appear so. Initially, she tried to convince me it was her husband's, but that was too hard to swallow, even for me. That old man was desperately ill for many months before he died. Roddy, I fear that I've explained this rather badly. Out of sequence as it were, but I'm rather shaken by the way events have unfolded."

"Who would expect otherwise!" Roddy reached out and laid a consoling hand on his friend's arm. "Well, that's right," Tubby said, seeming reassured by the supportive gesture. "She told me that she and Goodman had intended to move away and get married when her husband died. But then came the shock of Goodman's murder. And after that, the reading of Mr. Whatson's Will was delayed due to some investigations by his lawyer. Quite a complicated Will by all accounts. Now it seems that the lady has use of, but not ownership of, those properties he left to her. All this has taken time. And now she is beginning to 'show'". Tubby tapped his stomach. "So she is getting desperate. I believe that's why she chose me."

He must have done a poor job of hiding his shock, because Tubby hesitated, anticipating his next comment. "She chose you?" he said. "You didn't propose marriage?"

"Oh, no, she knew that I admired her, of course. I'm afraid I was rather transparent in that regard. But who wouldn't admire her? She's a very handsome woman." He blushed again.

"But, Tubby, there has to be some returned affection surely. You shouldn't marry purely for her convenience."

"Well, she said she was fond of me and was sure that in time that fondness would grow into love. She's frightened, you see."

"Tubby, I don't think that lady has ever been frightened in her life. She is a very strong-willed and astute woman. I'm sure that she would be a survivor in circumstances where most men would fail."

"No, Roddy; you are wrong. Quite wrong, I assure you. She was crying to me the other night as she was explaining her predicament. Especially after I challenged her on her initial assertion that Mr. Whatson was the father of the child. She was like a lost soul. I had to help. I just had to."

"Does the bishop know?"

"No! Not yet. I don't know how to tell him. I'm dreading his reaction. He may object to the marriage. Or, even simply dismiss me."

"So, when do you plan to marry? And where?"

"I don't know. I hoped that you might be able to give me some suggestions."

"Me?" Roddy sat bolt upright in his chair.

"Well, you always seem so capable."

"What does Mrs. Whatson have to say in the matter?"

"She said she'd leave it for me to decide. Me, being the man, as it were."

"Are you sure you really want to go through with this?"

"I've given her my word, Roddy," said Tubby, with a set to his jaw that Roddy had not seen before. "She depends on me now. But truthfully, I am concerned." He paused for a few moments, as though searching for the right words again. "I do have some concerns, Roddy. What if I cannot meet her needs either? I'm worried in case she may want me to agree to the same arrangement of another male companion."

Roddy set his glass aside and stood beside Tubby, laying one hand on his shoulder. "Forgive me, Tubby, but you know the marriage ceremony better than I. 'To the exclusion of all others' springs quickly to mind. Your questions plainly say that you are not ready for this relationship. It seems you fear you are being used. The lady wants respectability without responsibility. What better than to have a man of your calling and dutiful nature satisfy both of those needs? But tongues will wag, that's for sure and not kindly for the most part. Frankly, Tubby, even without the complication of the child, this is all too soon after Mr. Whatson's death for her circle of friends to consider it acceptable. If you go through with this marriage, I believe they will assume you to be the father of the child and conclude that you had been 'carrying on' behind Mr. Whatson's back." Tubby hung his head. "Well, I had hoped to spare her that. The 'carrying on' part, I mean. She would want people to believe that the child was Mr. Whatson's."

"Frankly, my friend, we have no control over what others think. But you'd be surprised at how quickly people can subtract nine months from a birth date and remember events as relevant as a mortally ill and aged husband. Personally, I believe it would be in Mrs. Whatson's best interests to leave Nextwest until after the baby is born and only return here after that. That way people might conclude that the child is Mr. Whatson's. Time will allow people's memories to cloud. They will be less likely to remember when she started to 'show' and relate that to the death of her husband."

"But where would she go?"

"I don't know, Tubby!" His impatience was showing. "Has she no parents, sisters, or other relatives?"

"I've no idea."

"Well, you certainly thought this through before committing yourself, didn't you, Tubby?" The sarcasm was not lost on Tubby, who blushed and hung his head. "You really must have fallen hard for her. Frankly, my friend, I'm concerned that she is merely taking advantage of your good nature. You are putting the rest of your life at risk in order to save this lady from the embarrassing consequences of her own indiscretion. And to boot, we only have her word regarding the agreement between her and her husband." Tubby was swiftly on his feet. His face was flushed, and he was bent on defending his lady. "Really, Roddy, I had expected better of you, especially in view of this lady's plight. It appears that I have misplaced my confidence."

"Calm down, Tubby, calm down! Obviously, I will do what I can to help." Roddy felt exasperated. "Why don't you visit the lady again?" he said. "Put to her the suggestion that she leave Nextwest as I suggested. Use whatever pretext she is comfortable with. See if she has family that could look after her until the child is born so that she can return here when all is settled. She has the financial means. She may even want to have the child adopted. Maybe that would be the time to see if she wants to spend the rest of her life with you or you with her. Time is a great healer, Tubby, and fading memory is one of its strongest medicines in cases like this." Roddy looked at the clock. "Let me know how things go, my friend. As I said: I will do what I can to help. But don't let yourself be rushed into this marriage for the wrong reasons. Think things through. I'm sorry, Tubby, I must leave to pick up Bessie now. She'll be wondering where I've got to." And so, Roddy took leave of his troubled friend and made his way to Marie's.

On the way back to Ryeport, he told Bessie of the situation with Tubby. She and Roddy had become fast friends and trusted each other implicitly with their secrets. Bessie was most indignant. "That woman's just usin' 'im. The poor little sod don't know what 'e's in for. Sounds like she's a real 'ard case, that one. O' course, 'e's an easy mark too. I've never known anyone so gullible an' trustin'. You're just goin' to wait an' see what 'appens when 'e asks about 'er relatives then, Father?" Roddy nodded. "He's a nice man, Bessie. Not very self-assured or worldly wise, but there's no harm in him, and he's always anxious to help and please others. I hate to see him used like this. There's the added problem of the child too. Tubby is small in stature. So is Mrs. Whatson. If the child takes after his father with his build, there will be considerable speculation. And what if the child should inherit Goodman's nature? God knows what problems might result from that."

The following day, Bessie breezed into his cottage, full of bounce and good humour. "Mornin', Father, how's things? Ready for Sunday's sermon, are ye?" He had been engrossed by his model of The Guiding Light Church and was a little startled by his housekeeper's effervescent mood. "Well, not quite, Bessie. I was just putting a few finishing touches to my model. I have plenty of time for the sermon. There's not much of anything else to demand my attention." He smiled, feeling that all was under control in the slow-paced village life. "Is that right, Father? Does that mean you've looked after the Bridget affair then?" Roddy had a sudden sense of panic. "Why? What about Bridget? Is she causing problems? Talking at the well perhaps?"

"Well, she 'as told the women that she's been to see you and that you've arranged to see 'er again – privately." She raised her eyebrows as she said 'privately.' "Caused a few raised eyebrows that did and a few sniggers. I wondered what you've decided about that situation. If you leave it lie as it is now, she will likely make up stories to tell at the well. She loves the attention. What 'ave you decided?"

"Well, nothing. Everything seemed to have died a natural death. I didn't want to resurrect it."

"You promised 'er an answer, Father. That was weeks ago. An' I think you'd better get to that pretty sharp like, or she'll be tellin' tales that'll make 'er a celebrity again."

"Well, I don't know, Bessie. I'll just have to tell her that I can't be involved, certainly not as my predecessor was, at least. I'll refuse to see her unless she is accompanied by another woman. That's it."

"She'll ignore that, Father. Unless the villagers know you won't pick up where Reverend Cole left off, she'll paint some pretty colourful pictures for the women. An' if you reject 'er too publicly, she'll find some way to pay you back. I was thinkin' that you could tell 'er in front of the women in the sewing circle. Careful like, so as they'll understand – but without 'er realisin' what it is they're understandin'. She don't catch on too quick, remember. She'll be at the sewin' circle this afternoon. We're 'elpin' to fit 'er with a pretty blue dress from the last batch we got from Nextwest. We will 'ave to let the bust out quite a bit though." Then she smiled that mischievous smile that was usually the precursor to a joke at his expense. "Maybe you should get Reverend Cole's book out. See if she is developin' proper."

"Bessie! That's not funny. And how can I possibly reject her, publicly, without embarrassing her and myself?"

"Why don't you walk in on the sewing circle, 'ave a chat with the ladies for a minute or two, then say: "By the way, Bridget, I'll not be able to 'elp you with that problem you asked me about. Sorry, but I'm afraid you'll have to find your answer elsewhere." You won't need to say what 'er problem is for the women to catch on. But you watch 'er. She'll look around an' try an' read their expressions. But if you don't say what 'er problem is, the women will ask 'er after you've gone. Then she'll be able to make up any story she wants. They'll know though. You'll be 'off the 'ook' as far as the village is concerned. They won't believe any stories about you an' 'er after that. But they will keep a closer eye on their menfolk though. I'll keep an eye on Bridget for you. If I see anythin' sneaky goin' on, I'll let you know. We'll work somethin' out. Would you like a cuppa' tea?"

"Bessie! You dump a problem like this in my lap; then you seem to think a 'cuppa tea' will make everything right."

"I didn't dump it in your lap, Father. Just brought it to your attention is all. Just like sayin': Mind you don't step in that packet of dog poop. Would you rather I kept quiet?"

Roddy's brief meeting with the ladies at the sewing circle went well, but he couldn't bring himself to follow Bessie's suggestion and address Bridget in front of the ladies. The problem was still unresolved but very much on his mind when he had lunch with Pru in his cottage, after Sunday's service. Pru, recognising his worried state, finally coaxed all the details out of him. "Which one is Bridget?" she asked. "She was the buxom, young woman with the blond hair and freckles," he said. "She wore her new blue dress in church today. Why?"

"Oh, I've not met her," she said with a smile. "I think I owe it to myself to meet 'the-temptress-of-Ryeport'. She's after my man, you know. That could mean trouble."

"Pru, don't you dare! This is my problem, and it's a very sensitive and private matter. Now you've really got me worried. If word of this ever reached the ears of the bishop, he would sack me without a moment's hesitation, and you know what that would mean as far as my inheritance is concerned. I'd be sacked for sure, Pru!"

"Oh, don't worry, Roddy. I'll be discreet."

"Pru, that woman's not all there!" he said tapping his temple with his fingers. "You can't reason with her. She has the mind of a child – a very cunning and spiteful child. She'd find a way to get back at us, in ways you wouldn't dream of."

"Oh, I can dream pretty good, Roddy!" Pru excused herself from the evening service. "I have a terrible headache," she said. "Please excuse me, Roddy. I will lie down for a while with a wet towel on my forehead."

• • •

On the same morning that Mrs. Drew was prodding Roddy for action on the Bridget problem, Tubby had come to a decision regarding his involvement with Mrs. Whatson. Fletcher harnessed the wagon and brought it to the door of the manse. Tubby hardly acknowledged the stableman as he climbed lethargically into the driver's seat. His unusually miserable demeanour prompted Fletcher to enquire: "You alright, Father? Feelin' under the weather, are ye? You don't seem your usual cheery self t'day."

Tubby, looking as though all the troubles of the world were on his shoulders, responded with a weak smile: "I'm alright, Fletcher. Thank you for your concern. I just have a lot on my mind right now. I'll be back in an hour or so," and he left for Mrs. Whatson's house, to put Roddy's suggestions to the lady. But he was desperately afraid of confrontation at any time, and this would be a particularly difficult situation. He was soon seated in the lady's parlour, and a sweetly smiling Mrs. Whatson poured him some tea. After the usual pleasantries, he decided to come to the point of his visit. He was very conscious of the fact that his face was flushed and his stomach was uncomfortable.

"Dear lady, I have given your present situation considerable thought – with only your best interests in mind, of course. I am concerned that for us to marry, so soon after the passing of your beloved husband, might cause your friends and acquaintances to attribute improper reasons to our marriage. In fact, in our haste to save you any embarrassment, we might actually provoke it. Your friends might improperly assume that we… that we had… er… had been… carrying on a relationship behind your husband's back for some time? Er…. I must confess that I am concerned that this could cause you considerable embarrassment. Me too, of course. Because of these concerns, I….er….I thought it would be in our best interests to explore other possibilities – other than a speedy marriage, that is – to solve your immediate problem." Mrs. Whatson paused, with her cup poised halfway to her lips; her smile had disappeared and her jaw tightly clenched. "Are you about to renege on your promise of marriage, Reverend Tubbs?" She leaned towards him in a very aggressive manner, staring intently into his eyes.

"No, no, dear lady. I simply feel that the timing is inappropriate. I was about to suggest…"

"Suggest nothing! It is clear to me that you have no intention of marrying me. You merely wanted to take advantage of my distress for you own lecherous desires. Don't think I haven't noticed you watching me in a most inappropriate manner." Tubby's colour heightened even more. He was scared. Her attack continued: "However, I know how to handle opportunistic lechers, Reverend Tubbs. I shall inform the bishop that I'm carrying your child but that you have no intention of honouring your responsibilities by giving your name to your baby and myself. I shall tell the bishop that you forced yourself on me at a time when I was most vulnerable and desperate for your spiritual help and consolation. Then we'll see just how well your deceit pays off."

If she had expected Tubby to backtrack in the face of her attack, she was disappointed. The injustice of her attitude, plus the fact that she would lie, and name him as her child's father, seemed to stiffen the backbone of the timid cleric. It was an unfamiliar experience for him, but he was angry.

"Madam, the injustice of your attitude is unworthy of you. However, I shall make allowance for the stress that you are under and forgive the malice that you are showing me. I also insist that you hear me out, for your own good. You should make your judgement only after you have considered the possible consequences and heard the alternatives that I propose." And so, in the face of an unrepentant and hostile Mrs. Whatson, Tubby reviewed the scenarios that Roddy had outlined.

Mrs. Whatson was not receptive. The uppermost thought in her mind was that Tubby was reneging on his promise to marry her. Her pregnancy was forgotten. This man was deliberately slighting her. Even worse: that slight was coming from a person she considered her inferior. Her injured pride obscured all reason. Unable to tolerate the situation any longer, she jumped to her feet, grabbed Tubby by the sleeve, pulled him from his seat and hustled him into the hall. "Get out of my house, you lecherous welcher. Never dare to show your face here again." She almost spat the words at him as she pushed him through the front door and slammed it closed behind him. Tubby's face was aflame with embarrassment, but he managed to retain some appearance of dignity and composure as he made his way to his wagon. The predominant thought in his mind now was whether or not she might follow through on her threat of naming him as the father of her child to the bishop. "That didn't go too well, Betsy," he muttered to the horse as he unhitched her. "Perhaps I should advise the bishop of this situation before she does."

He wondered how Roddy might have handled this situation. Halfway back to the manse, with his nerves strung as tightly as a bow-string, he had a sudden mental image of Roddy laughing and saying: 'She wouldn't dare. No matter how she goes about it, she could never come out of that situation with her own image intact. And her needs will always predominate. Certainly, she wouldn't risk her reputation just for revenge or spite." Tubby then considered himself 'off the hook'. The surge of relief that swept over him at that moment was like a welcome breeze on a hot summer's day. "Just imagine having to spend a lifetime with that woman," he exclaimed aloud. Disregarding Mrs. Whatson's threat, he burst out laughing. He spent the rest of the journey back to the manse rehearsing how he was going to tell Roddy just how masterful he had been. Fletcher raised his eyebrows in surprise when Tubby handed him Betsy's reins, wearing a broad smile.

"Well, Father," said the stableman. "It looks as though you got an awful load off your mind in a real 'urry. Glad to see you're feeling better."

"Thank you, Fletcher. Yes, indeed, I do feel better. Face your problems head on like a man. That's what I always say."

"What was that all about, Betsy?" Fletch asked the horse as he watched Tubby square his shoulders and stride purposefully to the manse.

• • •

With some extra help from Sailmaker, the model of the proposed church, complete with a 'guiding light', was finished. Now Roddy needed to sell the idea to people that could make it happen. Ideally, he should have been able to take his idea directly to the bishop. However, the bishop had proven himself a closed-minded individual, who made no secret of the fact that he thoroughly disliked him. He was certain that Bishop West would take great satisfaction in dismissing any idea of his out of hand. However, he reasoned, if his father would back him, and then invoke the aid of his friend, Bishop Mason, his idea might have a chance of a fair hearing. Even if it got no farther than a meeting with his father and Bishop Mason, surely that effort alone should score some points with his father.

He needed an acceptable reason to request a leave of absence from his parish. He recalled an earlier letter from his mother that had mentioned that his father had been very sick and that she was worried about his lack of concern for his own health. His father's doctor had warned him to take better care of himself because his heart was not as strong as it should be. That could be sufficient reason for a leave of absence. The bishop agreed, and Roddy was granted ten days of compassionate leave to visit his parents. Tubby was to assume his duties whilst he was away.

On the Monday following his meeting with Bishop West, Roddy carefully loaded the box containing the model of his proposed church and boarded the eastbound coach. Three days later, he arrived in London, tired and grubby, and far more apprehensive than when he'd started out. He had been obsessively careful with the box, taking great pains to caution all who handled it to be careful. Arriving in London, with a severe case of travel fatigue, he took a hackney carriage to his parents' home. Tired as he was, the familiar sights and sounds of the city lifted his flagging spirits. Surely, his initiative would help him regain his father's goodwill and possible reinstatement in his ill, together with all the privileges that he used to enjoy. "Fat chance!" he muttered, as a sense of reality returned to destroy his dreams.

The cost of the round trip, from Ryeport to London, had almost exhausted the paltry savings he'd skimped from his stipend as the Vicar of Ryeport – a sum that he would have spent without concern whilst living at home. He was financially desperate and would have to rely on his father for any extra money that this visit might require. Certainly, he would have to depend on his parents' goodwill for food and shelter. On arrival at their house, he paid the driver with some silver and held out his hand for the meagre change. The driver looked at his outstretched hand with raised eyebrows. Then he restored eye contact, without making any attempt to offer change. They looked at each other in silence for a few seconds, until Roddy gave a little shrug, broke eye contact, and dropped his outstretched hand. The driver smiled derisively, as he lightly touched the brim of his hat, slapped the reins on the pony's back, and made a clucking noise to the animal. The carriage moved off, leaving him standing at the kerb, dejected and almost penniless. The door was answered by an unfamiliar face, but once he introduced himself, he was quickly ushered into the house.

His mother wept and threw her arms around him. "Roddy, oh, Roddy! You look so thin and tired; are you ill? Why are you here? Have you lost your position in Ryeport? Does your father know you are coming? Why did you not write? Are you in any trouble?" He gently removed his mother's arms from around his neck and, taking both her hands in his, planted a kiss on her cheek. "Mother: please do not distress yourself so. Anyone would think I've returned from the dead. Now, come to think of it, that may be a fitting analogy."

"You have been sick then? Nearly died?" Mother raised a kerchief to her mouth in horror as she studied his tired features and travel-worn appearance. "No, Mother. That was meant to be a little joke. I've been fine. And to answer the rest of your questions: No, I have not lost my position in Ryeport. No, Father does not know I'm coming. And the reason that I am here is that I have been granted leave of absence. I needed Father's advice on an important church project that I have initiated. I believe it will interest him. I knew from your letters that he is off to France in a few days. So, there was no time to write if I wanted to see him before then. I decided that a surprise visit was my only option. Will Father be annoyed?" He screwed up his face – dreading the answer.

"Roddy. You've met our new housekeeper. Your father discharged Mrs. Green. It seems that she had been gossiping about you, and our family troubles, over a glass or two of stout at the local public house. Her tales about you – embellished I'm sure – were repeated until a friend of your father's heard of them and made it his business to discover their origin. When he did, he informed your father. He left his office immediately and rushed home here in a terrible rage. He dismissed Mrs. Green on the spot, without a reference. He was furious. He said that she had betrayed a trust and caused the family that provided her with her living terrible and unwarranted distress. He would not tolerate such disloyalty. She had to pack her bags and leave immediately. He actually threw her bags into the street himself. You will need to be very careful, Roddy. I fear it will be a very long time before he will accept you with the same grace you enjoyed when he was grooming you to take over his business."

Roddy grimaced and slumped into a nearby chair. "What a rotten sense of timing! Mother, I hope that you at least realise that I am deeply repentant of my past behaviour. If I could undo all of the things that gave Father cause for anger or pain, surely you know I would, at whatever cost to myself. It just isn't possible to turn back the clock. However, Mother, I have been reflecting on why I behaved so badly. I wonder if my life was meant to be sent on a radically different course. Maybe I was destined to help the poor people of Ryeport. That is what this visit is really about, helping the villagers. Please, Mother, try to persuade him to hear me out. It really is very important. Some of our villagers' very lives could depend on it. And I have spent my last penny on the coach trip, just to present their case."

He could see that his mother was impressed. This was the first time she had heard her son ask for something on behalf of someone other than himself. She looked at him curiously for a few seconds, before giving her usual warm smile. "Of course, I will speak to him, Roddy. He will be home shortly though, and I think it would be unwise for him to see you before I prepare him. Why don't you go to your room and freshen up? It really would be much better if I speak with him first. Take all your things with you. I will wait on the door to be sure the housekeeper does not tell him you are home. Stay in your room until she calls you for dinner. By then your father should have calmed down enough to listen to what you have to say."

Roddy washed, changed, and sat dejectedly on the edge of his bed, staring at the model church that he'd carried so carefully from Ryeport. How he'd wanted to relax in this, his old bedroom, and savour the comfort that he had once taken for granted. Instead, he waited, like an unwelcome stranger, for a servant to summon him to Father's critical presence. He began to regret his initiative and wished he'd stayed in Ryeport. The model church was a simple design. Its only exceptional feature was the large crucifix window, in one end wall. He had also brought a number of drawings he'd made of Ryeport. They were mostly of the harbour and the seaward entrance. One showing his model church, rather tall, located on a high cliff, with the crucifix window facing out to sea. He had also drawn a bird's eye view of the harbour from the high western cliff. It illustrated the difficult harbour access and the beacon locations. "I should just give up," he muttered. "Surely, I could run off and find lodging with some friends. I must be able to find some way to make an easier and more pleasant living than I have in stinky Ryeport." He was still bemoaning his fate when he heard his mother greet his father at the door. Their conversation was muffled, so he quietly opened the door a little and stood with his ear to the opening. Mother was obviously doing her best to make her husband relax.

He heard his father reply to the offer of a glass of sherry. "Yes, please, that sounds most tempting." He smiled. His mother believed she was subtle, but by now, his father would be well aware that the extra attention was meant to 'soften him up'. The only question in his mind would be: for what? Roddy could visualise his father's familiar, wary, half smile from the many times that he'd seen his mother 'charm' him into granting her wish.

The voices downstairs quietened, and Roddy knew this meant his mother would be explaining how their son was working hard for the benefit of others, etcetera. He was about to close the door when he heard his father angrily exclaim: "The devil he is! Here? Now?" He closed the door and went back to sitting on the bed. His heart sank. He knew he truly was in his mother's hands now. The voices quietened, and eventually, the housekeeper tapped at his door to summon him to dinner. All things considered, their meeting went quite well. Father was stiffly polite but did offer his hand. Roddy shook it and asked after his health. He also apologised for arriving without notice or invitation, stating that he desperately needed his advice. That caused Father to raise his head in surprise. That was a novel admission, and the quick glance that passed between his parents conveyed more than words.

After dinner, they relaxed with a glass of sherry, and he gave a brief overview of Ryeport, the hazards faced by boats entering the harbour on dark or stormy nights and the consequent risks that had become accepted as part of the cost of earning a living from the sea. Then he told the story of Mick Drew, his efforts to comfort the sick and his first funeral service. How he'd arranged for the richer people of Nextwest to provide hand-me-downs for his parishioners and so on. Obviously, he omitted the self-gratifying reasons for his good deeds and also his exploits on behalf of the smugglers.

Then he explained his friendship with Sailmaker and how he had taken him through the harbour explaining the hazards and supported him, even helped him to build the model despite his conviction that 'The Guiding Light Church' would never be built. Roddy's father looked thoughtful, and Roddy realised that he was seeing a side of him that he'd not seen before. He said: "Please show us the model you have built, Roddy. The concept sounds most interesting. I'm sure Bishop Mason would also be interested to learn of your progress. He could prove a powerful ally in promoting this venture."

Roddy brought the model into the living room and placed it on a stack of books on the table. He needed the model church to be well above eye level from his parents seated positions. When they rose to look at it, he asked that they return to their seats for a while. He lifted the roof of the model and lit a small candle behind the window. Then he reduced the room lights and closed the heavy drapes. The crucifix window shone brightly in the darkened room. His mother was most impressed with that. Then he placed a single chair several paces in front of the model and, after testing the view for himself, he asked his father to sit there. "Father, I want you to imagine that you are at sea and viewing the lighted crucifix from the deck of a ship or small boat. The crucifix is perfectly symmetrical from that position, isn't it, Sir?"

"Yes," he answered. "Now, Sir, I want you to move your chair to the right by two or three feet and tell me what you see." His father complied. "Well, the right arm of the cross is almost completely cut off by the extended side wall of the church. If you did away with the extended wall of the church though, you would be able to see the full cross."

"That's true. Now move an equal distance to the left of centre, as you did to the right."

"Same thing," said his father. "Only this time, it is the left arm of the cross that is cut off. Aha! I see, if you steer the ship to maintain a perfect crucifix, then you are steering into a safe channel!"

"Correct. I didn't need to explain it. Your natural reaction would be to keep the crucifix perfect. So, even for a complete stranger, it would be a guiding light. If you steer a true course, at sea, as in life, the same truth prevails."

"I'm impressed," said his father. "But how do the ships know when to turn left to avoid the submerged rocks that you referred to earlier?"

"Move back to centre, Sir. Now move closer in stages, towards the crucifix, and tell me what you see. "

"There is something masking the lower part of the crucifix. The closer I get, the shorter the lower part of the crucifix becomes. Am I doing something wrong? Should I move back?"

"No. You are on a ship. Just keep going forward." His father slowly edged his chair towards the crucifix. "Ah! What I thought was a mask is a bar of some sort. The closer I get, the higher the bar moves. Ah! Now the bar has become two bars, separated by a strip of light. And now the top bar completely masks that portion of the crucifix above the horizontal arm, and the lower bar masks the rest. That leaves just the horizontal bar of light, and that now forms an arrowhead."

"So what do you – as captain of the ship – do?"

"I turn left."

"And if you wait?"

"I end up on the rocks?"

"Correct."

"Wow!"

"I want to see! I want to see!" His mother was excited because of his father's enthusiasm. "Roddy, that is impressive," he said, as he rose from his chair. He replaced the chair at the starting position for his wife. "Here, my dear. Follow Roddy's instructions. This is very good, very good indeed." Mother went through the procedure but without the same insights as her husband since she had not really understood the maps or his explanation of the difficulties of the harbour entrance. However, once these were again explained to her, she too was most excited. "Of course, of course! I see it! Steer to maintain a perfect crucifix. Follow Christ's teachings, and his crucifix will guide and save you."

"That's right, Mother." Roddy was beginning to catch their excitement too, more than at any other time in the development of his idea. His parents' enthusiasm was contagious. He went on to explain how difficult it was to get the villagers to attend church. How they felt that their religion had failed them and believed they were alone. That God had turned His back on them. "If we can build this church, it will be a beacon to all seafarers. 'Follow The Guiding Light' will become synonymous with 'Live right, follow Christ, and be saved, physically and spiritually.' That is why I believe we should call it 'The Guiding Light Church.'"

"Have you taken this idea to your bishop?" asked Roddy's father. Roddy shook his head. "No, this is only an idea. I wanted the opinions of wiser heads than mine before I raised this issue with Bishop West. I will only get one opportunity to present this. If I do it badly, more parishioners will die, and many others will turn away from the church. Remember, I am in Ryeport under sufferance. Bishop West would remove me if he could. He even tried to stop my initiative with the clothes for the villagers. And when the donors objected and insisted that my plan be followed, he blamed me for his loss of face. I'm afraid he will be a major obstacle to any venture that I propose, even if money were no object." He could see that his father was impressed. Humility and concern for others were not traits that he was known for. He refilled their sherry glasses and walked over to the model again. "Let's re-light the other room candles, Roddy, and show me that map of the harbour again. We must have our presentation well prepared before we speak with Bishop Mason. He is a good friend but also a shrewd businessman. And this is a business he knows very well." "Thank you, Father. It is a great comfort to know that you see merit in this idea."

Roddy slept well that night, and his mother fussed and coddled him most of the following day. They even went out to lunch, and his mother made sure she introduced her son whenever she could. "My son is the Vicar of Ryeport, you know. He is doing wonderful things for the poor people of that community!" She knew, of course, that the embarrassing stories were widely known in her social circles, but she obviously wanted everyone to know that she was proud of her son, and in her heart, she believed he would justify her faith in him.

Over supper that night, his father announced he had arranged for both of them to have supper with Bishop Mason the following day. The bishop was too busy during the day but had yielded to his father's pressure when he told him Roddy had travelled to London at his own expense and had only one day left to present a life-and- soul-saving idea and saying that it was an idea that the church could take credit for. The bishop had arranged for his recently retired brother, a Master Mason, to join them. "His input regarding feasibility and costs could be invaluable," he said. Roddy was feeling very positive about the situation now and chided himself for his negative attitudes of the day before. Everything was falling into place just as he had visualised, given the most favourable circumstances. His father's encouragement gave him reason to believe that he had regained some ground with him. His mother, always his friend and supporter, went misty-eyed every time she caught his eye. And, joy of joys, supper was roast beef. Of all the good news and experiences of that day, he most enjoyed the roast beef.

The following morning broke bright and clear. Breakfast was light-hearted, and his father was enthusiastic about their supper appointment with the bishop. In his newfound optimism, the opportunities seemed endless. The day passed slowly, but eventually, his father arrived in a hackney carriage to whisk him and his precious model away to the bishop's residence. The greeting was cordial, and the bishop seemed genuinely interested in how he had fared since being transferred to Ryeport. From his questions, it was obvious that his father had advised the bishop of his initiatives on behalf of his new parish, and Roddy was grateful that the 'ground' had been prepared. However, he still felt awkward in the bishop's presence. They were soon advised that supper was ready and made their way to the dining room. The bishop apologised for the fact that his brother, Gerry, had not yet arrived. "To be truthful," he said, "I am very concerned about him. His wife passed away three months ago. He has taken the loss very badly, and he has been rather unreliable ever since. However, I did stress that this was an urgent meeting and felt sure that he would be here. His wife fell ill, quite suddenly, and passed away just days short of Gerry finishing his final project. It was very sad, and Gerry was heartbroken. He lost both his wife and his business interests, almost simultaneously. He began to drink rather heavily. I hope that phase will soon pass. Again, I do apologise for his not being here. But I promise that I will go over your plans with him myself and advise you of his opinions and recommendations."

They had barely finished their soup when they were aware of a disturbance at the front door. The argumentative voices grew closer until suddenly, the dining room door was flung open, and the rather harassed looking housekeeper appeared. "I'm sorry for the disturbance, Your Grace. Your brother has arrived. Not suitably dressed, I'm afraid. I tried to persuade him to change in your quarters…."

"But I said I'd rather change in hers." These last words were spoken by a tall, dishevelled looking man, obviously the worse for drink, who pushed past the flustered housekeeper, pulling her apron strings undone in the process. "There is no need to introduce me, Ma'am. My brother knows me well enough." The bishop rose to his feet, obviously embarrassed. His father looked on, disapprovingly, but Roddy had difficulty suppressing a smile. "Even bishops can have problems in their private lives," he thought.

"Too late to be fed, am I? Some bread and a slice of beef or cheese would do, my dear." This concession to the tormented housekeeper was accompanied by what Gerry Mason likely believed to be a charming smile. Actually, it looked more like a leer. "Funny how drink can do that to your judgement," Roddy thought and wondered how often his 'polite smile' had actually become a drunken leer.

 "Sit down, Gerry, for goodness sake. Yes, you are late but not too late. Please serve as arranged, Mrs. Hopkins." The flustered bishop turned to his guests: "Gentlemen: This is my brother Gerry, about whom I was just speaking. I hope you will forgive his show of bad manners. Quite out of character, I assure you. I know that we will be safe in counting on your discretion. Gerry, allow me to introduce my long-standing friend Mr. McDowd and his son, Roddy, the vicar of Ryeport. You will recall that these gentlemen were hoping for your opinion on the design of a small, but unique, church."

Gerry Mason stumbled from the stability of the chair that he had gratefully accepted so recently, just long enough for a quick bow in their direction. "Honoured, I'm sure gentlemen. Please forgive my poor manners. I had a problem that needed attending to most urgently. It made me late, so it did." He smiled a silly little smile and returned, rather awkwardly, to the safety of the chair. "Some food might help," said the bishop. "When did you last eat?"

"When was I last here?" responded Gerry Mason. As if on cue, the housekeeper appeared with the main course. She set the meals in front of them, intuitively leaving the new arrival until last. "Thank you," said Gerry Mason and promptly set to, apparently oblivious of the other diners and eating as though he had not been fed for a week. He appeared to ignore the conversation between them, until after he finished his meal. Then he reached for the wine carafe, too quickly for his brother to stop him. He filled his glass, drained it, and immediately refilled it. "Anybody else want some of this?" he asked, waving the carafe in the air. They all shook their heads: "No, thank you." Gerry looked around the table with an expression of disbelief. "Well, then, I assume that the rest is mine," he said. The bishop looked embarrassed. "Here, I'll be pleased to join you, Sir," Roddy offered. "It's sad to see a man drink alone."

"Then hold your damned glass still," said the inebriated Mason, as he waved the carafe in the general direction of Roddy, who caught his hand and steadied it whilst he filled his glass. "Not much of this left," Gerry said, waving the carafe at his brother. "Better open up the cellar, little brother. Your guests are thirsty." Dessert was apple pie and cream for the three early diners. For Gerry, it was the remainder of the carafe. All four of them retired to the library and, over another glass of wine, Roddy's father explained how Roddy was concerned about some serious problems in Ryeport and had designed a solution, which he believed would help solve them: a new church.

"Just what everyone needs! Another church!" Gerry, for all that his eyes were half closed, was obviously paying attention. "Ah, but this is not just a church. It is also a beacon to guide seamen to a safe harbour where, right now, danger prevails. I will let my son explain: Roddy." And so, Roddy repeated the history of Ryeport and the demonstration that he had given his parents earlier. Gerry seemed all but out of it, but the bishop was impressed. Every so often Gerry's eyelids flickered with some signs of life. However, for Roddy, it was a bitterly disappointing end to a promising evening. Eventually, they rose to take their leave. Roddy started to gather up the model and plans. "Leave that there." Gerry's eyes were bloodshot but open. "I beg your pardon?" Roddy asked. His disappointment prevented him from hiding the hostility he was feeling for this man who had so unfeelingly crushed his high expectations. "Don't beg! Just leave the model and the drawings. There's a problem with the design. It needs work. I'll look at it in the morning."

"I can't leave it. I am returning to Ryeport on the morning stage."

"That's alright. I don't need you here while I study it."

"Sir, I hardly think that you looking at it will solve any problems. And tomorrow may be too soon for you to see it clearly anyway." The bishop shook his head at him. "Please leave it, Roddy. I will guarantee its safety.

Gerry says he will look at it tomorrow, and I guarantee that he will. I will write you in detail regarding his findings. Your father will help me fill in any detail of your plans that I might overlook." Roddy stood silently for a few seconds, his shoulders slumped and looking utterly defeated. "Your Grace, I'm sure that I had just this one chance to make the idea take hold. Months of work were dependant on this one chance...on this very meeting. Now I find that all my effort was in vain."

The bishop smiled. "You must learn to have more faith, my son, even when all about you have abandoned theirs. Faith is your new mission in life, Roddy. It needs to become your strength. These are early days indeed for you to give up on such a promising venture. Have faith! Be depended upon for that. Your parishioners will look to you for example in this above all else. If they see you falter, they will certainly abandon their newfound hope too. Then the very circumstance that you described earlier – that of their turning their backs on the church and believing that God Himself has deserted them – will reassert itself."

His father put his hand on his shoulder. "Come, son. Leave your model here. His Grace has promised you an opinion in detail, and I know that is what you will get. God works in mysterious ways, Roddy. You are an example." Their carriage arrived promptly at ten o'clock, as arranged, and they said their goodbyes to the bishop and his housekeeper. Gerry was snoring quietly in the armchair when they left the library. Roddy was silent most of the way home. What had started as a promising evening had developed into a disaster. "I'll say goodbye to you now, Father. I have to leave very early in the morning before you are due to rise. I wonder if you might be kind enough to arrange for this cabby to pick me up and take me to the Coaching Inn tomorrow. I'm afraid that I don't have enough money left for that."

"I'll do better than that, son. I'll arrange for the cab certainly, but your mother and I will see you safely aboard at the inn. The cabby can then take your mother home before taking me on to my office. Do not be too disappointed at this early setback, Roddy. Anything worth having is generally achieved only after a long struggle. I believe you will triumph in the end. I also believe that you are a far different man than the one I sent away to be a cleric."

They recounted the events of the evening to his mother, and Roddy went to bed with a heavy heart. His parent's words of consolation fell on deaf ears.

The following day, they were all up at the crack of dawn. His mother had made breakfast herself. "I wanted this to be a family affair," she said. They all piled into the carriage, and his parents bade him goodbye as he boarded the stagecoach. The driver took his bag and gave him a quizzical look. "I'm sorry for your loss, Father," he said

"I don't understand," Roddy replied, frowning.

"Well, you've lost that bloody box you were so attached to on the trip down 'ere!" he said. "For a while there, I thought it was growing out of your armpit." Roddy managed a weak smile. The coincidence of having this same driver on this stage of the journey was welcome, however. He was a pleasant though somewhat irreverent man, and he had been glad of his company at the stops along the way. His mother borrowed his father's handkerchief again, and the coach clattered out of the inn's cobbled yard, bearing her son away once more. He was alone in the carriage at this stage of the journey and stared out the window, soaking up as much of the sights and sounds as he could. He felt the need to store these memories, much as one might store food in preparation for a famine. It could be a long time before he revisited London. "Back to stinky Ryeport and fish, fish, fish," he snarled.

He thrust his hands dejectedly into the pockets of Reverend Cole's altered coat, where he was surprised to find an unfamiliar wallet. Opening it, he discovered a sheet of his father's notepaper, on which the words 'Good beginnings' were written in his familiar hand. In the wallet itself, he found two guineas. He threw his head back against the headrest with a sigh of relief. Not a total loss after all. Obviously, of far greater value than the badly needed money, restoration of the essential goodwill was still possible.

CHAPTER 8

A matter of trust

The elaborate peal of a post horn startled the vicar from a most uncomfortable sleep in the bouncing coach. He was well known to this particular pair of coachmen – the storyteller and his mate – and they intended to announce his return to Ryeport in grand style. He was alone in the coach and had removed his shoes and laid out on the seat. Lacking a headrest or pillow, his neck was bent awkwardly, and it pained him when he sat up. He looked out the window at the familiar, straggly line of cottages and the harbour just now coming into view. A couple of minutes later, he was surrounded by a large gathering of well-wishers at The Harbour Light. The warm welcome only served to heighten his sense of disappointment. The villagers knew he had taken the model church with him and, although they would realise that his allegedly sick father would be his main concern, they would have anticipated him using some time to advance his 'crazy idea' of The Guiding Light Church. Unfortunately, he had no good news to give them on that score.

Sailmaker took his bag, and the crowd moved into the inn. After he had responded to their concerns regarding his father's health, their questions regarding the church quickly followed. He asked that he be allowed to have some refreshments before answering those and taking the vicar's cue, Ernie moved into his usual routine of setting up ale and food for the coachmen and villagers. Soon the barroom was echoing to the sound of laughter as the coachman regaled them with his latest tale. Their good humour left Roddy feeling more isolated than ever. At the back of the crowd, Roddy spotted an unexpected face. Bridget was staring at him in a most malevolent manner.

"What in Heaven's name is she doing here?" he muttered. "She never comes to the inn." As soon as their eyes met, she abruptly turned and left the inn.

Once the coachmen left, the vicar was again the centre of attention and obliged to tell the story of his visit to London. He decided to put a brave face on what he considered a devastating setback and try to leave everyone with the impression that there had been positive interest, but that considerable study would be required before any decision. The group finally broke up, and Roddy returned to his cottage, hoping for an hour or so on his bed. Bessie Drew put a hand on his shoulder. "I can see you're disappointed, Father. But take 'eart, this is a big project. It'll take time. I'm sure it'll work out eventually."

"I'll try, Bessie," he said. "But it seems there are more people trying to block my efforts than there are willing to give the idea a fair hearing."

"Don't confuse Ryeport with London, Father. Everyone 'ere is trying to help. Those others in London don't know you as well as we do. 'ave faith."

"That's what Bishop Mason said."

"Well, that doesn't sound like 'e's against you or your idea. Take 'is advice."

"You're right, Bessie! Sorry, I'm such a 'wet-blanket'. If the bishop's brother hadn't been drunk, the visit might have had a better outcome. By the way: I saw Bridget at the inn. She gave me a very hostile look and then left. I don't recall seeing her at the inn before. Have you any idea what that was all about?" Bessie slumped into a chair opposite the vicar. She made only brief eye contact before appearing to study her teacup. Now it was she who looked depressed. "I'm afraid I'm the problem, Father. I made a mess of tryin' to improve the situation. Do you remember the Sunday before you left for London? Miss Prudence didn't attend the evening service – said she 'ad an 'eadache. Well, she didn't really 'ave an 'eadache; she intended to give Bridget one. I saw 'er marchin' off along the harbour front, an' asked 'er where she was goin'. Friendly like, not nosy. She knows you an' me share a few secrets, so she told me she was goin' to see Bridget and tell 'er to keep away from you. I was shocked. Prudence was real angry. I've never seen 'er like that before. It took me quite a while to calm 'er down and explain 'ow careful this 'ad to be 'andled, or we'd 'ave Bridget tellin' a bunch of lies about you that might get back to the bishop. That seemed to cool 'er off a bit. Impulsive lady, ain't she?" Bessie gave the vicar an anxious glance. He smiled, but there was no amusement there. Bessie continued. "We 'ad a chat, over a cuppa' tea in my cottage, an' I promised that I would 'andle Bridget. I told 'er I would confront Bridget, in front of the other women at the well. I said I would say that I'd 'eard you tell 'er that you couldn't 'elp 'er with 'er problem, when I was passin' your window. I told Prudence that would put an end to the problem and she seemed to calm down. She thanked me, an' told me I was a good friend. We thought we'd found a way to silence Miss Bridget." Roddy was looking at Bessie like a condemned man awaiting sentence.

Bessie's expression betrayed her anxiety. "Sorry, Father. I messed up. Bridget was at the well with a crowd of women, when one of them asked 'er what 'ad 'appened at 'er private meetin' with you. Bridget smiled, an' said you were goin' to 'elp 'er just like Reverend Cole did. I did warn you somethin' like that might 'appen, Father," she said, as she gave him a reproachful look. "Anyway, that's when I piped up. 'That's not true,' I said. 'I 'appened to drop some kindlin' outside 'is cottage window, and I 'eard you both talkin' when I was pickin' it up. An' I 'eard 'im tell you 'e couldn't do what Father Cole did for you. So just you stop makin' up lies about 'im Bridget,' I said. 'Leave the man alone.' Ye see I didn't want 'er to know that you'd told me about 'er strippin' off for you. So I lied about over 'earin' your conversation. The women all stopped what they were doin', an' looked at Bridget, waitin' for 'er to change 'er story. But she didn't. 'You're a liar, Bessie Drew,' she said. 'When I left the vicar's cottage that time, I saw you talkin' with Kathleen Archer across the street. You weren't anywhere near 'is cottage while I was talkin' to 'im.' Then she looked around all the women at the well – all triumphant like. 'What do you think of your wonderful Bessie Drew now?' she said. 'Now you know she's a liar?' Then she put 'er nose in the air, an' walked off, all snotty like.

"So, now she knows that you an' me must have talked about 'er. An' she also knows I lied to protect you. The women at the well put two an' two together alright. I could see that. So I told 'em straight out, that you 'ad asked my advice about Bridget an' we were workin' together to try an' let 'er down lightly because of 'ow badly she acts when she thinks she's been slighted. They all know 'ow spiteful she can be. They understood; they nodded an' agreed about that. They also know I wasn't the only one lyin' about what 'appened when Bridget visited you. I told the women that you'd refused to take over for Reverend Cole. I left out the bit about 'er strippin' off for you." There were no smiles from Bessie this time. "So the village knows now that you won't get involved with 'er. No more worries on that score. But she knows that too. She won't be able to use you in order to be the centre of attention at the well like she wanted to. Sorry, Father. It went badly, I never should've lied, but I was caught off-guard. Anyway, you're off the 'ook, as far as the village is concerned. But you'll really 'ave to watch Bridget now. Don't give 'er any opportunity to pay you back. I'll 'ave to watch out too. Maybe we should 'ave somethin' stronger than a cuppa tea, Father. Might cheer us up?"

Roddy put his hand on Bessie's. "Thank you, Bessie. You're a good friend. I know you had my best interests at heart, and I'm sure everything will work out alright."

• • •

Bannerman and the Sullivans continued to creep-up the last of their sunken contraband, bringing it ashore in dribs and drabs, and storing it in a hide-away somewhere along the coast. Jed Pringle would make the occasional visit, bringing hay or collecting firewood, and after he left, some people seemed a little freer with their money than before his visit. Jed was a gruff but loyal fellow, and it was obvious that he cherished the comradeship that had been established during the Goodman and Godfrey affair.

Reverend Cole's wine cupboard had been re-stocked, and there was also an anker of rum in the scullery. And that even bore the King's mark. That was by courtesy of Bannerman. He would buy up empty casks, while selling dried fish along the coast. "We refill the empties," he said. "Just a precaution and no charge to you, Vicar. You've paid your dues. But this is just between us. Sailmaker 'as 'is two guineas now and a little extra. So Goodman did pay-up after all." He gave the vicar a grin and a broad wink. "An' Bessie 'as a bit of extra money too. No need to worry about Marie either. Fletch is 'lookin' after 'er." Bannerman was smiling happily. "We're plannin' a little business of our own now, Vicar. Next time we run some smoked fish and pickled 'erring along the coast, we'll be meetin' a couple o' Frenchies we know. We'll buy ourselves some brandy and other stuff, usin' some of the money from the sale of Goodman's stuff. Just a little; we're not greedy. We won't be bringin' it back with us from that trip neither. We've found a real safe 'ideaway for that. We'll let it lie awhile. Only get it when we need it."

"Oh, one more thing, Vicar. You may 'ave 'eard this already; I've bought a share in Sullivan's boat. I've given up the idea of 'avin a boat of me own. As I recall, you 'ad an 'and in decidin' I wasn't to 'ave a boat of me own."

Roddy gave Bannerman a punch on his arm. Bannerman smiled. "Bloody glad you did too. Vicar, Doc 'udson pointed out a problem that we'd all overlooked. 'e said that we were lucky that Whitestone's men 'ad taken it for granted that it was my old boat still under that bit of canvas at the landin'. If the kids were to play' 'ide an' seek under there, they'd tell everyone there's no boat there anymore. Then we'd be in real trouble! Don't worry though, Vicar. It's all arranged. We're goin' to burn it again this weekend. We're goin' to throw a party to celebrate my joinin' Sully an' Fred, by burnin' my old boat. We'll 'ave some games for the kids in the afternoon. Jenny Sullivan is makin' some toffee apples for 'em. We thought we could set up some tables at the landin' an' 'ave a potluck supper." The vicar was looking anxious. "But there's no boat left to burn." Bannerman smiled. "Oh, yes, there is a boat to burn. We found a similar wreck down the coast a few weeks ago. Sailmaker helped us put a couple of patches on it an' we dragged it into the 'arbour an' put it under the old sail. Then, last Sunday, while you lot was singin' your 'eads off in church, we pulled it into a clear spot, well above 'igh tide, piled driftwood around it, got it ready to burn and covered it up again, with that same old bit of sail. It wouldn't pass close inspection – no broken keel f'r instance – but we'll have 'er blazin' before anyone gets close enough to see that. And if the Customs people ever get curious about my old boat in the future, people will remember 'ow we 'threw a party to burn it – and that it was weeks after the ambush. They'll remember because of the potluck supper an' the party." Bannerman raised his hands in triumph. "Mission accomplished!"

That Saturday afternoon the village kids participated in sack, egg and spoon and three-legged races, amongst other games and stuffed themselves with toffee apples and other homemade treats. The villagers enjoyed the unexpected celebration. The bonfire was lit at dusk and proved a great success. Ernie sold a lot of ale to people who sang and told tales around the fire, well into the late hours. The vicar spotted Doc Hudson raising his jug to Bannerman as he gave him a 'thumbs-up' signal with his free hand. His smiling face made the conspirators feel a little safer. However, after that, life in Ryeport immediately slumped back into its regular routine: A lot of fishing, a little smuggling; coachmen's stories, Sunday sermons, and the sewing circle. Life was totally unremarkable. Bessie and the Vicar were bored stiff. No one saw much of Bridget unless some visiting admirers saw her in secret of course. If so, they would likely see as much of Bridget as they wanted.

• • •

Marie and Fletch were gradually moving furniture to the refurbished flat above the carpenter's shop. Fletch still kept his job at the church. Not quite ready to strike out on his own yet. Marie and Bessie were steadily expanding their delivery route in Nextwest. Bessie even delivered to Whitestone's house now. That would have strengthened her credibility with the Customs officer as far as her first deliveries were concerned. However, it did seem that the sister's incomes had improved beyond what one might expect from their new business. Surely, that couldn't have anything to do with the goods that had gone missing from the secret cupboard. Bessie's pie deliveries still had to be restricted to Thursday afternoons and Friday mornings, of course, and would remain so until they could afford a horse and wagon of their own. The bishop was unaware of Bessie's use of the church's wagon, and the vicar didn't consider he was lying, by not mentioning it.

However, one really terrible and unexpected event had occurred during Roddy's visit to London. Tubby had been secretly and forcibly married to Mrs. Whatson. Tubby's belief that he had quashed his problems by using Roddy's suggestions proved erroneous. True, she had adopted one of his suggestions – that of moving away until after the birth of her child – but she had also made good on her threat to name Tubby as the father of her child. She tearfully told the bishop that Tubby had taken advantage of her in her time of grief and that when she told him she was now carrying his child, he had reneged on his offer of marriage and left her in a state of shock and distress. Roddy learned the shocking news on his next trip to Marie's. He broke routine and left Bessie at Marie's whilst he went to the manse to get the details from Tubby.

Bishop West had accepted Mrs. Whatson's story without question. He was intent on retaining the support of this influential lady and her rich friends. In front of Mrs. Whatson, he berated the timid and insecure Reverend Tubbs, saying: 'If, Reverend Tubbs, you want to remain a member of the clergy, you will honour your obligations. You will quietly marry Mrs. Whatson at the earliest opportunity. Today would be a good time. Reverend Watkins could perform the service. Fletcher and the cook could witness the ceremony.' It was to be a discreet marriage, after which the bishop himself would drive the lady to her friend's home in Bristol, where she would remain until after the birth of the child. 'What say you, Tubbs? Are you a man, or just a contemptible rake?'

Tubby told Roddy his protests of innocence were beaten down and Roddy knew first-hand that the bishop was at his best when bullying a subordinate. Tubby told him that Whatson's self-satisfied smirk had expanded into a triumphant grin when he finally capitulated. They were married within the hour and had lunch with the bishop whilst Fletcher prepared the bishop's coach. Tubby was to stay in Nextwest and continue with his work at the church. Other than by letter, he would not be allowed contact with his new wife until after the confinement. The bishop told him that would give him time to reflect on his conduct and consider how to make retribution for his contemptible failings. He would, of course, make support payments to Mrs. Whatson. The bishop would arrange the necessary deductions from his stipend for that.

"How on earth did this happen, Tubby?" Roddy asked. "You told me that she practically threw you out of the house when you were last there. And why would you agree to marry her after the way she lied about you?"

"I don't know, Roddy," responded the downcast cleric. "I was having a good day until the bishop summoned me to his office. My heart sank when I saw Mrs. Whatson sitting there. He attacked me as soon as I closed the door, calling me all sorts of names. He threatened to sack me and refused to listen to one word of mine. His mind was made up; my fate had been decided before I entered the room. I've got no family Roddy. No independent income. No employable skills other than those suited to the church. And his Grace assured me I'd never get another position with the church unless I went along with his demands. What was I to do? She is a vile and vicious woman Roddy. And she has destroyed my life." His shoulders slumped, and he set aside his glass of wine looking utterly defeated.

Roddy too was despondent. He knew that Tubby had depended on his advice and suggestions, and he had underestimated Mrs. Whatson's vindictiveness. He felt that he'd failed his friend. Tubbs was no match for the bishop, and Roddy knew he would have enjoyed the opportunity to browbeat his subordinate in front of Mrs. Whatson. Try as he might, Roddy could think of no solution to his friend's problem or even meaningful words of comfort. After a long period of silence, Roddy rose, put his hand on Tubby's shoulder and said, "Tubby, I know that things seem bleak and impossible now, but try to keep your spirits up. There's always a way out. It may be difficult to see right now, but unless one presents itself naturally, we shall make one. Remember, my friend, you are not alone in this. You have friends, and we will do our best to help you." Tubby was not encouraged. "Thank you, Roddy. I know you mean well, but I think the bishop will make sure I remain in this trap." Roddy bade Tubby goodbye and left. Bessie drove him to Pru's, where he gave her the sad details. Apart from this depressing event, their lives were quiet and continued so for about three more months.

• • •

One Friday evening, following their weekly visit to Nextwest, Bessie and Roddy arrived back at The Harbour Light. Except for the fact that Tubby was sinking ever deeper into depression, the trip had been pleasant. Bessie was happy with the success that she and Marie were having with their new business, and they were realising positive financial advantage from their efforts now. Bessie was now better off than she had been since losing Mick.

As Tom was taking Slondosh from the shafts, he said: "Dad wants to see you, Father. A gent' arrived on the coach this mornin' an' asked for you. Dad'll tell you all about it. I'll put Slondosh and the wagon away."

Ernie described the man that had been asking for him. "Tall gent," said the innkeeper. Well-dressed, talks a bit posh. He carries a heavy looking walking stick with a big silver knob on the top with a design on it. Hawksworth spoke with him. They shook hands."

"Where is he now? Did he give his name?" Roddy was puzzled but began to suspect it might be Bishop Mason's brother, Gerry, and wondered if he was sober.

"He's up on the cliff, walkin' about in the area where you lit that fiery cross. Says 'is name's Mason." Roddy jumped up from his seat. "I must go and find him – how long has he been gone?"

"Came in on the Westbound stage, around noon. He had a bite to eat, asked a few questions, booked a room and took off." At that moment, the door opened, and Gerry Mason ducked his head under the low lintel, and carefully stepped down onto the brick floor. He stood there for a few moments, allowing his eyes to adjust to the dark interior. And then he spotted Roddy. "Ah, there you are, Father. I've been looking for you. We need to talk. Is there somewhere we could go, for a private chat? Your place perhaps?" The distinguished looking Gerry Mason certainly looked out of place in The Harbour Light.

"No problems with drunkenness today," thought Roddy as they shook hands. "Well, Mr. Mason, it's been some months since you offered to study my proposal. You needn't have come all this way to give me bad news. A letter would have sufficed." There was an awkward silence for a few moments as Mason studied his face before deciding how to answer the scarcely veiled rebuke. "You're right, of course, Sir. A letter would have sufficed for a negative decision. So, why then am I here? Why would I endure three days of a bone-shaking coach ride, in poor company, all the way from London, just to give you bad news? Could it be that I need more information to complete my evaluation? Perhaps, my young friend, you could rid yourself of your negative assumptions, long enough for us to discuss some suggestions that I have for you. In a more private setting – if you please."

The bar had gone quiet. Everyone was focused on them, and Roddy was embarrassed. "My apologies, Sir. That was churlish of me. I'm afraid I had assumed the matter was long since decided. Please, walk with me to my cottage." Turning to Ernie, he said: "Ernie, Mr. Mason and I would like to have supper in my cottage. Would you be kind enough to arrange that for me? Some of your best wine too, if you please." The short walk from The Harbour Light to his cottage was accomplished in silence. Obviously, the terse verbal exchange between Mason and he had set an uncomfortable atmosphere.

Roddy ushered his tall guest through the door of his cottage. "Welcome to my humble abode, Mr. Mason. Please make yourself comfortable whilst I pour us some wine." He gave the slumbering fire a poke, arousing a flurry of small flames. Then he selected his best wine from the cupboard. As usual, Moggy was occupying the best seat in the house – the wing chair by the fireplace. Mason gave the reluctant cat a gentle push and settled into the warmth of the freshly vacated cushion before looking around, obviously taking note of the sparse furnishings. "Not quite the standard of living that you were accustomed to, Father?

"No. But I'm becoming acclimatised."

"Is this the best they could do for you?"

"Yes. And it's better than most of the villagers have, so I can't complain."

"Can't, or won't?"

"Same thing, really! I'm already enjoying a living as good as the better-off villagers, so it wouldn't generate much goodwill if I were to complain. They work a lot harder for their small comforts than I. So even when I feel like complaining, I won't."

"How do you find the people here? Not your style either, I imagine."

"They're good people. Although I must confess that wasn't my first impression. They are hardworking, very loyal and supportive of each other. It takes a while to earn acceptance in such a tight-knit community. They have bonded through many years of mutual hardship. It's especially hard for priests to be accepted. Over the years, the villagers have developed a mistrust of religion and its advocates. No matter how diligently they followed the teachings of the clergy, pain and misfortune followed them most of their lives anyway. Many of the fishermen mount a crucifix to their boat's mast, touch it and say a prayer every time they go to sea. They repeat that and give thanks for each safe return or good catch. I don't recall ever seeing devotion such as that in London. To make matters worse, the most devout villagers seem to be singled out for the worst misery. My housekeeper for instance: First her husband drowned, almost three years ago. Then on my first night here, her only son drowned in the wreckage of a fishing boat. The other two crewmen were badly injured. They are still unable to work. That means no income for three families.

"In all honesty, they'd practised good Christian values all their lives, without the need for a priest to guide them. But, I discovered that when they had a resident priest, he did nothing to understand them or ease their problems. He just kept throwing words at them. Telling them to repent and pray more. Can you wonder they became disillusioned and gave up on the clergy? At the same time, this same priest was living a better life and in more comfort than they, without enduring any of the risks or hardships they faced." He shrugged. "It's hardly surprising that they developed a very cynical attitude about the church and the people that represent it."

"So you're still an outsider?" said Mason, as he waved his glass at Roddy.

"Not so much now. At first, I felt that I'd been thrown to the wolves. During my first weeks here, it was made abundantly clear to me that some of the villagers would sooner see me dead than have me as their vicar. A couple of them even roughed me up a little, promising to be the instrument of my demise."

"Are you serious?" Mason was looking at him in shocked disbelief. "How did you overcome that?"

It was obvious that the vicar had his full attention now. "Oh, largely through the intervention of a couple of good souls who protected me. Then I managed to start a couple of programmes that benefited the villagers a little. That slowly eased the tension. I decided that I needed to understand them better. So I went out fishing with them a couple of times. I wanted to see for myself what their life was all about. That's how I got to understand the dangers of this harbour. I needed to improve the safety of the entry because that was the reason for their worst disasters. The fishermen thought, as you did, that I was not qualified to give them any advice on that score and brushed off my suggestions. However, they did give me credit for trying. Because of that, they tolerated my questions and ideas, appreciating my efforts, however useless they thought they were. They tolerated me. I was being given a second chance. The women were more receptive than the men."

"You've had a rough time of it. Most would have packed their bags and left." Roddy shrugged again. "Where would I go?" Mason was thoughtful for a few moments then asked: "How many in the parish?"

"About one hundred and ninety-two."

"One-ninety-two. That's a pretty precise number for an approximation."

"I made the count in the church registry. That number includes some local farmers from outside the village. I've not met all of them, and there may have been births and deaths not recorded, because of that."

"Ah! And how many of these good people attend the church?"

"Not many. About thirty, mostly women and children, plus a few older folk. Weddings, baptisms, and funerals dramatically increase the attendance. We usually see about thirty now, forty on a good day. My first service was a funeral, and the church was full. During my next service, the count was down to seven." He managed to add a small smile. "You certainly ask a lot of questions." Mason returned the smile. "I've always found that the best way to learn. Besides, I need to get a feel for the place if I am to sell your idea to the powers-that-be."

It was Roddy's turn to look surprised. "Does that mean that you will try to sell it?"

"A lot depends on you and the answers that I get over the next couple of days."

"So what do you expect from me?"

"Now you're the one asking all the questions."

"Hey, I answered yours."

"That's true. Nice wine," he said, handing Roddy his empty glass. He took the glass but paused, looking thoughtfully at his guest for a few seconds, without saying anything. "Yes, please," he said. "I would like another, but don't worry I'll not get drunk. With a little help from you, it's quite possible I'll never get drunk again." They eyed each other thoughtfully for a while, trying to get each other's measure. Roddy broke the silence. "What sort of help do you need from me?"

"Nothing momentous. Only a purpose for my life." Roddy searched Mason's face, hoping for some clue or further clarification of his remark. None was forthcoming, so he dutifully refilled his glass and returned it to him. "Frankly, Sir, I don't think I'm qualified," he said. "To give you a purpose for your life, I mean. Your brother would be better able to help you in that regard." Mason twirled the stem of the glass slowly; his eyes were directed towards the dark liquid but did not appear to be focused. When he raised his eyes again, to re-establish contact with Roddy, they appeared sharper...more critical. "For this enterprise to succeed, Father, we will need to work together. That will demand mutual understanding and respect. If I had to rely on our first meeting to judge that possibility, it would have been negative. I'm still not sure if we would be compatible."

Roddy was about to interrupt, but Mason held up his hand. "Hear me out, please. I was about to say: I am aware that I was the reason for our sour relationship. For that, I do apologise most sincerely. I treated you disrespectfully by turning up drunk for that first, important, meeting. I had no right to do that. It was extremely bad mannered of me. I compounded that bad behaviour by embarrassing my brother in front of his guests. Unforgivable really! He was certainly entitled to more respect. As were you, and your father of course. You had obviously put a great deal of thought and effort into your proposal, and without giving you due consideration, I appeared to dismiss it out of hand. That was partly because I felt you were not qualified to make the proposal in the first place, but also because I knew of your reputation. Incidentally, my contacts in the city believe that your present vocation – and location – are an attempt to hide you away forever. That information caused me to believe that this wildly ambitious proposal of yours was most likely a ploy to curry favour and regain some lost goodwill and status." He raised his hand again. "Before you make any assumptions regarding my sources of information, you should know that I have many contacts, both in the city and in the church. And none of my information concerning you came from my brother. He would have considered that a breach of trust. I must also say, however, that my contacts advised me you did your father a grave disservice with your – shall we call them exploits? Were you aware, for instance, that his French associate initially cut off all supplies to him, offering his wines instead to your father's competitors and at reduced prices? All in an effort to drive down your father's business. How your father eventually made his peace with the Frenchman, I'll never know."

Roddy hung his head. "No, Sir, I didn't know that."

"I'm sure that's true. Your father is a strong-willed and honourable man. I doubt that even your mother is aware of the full extent of the problems he faced. Now, back to my own situation, something you would not be privy to. I love building. Always have. I have worked with many great architects, but never have I been involved on any landmark or major works. And lack of talent or expertise had nothing to do with that. Despite my many excellent referrals and contacts, it seemed timing and prior obligations always kept me out of the running for such projects. So, as I said before, I have worked on nothing unique or nationally prestigious. I was growing older, and any chance of being identified with a building of note was extremely unlikely. I confided my disappointment to my dear wife, who never really understood my need for peer group recognition. She would console me, as best she could, by listing my various accomplishments, etcetera, but she also did her best to persuade me that it was time for us to consider some time for our own personal pleasures. To retire, in fact.

"We have two sons. Our youngest is a lieutenant in the King's Navy. The oldest, Robert, has made a life for himself in America. My wife wanted to visit him there, meet his family and see our grandchildren for the first time. In truth though, Robert and I never saw eye to eye on much at all. I'm not sure that I would be welcome.

"However, my wife loved to see new places, and this trip would have given her great pleasure. Money would not be a problem. She once told me that her only regret about our marriage was that we never spent enough time together as a family. I was always working, often at the other end of the country. So I promised her that my current commitment would be my last. I would retire and devote the rest of my life to making up for her lack of family companionship. We would take a voyage of her choosing, as soon as my current project was complete. She undertook to select and plan the trip, during my last few weeks of work.

"Sadly, she was suddenly taken ill and died shortly before my project was finished." He paused, taking a few seconds to recover from an obviously painful memory. "I wasn't even at her bedside when she passed away. Nor was I there when our two children were born. Too late now for regrets! Hindsight, of course, is always crystal clear. It also underscores our poor sense of values and priorities." He waved his free hand despairingly. "So, with my career ended, and without the company of my dear wife or other family members who needed me, I was left to my own devices. I was a lost soul, without motivation, hobbies or other interests. So I indulged myself in petty pleasures. Hence, my temporary drinking problem and I do stress, temporary. This is my first alcoholic drink since you, and I last met. I enjoy good wines; I'll not deny that. But I don't need it. I've avoided such beverages since our last meeting for the sole reason of proving that fact to my brother. However, if I happen to sink to that level of despair again – most likely through a lack of purpose for my life – then I fear I might return to the taverns and the demon drink once more.

Again, I apologise for my drunken state at our first meeting. However, I've come to realise that that meeting might possibly save my life. Even in my befuddled state that night, I was able to see a unique concept in your proposed building. Not a national treasure, of course, but something unique and prestigious. A building with practical, lifesaving benefits that I might perhaps be associated with. Possibly even be remembered for. That is why I asked you to leave your model that night, for my more sober consideration! Since then I have visited other masons, for their discreet opinions, and bearing in mind the objections that the project is bound to face, the possibility of some material help. If only it could work! If only it could be funded! And, of course, if your bishop would approve it.

"I'm sure you are aware, your bishop has a strong and active dislike for you and no particular love for your parish either. So the 'ifs' become even more significant. And there are so many of them. Here's another: 'If', we could work together. And another: If the villagers are prepared to back you – us – in this venture. So, you see, it is imperative that we build a strong, mutually respectful, working relationship if this unique church of yours is to have any chance at all. Well, I have shared as much of my soul as I am prepared to at this stage of the proceedings. Actually, you now have as much information as my brother regarding my personal motives and ambitions. I hope you will respect my confidence. Otherwise, we certainly could not get along, and all would be lost. Now it's your turn." Mason took a sip from his recently replenished glass, just as a knock came at the door. It proved to be supper. Meg and Tom stood in the doorway carrying a large, heated kettle between them. "My dad's idea," said Tom. "Put the dishes in a heated kettle, and cover them with clean hot towels. It'll keep the food hot he said." Tom was beaming, pleased to be the news bearer for such a worthy innovation.

"My mother's compliments, gentlemen," piped up his smiling sister. "She hopes that roast beef, Brussel sprouts, roast'taters 'n' carrots will be acceptable. Apple pie and cheese for afters."

"My father's compliments too, Sirs," added Tom. "He said he finds this wine excellent and hopes you will enjoy it as much as he does." He proffered two large bottles that he held in his spare hand. Meg quickly prepared the table, and they were soon seated. "Well, Father," commented his obviously enthused guest, "I'm sure you will agree that our business must await our full and undivided enjoyment of this excellently prepared meal. Thank you, young lady and you too, Master Tom. You certainly do your parents credit." His smile was as warm as his words. Roddy added his appreciation: "My thanks to Meg and Tom. Please thank your parents for me. This is a truly excellent surprise and piping hot too. That was an excellent idea of your father's." He smiled. "I must confess, I half-expected fish."

After the meal, over a second glass of Ernie's excellent Bordeaux – and with considerable trepidation – Roddy produced his journal for Gerry Mason. "This was meant for no eyes other than my own," he said. "That will be very clear to you from the opening statements. I intended this as a reference point from which to measure my personal improvement. I only produce it now, because it will be obvious that it was not contrived for your approval. In this journal, I admit to the motives that you suspected of me, and that my priority was to regain my place in my father's Will, by performing well in this trying situation. It does not reveal me in a very good light. But you already know I'm no saint. However, I have become truly concerned for these villagers. To my surprise, in the short time that I have been here, I have made more genuine friends, than I have ever known before. So, I am being as frank with you as possible. I also ask for your discretion. Firstly, for the same reasons as you sought mine – mutual trust and respect – but also because in allowing you to read this journal, I will be revealing confidential information that could prove harmful, life-threatening even, to good people that I truly care about. People who have earned my trust and rely on me to respect their confidences. You will need an open mind and some appreciation of how difficult life can be here if you are to make an enlightened judgement. But, before you open this book, I need your word of honour, that you will never reveal any of its contents to another soul without my explicit permission. If, after reading the journal, you find yourself unable to work with me, I would appreciate your being equally as frank and direct as my journal." He placed lighted candles on the table, one on either side of the journal, refilled Mason's glass and placed the bottle within his easy reach.

Mason studied his face, for what seemed an eternity, before he asked: "Is there anything unlawful described in this book?"

"Yes."

"Are there justifiable grounds for these illegalities?"

"You must judge that for yourself. But I certainly believe so."

"How long will it take me to read what you have written here?"

Roddy smiled. "Roughly: the rest of that bottle. My life is in your hands, Mason. Do you agree that the journal's contents will remain confidential, regardless of any decision you make regarding me or the project? The contents must remain between us alone. If you don't agree, despite the many hours of labour that it represents, I shall burn the journal here and now and deny that it ever existed. I could not bear for it to be discovered by the wrong person. At present, only you and I even know of its existence."

Gerry Mason hesitated, looking very troubled. "The fact that you would burn it indicates something very damning in its contents."

Roddy picked up the journal and moved towards the fireplace. Mason held up his hand. "Stay, Father! Don't be so hasty. I have no idea what I'm agreeing to here. I'm an honest man and proud to be so. Are you putting me in an untenable situation?" Roddy shrugged. "Are you merely honest?

Or might you agree that honesty sometimes needs to be silent, in the cause of justice?"

"Don't mince words, man! Is this a book of debauchery and corruption, of evildoings and illegal acts?"

"There are some illegal acts; the same illegal acts that happen on a daily basis all around our coast. Mainly they deprive the King of some revenue."

"Smuggling?"

"Yes, and some of its consequences!"

"Are you involved?"

"Yes, but not for personal gain. Only to protect some villagers. I do not run with smugglers, nor do I share profit from their endeavours in 'the trade'". Mason was about to frame another question, but Roddy held up his hand. "Either swear to keep this matter strictly between us now or it goes in the fire. In that event, our business here is finished. The mutual trust you seek could never exist." Mason stood quietly, studying his face. "I believe that you are risking more than I by this action. I also believe that you are a different man than your reputation describes. So, I will so swear. Do I need to swear this on a Bible?"

"No. I trust your word." He handed the journal to Mason and retreated to the wing chair, transferring Moggy from the seat onto his lap. His glass in one hand, he stroked the purring cat with the other and gazed into the flickering flames as he tried to purge his mind of all the doubts and fears that had surfaced by giving such open access to a man he hardly knew. Somehow though, despite their poor beginnings, he had the feeling that he could trust Gerry Mason. Time was not accurately measured by Mason's consumption of the wine. A second bottle was opened and shared between them before he was finished reading. He had read and re-read certain passages, turned on occasion as though to question Roddy but thought better of it. Eventually, he snapped the cover closed, rose stiffly from his seat, and stood before him, with both hands pressed to his lower back. "Well, Sir . . . I hardly know what to say. You appear to have experienced more of life in the past year than a normal man might see in several lifetimes." Roddy looked up at him in silence, contributing nothing. Mason continued. "Your initial motives – as you confess – whilst understandable do you no credit, but your methods of achieving your goals have only resulted in benefits to others, not yourself. I don't know what to say."

"Will you honour our agreement? That the contents of the journal are to remain between us alone?" he asked.

"Yes. I already gave you my word on that." Mason's expression was very solemn.

"Then why don't you sleep on the other decisions? Wait until you have what other facts you need, before finally proceeding. Frankly, I would never have believed the events in my journal possible a year ago. Now, however, they are part of my very existence. Take whatever time you need, now that I have your word concerning my friends. Come, let me walk you back to the inn." He put Moggy back in the wing chair, retrieved the Mason's topcoat and ornamented walking stick and escorted his thoughtful guest back to the inn.

• • •

The Harbour Light was unusually busy for breakfast the next morning. The lively curiosity of the villagers was piqued by the well-dressed visitor who had spent most of yesterday afternoon walking alone on the cliff top. That same cliff-top where the 'Ryeport Players' had caused so much amusement months before when they burned a large crucifix. However, the vicar was no longer the same object of scorn and ridicule that he'd been in those early days. It was true that only a few of the villagers knew the full extent of his involvement in the affairs of the village, but those few, without disclosing the reasons for their changed attitudes, now supported him. Now it appeared that this 'toff', from London, was also very interested in the vicar's idea of a 'guiding light' on the cliff top. No one would make the long and tiring trip from London lightly. That gave more credibility to the vicar.

The morning was bright and cheerful, with a light breeze. The fishing boats had already been at sea for over an hour when those curious villagers, able to spare an extra copper or two, visited the inn, hoping to pick up some interesting information no doubt. Ernie had a big smile on his face as he bustled around his busy inn, his arms loaded with plates of food. He bent low as he passed Archer's chair and whispered in his friend's ear: "This is an even better business than when the coachmen visit."

Mason and the vicar were quietly chatting at a corner table when Sailmaker came in. The vicar called him over and introduced him to Mason, explaining how helpful Sailmaker had been in rowing him around the harbour and detailing the problems of the entrance. Mason, recalling his reading of the journal last evening, was especially interested to meet Sailmaker. However, remembering his promise to the vicar, he was careful to behave as though he had no knowledge of their recent history. "Well, young Sir," said Mason. "If it's at all possible, I would like to take your tour around the harbour myself. I imagine Reverend McDowd might also want to join us. He would be better able to explain his ideas from that vantage point than sitting here. Could you possibly arrange that for us?"

"Certainly Sir. Right after breakfast, if that's alright with you."

"Excellent. No time like the present."

"I would suggest, Sir," said Sailmaker, "some warmer and less formal clothing if that's possible. Mine is a working boat and not kind to fine clothing."

"I'll see what I can do." About an hour later, Sailmaker was rowing them around the protected harbour. Then they left, by way of The Chute and Sorry Cove. Sailmaker raised the sail, and they did a quick tour along the coastline, west of the harbour, as far as Carter's Rock, then back east again and along the Dragon's Tail, to demonstrate the route that the fishing boats would have to take. Sailmaker would pause here and there, whilst he pointed out a particular hazard or the scene of a wreck. A calm sea and a gentle breeze allowed them a comfortable and relaxed tour. As they turned into the dogleg of the harbour entrance, Sailmaker explained how the inn had earned its name: The Harbour Light.

"What a striking array of features and so aptly and colourfully named." Mason's face was aglow with genuine pleasure and interest. "This has been a most interesting and delightful tour." They paused in the access channel to the harbour, to study the proposed cliff-top location for the church. Mason had Sailmaker come about and re-enter the channel a couple more times in order to familiarise himself regarding the proposed siting of the 'Guiding Light'. Then Sailmaker took them back out to sea again to re-enter the harbour by way of The Chute, pointing out Archer's bridge and telling the story of The Lucky Lady. Mason was generous in showing his appreciation to Sailmaker. "What a splendid way to spend a morning! That was most enjoyable, young man. Thank you very much; that was most enlightening. Don't you agree, Father?" Sailmaker smiled broadly and knuckled his forehead as he thanked his guest for his generosity.

They arrived back at the inn just before noon, only minutes ahead of the stagecoach. Mason was still enthusing over the tour. "I feel I have a much better understanding of the dangers now and your solution, Father," he said.

Hawksworth had ridden in to meet the coach and to exchange leather mailbags. Once again Ernie was very busy. "What a day," he said to Meg. "If only we could have a couple of days like this every week." Hawksworth asked Ernie to enquire if he might join Mason's group for lunch and was quickly welcomed. Then Ernie asked for quietness whilst the coachman dispensed the latest news. The news was hardly momentous, however, and after a quick lunch, the coachmen were soon away.

Then Mason shocked everyone. He reached across the table to tap Hawksworth's leather mailbag. "That's a very official looking mailbag you have there, Hawksworth. Looks like government business. I thought you had retired from the service. What's that all about?" At once everyone within earshot fell silent. The sudden silence felt like an impact on everybody's ears. Sensing that he had committed a serious breach of etiquette, Mason, looking very embarrassed, quickly apologised. "My God, man. I'm sorry! That was ill-mannered of me. None of my business, of course! Please, forgive me, and forget I even asked." The bar remained silent as they waited for Hawksworth's response.

The captain's solemn expression soon gave way to a broad grin and, as he looked around the bar, it became an infectious chuckle. He took a few moments to compose himself before giving Mason a reassuring smile. "It's no problem, my friend. It's my perverted sense of humour that is to blame for your embarrassment. Everyone here has had their eye on this bag ever since I started to collect my mail here. I must confess that it amused me greatly to see them so curious. So much so, that I vowed to keep the mystery going as long as I could. I derived great pleasure from watching these good folk eye this pouch so suspiciously, and then endeavour to look disinterested if I happened to catch their eye. This pouch provided me a certain air of mystery. Notoriety might be a better description. I was prepared to keep everyone guessing forever, just to satisfy my warped sense of humour. I'm sure the whole village believed I was an undercover Customs officer. The local Customs officer, Whitestone, drafted me into secretarial duties during a smuggling investigation here. I'm sure that convinced everyone that I was a spy. What say you, Father? Or you, Innkeeper? Am I a Revenue spy?" He laughed again. "After all, Whitestone and I do know each other quite well. We served on the same ship some years ago."

Hawksworth held the mailbag at arm's length, using it as a pointer to single out individuals here and there. He would raise his eyebrows, inviting a response to his question: "Am I a Revenue spy?" And then pause, to listen to that individual's blustering protests of innocence. Archer, in particular, was caught off-guard and huffed and puffed in a most unconvincing manner. "Certainly never thought you was a Customs spy," he stammered. "Bloody bag's of no consequence to me." Hawksworth knew better and laughed ever louder at each new disclaimer. Mason too was smiling, obviously enjoying the interaction and banter. Eventually, Hawksworth wiped the tears from his eyes, borrowed a towel and dried a convenient table before shocking them all by opening the bag. He then spread the contents of the bag over the table. Several sheets of handwritten script and some crude drawings of parts of a ship and related objects were spread before the inn's customers. People from the other end of the bar crowded around to view the contents, smiling all the while. Most of them couldn't read, but they looked anyway. At least the drawings were of familiar items.

Hawksworth explained: "I have an old friend in London who is writing a novel. It's a story about life at sea in a man-o-war. The problem is: he's not very good at the seafaring side of things. He's a doctor, a surgeon actually, and a damned good one. He has a practice in London, with a well-to-do clientele. Anyway, he got bored with pampering all these spoiled people and decided to go to sea. He wanted adventure. So he got himself a position as a surgeon in a King's ship-a frigate actually. On his very first voyage, he saw action when they engaged a French privateer off the coast of Portugal. His services were soon in demand, and a number of the crew were injured. He was on deck, putting a tourniquet on the captain's leg when a shot smashed through the ship's side, and a large chunk of splintered oak tore away most of the calf of his right leg." Hawksworth's good humour gave way to an expression of concern. "His helpers carried him below and amputated his leg at the knee. He was lucky to survive their butchery. His 'surgeon' was a 'loblolly boy' – one of two men assigned to hold a patient down during amputations. His only surgical experience was his ability to do that – hold injured seamen still – whilst the surgeon maimed his patient, in an effort to save his life. My friend was lucky to survive. However, that was enough adventure for him, and he decided to start a fresh practice in London. But most of his patients didn't like him stomping around, making bad jokes about his wooden leg, while he treated them. That was especially true of the ladies; some had been his patients when he still had two good legs, and they had wanted the chance to marry the young, handsome doctor. His practice began to decline when he tired of pampering these spoiled people.

However, that didn't bother him; he had inherited lots of money.

"So, out of boredom, he started writing a book: a seafaring, adventure novel in which he drew on his limited experiences at sea. He showed me his first draft and asked my opinion. I had to point out that, although his story was entertaining, the description of the battles and anything else pertaining to ship's business was seriously flawed. To make a long story short, I got the job of correcting those parts of the story involving ships and seamanship. He sends me his drafts, in this very suspicious leather pouch." He struck a villainous pose – hiding his face behind an imaginary cloak – whilst looking around in a theatrically suspicious manner, before breaking into a fresh fit of laughter. Once the chuckles subsided, he resumed his normal posture and continued: "I mark his drafts, with my suggestions and send them back for re-write.

"Now!" He threw up his hands. "There goes all the mystery surrounding the suspicious, secret life of Cap'n Hawksworth. And along with it goes all the fun and smiles that I enjoyed so much by feeding your suspicions. He burst out laughing again. "But you know, it's been worth it. Just to hear you all protesting your innocence. Best laugh I've had in a long while." Again, he pointed at various patrons in turn, mimicking their protests and laughing afresh at each repeated protest of innocence. Archer was looking particularly annoyed. Hawksworth's laughter was so infectious, however, that the whole barroom was caught up in his merriment. Hawksworth wiped tears from his eyes and took a quick look around the bar. "Ernie, buy the house a round on me. Just to thank you all for the fun you've given me, these past months."

"Aye, aye, Cap'n!" said the smiling Ernie. Once all were served, the innkeeper raised his own tankard. "To Cap'n Hawksworth's health lads," he called loudly. "Aye! Cap'n Hawksworth!" they all echoed and raised their jugs to the man that had held their suspicions for nearly a year. Hawksworth gave them all a wave before excusing himself from the table and beckoning Ernie to a quiet spot at the bar. "Ernie, I've just had a thought. I know how concerned you are about Doc Hudson. He's getting on in years, and the problems he's had to face these past few months have been a big strain on him."

"Aye, that's true," replied the innkeeper.

"I know too that you would be hard pressed to find a replacement for the village. Let's face it, a man couldn't earn a living here as a doctor. Firstly there wouldn't be enough patients, and what patients there might be would have little or no money. No potential for a lucrative practice here. The villagers, including Doc Hudson, help each other out, free of charge. Very commendable but not the sort of place an ambitious doctor would want to start a practice."

"No argument there. What's your point?"

"I was wondering if my doctor friend – the would-be-author, Will Simms – might be interested in the job. He doesn't need money and doesn't like pampered people, but he loves the sea and boats. He would have plenty of time to write down here. The demand on Doc Hudson tends to be sporadic and only busy in times of disaster. Will and I would be closer to cooperate on his writing. It seems to me that it would be a good fit. How do you see it? Do you think that he and Doc Hudson might be able to work together until the Doc decides to retire?"

Ernie's brow furrowed in a heavy frown. "I don't know. Doc might think we are trying to push him out."

"Never! He's too well liked and respected. Loved might be a more appropriate word."

Ernie thought for a few seconds. "There's no denying that Doc Hudson should retire, and soon, for the sake of his own health. Do you want me to talk to him about it?"

"No. Not yet," said Hawksworth. "Let me see what my friend might think of the idea first. No point in causing any concerns if Will's not interested. He might even come down here for a visit. He could even stay at my place until Doc retires. I hadn't thought of that."

"Is he married?"

"No. He was engaged when he went off to sea, but the lady thought better of it when he came stomping home on a wooden leg. It was a pretty crude job, made in a hurry by the carpenter's mate. The carpenter was one of those killed in the action." Hawksworth smiled. "Will told his betrothed he would get a new leg just to please her. When he asked her if she would like it to match the chairs in the dining room, she ran from the house crying and was sick outside. It's just as well it ended then. She was a pretty lady but far too coddled to be of much use to Will."

Ernie smiled. "No other marital prospects then?"

"Not that I'm aware of."

"Not likely to find much of a match here."

"That's true."

"I'll leave it up to you to sound out your friend then, Cap'n. Meantime, this stays between us, alright?"

"Certainly," said Hawksworth and rejoined the group at Mason's table just as they were about to leave for the cliff top. Tom brought the wagon around. Sailmaker, Mason and the vicar climbed aboard to take the less arduous route to the cliff-top, rather than the rough path taken by Mason the day before. "Why ever didn't someone tell me that I could have got to the cliff-top in a buggy yesterday?" grumbled Mason. "I could have done without that climb, especially after that bone-shaking coach trip."

"Vicar's wagon wasn't 'ere yesterday, Sir," piped up Tom with a big grin. " 'ardly ever is lately." Hawksworth was smiling as he mounted his horse, waved the famous mailbag in farewell and rode off. Minutes later, the three passengers in the buggy also smiled as the light breeze carried a sudden peal of Hawksworth's laughter back to them.

CHAPTER 9

The lamp maker

The vicar and Mason had shaken hands on their agreement to work together. The necessary trust and respect appeared to be a condition both men wanted to nurture. However, it was now Sunday, and they were obliged to put their enthusiasm for their project on hold. Mason attended both of Roddy's services, which were graced by at least 20 more people than usual. Most of the pews were occupied, rather than just the rows closer to the pulpit. Roddy was quite startled at the size of the congregation. Many of the villagers were also dressed in their new clothes, and looked quite sophisticated as they turned the pages of their hymn books, looking for the markers that Meg had discretely left for them. Mason was quite impressed.

Bessie came by to tidy up the house soon after he'd left, and the vicar was anxious to hear what she thought about the increased congregation. "Was it the new clothes that brought all those extra people to church, Bessie?"

"That was part of it, Father; they really wanted to see Mister Mason, but they also wanted 'im to see them as well. We haven't 'ad that many people in church for years. You seem to be doin' all sorts of things to bring the people back, Father. It won't 'urt when Mister Mason tells 'is brother about that neither. Shows the villagers are respondin' to you."

Monday morning broke bright and clear, and the vicar and Mason were on the cliff-top early. Mason spent nearly an hour examining the rock that formed the cliff-top, even venturing on a hazardous climb to lower levels of the cliff-face. Roddy and Sailmaker were left basically twiddling-their-thumbs, whilst speculating on what Mason found so interesting about the cliff. When he finally resurfaced, he had a broad smile on his face. "Solid as a rock," he said. "No pun intended."

Mason retrieved his unusual walking stick from the wagon and twisted the silver handle, causing a second, thinner, leg to spring loose from the main body of the stick. That inner leg was hinged about three inches below the handle and had a locking brace attached to it. Mason adjusted that brace, referring to a scale engraved on the thinner leg, before locking it in place. Now his walking stick became a set of dividers or pacing stick. He then took a small compass from his pocket and led Sailmaker to a position about a hundred feet back from the edge of the cliff. Taking a sighting with his compass, he began walking away from the cliff, on his chosen bearing, towards Sailmaker, swinging the pacing stick as he went. In this fashion, he measured his chosen distance before stopping. "Please stand here for a moment, Father, just whilst I find something to mark the spot."

 "What exactly are you doing, Mason? I feel like a pawn in a very boring chess game." Mason's single-minded attitude had relegated the vicar and Sailmaker to nothing more than mobile markers.

"Sorry, old chap. My idea could make this project much more affordable. I failed to bring paper and pencil with me because I only intended to examine the cliff for flaws and faults. So, without drawings to mark and refer to, I have to keep the details in my head whilst I evaluate viability. Just a few minutes more." As soon as he got back to the inn, Mason hurriedly borrowed a pencil and paper from Ernie and made some quick notes. Then, at last, seated with a jug of ale and a ploughman's lunch he heaved a sigh and revealed the reason for his prolonged silence. "I'm sorry for my lack of communication, my friends; I was trying to keep too much in my head. Whilst I was examining the cliff, I had an idea which, providing there were no flaws in the cliff, could save us a great deal of money in the construction. Your design for The Guiding Light, Father, is sound. However, as your model shows, it would require a very tall building to accommo-date the large crucifix window. That would mean a tall church, much taller than a two-storied house in fact. That would be disproportionately tall for the area required to accommodate your modestly sized congregation and would prove very expensive. I'm sure that the powers that control the purse strings will say it will be too expensive. You will remember, Roddy, that we agreed that a lot of 'ifs' would have to be satisfied before we could make a successful presentation for this project. Cost is always a major 'if'". The vicar acknowledged, with a nod, and Mason continued: "Well, my idea is to build the church as two integrated parts. The first part will be the lamp-house: essentially a tower to accommodate the large window, and the means to illuminate it. The second part will be the church itself. My idea is to build the lower half of the lamp-house part way down the cliff-face. A more conventionally sized church – more in keeping with the needs of the congregation – would be built on the cliff-top and tied into the upper section of the lamp-house. By starting the lamp-house lower down the cliff, we can reduce the material costs involved in building such a tall church. It would look something like this:" He made a quick sketch of a basic church and then added a taller, vertical section on one end but with the lower half of the 'tower' hanging below the floor level of the church. Then he sketched in the cliff around it.

"I was checking the integrity of the rock there to ensure that it will provide a solid foundation when the idea came to me. There is another benefit to this idea. We will be able to quarry the stone we need to remove and use that in the construction. It's a colourful stone, pinkish grey-brown with thin, coloured veins running through it. We won't need to dress it too finely, and it will be free for the taking. I also believe I can scrounge enough fine ashlar to frame the building's corners, door and window arches. That will make a good contrast with the walls. The floor too can be built using local stone. It should be very attractive."

Roddy shrugged, looked at Sailmaker and then back to Mason, before saying: "Gerry, we sited the church farther back because we needed space for the blocking walls that would mask the arms of the cross should the boats deviate from the safe channel. That is how The Guiding Light will work. Now you would change all that." Mason smiled. "I understand, Roddy, but we can achieve the same ends, and more effectively, by extending the side walls of the lamp-house; that would be a minor alteration to the design. I'll be able to show you better, by modifying the model back at your cottage. What say we finish our ale and retire there? Then we will re-examine the site tomorrow." He turned to Sailmaker: "I will need your help for that, my friend. Provided that you are available, of course? We will need you in your boat and some system of signalling between us. Could you help us with that? I will pay for your time, of course." Sailmaker smiled. "Certainly, Mr. Mason. Be pleased to."

The candles burned late at Roddy's cottage that night. Bessie Drew arrived, prepared supper and cleared away. Later she confided to Ernie: "I don't think these two will ever be able to work together. At logger'eads they are. Mr. Mason started to alter the vicar's model, and the vicar was protesting over this change an' that, as 'e watched months of 'is work taken apart before 'is very eyes. Mr. Mason replaced it with a much smaller buildin'. The 'Guiding Light' part remained the main feature though. I think they might've come to blows if Mister Mason 'ad tried to change that."

The vicar was still sleeping when Bessie arrived to make breakfast the following morning. Moggy was curled up on the vicar's bed, tucked in behind Roddy's knees, as usual.

Bessie clapped both hands to her face as she saw how drastically the model had changed. The height of the church had been reduced to almost half its original size – except for the part that accommodated the featured window. But half of that was now overhanging the edge of the table, and the side walls had been extended seaward. "Like looking into the open end of a box," she muttered, as she examined the 'lamp-house' portion, dangling over the table's edge.

At breakfast, she expressed her concern to the vicar. "Mercy, Father! Whatever did that man do to your model?"

"Oh, Bessie, he really had me upset at times," said Roddy as he stretched and rubbed his tired eyes. "He said it would cost too much money the way I had it set up. He plans to have the seaward end cut into the cliff, just as the model hangs over the table. The rest of the church will not be as tall as my original design. Not much bigger than our present church actually. 'Less expensive to build', he said. And, because of that, we will have a better chance of our proposal getting accepted. I think it'll work. We'll work out a few more details today, and then he plans to take the model back to London, and 'sell' the idea to his brother. Then he'll enlist his brother's help to sell it to Bishop West."

"Take all the credit for the design 'imself too, I s'pect?"

"No, I don't think so, Bessie. I like this man. I believe he's honest, and a good friend."

"Didn't much sound like you were good friends last night, Father."

Roddy smiled. "Good friends reserve the right to disagree and still remain friends, Bessie. I believe this man will do everything in his power to help us build this church."

"Well – If you say so, Father."

"But so far we have only considered the building, Bessie. There are still the costs involved in designing and making the lamps to light the window. Mason knows a man whose firm makes lamps for all sorts of grand places. He's quite clever apparently and delights in the challenge of something new and different. The lamps will be a major part of the expense, Mason says. However he believes this lamp maker – his name is Albright – would love to tackle the job."

"Got the right name for the job too, ain't 'e, Father? Same as Mister Mason's got the right name for 'is job. Or are you just makin' that up? Sounds like it's too much of a coincidence."

"No, that's the man's real name, Bessie. Mason says he's a real hard-nosed businessman but very religious and willing to back any good new idea that he can be part of. A good man to have on our side, Gerry said. He has made all these changes to try and get the bishop to consider our proposal. Now it seems we will have to fight for the lamps too. Fight for this. Fight for that. Makes it sound like we're going into battle."

"Sounded like a bit of a battle in 'ere last night, Father. Tomorrow's Tuesday. We usually go to Nextwest on Thursdays. Will we still be goin'? Or will you be workin' on the model?" Roddy smiled. "Oh, I think one more day will finish whatever Gerry can do on this trip, Bessie. He'll take the model back to London, make fresh drawings and compile a list of materials. When he's got that sorted out, he'll be able to estimate a cost for the project. That will be the real test. Based on those figures, he'll decide on how to present the idea to his brother."

Roddy drove Mason to meet the coach on Wednesday morning. Mason carried the box containing the model church under his arm. The coachman gave Roddy a stern look when he saw Gerry carrying the box. "It must be catchin', Father. It looks like we'll all be walkin' about with boxes growin' out of our armpits if this keeps up." The vicar thanked Gerry for his help. Mason smiled. "This project has brought interest and challenge back into my life, Roddy. You have given me that purpose in life that I needed so desperately. You have my sincere thanks for that, as also your hospitality and friendship."

"Not a bad beginning after all, Slondosh," said Roddy, as the horse trotted back to Ryeport.

Gerry's first stop would be his brother's house. He decided to invite himself for dinner on the night of his arrival and solicit his brother's backing. Then he would visit Albright, the lamp maker, and see what ideas he might have regarding the lighting of the cruciform window. He too was a Lodge brother, so Mason anticipated an open-minded reception, despite the man's hard-nosed business style.

Bishop Mason was taken aback by his brother's enthusiasm. "Gerry! It is wonderful to see you so enthused and excited about your work again. You look the picture of health too. The sea air must agree with you. Did you sleep well? You've had such a problem getting a good night's rest these past months."

"Yes, yes, Steven. I've slept well. I'm fine. Moderate in my drinking too! I even wash the back of my neck and behind my ears. You really do mother me too much, Steven. I've got so much to tell and show you. Can you give me supper? I've come here directly from the Coaching Inn, and I'm famished." The bishop was smiling, happy to see such a positive change in his brother's attitude from just a few weeks ago. "Certainly, Gerry, you are always welcome here." Gerry was already unpacking the model of the church. Over a glass of wine, he explained the modifications that he had made in order to reduce the cost of the building. He talked all through supper, explaining how he could use the local stone for much of the work. Then he continued with his ideas of using surplus and discarded materials from other building projects and his intention to visit Albright the following day. His brother listened attentively, smiling and obviously delighted by his brother's enthusiasm.

"Gerry! I can't tell you how pleased I am to see you so excited again. You've had me so worried since you lost your beloved Julia. But now, you have regained the spark-of-life. It's wonderful! Just wonderful! I shall do every-thing I can to help. There will be some obstructions, of course. Bishop West has written to me on occasion about Reverend McDowd, and his remarks were not complimentary. I imagine he will oppose the idea of the new church, especially for a man he considers a waster and a liability. Then there is the matter of transporting any salvaged material to Ryeport. I fear those costs might eliminate any savings you hope to achieve. Also the matter of the lamps for this 'Guiding Light'. Albright's services do not come cheap, and this will be a particularly demanding project." He raised his hand to silence his brother's imminent objection. "Nevertheless, Gerry, we shall find a way to overcome these problems, I'm sure. You shall certainly have whatever help I can give."

The visit to Albright's workshop started poorly. Albright – known to be sadly lacking in social skills – was busy. As soon as he heard the word 'church,' he tried to usher Gerry out the door. Albright was about to close the door behind him when Gerry put his foot in the way and asked: "Who else could I speak to about this lighthouse? I've been told it would be impossible to adequately light the large cruciform window."

Albright's head snapped up, and he stopped dead in his tracks. He grabbed Mason's arm and practically dragged him back into his shop. "A lighthouse? I've always been interested in lighthouses. A chap named Winstanley built one on the Eddystone reef, off the Cornish coast. That was a marvellous feat. He was drowned, you know. It was around the turn of the century; a vicious hurricane struck off the Cornwall coast and did tremendous damage. It sank over a hundred ships, destroyed hundreds of windmills, ripped the roofs off churches and then destroyed Winstanley's lighthouse with him in it." Albright, a small pugnacious man, was waving his arms frantically as he described the fury of the storm.

"Winstanley's biggest challenge though wasn't the light itself but building a tower to hold it – on a reef out in the sea. What determination. It took a year just to secure some foundation posts for the tower. They cut deep holes in the rock and poured lead around the foundation posts to secure them. What determination! Then he had to leave it over the winter and continue only when the weather permitted. It didn't last long mind you, about five years I believe. But it saved countless lives in that short time. After the storm destroyed that lighthouse though, they built another – on the same spot. Winstanley had proven the value of his idea.

"I doubt there would ever have been a lighthouse there now but for Winstanley's initiative, resolve and ingenuity. I admire that man. After all, he was the one that proved it possible and in a seemingly impossible location. Is your lighthouse to be something like that? Out in the sea, I mean? Some groundbreaking new design perhaps? Is that a model that you have with you? Show me. Show me." Albright was bouncing with anticipation. Gerry had never realised that the man was capable of such excitement or known of his interest in lighthouses.

Mason smiled, unwrapped the model church and set it on Albright's desk, with the two-storied section hanging over the side away from the lamp maker. Albright straightened up, his face registering his deep disappointment. "This is just another church," he said impatiently. "You said you were building a lighthouse."

"This church is a lighthouse," responded Gerry, as he took Albright by the elbow and led him to the model's seaward side. He lifted the roof and lit the candle inside. The crucifix window glowed in the dimly lit shop. Albright paused, looked at Gerry, back to the model, then back to Gerry. "It'll never work like that," he grumbled. "The light needs to be focused." But his eyes were lit with interest, and there was the beginning of a smile on his face. Gerry unrolled Roddy's map of the harbour entrance and explained the thinking behind the light. Then he borrowed some books to raise the model higher on Albright's desk and proceeded with the same demonstration that Roddy had given weeks before; elaborating as he went on the dangers of the harbour, the loss of faith by the villagers, and how their new vicar was gradually rekindling that faith.

Albright insisted that they go to lunch so that Gerry could fill in all the details of the village, and the vicar's work there, without fear of interruption. It was a good lunch and an even better meeting. Gerry was convinced that he'd found a firm ally in Albright. The lamp maker insisted that he leave the model with him. "Take the dimensions, make a sketch, and build yourself another model. I need this one. I'll see you at the Lodge on Wednesday and let you know how I'm getting on with the lighting problem. It won't be cheap," he cautioned, raising a finger in Mason's face. "But, in the circumstances, I'm prepared to make some accommodations on the price." Gerry walked out with a sketch and a big smile on his face. He could hardly wait to tell his brother.

• • •

In Ryeport, life had returned to normal. Most of the people that had attended church for Mason's visit now attended regularly. Not that Bishop West would be impressed, but the regular congregation numbered about fifty now. Most of them wore the new clothes that had been modified at Bessie's sewing circle. Fifty hardly qualified as a full house, but it was a lot better than the ten or 11 that used to attend for Reverend Cole. And there were now more men amongst the regulars – Jamie Rooken being the most outstanding example.

True to his word, Hawksworth had written to his friend Will Simms to see if he might be interested in coming to Ryeport as a relief physician for Doc Hudson. Simms expressed only lukewarm interest but had nevertheless accepted Hawksworth's invitation to visit him for a week or so, to speed the final editing of his book. During that time, he promised to reconsider Hawksworth's proposition.

Bannerman and the Carters had retrieved all of the hidden contraband from the failed Goodman run and were now hungry for more of the same. They'd made fresh contact with the French cutter that had supplied that last consignment and purchased six ankers of brandy from the captain. However, the Frenchman made it clear the order was too small for him to be interested in working with Bannerman on a regular basis. That was a major disappointment to Bannerman and the Sullivans. They didn't have the funds, or the clientele, to offer a larger order. So, Bannerman decided to have a word with the Pringle brothers to again explore the possibility of resurrecting the old network.

• • •

Albright failed in his promise to meet Gerry Mason at the Lodge on Wednesday evening. Mason expressed his bitter disappointment to another Lodge brother who was aware of Gerry's new project. Gerry's friend smiled. "You know how Albright is with a new challenge. I tried to see him yesterday and was told that he would see no one, refusing to be disturbed or distracted in any way. His foreman said he was intensely focused on a new project. I'm told that the lights in his shop were burning late every night last week."

Bishop Mason also had some news for his brother. "Gerry: the Bishop of Salisbury paid me a visit yesterday. He was in town for some personal business. I described your new project to him, and he was very interested. When I mentioned the financial aspect of the case, and how you were looking for low-cost materials, he told me of a wealthy businessman in Salisbury, who had recently purchased a bankrupt estate, west of Southampton. The previous owner was having a mansion built there but went bankrupt when he lost two ships in less than a year. The new owner of the estate fell in love with the property but didn't like the design of the mansion that was being built. He ordered the builders to pull down the partly finished building and work instead on his new design. The original building was stone. The new building is almost entirely brick. A lot of materials had already been prepared. The doors had all been made and most of the roofing timbers. Other timbers were cut but still needed some finishing. Salisbury believes they might be available at a considerable discount. He's promised to get the details for me and some idea of a price. I thought you might be interested. It is a lot closer to Ryeport too. That could mean huge savings on cartage costs. Gerry: In the same vein – cost reduction – I had another thought. I have to arrange passage for two relief missionaries to Cuba, to relieve two older men coming home to retire. This is a month or more away yet, but I thought it might be possible for the same ship to pick up any supplies either here or along the coast. The ship could then deliver the goods directly to Ryeport. Albright's lamps too provided they were ready. What say you? I'll pay the freight. That will be my contribution to the building fund of The Guiding Light Church."

Gerry was dumbstruck for a while. "Steven, that is uncommonly generous of you. What a wonderful gesture. Unfortunately, I have no idea about the lamps and even less about the supplies Salisbury was mentioning. And not the faintest hope in hell of getting approval from Bishop West in such a short span of time. From what I understand of the man, he refuses to spend a penny on anything for Ryeport. So, even if the church were to be an absolutely free gift, we'd still have an uphill battle to get his approval. Added to that, there will always be the cost of the materials that I'll have to pay full price for, plus the labour of the craftsmen. That alone could amount to more than I imagine Bishop West would ever agree to. No, Steven. I'm afraid that I will have to do a lot of work before I can make a proposal of any sort to the bishop. I may even have to change the dimensions of the building, depending on what materials I manage to scrounge. It will be impossible to cost the project until I know what supplies and monies I can count on."

The bishop was thoughtful. "Gerry, why don't you take a trip to South-ampton, see what this man has to offer and whether it might be suitable? It might pay you to talk to your Lodge brothers down there, they may also have materials that you could use. You could also hire local masons to do the work. You will have to wait on Albright for a while whilst he experiments with his design. You could put that time to good use."

Three weeks later, Bishop Mason invited Reverend McDowd's father for a supper meeting. Albright and Gerry Mason were to complete the foursome at the bishop's residence. Gerry had made a very rewarding visit to Southampton and built a newly dimensioned model of the church as a result. Albright arrived with a large, flat crate, such as might be used to protect a valuable painting. Gerry helped him carry that into the bishop's drawing room. After supper, and over a few glasses of fine wine that McDowd Senior had supplied, the four men got into an involved discussion of the problems attendant upon building the new church. Bishop West, being the main obstacle, also became the main topic. As the problems unfolded, Albright became very agitated. He turned angrily to confront Gerry Mason. "Why would you have me put all my other works aside, Mason, to concentrate exclusively on your project when that project has no approval and no funding? My time is worth money. You should have told me that this lighthouse of yours is nothing more than a pipe dream."

Gerry regarded the indignant Albright with some amusement. "In the first place, Albright, I don't recall asking you to drop anything in favour of this project. You practically snatched the model out of my hands and wouldn't let it go, remember? It was largely because of your infatuation with Winstanley's lighthouse as I recall. Secondly, you of all people are well aware that all projects have a beginning, middle and an end. The beginning is usually some sort of a dream: a pipe dream, daydream, call it what you will. Some dreams are worthy enough to progress to the middle stage – the one that we are at now – and some actually reach completion. The motivation for completion, in this case, is particularly strong, saving lives with The Guiding Light, and souls too, by inspiring people to return to the church. Remember too that you were extremely interested in the village of Ryeport and its problems. You will recall that you insisted that we lunch together so that you could learn more about the villagers and their plight. To your credit, Sir, I thought you were about to gallop down to Ryeport on a white charger and save those villagers single-handed." Gerry's broad smile was repeated on his brother's and McDowd's faces. It was well known, amongst his associates, that Albright's gruff and grudging manner concealed a generous and caring nature. Albright was quiet for a few moments before saying: "Alright, I'll help get this project off the ground. Material cost only, labour and design: gratis." Then he put on his stern, business face again before adding: "Provided that I get due recognition for that and in areas where it will promote business for me. Shipping is to be your liability."

"Thank you, Albright. That is most generous," said Gerry. "I shall certainly see that you get full credit for your generosity and expertise. As far as shipping is concerned, my generous brother here has undertaken that expense. For my part: I shall provide my services free and commit to an initial donation of fifty pounds. I also have a valuable and extensive list of materials available to us for shipping costs only. These supplies include some fine masonry, roofing timbers, a fine pair of entrance doors and four other matching internal doors. They await our pick-up, from a site just west of Southampton. Some of the stone is already carved to suit those same doorways."

Turning to his brother, Gerry added: "Steven, your friend, the Bishop of Salisbury, used his considerable influence with that wealthy gentleman who purchased the bankrupt estate. Such materials as I can use from the cancelled project are now ours for the shipping and handling costs only. His only requirement, in exchange for this, was an invitation to the dedication ceremony. Thank you, Sir, for your wonderful intervention on our behalf. Because of that, a great deal of expensive material is now ours for transportation costs only.

"I've had to change some dimensions of the church, to better accommodate these gifts, but nothing that will adversely affect the essential features of The Guiding Light." There was a polite clapping from the group and smiles on all faces as their glasses were raised to Bishop Mason. Gerry continued: "We are making considerable inroads on the expense of the building. Our Lodge brothers have also offered to contribute, and I am sure we should be able to raise some help in the Ryeport area too. Young Reverend McDowd seems very capable at stimulating the generosity of his contacts in the area."

McDowd Senior smiled at Gerry Mason's good reference to his son and added: "My wife and I would be pleased to match your initial cash contribution, Sir, and stand ready for more support where necessary." In this positive atmosphere, Gerry unveiled his new model of the church. McDowd was quite impressed by the innovative way Gerry had reduced the size of the church itself, whilst retaining all of the essential features necessary for the function of The Guiding Light. He had also added a belfry since the villagers had told him that a warning bell would be much appreciated in foggy weather when the light might be less visible.

Then it was Albright's turn. His model was of the seaward end of the church-in-essence, the complete lamp-house. They set the model up on a sideboard, at the far side of the room. Albright lit some candles in the back, whilst the bishop snuffed out some around the room. The effect was startling. The window glowed with radiated light, whilst sharply retaining all of the character of the cruciform window. Albright's companions were most impressed. Ooh's and ah's abounded, and the lamp maker's smile was bigger than any of them recalled seeing before. "That is magnificent," said Gerry. "Absolutely," agreed the bishop. "Amazing," added McDowd. "How did you manage such a bright and even light?" Albright opened the hinged front wall of the model, to reveal racks of small candles and adjustable mirrors. "Focus," he said, "I used mirrors to concentrate the light on the glass of the window, instead of just raising the intensity of the light in the whole lamp-house. It will be cheaper to operate this way too."

"Does it still function as a guiding light though, by requiring the boats to steer so as to retain the full and complete image of a crucifix?" McDowd asked. "Certainly," responded Albright. "But that's a function of the building design. The extended side walls of the church partially obstruct your view of horizontal arms of the crucifix, unless you are centred in the safe channel." He placed a chair in front of his model and took them, one by one, through the same presentation that Roddy had with his original model. Moving the chair from side to side resulted in partial obstruction of the horizontal arms of the crucifix whenever they deviated from the safe approach.

"It will be up to Mason to arrange the signal to have the boats turn left at the appropriate time." Turning to Mason, he said: "I have taken the liberty of adding one more light, Mason. Although the extended side walls of the church function very well in keeping the boats centred in the safe channel, they also restrict The Guiding Light's visibility to a narrow area at sea. If the boats were too far east or west, they might not be able to see the light at all. They would need a broader ranging light to bring them to the one that will safely guide them into the harbour channel. So, I increased the size of your belfry to accommodate such a light." He placed a larger belfry on the roof of the lamp-house and lit some candles inside. A bright light radiated 'seaward' but over a much wider segment. Albright hung a rough drawing of Ryeport's coastline over his model. He had drawn a narrow inverted 'V' from the church wall, out into the sea. "Boats within this narrow 'V' will be guided appropriately," he said, "But those outside of it will have to find that narrow vector in order to get the guidance they need." Then he drew a broader 'V' from the same spot. "This broader light will be visible over a one hundred and twenty-degree area and guide the boats to the channel's 'Guiding Light'. I strongly suggest the addition of this other light for that purpose. It could easily be built into a larger belfry, Mason."

Gerry was quiet for a few moments before responding. "That is an excellent idea, Albright. You obviously derived more from the harbour sketches than I did. Thank you. I shall indeed incorporate your extra light into the belfry design." Then he gave the lamp maker a broad smile. "So, you got your lighthouse after all, Albright. Well done." The four men looked thoughtfully into each other's faces for a while, before Bishop Mason said: "I shall arrange a meeting with Bishop West as soon as possible. I might even get the Bishop of Salisbury to join me for that visit. I think that, with this presentation, we might persuade Bishop West to adopt this excellent proposal. Gentlemen, this has been a most entertaining and rewarding evening. We are on the verge of good things here. Mr. Albright, you have our special thanks for your special skills and generosity. Yours was an outstanding presentation. My brother Gerry is also deserving of our special thanks for both his inventive skills and the effort he has put into making this project financially feasible. But we must remember that none of this could have happened without the ingenuity, persistence and innovative talent of Reverend McDowd of Ryeport. Your son does you proud, my friend," he said as he extended his hand to McDowd Senior's. "Hear, hear!" responded the other guests.

• • •

A smile crossed Ernie's face as the post horn announced the arrival of the stagecoach. Hawksworth's now famous mailbag was the first thing off the coach, but there were also two letters for the vicar. Roddy recognised his father's distinctive hand on the first. Gerry Mason's was less familiar. Apart from the family news, both of these letters basically told the same story: The considerable progress in designing and building the lamps, the donations of materials and money to help build the church and the overall enthusiasm for the project.

In his letter, Gerry had also raised his concerns about Bishop West and that getting his approval would be difficult due to his lack of confidence in Roddy.

"I must advise you that your bishop still considers you a disruptive and willful fellow and mistrusts your motives. However, without committing himself, he will give consent to the proposal provided that you have adequate support from your village. He intends to have an unidentified observer attend your services every Sunday for the next few weeks. If the attendance is acceptable, he will consider the next step: the evaluation

of cost. Roddy, I cannot stress too strongly the need for your villagers to back you in this. The history of the village's support for the church over the past few years has been dismal, and you have had little time to correct that. Bishop West intends no reconsideration if the village fails this test, no matter how worthy your idea may be. He is bent on your proving to him that your past is not a predictor of your future behaviour, and that your influence on the villagers is beneficial and substantial."

Roddy carefully folded the letter and placed it in an inside pocket. He intended to read it once more, in the privacy of his cottage. However, Ernie had been watching him thoughtfully, noting his changing expressions as he dealt with its news. "Not bad news I hope, Father?" Ernie paused in his beer service as he made his anxious query. "Oh, no Ernie, quite good news, actually. I'll tell you more about it when we have more privacy."

Business had picked up a little. The coachmen had some fresh news, and a new joke or two – Ernie was happy. Hawksworth arrived for his mailbag and stayed for lunch. His popularity had increased greatly since the disclosure of the mailbag's contents, and more villagers were now inclined to stay for a chat and an extra jug of ale. Once the bar emptied, the vicar nodded towards the kitchen door and asked Ernie: "Can we have a private chat?"

"Certainly," said the innkeeper and led the way into the empty kitchen. First, Roddy gave Ernie the good news regarding the building considerations. The innkeeper was obviously surprised; his eyebrows lifted, and a smile spread over his face. "There is one serious problem though, Ernie," said the worried looking vicar, "and this could kill all our hopes. All that I tell you now must remain strictly secret. It would not only kill the project if this should ever leak out, but it will finish my career in the church. No one must know! No one!" Ernie's expression was very serious as the vicar explained Bishop West's strict condition. "The whole project will fail unless we fill our church, every Sunday, for the next few weeks. The bishop will have someone secretly monitor attendance for that time. I'm not supposed to know about that, and the villagers must never know about the fact that we are being monitored, but we have to pack the church every Sunday, or the new church will never be approved. Ernie, how can we possibly manage that? What can we possibly do to get everyone there without disclosing the reason?" The vicar threw his arms in the air in a gesture of despair. They both fell silent and were racking their brains for ways to solve their problem when Bessie Drew stepped into their non-productive silence. "Ah! There you are, Father. What are you two up to? Look like a real pair of conspirators, you do. Not very 'appy ones either."

So the vicar had to explain the situation to Bessie. Her first response was to hope that Tubby would be the monitor. "That's not likely, Bessie. The bishop knows we are friends." Despite her initial exuberance, she too fell quiet. When she did look up, there was a determined expression on her face. "Don't you worry, Father. We'll fill the church, won't we, Ernie? There's enough villagers that owe us two some support and, if we ask for it, we should be able to fill the church without having to bare our souls to get it. Father, this might be a good time to invite the good folks from Nextwest to come and see what their clothin' donations 'ave achieved. I'm sure we can count on the Pringle family, an' they will know some local layabouts that could be 'encouraged' to attend. Prudence would come. Maybe she could even start a Sunday school for the children. That should impress the spy." She laughed: "We might even get Bannerman and the Sullivan boys to attend. Come to think of it, if we could get them to attend, we could likely charge admission. It would be standin' room only to see those boys in church for somethin' other than a weddin' or a funeral. That would really be somethin'". She laughed again. "But don't give up on 'em. After all, we did get Jamie Rooken. We've got to stack the church, Ernie. We can do it. We'll 'ave a couple of choir practices durin' the week too. Impress 'em all to blazes with our singin', so we will. And 'ow about a 'fellowship' lunch or supper every Sunday?" Ideas were popping into Bessie's head, just as they had over the pie delivery business, and her enthusiasm was so contagious, Ernie and the vicar were smiling. The same light was shining in her eyes now as when she had confessed to enjoying the excitement of warning the smugglers. "Can't sit 'ere all day. There are things to do. I'm off to see Kathleen Archer. She can get 'er sister busy and a few others for starters. You and I could call in on the Pringles tomorrow, Father, on our way to Nextwest. Then you can go an' see Westerhof while you're there. Maybe Prudence can bring a coach load of 'is friends on Sunday. Ernie, you'd better get ready for some extra business. These folk from Nextwest will likely stay for a drink afterwards. Might 'ave to feed 'em at the church though. Don't want to offend their ladies by bringin' em into the 'arbour Light. They might be a bit too refined for that. No slight intended, Ernie. You know what I mean."

Sunday proved to be quite an event. Bessie had the church packed. To the amazement of the rest of the congregation, Bannerman and the Sullivan boys were there. The Rookens and the Pringle brother's and their families. There were also several new faces that Roddy didn't recognise. He wondered which of those might be the monitor. Westerhof brought a coach load, and Fletcher brought Marie and Prudence in a rented wagon. Roddy was a little taken aback by the size of the congregation. He praised the strength of community in the village. Then, without alluding to the clothing donations that now dressed so many villagers, Roddy welcomed their generous friends from Nextwest. Bessie led some appreciative hand clapping from the villagers. That brought smiles to the faces of Westerhof and his guests.

After the service, trestle tables were soon erected and covered with clean cloths and simple refreshments, all prepared by the ladies of the village. This enabled the congregation to mingle and socialise with the folks from Nextwest. The day was an outstanding success. Roddy made a point of thanking the villagers for their generosity, and Westerhof, beaming with pleasure, added his 'Hear! hear!'. "I've never, ever seen the villagers come together like this," said Ernie. "We're all looking forward to the new church, Father. This new spirit can make it happen. Bessie has done a wonderful job. You too, of course."

The following Sunday was packed too, but Westerhof and his friends were absent. The renewed enthusiasm was very evident, and choir practice was held twice that week. "For Those in Peril on the Sea' and 'Rock of Ages' were sung most lustily, and the singers enjoyed a social meal afterwards. The church was fast replacing the 'well' as the social centre of the village. The villagers were oblivious of the fact that the increased attendance was essential for the approval of the new church and that was forgotten too by the vicar and Ernie because they were so impressed by the villagers enjoying the social life that had become part of their new church routine. Bessie even had the ladies stitching articles for the church from the fancier leftover materials from her sewing circle. She also had them stitching their names into the work. That meant that she had to show those who couldn't read or write how to write their names. "No more making their marks, for these ladies. They sign their names properly," said Bessie, proudly.

On the third Sunday, the congregation included two coach loads from Nextwest. Westerhof had been so impressed by his previous visit that he had persuaded more friends to attend. The potluck lunch had become a regular event that was looked forward to by the villagers, and the church was full of laughing groups, sharing stories and enjoying their new friends from Nextwest. Bishop West arrived, unannounced, and he remained outside, in an unmarked coach with the curtains drawn. He eased the curtain aside and watched in pained disbelief, at the enthusiastic congregation enjoying the day. The vicar would never have known had Fletcher not decided to check that his pony was comfortable. He recognised Bishop West's coachman, and also the bishop's voice, when he ordered his driver to take him back to Nextwest. Fletch told the vicar of this when he re-entered the church and then pointed out an unfamiliar face in the crowd. "That's Samuel Wilson," he said. "He's a close friend of the bishop. He'll be your monitor for sure."

CHAPTER 10

The Seahorse

Gerry Mason returned to Ryeport on the following Wednesday; his new model of the church and Albright's detailed model of the seaward wall with the added belfry-light were unloaded with care. Gerry was in fine spirits and immediately arranged to give a presentation of the latest design to follow Sunday's service and potluck luncheon. He had also arranged for two masons to arrive on the following week. They were to mark out the site and prepare that piece of the cliff-face that would accommodate the footings and the lamp-house. Roddy could hardly believe his ears. "I must admit, Gerry, I never believed that Bishop West would permit this new church. However did you manage it?"

Gerry smiled. "The credit does not belong to me, old chap. You have convinced my brother that this is a worthwhile project and that, because of your efforts here, you are worthy of his support. As you know, he has also enlisted the aid of Salisbury, for this endeavour. Together, they persuaded your bishop that he should back you and your ideas." Gerry's expression then became more serious. "At first though, after agreeing to the building of the new church, he was insisting that he would place another vicar here. He said he had no intention of rewarding your past behaviour by giving you this new and very special church. My brother was furious, well controlled, but furious. Believe me, I know the signs."

'What you are overlooking,' Steven said, 'is that it was Reverend McDowd who conceived and initiated the whole concept of this church. He is also responsible for a massive return to the church of people who had abandoned it. The villagers obviously respond to him. Your own monitor has confirmed the exceptional attendance level at the church since he took over. The villagers are unlikely to respond to a new man with no understanding of their problems. He would certainly lack the credibility of a vicar who went to sea with them and then designed this solution to overcome their greatest danger. McDowd has done wonders for this village in the short time he has been there and he deserves to be acknowledged for that. I understand that he now has a young woman teaching Sunday school and another giving reading and writing lessons to interested villagers during the evenings.'

"Anyway, my friend, all is well. We start next week. Your bishop will still be watching, mind you. He may have given your new church his blessing, but he's not quite ready to do the same for you. The bishop has climbed down from his high horse, and the future has brightened for you again, Roddy. You will be master of your own church once more."

•　•　•

It was Friday morning. In Nextwest, Bessie was completing her usual round of deliveries with a call at Westerhof's house. He always attended on her calls personally and, being most interested to learn of the modifications for the new church, asked if he might attend Gerry's demonstration. "Why, certainly, Sir; you are always welcome in our village. We would be pleased to see you or your friends at any time." Westerhof beamed. He was really enjoying his popularity and involvement with the villagers.

Gerry Mason proved to be a good and entertaining speaker and interacted very well with his audience. After the presentation, Westerhof spent quite a long time talking to Gerry and was all smiles when he left. "You were having quite a chat with Westerhof," Roddy said to Gerry. "He seems to have become quite attached to our village."

"More than you know, Roddy. When he learned how this whole project came together, he offered a generous donation towards our building fund and also undertook to provide some furnishings for our mason's lodge. Oh, I forgot to tell you: My brother asked Bishop West if he would agree to my converting a couple of the disused cottages in the village to a lodge for our masons. He agreed."

Sailmaker and Meg were both smiling as they joined the two men. Sailmaker asked: "How is it, Father, that your crazy ideas always work out? Today's presentation is a far cry from our lighting of the fiery cross and your introduction of the Ryeport Players."

"Oh, I'm just fortunate in the backing I receive from my friends," said Roddy, as he put his arms around the young lovers and gave them a hug. The following week proved very busy. Just ahead of the stagecoach, three masons arrived with a wagon load of baggage and tools. Once again, there was a bustle of activity at the inn, and Ernie had a big smile on his face. Most of that day was spent setting up accommodations for the masons. The following morning brought moving day for Jamie and Emily Rooken. Jamie had recovered surprisingly well – a cure that he attributed to 'medicinal' brandy. However, he would never again be well enough for beacon master's duties, so the Rookens were exchanging cottages with Jeremy Higgins – his replacement – so that Higgins could be closer to the beacon. There were plenty of willing hands to move the two families, and Archer's cart was kept very busy. The Rookens would now be living just a few doors away from Emily's sister, Kathleen, her husband and Jamie's long-time friend and partner, Archer. The village hadn't seen so much hustle and bustle for years.

• • •

A month later, the cliff-face had been excavated and dressed square, and the footings for the lamp-house were established. Sailmaker had been given the job of installing lifting tackle for bringing some stone to the cliff-top, and a considerable amount had been salvaged and cut for the building. Some of the villagers had also found casual work, labouring for the masons and catering to their needs at their lodgings. The social life of the village had improved too because of the mason's presence and the extra income they generated. The masons always attended the Sunday services and were often invited to villagers' homes for supper afterwards. It was after one of those Sunday services that Sailmaker and Meg came to see Roddy. They seemed lost for words initially, and there was an embarrassing silence for a while as Sailmaker shuffled his feet and avoided eye contact with the vicar. Meg was smiling shyly, as she stole furtive glances, first at Sailmaker and then the Vicar. Finally, Sailmaker blurted out: "Father! Will you marry us?"

Roddy smiled. "Is that what you really want, Meg? To marry this young fellow, I mean?"

"Oh yes, please, Father." The vicar put on his most serious expression. "Really? Does your father approve of this, Meg?"

"Yes, of course, Father," she responded, sounding offended.

"Really! Well, there are some things that need to be considered first.

Marriage is a very serious matter. Not something to be entered into lightly, you understand." The smiles faded from their faces, and they stood solemnly before him, looking rather nervous. The vicar looked from one to the other searching their anxious faces as though he could read their innermost thoughts. But he couldn't sustain his serious expression for long, however, and – feeling guilty for teasing them so – he suddenly burst out laughing. "Of course, I'll marry you. Nothing would give me greater pleasure. Congratulations, Sailmaker, and you too, Meg. I wish you both every happiness this world has to offer. You two are amongst my dearest friends. I don't think I've ever known a couple more deserving of each other. When would you like this happy event to take place?" The two youngsters looked at each other as broad grins spread over their faces. Sailmaker hugged Meg, lifting her off her feet. "Sunday week, if you please, Father," Meg said, over Sailmaker's shoulder. "We need a little time to make my dress and such. My dad will give me away, and he says he will feed well-wishers at the inn afterwards. If that's alright with you, that is."

"Meg. I think that's wonderful. Sunday week it shall be. You will let me know what hymns you would like, of course, and if you have any special arrangements that you would want for the ceremony.

"Oh yes, Father. I can do that."

Roddy put on his serious face again: "Oh, just a moment; are you sure that you wouldn't prefer to wait until the new church is finished? You could be the first couple to be married there. It would be an historic event. Your wedding would be a foundation stone in the history of the new church." He spread his arms as he looked at them very seriously. "After all you were both influential in its creation." He waited silently as his two friends looked into each other's suddenly solemn faces.

Then Meg exploded: "Oh no, Father. We can't wait that long." She looked anxiously at Sailmaker. "No, Father. We can't wait that long," echoed the serious faced young man. "But thank you all the same," Ernie announced the upcoming wedding at lunchtime the following day. Meg's arthritic mother put in one of her rare appearances and added her blessing to the engagement. She managed to stand behind the bar during several toasts, looking bright and happy. The vicar bought a round for the house in celebration. Ernie followed that with another, and everyone raised their tankards to the happy couple. Bessie was smiling too, but the vicar thought that she was not her usual effusive self. Having been involved in so many dangerous incidents, together, they had each developed an understanding of the others moods. "Whatever is the matter, Bessie? You seem a little troubled. Surely you don't think there is a problem with this marriage." Bessie took him aside. "No, Father, they'll make a great couple. I'm sure God Himself couldn't have made a better match. I'm lookin' forward to their wedding. We've already got a really pretty dress for Meg. It just needs to be taken in a bit. But I do have a personal problem that I need your help with."

"Of course, Bessie; I'll certainly help if I can."

"Well, Father, it's about our pie and preserves business in Nextwest. As you know, it's doing very well. In fact, we've added several new customers, all by referral. The local baker also wants us to carry 'is bread. As you know, we don't make bread – an' 'e don't deliver. But 'e'll pay us to carry his. Father, I don't know 'ow to ask this really so I'll just come straight out with it. Would you mind very much getting yourself a new 'ouse-keeper?" She stepped back, so as to study his expression more completely. His face had gone blank. The likelihood that their door to door subterfuge might really become a successful business hadn't occurred to him. Bessie continued: "I'd really like to join Marie full-time, Father. We think we can make a real go of this business, an' we would be a lot better off, money-wise. Y'know, it's not been easy for me since I lost Mick. Marie lost some income too, remember, when Godfrey died. Fletch is buildin' a large, brick oven on the back of 'is shop, for Marie's bakin'. She'll need it to 'andle the extra business. Fletch 'as also got 'is eye on a closed wagon for the deliveries. It'll be better suited than your wagon Father – especially for carryin' bread, an' all. Don't mean to sound ungrateful mind, not at all."

"Well, Bessie, I must confess I hadn't realised your business would expand so quickly. Congratulations. I wish you all every success. By all means, Bessie, join Marie. I shall miss you terribly, but I can certainly manage. Isn't it strange that something as good and fortunate as this should come out of our desperate scheme to warn the smugglers?" He laughed. "I doubt anyone could have foreseen that." Bessie laughed too. "No, I think not. I was worried stiff when I told Goodman to read the message under the wax-paper." Then she fell serious. "We couldn't 'ave foreseen where that would lead either, Father. Nearly cost Sailmaker 'is life. Yours too, an' Jed 's, an' Miss Prudence as well. I think God was on your side that day, Father. I think He 'ad somethin' special in mind for you. The Guidin' Light church most likely."

"Well, that's all water under the bridge now, Bessie. Thank God indeed. We've come through a few troubles together, haven't we?"

"Yes, and we'll always be closer friends because of that. That's why I was so nervous to give you notice, as it were. But it really is gettin' 'ard to cope with all the work of the new business with just a few hours a week. I knew you would need someone to look after the 'ouse for you though, so I took the liberty of arrangin' that. I've already got approval from my replacement too. So everythin's all set up. Provide you approve, that is?" Bessie was all business now; her expression was serious, and she made firm eye contact as she 'ticked-off' points on her fingers. "I knew you'd need someone who was a good cook, keeps a clean 'ouse and would be obligin' when you needed a little extra something." The vicar was most anxious to hear who his new housekeeper would be. Bessie kept him waiting a few more seconds before saying: "So, I've arranged to show Bridget around your cottage tomorrow an' tell 'er about your special needs." She watched his calm expression dissolve into a look of shocked disbelief. "You did what?" he exclaimed.

"Well, like I said: Bridget, bein' single an' all, would be free to look after your needs no matter what time of day or night. So she was my first choice."

"Really, Bessie! You shock me! You should have consulted me before involving Bridget!"

"Well, like I said: Father, Bridget was my first choice, but I was concerned in case you couldn't meet all 'er needs." She exploded with laughter. "You should see your face!" She said, pointing at him, as he stood there open-mouthed. Then he realised he was being teased, and he couldn't suppress a smile of his own. "You are an unforgivable torment, Bessie Drew. That's for sure. Someday I'll pay you back for these terrible jokes you play on me. Who do you really have in mind for your job?" Bessie wiped the tears from her eyes. "Well, actually, I was askin' Emily Rooken if she might be int'rested in takin' over for me. I 'ope you won't be offended, Father. I didn't promise 'er the job or anything. But Emily's a good lass. Thinks the world of you, by the way; she keeps a clean 'ome, an' she's a good cook too. Likes to cook with wine. Kathleen used to pull 'er leg about that when she first told us. She used to say: 'Emily likes to cook with wine – an' sometimes she'll even put some in the food." They both laughed. "Emily will suit very well, Bessie. Thank you. But how will you manage as far as your cottage is concerned? You won't want to make that journey to Nextwest every day."

"No, Father, I'll be movin' to Nextwest. I'm goin' to take over Marie's old place. I thought I'd leave most of my furniture an' stuff 'ere, just take the personal bits. Marie will leave some of 'er things for me 'cause Fletch will bring stuff from 'is flat at the church. 'e gave 'is notice there last week. Glad to be away from the bishop, 'e says. Never forgave 'im for the way 'e treated poor Tubby. All this is only provided you agree Father. I won't go otherwise. We'll 'ave to find some other way. We're like family now, you an' me, after all we've been through. If it's alright with you though, I thought that Sailmaker an' Meg could move into my cottage. She'll still work for 'er dad, o'course. They'd really miss 'er around the inn. I think that things will work out pretty well this way. Emily could use a few extra shillin's now that Jamie can't look after the beacon anymore, Sailmaker an' Meg will 'ave a comfortable place to live, an you'll still 'ave a good 'ousekeeper." Bessie was looking anxiously at Roddy.

"Well, Bessie! That sounds just fine. You seem to have arranged everything beautifully, as always. I shall miss you, of course. But then again, we'll not be strangers. I'll see you on my trips to Nextwest. I'll always drop in for 'cuppa' and a piece of pie. " Bessie looked relieved. Her shoulders relaxed, and a smile replaced her anxious expression. "Bless you, Father. It's such a relief to know you're alright with this."

"When is this change to take place, Bessie?"

"Right after Meg's weddin', Father."

"That's fine. Just have Emily come and see me first. In case she needs any special wines for her cooking." They both laughed, and Bessie gave him a hug. "Thank you so much, Father...for everything."

• • •

Meg looked radiant at the wedding. Her gown was one of the more lavish of the gifts from the ladies of Nextwest, but it had been simplified and fitted specially for her. A veil was furnished from some of the materials saved from previous alterations, and fresh flowers adorned a halo that retained the veil. Sailmaker too was smartly turned out. They made a handsome couple and the wedding was a most joyous occasion. Ryeport was ecstatic, especially Ernie and his family.

• • •

Some weeks had passed since the village had celebrated the wedding, and the newlyweds had tolerated the inevitable round of ribbing that accompanies such events with their usual good humour. Fortunately, that ribbing had now run its course and they finally had some peace. Bessie's newly vacated cottage had become 'home', thanks to Meg's personal touches. They were feeling very comfortable there. Apart from this change of housing, their working lives continued much as before. Sailmaker, however, was getting restless. He was feeling more ambitious now, and eager to expand the business of his rigging shop and earn more money. It was a condition of Ernie's blessing that he swear a solemn oath to have no further involvement, of any kind, with the smugglers. One night, as he and Meg were eating supper, each using just one hand, because their other hands were clasped together across the tabletop, he remarked: "I'm hoping that more ships will be putting in here once the new church is built Meg. The Guiding Light may give merchant captains the confidence to use our harbour again. It's a good harbour Meg. It's just a problem to find the entrance in bad weather or darkness. The Guiding Light should change all that. It could mean a better living for all the villagers."

"Well, that would be nice," responded his new bride. "But don't fret over it. We are managing quite well just as we are. A little extra money would always be appreciated, but we are eating well and have a comfortable home. We're very lucky really."

"Aye, but it would be nice to have a little money to spare once in a while. I'd like to buy you some pretty things and take you places."

The following morning whilst Sailmaker was working at his shop, he was surprised to see a three-masted ship navigating the dogleg passage that led from the sea. It seemed like an answer to his dreams, and he was very excited. This was the first ship to enter Ryeport harbour in many years. Although there was little likelihood of any business from this particular visit, it was still a positive sign – almost as though a silent prayer had been answered. He watched, almost reverently, as the vessel slipped gracefully past his small dock and on into the harbour pool. The ship was very trim – more like a King's ship than a merchantman, he thought, as he admired the gold painted figurehead and read the vessel's name: "The Seahorse."

The ship turned gracefully to port, and her captain allowed the floodtide to gently broadside her to the harbour wall, spilling wind from the lone fore topsail as she went. The manoeuvre was so well-executed that the deck

From the author's sketchbook

hands were able to hand the mooring lines to the villagers, rather than throw them. From his working location on the cliff-top, Gerry Mason had seen the ship approaching. He had been eagerly awaiting its arrival, but no date had been scheduled. By the time the ship was secured, he was waiting on the dock for the gangplank to be set. "Mister Mason, I presume?" The captain smiled as he extended his hand. "Welcome aboard, Sir. I am Captain Currie. I believe you are waiting for some building materials."

"Indeed I am, Captain. Indeed I am. It really is a pleasure to see you. I hope you had a fair trip from London. Did you manage to pick up my extra supplies in Southampton?"

"I did, Sir. They're all safe and secure below. We shall have them all ashore for you before dark I expect. My purser, here, Mister Darby, has the manifest. Perhaps you will be kind enough to delegate someone to check your goods ashore. Then perhaps, you will do me the honour of sharing a glass or two of wine in my cabin."

"Thank you, Captain. I would enjoy that." Mason beckoned one of his group from the dock and placing his hand on the man's shoulder, he handed him a list. Turning to the purser, he said: "Mr. Darby, this is our Mister Ticehurst, a Master Mason; he will check off the supplies as they come ashore. Thank you, Sir, for your co-operation. And thank you too, Captain, for your hospitality. I would certainly enjoy a glass of wine right now. We have been waiting on these supplies to get our building started. I am particularly anxious to examine those supplies that were loaded in London."

In his cabin, the captain introduced Mason to two missionaries. "Mr. Mason, allow me to introduce two reverend gentlemen that we are taking to Cuba: Reverend George Wilson and Reverend Tobias Clyde. These two gentleman will be relieving two retiring colleagues who will then join us for our return trip." The captain smiled. "I get the impression, Mr. Mason that these gentlemen would welcome a turn ashore. Their sea-legs are not too well practised as yet, and they have changed colour a few times since we left London. Their complexions, I mean, not their legs. Ha-ha!"

"Well, we would be pleased to show them some hospitality Captain," responded Mason. "I believe I saw our vicar approaching the ship as we went below. He would be delighted to show your passengers around and explain the unique design of our new church. It will also serve as a lighthouse you see, as well as a place of worship. I'm sure these gentlemen would find it most interesting."

The atmosphere in the village was very happy. Archer's cart was kept busy all day, transporting stone and other construction material to the building site. The last items off The Seahorse were the crates loaded in London. They contained Albright's lighting fittings. Before unloading these, the captain handed a letter to Mason, in which Albright insisted that these be stored indoors. Albright was most concerned that the mirrors in the crates should not be left outdoors, at the mercy of the salt sea air, for the months that it would take to build the lamp-house. He also insisted that he be present for the installation of his equipment, requesting ample notice for that event. Mason smiled. Albright was treating this particular installation as his personal project. He was grateful for that. The lighting of the cross was the hinge pin on which the success of the whole venture would depend. A quick conversation with the vicar resulted in a vacant cottage, close to the building site, being made available for those crucial supplies.

Roddy had been happy to entertain the missionaries, who were as grateful for a spell ashore as he was for news of the outside world. They were intrigued by the models of the church and the explanation that Roddy gave them. Later, they met with Mason and Captain Currie for a meal at the inn. The vicar stood at the entrance of The Harbour Light to warn them of the unusual 'step down' entry to the inn. "Watch your step. You will have to duck under the lintel. The floor is a goodly step down inside. Thousands of left feet have been pounding that same spot for a couple of centuries."

By dusk, the materials were all ashore, and many of the fishing boats had returned to the harbour. The Seahorse crew, with the exception of some watchmen, were allowed ashore and made straight for The Harbour Light. The vicar arranged for Ernie's son, Tom, to warn them about the entrance to the inn. Ernie was smiling at the increased business but, having been a sailor himself, had a word with the captain, asking that he ensure his crew behave.

"There'll be no problem there, innkeeper. Half of them – the first watch – will go aboard for supper. They are to make sure that all is secure for our morning departure. I shall be here to watch the others until roughly halfway through the first watch, about ten o'clock. Then we shall all go aboard. I want no hands too drunk to workship tomorrow – or any left ashore. Our crew is adequate, but we carry no spare hands. It's too expensive."

The sailors from The Seahorse made the inn unusually noisy, and Ernie and Tom were kept very busy all evening. True to his word, Captain Currie sent half the men back to the ship around seven p.m. They had behaved well enough, but for noisy complaints about the lack of female company. Business eventually quietened enough to allow Ernie to get some supper. "Meg will be here shortly, Tom," he said. "She can help out while I get some supper. By then business should be down to our regulars, plus some of the ship's officers. When they leave, we can all turn in." Ernie went into the kitchen for his meal. About an hour later, when Meg peeked through the door into the kitchen, her father was asleep; his arms were folded on the table, pillowing his head, and he was snoring quietly. She decided to let him rest.

Meg found that only the captain's table was in need of any attention now. A few locals remained, nursing a last pot of ale when Tom went to the yard for more firewood. Archer, having checked that all the village boats had returned, had joined Rooken and other regulars. As always, they were disputing some issue or other, and although the overall noise in the bar had lessened considerably, it was still much louder than normal.

Captain Currie and the purser, Darby, plus his first mate, the cook and one other hand were all seated together, enjoying Ernie's ale. All of the men at this table were old shipmates, most of them having served with Currie during his command of a King's ship. The captain 'signalled' another round to Meg, and she smiled her acknowledgement as she went to the bar to draw a fresh jug. "Now there's a likely wench," said the captain to his first mate, Ruddock. "She could warm my bed any night." Ruddock laughed: "I'd not kick her out of bed either." The group sniggered, all agreeing that they would like to enjoy Meg's undivided attention in bed for a while. Meg returned to the table and began filling their pots. The purser was the farthest away and did nothing to move his pot closer for her, and she had to stretch across the table to fill it. That was when the captain grabbed her backside. "Steady, lass. Don't fall now," he smirked, allowing his hand more licence than was decent. Meg jumped back, flushed and angry. "Keep your hands to yourself, Sir. Don't take liberties."

Captain Currie smiled – it was more of a leer actually – as he mimicked Meg. 'Don't take liberties'. "Did you hear that, lads? The tavern wench says I'm taking liberties. I'll take whatever I want, wench. Don't put on airs and graces with me." He stood and grabbed Meg's wrist with one hand, as he groped her breast with the other.

"Let go of me, you drunken pig!" Meg yelled, but her voice was lost in the general hubbub of the bar. Her father was sleeping in the kitchen, and Tom was still outside, collecting wood for the fire. The captain continued to take liberties, but Meg threw the contents of the jug in his face striking him in the mouth with the jug as she did so. Currie jumped back, the front of his clothing soaked with ale and blood starting from his lip where the jug had struck. Had he not been the worse for drink, he might have been able to fend off Meg's second blow, but her jug caught him on the side of his head, cutting his ear. Then she turned and hurried for the kitchen. Archer had witnessed the second blow and stood up as the scowling captain started after Meg, with blood running from his lip and ear. "Come here, you bitch!" he yelled, and managed to grab her wrist before she could get behind the bar. That was the moment that Sailmaker came through the door and saw his young bride being assaulted. His right fist was 'cocked' as he charged at Currie. The captain, sensing a new assailant turned, obligingly presenting his nose as the target of choice. Sailmaker's fist spread that target all over his face.

The captain reeled against the bar, hands held to his bloody and broken nose, unable to clearly see his attacker. The captain's cronies jumped up from the table and moved to assist him, but Archer and other locals barred their way. "One on one is fair play, lads." Archer said, "'specially when a man's defendin' his wife. Try to change those odds, and you'll have the whole village to deal with, and I guarantee your ship will be short a few hands tomorrow. The captain had recovered somewhat and charged Sailmaker, headbutting him in the stomach and driving him against a table. Sailmaker gasped, partially winded, but grabbed the captain's shoulders and pushed him away and brought his knee up hard into the man's damaged face. As the captain's head snapped back, Sailmaker hit him alongside the head with a double-handed blow, dropping him to the floor. At that moment, Meg dragged her bleary-eyed father, into the bar.

The innkeeper shoved his way through the locals that were preventing the sailors from getting to Sailmaker. "What happened here?" Meg quickly explained how Currie had grabbed her and, on hearing that, Sailmaker's temper flared even hotter. He bent and gave the kneeling captain another heavy fist to his left eye, before being restrained by the villagers. The captain's cronies helped the dazed and bloodied Currie to his feet. Ernie's expression was vicious too, as he moved to intercept the captain intent on adding to his pain. Archer and Rooken blocked his way, however. "Don't bother yourself, Ernie. Sailmaker gave him more than he could handle," said the lanky beacon minder. Seconds later, all the sailors were gone from the inn. The first mate and the purser were half carrying the captain. "Don't you ever show your faces in here again," Ernie yelled after them. "If any of you bastards even attempt to touch my daughter again, I'll kill you." Ernie was struggling to free himself from his friend's restraining grasp, his anger building with every breath. Fortunately, Archer and the others did a credible job in restraining him. "Steady, Ernie! Steady! Meg's husband gave him something to remember this night by. I doubt his nose will ever look normal again. They'll all be leaving on the morning tide. It's not likely we'll ever see them again. Let it go, Ernie. Meg's alright, aren't you, lass?"

"Aye, Archer, I'm alright, but I wish someone had stepped in earlier. I was just lucky Sailmaker came in when he did."

"Well, I'm sorry too, lass, but the noise in here has been goin' steady all night long. We'd got used to it, and when you started hollerin', it was lost in all that racket. We were on our feet as soon as we saw you were in trouble, but your man beat us to it." He patted Sailmaker's back as the young man comforted his wife. "Bloody sailors," growled Ernie. "They think any woman is fair game once they've had a couple of pints. But you would expect better from their captain."

"Aye," responded Archer. "But did you see the way some of his crew – those at the window table – were grinnin'. They enjoyed seeing him get a shellackin'. I'd bet he's a miserable bastard to his crew. I'd be willing to bet that the story of what happened here will be all over the ship in half an hour. I heard some of the other watch talkin', afore they went back on board. Currie's an ex navy commander by all accounts. He's a damned good navigator and sailor, they say, but a tyrant to 'is crew. When 'is last ship paid-off, there wasn't another King's ship available. Not for him anyway. He was lucky to get this missionary ship to command. Some of his crew are old shipmates; the rest are pick up crew. That won't be a happy ship, I'm thinkin'. A bunch of the captain's cronies on the one hand, and a luckless bunch to be whipped and bullied on the other."

Ernie checked to make sure his daughter was alright before giving Sailmaker a friendly cuff alongside the ear. "Good for you, lad! I'm glad Meg's got you to protect her." He closed and bolted the bar door. "Sit down, and I'll get you all a drink. Thank you all for helping out here tonight." A brandy bottle and some glasses had been set on the table when Tom came in through the kitchen to dump some logs on the hearth. He smiled as he brushed wood debris from his apron front. "What goin' on here?" he said. "I thought the sailors would have stayed another hour or so."

• • •

A crowd of villagers were at the harbour wall early the following morning, waiting to see The Seahorse leave. The Cobbe brothers and Carter were already leaving the harbour, but some fishermen had wanted to see the ship leave and head out through the dogleg to the sea. Despite the problems at the inn last night, they all knew that having a few merchantmen put in here could improve the living standard of the whole village. They could handle the rough stuff. They just hadn't been prepared for it this time.

Sailmaker had been in his rigging shop since first light. He was still mad about Currie manhandling his wife that way and hadn't slept well because of it, but now the ship was leaving. Pleased as he had been to see it arrive, now he wanted it gone from his sight forever. Through the window, across the harbour pool, he could see the crowd waiting to see The Seahorse leave. Something was happening on board though. It looked like a fight. The villager's attention was firmly fixed on that. He stepped outside to get a better view – and everything went black.

The first mate threw aside his belaying pin and motioned to the crewmen working with him. "Look lively now; roll 'im in this sailcloth and get 'im in the jolly boat, while the villagers are watchin' the fight." Minutes later the jolly boat was being swung aboard, with the unconscious Sailmaker lying in the bottom. The villagers had been so distracted by the 'staged' fight, that they hadn't even been aware of the boat until it was brought inboard and secured on the midship hatch. "Leave that there, lads," called the captain. "We'll proceed to sea. Foretops'l an' jib, Mister Ruddock."

Then, as the sails bellied in the offshore breeze, he called: "Stand by stern line, let go forra'd. Helmsman; let the breeze move the pointy end towards the channel. Steady now, steady. Stand by stern line." The captain waited until the bow was almost aligned with the seaward channel before calling: "Let go aft. Stand by maintops'l, Mister Ruddock!" And the hands hurried aloft. It was a well-executed departure, and The Seahorse moved smoothly into the dogleg, passing Sailmaker's dock and his empty dinghy, off the port side. The shanghaied prisoner groaned and began to stir in the bottom of the jolly boat. Five minutes later, The Seahorse was well clear of the Dragon's Tail, topsails set and heading westward. " 'courses, Mister Ruddock. Lively now," called the captain, and Ryeport quickly fell astern.

The villagers didn't miss Sailmaker until noontime when he failed to show up for lunch. Meg wandered down to his rigging shop, looking for her husband. His boat was still tied up, but there was no sign of him. She shrugged and walked to the vicar's cottage, knowing that they often got involved together and would sometimes lose track of time. No, the vicar hadn't seen Sailmaker at all today. Sudden apprehension gripped Meg, and she became fearful. She began calling out to everyone she passed: "Have you seen Sailmaker?" But no one had. She hurried back to the inn calling for her father as she ran.

The Seahorse was making seven knots, under full sail and a stiffening wind. She was now about thirty miles west of Ryeport. Captain Currie was on the quarterdeck, having to breathe through his mouth because of his disfigured nose. His left eye was badly bruised and cut. "Mister Ruddock: Rig the grating and muster the ship's company to witness punishment." The men were soon assembled, and the grating rigged to receive the luckless offenders. Sailmaker was brought from the hold and thrust into a lineup between two others. "Read out the list of offenders and their offences, Mister Ruddock."

"Aye, Sir. First offence, Sir, is ordinary seaman, Midson. The offence is theft. He was caught stealing from the cook's sea chest, Sir."

"I'll not allow thieves to prosper on my ship, Midson," said the captain. "What have you to say for yourself?"

"I didn'y steal nothin', Captain. I dropped me knife as I was passin' cook's sea chest, is all. Stooped to pick it up an' Cook accuses me of 'avin' me 'and in 'is sea chest, Sir. 'tain't true. All I did was pick up me knife, Sir."

"I find that hard to believe, Midson. Cook and I have sailed together for several years now and I have always found him to be an honest man. However, I will be lenient this time. Mister Ruddock, six lashes for this man. Seize him up." Midson's shirt was removed, and he was spread-eagled against the grating. The first mate laid on the six lashes with a will. Midson's back was a bleeding and sorry mess when two other hands were given the task of taking him below decks.

"Next charge, if you please, Mister Ruddock," said the captain.

"Aye, Sir. New hand, Sir: Sailmaker. The charge is striking an officer, namely yourself, Sir."

"Ah yes, Sailmaker, the man who attacked me from behind. The penalty for striking an officer is death by hanging, of course. What have you to say for yourself, Sailmaker? Thinking better of that cowardly attack now, are you?" Sailmaker was thrust forward by men holding him on either side, his hands tied behind his back and secured to his belt.

"Aye! I've got something to say," he yelled. "First of all, I was defending my wife, who you were molesting. Secondly, if I attacked you from behind, how is it that your nose took the first blow?" There were a few stifled sniggers from the crew, but these were quickly silenced by the captain's angry glare. "Thirdly: I'm not a member of this crew and you're no officer of mine. And our fight took place ashore. You had me shanghai'd aboard this vessel. You should be the one on trial here."

The captain bridled and his body tensed. "Well, well! Fiery little liar, isn't he, Mister Ruddock? I believe you have his mark on the ship's papers as a new crewman. That was dated the day we arrived in Ryeport was it not?"

"Aye, Sir, that I do," and Ruddock held a document aloft. I witnessed 'im make 'is mark meself, so I did."

"You're a liar," screamed Sailmaker. "In the first place, I can read and write. I don't need to make a mark. That's just forgery. Secondly: I was married only weeks ago and have my own business in Ryeport. I had no intention of ever going to sea again."

"Amazin', Sir, what a few drinks will do to a man's mem'ry," said Ruddock, with a smirk.

"Well, Sailmaker. It seems that you have been found guilty as charged," said the captain, with a sneer. Prepare to hang this man, Mister Ruddock, Maintops'l yard, port side. He can watch Cornwall slip away from that vantage point. May the Lord have mercy on his soul!"

The two missionaries had been standing unnoticed behind the crew, but now the smaller of the two men stepped forward. "Captain Currie, Sir," said Reverend Tobias Clyde. "My colleague and I spent some pleasant hours ashore yesterday, thanks to your kind officers. During most of that time, we were with the vicar and this man – Sailmaker. He certainly signed no papers that we were witness to. The only time that we saw Mister Ruddock during all of that time was when he had lunch at the inn. Sailmaker never signed any papers there either. You were also present for that lunch, Sir. I'm sure you would remember if he was signed aboard since that would require your approval. When Sailmaker left us, after showing us around the village, he went straight to the inn, stating that he was to meet his wife there. I believe Sir, that was the time of your confrontation. I am bound to say, Captain, that Mister Ruddock is either mistaken or trying to deceive you. Perhaps it was he that had a few too many drinks." The captain looked very angry. "Indeed, Reverend Clyde, and just where did you spring from? I don't recall either of you being part of this ship's company, so you certainly weren't summoned for this ship's business."

"Well, Captain: you never told us that we were not allowed on deck. And we were very interested to see how justice was handled on board this missionary ship. Otherwise, we would have only rumours to rely on. I'm certain that justice is uppermost in your mind, Captain, not revenge. At least that is what I hope to report to my superiors: the owners of this vessel." The murmuring that had started at the missionary's intervention stopped, as the angry captain returned his gaze to the crew, seeming to make direct eye contact with certain individuals.

"Very well! Never let it be said that I do not defend justice. Mister Ruddock: paper and pen, if you please. If Sailmaker can write his name, as he claims, I shall concede that a mistake was made regarding his signing with this ship yesterday. However," and his mouth set in a grim line, "he will sign aboard today or otherwise I shall deal with him as a stowaway." While awaiting on Ruddock, the third offender was dealt with. Then Sailmaker signed ships papers in a clear, legible hand: "Stephen Riggs."

"Assign this man duty in the foretop, Mister Ruddock, but watch him closely. I believe he will sorely try our patience before this voyage is over. Dismiss the crew." The captain stormed off to his cabin. Sailmaker nodded to the missionary "Thank you, Sir. I am most indebted to you. He would have hanged me for sure."

"Aye, lad, I believe he would," said Clyde. "But you will have to watch yourself now. You are signed aboard as crew, on a ship where he is lord and master. You have now bested him twice. Once at the inn and now on board his ship, and in front of his crew on both occasions." The missionary's expression was grim. "We will watch, and try to ensure fair play, young Sir, but he'll not tolerate our interference for long, I'm thinking."

• • •

It was not the first time that Ryeport had mounted a search for Sailmaker, but last night's fight with Captain Currie, plus the swift departure of The Seahorse, heightened the feelings of foul play this time. The villagers, talking quietly, and out of earshot of Meg, suspected that Sailmaker might already be dead and his body dumped overboard. There was no possible way they could overtake The Seahorse, so the only thing they could do was organise another local search and hope their suspicions were wrong. A day later, they agreed they could do no more and called off the search. No clues had been found as to his whereabouts. However, they did recall the rather theatrical fight, on the foredeck of The Seahorse, and also the hurried hauling aboard of the ship's jolly boat. These memories added to the villagers' suspicions that Sailmaker had been shanghaied. Their only hope now was that he would be kept alive because of his value as a skilled crew member. In that event, it was possible that he would be returned to them when the ship arrived back in England. What condition he might be in that time, they could only speculate.

Meg was distraught. The villagers did their best to comfort her, and the vicar wrote a letter to Bishop Mason, outlining the details of the confrontation, and their suspicions. Hawksworth also wrote to his contacts in the navy, asking that they alert the ships along the route of The Seahorse to look for news of Sailmaker. Gerry Mason told Meg that The Seahorse was one of three vessels owned by "The Friends of the Missionary Society" and that there was frequent communication between vessels in foreign ports. He assured her that his brother would use all the means at his disposal to learn about her husband and ask for intervention on the part of other captains if any opportunity presented itself. The stagecoach bore the letters away in great haste with the driver electing to forego his usual storytelling and the benefits associated with it. Now, all the village could do was to wait for news and try to console Meg.

Story continues in

BOOK THREE

DEATH OF THE SEXTON

ABOUT THE AUTHOR

Les was born in London, England in 1930. He, and his wife Joyce, immigrated to Ontario, Canada in 1965 where they raised their family in the scenic Hockley Valley.

Les was always a gifted storyteller who entertained family and friends regularly with his embellished versions of classic fairy tales and a host of made up words that he used to make every day conversation more colourful.

His first novel became a labour of love during his retirement years and was nearing completion when he suffered a serious stroke which robbed him of his wonderful communication skills. Happily with the help of his family, the original version, *The Fo'c's'le Door*, was published in 2013 and he was able to hold a copy in his hands prior to his death in 2016.

It is a long and captivating mystery involving adventures in smuggling, murder and the supernatural and met with great reviews from those who read it.

The Ryeport Redemption is a republication by his family of the original novel, with the help of a new publisher, in order to give this wonderful adventure the recognition it deserves. It is an opportunity for them to complete this part of his legacy and share their Dad's imagination and storytelling skills with the world in honour of his memory.

lescribb.com
https://www.facebook.com/AuthorLesCribb/

With every donation, a voice will be given to
the creativity that lies within the hearts of
our children living with diverse challenges.

By making this difference, children that may
not have been given the opportunity to have their
Heart Heard will have the freedom to create
beautiful works of art and musical creations.

Donate by visiting

HeartstobeHeard.com

We thank you.

www.ingramcontent.com/pod-product-compliance
Lightning Source LLC
Chambersburg PA
CBHW030907060726
47591CB00005B/1448